THE WOMEN'S WAR

THE
WOMEN'S
WAR

JENNA GLASS

DEL REY   NEW YORK

Copyright © 2019 by Jenna Glass
Map copyright © 2019 by David Lindroth, Inc.

Published in the United States by Del Rey,
an imprint of Random House, a division of
Penguin Random House LLC, New York.

Del Rey and the House colophon are registered trademarks of
Penguin Random House LLC.

LIBRARY OF CONGRESS CATALOGING-IN-PUBLICATION DATA

Names: Glass, Jenna, author.
Title: The women's war / Jenna Glass.
Description: First edition. | New York : Del Rey, [2019] | Series: Women's war
Identifiers: LCCN 2018015835 | ISBN 9781984817204 (hardcover) |
ISBN 9780525481515 (ebook)
Subjects: | GSAFD: Fantasy fiction.
Classification: LCC PS3602.L288 Q44 2019 | DDC 813/.6—dc23
LC record available at https://lccn.loc.gov/2018015835

Printed in the United States of America on acid-free paper

randomhousebooks.com

2 4 6 8 9 7 5 3 1

First Edition

Book design by Elizabeth A. D. Eno

To all the feminists—past and present—
who have fought for women's rights.
You are my heroes.

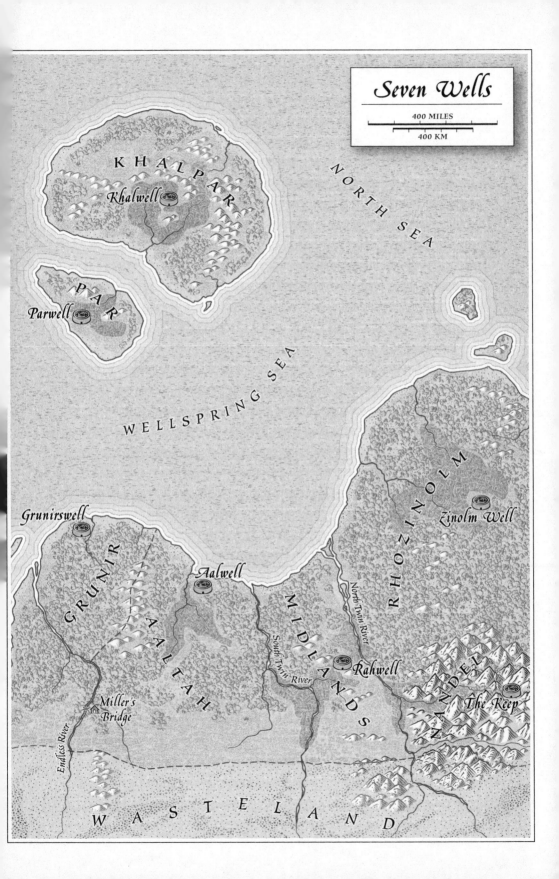

THE WOMEN'S WAR

Part One

THE CURSE

CHAPTER ONE

Every year, when the long days of summer began their inevitable decline into fall, the winds in Aalwell changed direction. Instead of skimming along the coast, they began to blow inland, carrying the scent of sea and salt over the low-lying lands at the base of the cliffs. Unfortunately, they also carried the scent of the harbor, of rotting fish, of soggy streets, of too many unwashed bodies. The cliffs trapped most of the scent, confining all but the occasional foul whiff to the Harbor District. And this year when that wind change came, Alysoon Rai-Brynna reconsidered her decision to continue living in her late husband's manor house rather than taking up residence in the royal palace above the cliffs. Her father had all but begged her to pack up her children and join him, but decades after he'd divorced her mother and made Alys and her brother technically illegitimate, she still hadn't forgiven him. If the king wanted to spend time with his bastard daughter and his grandchildren, he could come down to the Terrace District; Alys would not go to him. Besides, the manor house was her home and had been for more than twenty years. She'd learned to live with the occasional foul whiff long ago.

On the most oppressive of autumn days, the gentry of the Terrace District either stayed inside their perfumed homes or flocked to the risers for a trip up to the Business District at the top of the cliffs. The merchants of the Business District loved oppressive autumn days above all others. Alys and her children had spent the last two days shopping, and if her eighteen-year-old daughter, Jinnell, had her way, they would spend a third. And probably a fourth. And a fifth. But Alysoon wasn't about to let a few smelly breezes keep her from her weekly visit to the Abbey of the Unwanted, where her mother had resided since the divorce.

"But the Abbey will be intolerable!" Jinnell protested. "And you need some new gowns for winter now that you're out of mourning."

Alys suppressed a smile. She knew a disingenuous argument when she heard one, just as she knew the moment they reached the Business District, it wouldn't be her own gowns they ended up shopping for.

"I do need new gowns," Alys agreed, because it was true. Her winter wardrobe was almost two years out of date thanks to her year of official mourning. She doubted that her *true* mourning would ever end, but at least the grief was no longer quite so sharp as it had once been. "But I don't need them today. And your grandmother is expecting me."

Jinnell groaned dramatically as only a teenager could do. "Every time you visit the Abbey, people talk—and that's not doing my marriage prospects any favors."

Alys resisted the urge to roll her eyes. As long as the king was providing a generous dowry—over and above what Alysoon herself could offer from her husband's estate—Jinnell's marriage prospects were in no danger. As her daughter was well aware.

"I've been visiting the Abbey once a week since before you were born," Alys said. "The damage is done, and I promise I'll find you a nice goat farmer to settle down with. I'm sure we can find one under the age of sixty who will take you despite the disgrace I've brought down upon you."

"Very amusing," Jinnell said with a sour look on her usually sweet face. "I'll die of boredom here. All my friends are shopping today."

"You might try reading a book," Alys suggested, receiving in response exactly the expression of disdain she expected. Alys had spent her whole life rebelling against the prevailing opinion that girls need not be educated beyond the basics required for managing a household, and jumped at every chance to read—especially if the subject matter was considered useless or inappropriate for females. Her daughter, however, would never dream of cracking open a book unless it was forced upon her.

"As you wish," Alys continued with a careless shrug. "I'm going to the Abbey, and if you're worried about death by boredom, you can always come with me. Your grandmother would love to see you."

Jinnell wrinkled her nose. "Maybe in a month or so when the winds change again."

Alys wasn't surprised by the answer, and while she did on occasion force both of her children to accompany her on these visits, Jinnell was right and today would be especially unpleasant, thanks to the wind.

Leaving her daughter to sulk and her son to catch up on some lessons he'd neglected, Alys headed to the coach-house, which housed her carriages, horses, and chevals. Her groom was currying Smoke, her late husband's horse, when she entered the coach-house. The poor creature was a shadow of his former self, his coat no longer gleaming, his head hanging in a habitual droop. Unlike Alys, Smoke had no friends and family to help ease the pain of loss and relieve the loneliness. Although Alys knew how to ride a horse, it was considered highly improper for a woman of her station to do so, and her son preferred his own horse to his father's. Alysoon fed the horse a lump of sugar as an echo of grief stabbed through her and tightened her throat.

"Which cheval would you like, my lady?" the groom asked.

Alysoon swallowed her grief and glanced over the row of inert chevals against one wall. "The black, I should think," she said. It was the least lovely of the chevals, covered in plain black leather with no adornments, but it would show the dirt of the Harbor District the least.

The groom bowed, then moved to the chosen cheval. His eyes turned milky white as he opened his Mindseye and fed some Rho into the cheval, which promptly came to life and gave a very horse-like snort and stamped one wood-and-leather leg. As if the crafter who'd made it thought someone might mistake it for a real horse despite its lifeless eyes or its complete lack of personality. Then again, it wasn't temperamental or missing its master, as the real horses were.

The groom hitched the cheval to Alysoon's smallest carriage as her coachman, Noble, emerged from the servants' quarters in the rear of the coach-house.

"The Abbey, my lady?" he asked as he helped her into the carriage, but it wasn't really a question, for he knew her routine by heart—as did the rest of her household.

Falcor, her master of the guard, arrived right on Noble's heels. He would sooner fall on his sword than allow Alys to leave the house unaccompanied. She had nothing against the men of her honor guard, but they were just one more reason she longed for the days when Sylnin was alive. As long as she'd had a husband to "look after" her, her father had allowed her to refuse the honor guard that was her due as a king's daughter. But the day after Sylnin had passed, Falcor and his men had shown up on her doorstep and refused to leave. She frequently had to remind herself not to be unkind to the men who had no choice but to follow orders.

Alys allowed Falcor to climb onto the back of the coach without demur, having long ago resigned herself to the intrusion. Many women enjoyed *more* freedom when they became widows, but thanks to her royal lineage, Alys had less. She drew the sheers over the carriage's windows.

The carriage descended the three sets of terraces, then clattered through the crowded streets of the Harbor District, the cheval expertly dodging pedestrians and horse-drawn carts and pits in the road, passing fish markets and taverns and storehouses all teeming with noonday business. Alys's cheval carriage was well-known along this route, and while the street merchants eyed it longingly, none tried to approach and offer her their wares. It was unseemly enough for a woman of her stature to set foot in the Harbor District. To make purchases there was unthinkable.

The carriage eventually wended its way to the half-moon-shaped Front Street, which ran from one end of the harbor clear to the other. A massive warship was docked at the naval base near the Citadel, its crew and a platoon of dock workers busily repairing and refitting it after its tour of duty. Several smaller warships were docked quietly nearby, and one was putting out to sea, most likely for patrol duty. Aaltah hadn't seen true war since Alys was a child, and these days Aaltah's navy mostly did battle with pirates and smugglers. But the Lord Commander of the Citadel made sure all soldiers and sailors were kept battle-ready, for the kingdoms and principalities of Seven Wells had a habit of war that stretched back to the very beginnings of recorded history.

Between the naval base and the dockyard at the other end of the harbor, the water was packed tight with a ragged flotilla. Here was where the commoners who weren't rich enough to afford a home on land settled, with their rickety crafts of questionable seaworthiness. Whole families lived on tiny boats with open cabins, braving the weather for easy access to Aal, the primary element produced by Aaltah's Well. Thanks to the Well, Aal was almost as plentiful here as Rho, the most common of all elements. Aal was the primary element in many spells associated with movement—including the spell that powered the cheval—and was thus one of the mainstays of Aaltah's economy.

The flotilla was responsible for a good deal of the Harbor District's stink, and it seemed that every year at this time, some city councilman would bring a proposal to the king to outlaw it. And every year, the king refused, because having so many commoners who could see Aal was convenient when a great deal of Aaltah's economy relied on the export of Aal-infused magic items.

As the carriage made its way down Front Street to the Abbey at the far end of the harbor, Alys opened her Mindseye, secure in the knowledge that no one would see her doing it through the window sheers. Her physical vision blurred and became indistinct as the elements of magic came into crisp focus.

As with anywhere in the known world, the most immediately visible element was Rho—pure white globes the size of pebbles. Every living thing was surrounded by sparkling motes of Rho, and the Well spilled thick clouds of it into the atmosphere. The second-most common element this near the Well was, of course, Aal, which in Mindsight looked like a child's glass marble in a mixture of white and cloudy blue. Mingled with the motes of Aal and Rho were countless other elements, forming a beautiful tapestry of colors that never failed to take her breath away. Alys reached out to touch a radiant royal blue mote with flecks of gold in it, and for the millionth time, she wished she'd been born a man so that the world of magic were open to her. Her son, Corlin, was just beginning his magical education as adolescence developed his Mindseye. Many times she had been tempted to crack open his primer, which he often left lying around after his lessons, but she had so far resisted the urge.

Reluctantly, Alys closed her Mindseye. It was her particular form of self-torture to gaze longingly at that which was forbidden to her. Every time she opened her Mindseye, she told herself that this would be the last time, that she would not allow herself to be tempted yet again. But it was always a lie, and in the privacy of her home, with her husband gone and a locked door between herself and the rest of the household, she had occasionally been known to dabble. Very little, however. Forbidden to read spell compendiums and able to recognize and name only a handful of the myriad elements she could see, it was too dangerous for her to do any serious experimentation.

The Abbey walls loomed before her, twice again as tall as the nearest buildings. While the place was not technically a prison, no one had seen fit to inform its designers of the fact. Built of cold gray stone, with narrow windows and unlovely blocklike towers, it inspired a sense of foreboding in Alys's heart every time she passed through its gates. It was a stark reminder of what would happen to her if she were ever caught "dabbling" in magic. Being the king's daughter afforded her many freedoms that other women lacked, but that freedom had its limits.

Just past the Abbey's walls lay the purpose of the Abbey's existence: the Women's Market. Stalls and booths were set up all along the courtyard's perimeter, each manned by at least one red-robed abigail and selling the magic that only women could create. Love charms, minor healing potions, beauty enhancers, sex enhancers— and sex. This was called the Abbey of the Unwanted because it was filled with women no one wanted as wives. Women who were unchaste—or at least accused of being so. Women who were disobedient, who caused trouble, or who inconvenienced their husbands or fathers. Women like Alys's mother, who had gotten in the way of her husband's desire to marry another.

All were tainted beyond redemption in the eyes of society, and with that taint and the virtual imprisonment that resulted came the permission to practice magic. Polite society might frown upon women practicing magic, but that didn't stop polite society from buying and using the magic created by these ruined women. Likewise, polite society might consider it inappropriate for a woman to have sexual relations with anyone but her husband, but that didn't stop Aaltah's men from buying the sexual favors of whichever young and pretty abigail caught their eye.

The stalls selling magic items were dwarfed by the pavilion at the far end of the courtyard, where the Abbey's most desirable displayed themselves as merchandise, their long red robes put aside for tiny scraps of red fabric that covered the bare minimum of their bodies. Men mobbed the pavilion, placing bids on their favorites, competing with one another in bidding wars that sometimes devolved into brawls.

Once upon a time, Alys's mother had been one of those women.

Thirty years old when she was set aside, Brynna Rah-Malrye would have been considered too old to work the pavilion had she been any other woman. But a woman who had once been queen was too profitable a commodity to pass up, commanding a higher price than any three women combined. The thought that her father had allowed her mother to be so humiliated and abused lit a fire in Alys's veins every time she entered the Abbey's courtyard and saw the pavilion. He could shower her with gifts and affection until the day he died, and still she would never forgive him.

It was a time Brynna never spoke about with her daughter, and Alys was happy to keep the silence. She was also glad that when she'd visited her mother in the Abbey as a child, she hadn't understood what those women in the pavilion were selling.

Now, after more than three decades as an abigail, Brynna was the abbess, the highest authority within the Abbey. Queen of the Unwanted Women, as it were. It was small comfort to the woman who'd once been the Queen of Aaltah.

Alys was expected, and her carriage was met by a young abigail whose face was marred by an enormous wine-colored stain over the pale gold skin of her right cheek and the bridge of her nose. The deep crimson robes emphasized the mark, and Alys noticed the girl stood at a slight angle to greet her, as if trying to keep that side of her face in shadow.

"The abbess is ready for you, my lady," the girl said in a voice barely above a whisper, her body still canted as she dropped a curtsy.

Alys wanted to tell the poor child that the mark was not a cause for shame—or at least that it *should* not be—but doubted it would do much good. Odds were high the girl had been relegated to the Abbey precisely because her family had been ashamed of her appearance and deemed her unmarriageable. At least the stain meant she didn't have to work the pavilion.

The shy abigail led Alys to the abbess's office, within the Abbey's highest tower. The room was large by the Abbey's standards, and even relatively comfortable. Small windows on three walls provided more natural light than in other parts of the Abbey, and a candelabra fitted with large luminants made the room even brighter. The luminants were an indulgence, which Alys had gifted to the Abbey so that her mother and the abigails did not have to live in gloom. But while the abbess was in charge of the Abbey's day-to-day working, she had to answer to the king and the king's council—including the lord high treasurer, who'd declared Alys's gift fully taxable. Over Alys's strenuous objections, the treasury had seized all the luminants but five, allowing the abbess to keep them as long as she used them only for herself as a personal gift from her daughter.

The cold stone floor was covered with a warm red rug that was growing threadbare in patches, and there was a cozy seating area with a ragtag collection of mismatched chairs situated before the fireplace. More evidence of the treasurer's greed, allowing the women of the Abbey no more than the bare minimum of comfort while they debased themselves to fill the Crown's coffers.

The abbess was sitting in one of those chairs, sipping from a steaming cup of tea, when Alys was shown in. She set the tea aside when Alys entered, rising slowly to her feet and mustering a wan smile as she held out her hands to her daughter.

Brynna Rah-Malrye had once been a stunning beauty, with perfectly smooth tawny skin, a cascade of raven-black curls, and deep brown eyes that radiated warmth. The Abbey—and time—had stolen much of that beauty. Stress and austere living had etched her face in lines and wrinkles, and her glorious hair, now iron-gray, was perpetually hidden under a red wimple. Even her eyes had lost their luster as cataracts encroached.

Alys took her mother's gnarled hands and gave them a squeeze. Ordinarily, the abbess's dull eyes came to life when Alys visited, reminding her of the vibrant woman she'd once known. Today, the abbess managed a smile, but the expression didn't reach her eyes, and Alys could see the tension written on her face in bold print.

"Mama, what's wrong?" Alys asked as the two women hugged.

"Nothing, my child," the abbess said, though she held the embrace for longer than usual.

Alys shook her head and peered into her mother's face. She was not imagining those shadows under her mother's eyes or the sharp crease between her brows.

The door squeaked as the young abigail closed it, and Alys could hear the soft shuffle of the girl's footsteps as she retreated. She watched the door and waited until she could no longer hear footsteps before turning to her mother once more.

"What is it?" she demanded.

Her mother gave her another wan smile and gestured toward one of the chairs. "Please sit. And have some tea."

Alys sat on the very edge of the chair but didn't even glance at the tea set. "Tell me what's wrong."

The abbess slowly resumed her seat, the slight tightening around the corners of her eyes telling Alys that her arthritis was giving her trouble again. There were potions that could ease her symptoms, but they were pricey imports and beyond the Abbey's meager budget. Alys didn't like to think of her mother as an old woman, but the abbess was sixty-two, and today she looked more like eighty.

"There is truly nothing wrong, my child," the abbess said. "I am fine."

"But—"

The abbess held up her hand to interrupt Alys's protest. "I am fine, all is well, but I have something important I must speak to you about." She sighed and shook her head. "I have struggled to figure out how to start."

Alys smoothed her skirts just so her hands would have something to do. All was clearly *not* well, no matter what her mother said. But her mother never spoke without thinking long and hard about her words, and there was no use getting impatient with her. Even if patience was a trait Alys herself lacked.

The abbess sighed heavily, and a corner of her mouth lifted in a wry smile. "I must apologize in advance for the incomplete information I am about to give you. I know you will have questions, and most of them I will not be able to answer."

Alys almost groaned at that, holding back the sound with an effort. Her mother spouted off cryptic, nearly unintelligible warnings and advice all the time, and never seemed to notice or care that Alys didn't understand. If she was apologizing in advance, this was going to be far worse than usual.

Alys must have made a face, because her mother chuckled, the sadness momentarily lifting. "Yes, I know I often say things you don't understand. You're just going to have to trust me when I say it's for a good reason."

Alys arched a brow. "You mean other than because you enjoy tormenting me?"

"Well, there's that, too." Unexpectedly, she reached out and squeezed Alys's hand. "I can never adequately convey how much it's meant to me that you've continued to visit me all these years."

Alys shook that off. "I don't understand how anyone can just pretend you don't exist." As the king did. As Alys's brother did. As all her mother's old friends did.

Her mother shrugged. "It's the custom, and most people don't have the courage to defy custom."

Alys would hardly label her own defiance as courage. Everyone knew she was the king's favorite—if only because she alone withheld her affection. And the king's favorite could flout some of the most rigid customs without undue hardship. Of course her father wouldn't be around forever, and her relationship with his heir—her half-brother, Delnamal—was nowhere near as cordial. He had more than once promised to bring her to heel when he became king.

"You're my mother," Alys said simply. "You will always be my mother, no matter what happens."

"Yes, and that may well cause you some . . . difficulties in the days to come."

"What do you mean?"

"Something is going to happen tonight. Something . . . momentous. Something that will change the world in ways I can't entirely foresee."

Alys's stomach knotted, and her chest felt tight. Her mother was not prone to hyperbole—much the opposite, in fact—and if she said something world-changing was going to happen, she meant it literally. "What is it?" Alys asked, her voice coming out high and breathless.

"I can't tell you."

Alys let out a sound between a sigh and a growl, bunching her skirts up in her fists to keep from grabbing her mother by the shoulders and giving her a good shake. "You can't do that! You can't tell me something momentous is going to happen and refuse to tell me what!"

"Of course I can," her mother responded with an incongruous half-smile. "I'm a seer. It's what we do."

Alys had never been able to determine whether her mother could genuinely foresee the future or whether she meant that in a more figurative manner. There were rumors of spells that allowed women to see the future, but conventional wisdom labeled those rumors false. Alys was not so sure. "Mama—"

"There's a reason I can't tell you, Alysoon. Trust me."

Alys jumped up from her chair and started pacing before the unlit fireplace, unable to contain the angry energy that coursed through her blood.

She loved her mother, she really did. But did she *trust* her? Even before her mother had been banished to the Abbey, she'd had a hard streak in her, a level of brutal practicality that Alys could never match. Life in the Abbey had certainly not softened her, and though she was not unkind, she was not especially kind, either. It was all too easy to imagine the reason she "couldn't" tell Alys what was going to happen was that she knew Alys would not like it.

"It makes no sense to give me a vague and ominous warning when you have no intention of explaining," Alys snapped.

The abbess pushed to her feet once more, drawing herself up to her full height and putting on her sternest, most repressive expression. "You'll understand soon enough, and throwing a tantrum won't aid your cause."

"I don't have a cause," Alys said petulantly, but she knew continuing the argument was pointless. Her mother was an immovable object when she wanted to be.

The abbess reached into the folds of her crimson robes and pulled out a small book bound in blood-red leather and stamped with gold leaf. Some of the gold leaf had been worn off, as if from too much handling, and the spine was cracked almost to the point of coming apart. She held the book out to Alys, who took it from her and frowned at it.

Heart of My Heart, the title declared, and Alys's lip curled in distaste. She'd known at once from the red binding that it was a book meant for women, but the title declared it was some kind of romantic drivel, with which Alys had no patience. She quickly thumbed through the pages, just to confirm her initial impression, and saw it was even worse than she'd thought—not just a love story, but love *poems.* She tried to hand the book back to her mother, but the abbess didn't take it.

"It's for you," her mother said.

Alys rolled her eyes. "I *might* read love poems if someone held a sword to my throat and threatened me with death, but there's no guarantee." She was much more apt to read about adventures on the high seas, or accounts of great battles, or biographies of kings past. Anything that wasn't considered appropriate reading material for a woman, she found intensely intriguing.

The abbess smiled with genuine humor. "Alysoon, my child, I have known you for quite a long time, and I'm not expecting you to develop a sudden passion for love poetry."

Alys frowned and peered more closely at the book, scanning through a few lines on a random page. It was definitely love poetry, of just the treacly sweet flavor that set her teeth on edge. She couldn't see her mother reading it, much less herself. And yet the book was worn and clearly well-loved.

"I don't understand."

"But you will. After tonight's events, feed three motes of Rho into the book and you will see why I've given it to you."

Her mother was telling her to use magic? All Alys's life, her mother had warned her to keep her Mindseye firmly closed, to re-sist the temptation to explore. To the point that Alys could practically recite the lectures word for word. (Which, come to think of it, she had, though Jinnell was so painfully proper by nature it had never seemed necessary.)

What had changed?

Alys opened her Mindseye, sure it was safe here in the abbess's closed office. She expected to see the book teeming with elements, all bound together in some complex spell that required only Rho to complete it. Instead, what she saw was . . . a plain book of love poetry. Perhaps not surprising, as paper was considered nearly useless as a spell vessel, but feeding Rho into an ordinary book would have no effect whatsoever.

Alys looked at her mother, just to make sure her Mindseye hadn't suddenly gone blind, and there was indeed a halo of Rho surrounding the older woman. The luminants in the candelabra were filled with some red-orange element Alys didn't recognize, and the air in the room was swimming with motes like dust in the sunlight. Either the book was filled with elements beyond Alys's ability to see, or it was exactly what it looked like.

"I can't see any elements in it," Alys said, closing her Mindseye so she could see her mother's face more clearly.

"That's rather the point, my child. No one looking at it would have any reason to suspect it isn't exactly what it appears."

Alys shivered. "Why?" she asked, knowing full well she would not get an answer. At least not a satisfactory one. "Why don't you want anyone to know it's a magic item?"

"That's another question you will learn the answer to before the sun next rises."

Alys was tempted to throw the book to the floor and stomp on it. Of all the mysterious and frustrating conversations she'd ever had with her mother, this was by far the worst.

"Would it kill you to give me a straight, clear answer?"

"No, but it might change things that must not be changed. What will happen tonight will be difficult for a great many people—especially for you—but it is for the greater good, and I can't risk altering what I've foreseen."

Alys sank back down into the chair, her anger draining as dread pooled in the pit of her stomach. What was going to happen tonight?

Her mother laid the back of her hand against Alys's cheek, a comforting gesture that did nothing to soothe the turmoil that roiled within her.

"I love you very much," her mother said, and there was a catch in her voice that made Alys's eyes sting with tears. "Never doubt that."

Alys looked up at her mother's face, shivering to see and hear so many unguarded emotions from a woman so determinedly stoic. "Is something going to happen to you tonight?" Because in light of all the ominous warnings, the sadness in her mother's eyes suddenly looked very like a goodbye.

The abbess didn't answer. But perhaps her silence was an answer in and of itself.

CHAPTER TWO

Nadeen Rai-Brynna awoke with a start, shocked she'd managed to fall asleep at all, if only for a few minutes. A glance out her narrow window showed the moon high in the sky.

The time had come, Nadeen realized with a potent mixture of excitement and terror, hope and dread.

The bed creaked as, beside her, Kamlee stirred sleepily, missing her warmth. She held her breath, hoping she hadn't made a tragic mistake by letting him spend the night. He ordinarily slept like the dead, and she'd been sure she could slip out without waking him. Fully aware that she was taking an unacceptable risk by spending the night with her forbidden lover, Nadeen had done it anyway. If she woke him and he somehow interfered . . . But she couldn't face what she had to do tonight without showing him one more time how much she loved him. It was all she could do not to dive back under the covers and snuggle up to the man who'd made the last few years of her life the happiest she'd ever known. Her mother, the abbess, would be livid if she knew, would pile on the shame and guilt until Nadeen staggered under the weight of it.

Nadeen let out a slow, shuddering breath as she slid out of the bed. A moonbeam provided just enough light for her to find her robes and pull them on. How she wanted to light a candle so she could look at Kamlee's face one last time, but that might make this night even harder.

She hesitated in the doorway, dizzy and disbelieving, her mind repeating the sentence *the time has come* in an endless, echoing loop. A part of her had never truly believed this was going to happen, had been sure something would stop them. Surely the Wellspring would rise up to prevent their assault on its very essence. Maybe someone would wonder at the coincidence that both the abbess and her daughter conceived and bore children in the Abbey, despite the easy access to contraceptive potions that were almost always effective. Or maybe Vondeen, Nadeen's daughter, would lose her virginity before they had a chance to perform the ritual. Such was not uncommon in the Abbey, where a pretty girl was expected to begin working the pavilion the moment she became a woman. But of course the abbess had planned for that and declared they would perform the ritual on the night Vondeen shed her first woman's blood. Tonight.

Tears stung Nadeen's eyes as she made her way through the Abbey's dark and silent halls toward the abbess's office. Vondeen was only fourteen years old, and Nadeen had never known a kinder, purer soul. It was her sacred duty as a mother to protect her daughter, and in that most vital of all women's duties, she was about to fail.

Both the abbess and Vondeen were already present when Nadeen entered the office, which was brightly lit with luminants. She had blinked the tears out of her eyes before stepping inside, but they welled again the moment she caught sight of her daughter, with the pale skin and green-gray eyes she'd inherited from her Nandel-born father. Today, the girl had donned her red abigail's robes for the first time, but she looked to Nadeen like a child playing dress-up. Certainly too young to give her life, even for a great cause. It was all Nadeen could do not to burst into sobs.

Vondeen leapt from her chair and hurried to embrace her.

"It's all right, Mama," the girl said, hugging her tight. "I'm ready, and I'm not afraid."

Nadeen hugged her daughter back fiercely, not sure she could bear to let go. The spell they were set to cast tonight had been generations in the making, built by a succession of gifted abbesses who'd seen what no one else had seen—and who'd had the courage to act on it. It was well known that magical aptitude ran in certain families. In the Abbeys, it was similarly well known that the rarer feminine gift of foresight also ran in families, though only women who inherited that gift from both sides of their families could use it. And so the abbesses of Aaltah had set about manipulating bloodlines based on what they saw, strengthening and concentrating the abilities they needed. A love potion slipped into a client's drink. A contraceptive potion withheld. A marriage falsely predicted to be unfruitful when the bloodlines were analyzed . . . The fate of the world rested on these small acts of feminine defiance.

Brynna Rah-Malrye had completed the process by bearing Nadeen and breeding her with that repulsive Nandel princeling to produce Vondeen. Generations had labored to produce these three women—the virgin, the mother, and the crone—who were the only ones who could complete this epic spell.

There was no turning back, no matter how high the cost or how much it hurt.

The abbess joined in the embrace, hugging her daughter and her granddaughter. "I hope you know I love you both," the abbess whispered.

"I love you, too," Vondeen said with no hesitation.

Nadeen's throat tightened to the point she couldn't speak, could hardly breathe. She respected her mother a great deal, but respect was not the same as love. How could she love a woman who'd brought her into this world only because she was needed for this spell? How could she love a woman who'd ordered her into a known rapist's bed and even ordered her to conceive by him, shaming Nadeen into not taking the contraceptive potion that all women in the Abbey drank when they were working the pavilion?

No, Nadeen couldn't truthfully say she loved her mother, and she had a hard time believing her mother loved anyone at all. Even her first daughter, Alysoon, who was conceived and born out of love, was now but a tool for the abbess's use. Nadeen had never met her half-sister—she suspected Alysoon didn't even know she existed—and wondered if the woman had any idea how her life was about to change, what her mother planned to put her through.

The abbess rubbed Nadeen's back as if comforting a small child. "I don't expect you to say it back, daughter."

"Mama loves you, Gran," Vondeen said. "Even if she doesn't know it."

That brought a hiccup of near laughter from Nadeen's throat. Vondeen always saw the best in people despite Nadeen's efforts to warn her how dangerous—and disappointing—that could be. Despite knowing she'd been bred to fulfill a purpose, like a horse. It was unthinkable that Nadeen could allow this precious girl to be sacrificed.

"I can't do it!" she said, twisting out of the shared embrace. The tears she'd been fighting so hard to hold off refused to be denied, and her whole body shook as she backed away.

She expected a rebuke and a lecture about her responsibilities from her mother, but instead it was Vondeen who stepped forward and took hold of her shoulders in a firm grip.

"You have to, Mama," the girl said. Her voice was calm and steady, her eyes showing no hint of fear or doubt. "We were born to change the world. It's our purpose, and it's noble, and it's worth any sacrifice."

How could a fourteen-year-old girl be so ready to sacrifice her own life for the greater good? Just like her daughter, Nadeen had been raised knowing her destiny, but when she'd been fourteen, she had resisted that destiny with every bone in her body. With more than half her life still ahead of her, she'd cried that it wasn't enough and had gone so far as to try to flee the Abbey and her fate. She'd been caught before she'd set foot outside the gate, and soundly beaten for her efforts. Not yet abbess, her mother had begged for leniency, and Nadeen knew the beating could have been far worse.

How could Nadeen's daughter be such a pillar of serenity and fearlessness when Nadeen herself was made of fear and pain and doubt?

She was weak. Selfish. Unworthy.

Still the abbess said nothing, made no attempt to soothe Nadeen's terror nor even remind her of her duty. Nadeen didn't look at her mother, couldn't bear to see the look of stern disapproval, maybe even contempt, as she proved herself too cowardly to fulfill her life's purpose. She shuddered, her knees going weak, and sank to the floor. Vondeen, still holding her shoulders, sank with her, until both women were kneeling on the threadbare rug.

Nadeen buried her face in her hands as undignified sobs rose from her chest. She was a liar and a fraud along with all her other faults. It wasn't Vondeen's life she was so desperate to save: it was her own. Even after a lifetime of preparation, she wasn't ready to die for their cause, and a wave of humiliation broke over her and nearly drowned her.

She felt Vondeen move closer, drape her arm over her back as the girl whispered soothing words and crooned like a mother with a crying child. Completing the humiliation.

Nadeen felt as if she were being torn in two. Half of her was the sobbing, terrified woman who cowered on the floor and required her fourteen-year-old daughter to offer comfort and aid. The other was the avenger of women who'd been bound since birth to a cause she believed in with all her heart and to which she had pledged her life.

But it was so much easier to give one's life to a hypothetical future, especially one that might never exist. Certainly the sacrifice had never seemed real to Nadeen. Even a few hours ago when she'd taken Kamlee to her bed in what was meant to be a final farewell, some part of her had never truly believed she wouldn't return to her lover's arms.

"Please, Mama," she heard her daughter whisper into her ear. "We have to do this. You promised me I would never have to sell my body in the pavilion, and that is exactly what I shall have to do if we don't cast this spell. I will be just one more unwanted woman in this world with no higher purpose to lend me the strength to endure. Surely that's not what you want for me."

Nadeen sucked in a great gasp of air. She hadn't for a moment considered what the consequences of her refusal would be, had thought only about the continuation of her own life and Vondeen's. But Vondeen was too beautiful to escape the pavilion, where she would sell herself day after day, night after night, for the Abbey's coffers, lying with any man who bid for her, no matter how cruel or venal or sickening. All so that the Abbey could turn over the lion's share of its profits to the Crown while its women lived in near poverty.

Nadeen knew exactly how dreadful it was to work the pavilion, how degrading and painful and soul-crushing. She'd survived nearly fifteen years of it herself before she'd become too old to bring a good price, and on those nights when she'd suffered the most repulsive of her clients, she'd retreated to a place where she could dream of fulfilling her destiny, a place where all her suffering was worth it.

Vondeen would not have that same shield if Nadeen couldn't find the courage to do what she must. How much worse would the humiliation and pain be when she knew she'd suffered it for no purpose, that she'd been lied to and betrayed by the woman who'd brought her into this world and promised her an important place in it?

Nadeen drew in another deep breath, pushing down the fear that had escaped the containment she'd built inside her chest. She was still racked with tremors, her nose stuffed and her eyes swollen, but she stiffened her spine and sat up straighter, looking into her daughter's eyes. Eyes that still showed no fear, only steely determination. Eyes that would show fury and pain, contempt and betrayal, if Nadeen let her fear win. She swallowed hard, willing that fear to drain away, or at least to go back into hiding where she could ignore it and move forward.

"What I want for you," she said in a voice hoarse and raspy with tears, "is a long and happy life."

"But that's not something within my reach," Vondeen answered swiftly. "It's beyond the reach of most women in this world, beyond their hopes, even. But we can change that for them."

Vondeen's eyes glowed with something uncomfortably close to fanaticism, but Nadeen supposed that was to be expected, given the girl's upbringing. Privately, Nadeen wasn't so sure their spell would have as positive an effect on the lives of women as Vondeen hoped. Not for the current generation, at least. But for the youngest girls and for girls born in the future, when the spell had had time to settle and the worst of the shock had worn off, the world *would* be better. Of that, Nadeen had no doubt.

Nadeen wiped her eyes and cheeks with the back of her hand, then dried her hand on her robes. One more shuddering breath, and she felt nearly like herself again. She gathered Vondeen into her arms for one last hug, then finally glanced up at her own mother, who hadn't spoken a word.

To Nadeen's surprise, the abbess's back was turned as she bent forward and gripped the back of a chair with white-knuckled hands. When she finally turned to face her daughter and granddaughter once more, there was a suspicious shine in her eyes, though her face looked composed, the expression an obvious mask over her emotions. Nadeen was oddly comforted to know her mother was not as unaffected as she pretended to be.

The abbess nodded briskly. "It is time," she said, then knelt on the floor with a wince of arthritic pain and pulled back one corner of the rug, revealing the flagstones beneath. The abbess's eyes went white, and she touched one of the stones, feeding Rho into it to trigger its spell. The stone rose into the air and slipped to the side, opening a twice-hidden compartment—hidden to the physical senses by the camouflaging stone and hidden to Mindsight by a secrecy spell so strong only a handful of people had the skill to see past it.

Inside the compartment lay a stemmed cup of hammered copper crusted with a hodgepodge of gems, some precious, some semi-precious. For nearly a century, each successive abbess had added those gems, each filled to capacity with elements—some exceedingly rare—from all across Seven Wells. Those elements, bound together, formed the makings of a spell more powerful than any yet imagined. It needed but one more element to be triggered—an element only these three women could produce.

The abbess lifted the cup gently from its compartment, setting it on the floor and drawing out the three daggers that were stored with it. Nadeen and Vondeen watched the abbess's slow, deliberate movements with a combination of terror and resolve. Their hands had come together, fingers gripping one another, sharing their love and courage.

The abbess placed the daggers in a triangle around the cup, taking a position behind one and waiting for Nadeen and Vondeen to join her. Nadeen found she was shaking, not sure how she would find the courage when the moment of truth arrived. Vondeen offered her an encouraging, courageous smile, then let go of her hand and went to kneel behind a second dagger. Not trusting herself to stand, Nadine shuffled into her own position on her knees.

In Mindsight, the cup was nearly blinding to look at, elements of all colors and sizes writhing and roiling within it. Most of them were feminine elements, though some were visible only to the most powerful women in the world. But some were masculine as well, elements that no woman should be able to see. Elements that Brynna, Nadeen, and Vondeen could see only because they had all been bred for the purpose.

Each woman reached for a dagger. The abbess brushed back the sleeve of her robes, revealing her wrinkled, age-spotted arm with its mapping of deep blue veins. With a steady hand, she placed the tip of the dagger against her skin, about halfway up her forearm. Then she slashed quickly downward to the wrist, laying open her flesh and letting loose a river of blood.

It was done with no hesitation, and only a slight tightening at the corners of her eyes indicated that it had hurt. She held out her bleeding arm, letting her blood splash into the waiting vessel. At first, Mindsight revealed only Rho, the element of life, in that blood. But as the blood continued to pour out unchecked, a new element shimmered into existence.

Kai. The death element. Elusive, powerful, and visible only to men of the noble houses—and to these three women.

Kai motes were unmistakable—crystalline in structure, whereas other elements were spherical. Their form and coloration were unique to the individual who produced them. Brynna's Kai was glossy black in color with three distinct crystals jutting out like teeth.

Fear escaped its captivity once more, and Nadeen's hand shook as she pushed up her own sleeve. The abbess had closed her eyes, whether because she couldn't bear to watch or because she was losing consciousness, Nadeen didn't know.

Nadeen bit down hard on her lip, hoping to distract herself with that little pain as she held her arm out over the vessel and lifted the dagger. *I'm doing this for all the women and girls who will come after me,* she reminded herself. She made the cut swiftly, giving herself no time to think. Her shaking hand made a mess of it, creating a jagged wound instead of her mother's neat slice, but the blood flowed freely, rushing to enter the vessel. She dropped the knife and almost knocked over the vessel, but the deed was done, and there was no turning back now. She whimpered when she saw her own Kai appear, proving that her cut was true and would take her life. Her Kai was a deep, heart's-blood red. She reached out with her trembling hand and nudged her Kai toward her mother's. The two motes fit together perfectly, creating a mostly smooth red and black crystal with one jagged gap.

Nadeen sobbed freely and without shame as her daughter calmly slashed her own wrist and held it over the vessel. Somehow, although they hadn't planned it that way, the three women ended up holding one another's hands as they bled their lives into the vessel, willing the spell it contained to rise up and spread over all the world.

Vondeen's Kai appeared. Pure white like Rho, Vondeen's Kai slid easily into the space left between Nadeen's and Brynna's. The three Kai motes now formed one large, multicolored crystal, which Vondeen nudged into the spell vessel. The crystal drew the trapped elements out of the vessel, binding and combining with them, the power of the spell's birth causing the copper to melt to a steaming pool.

One by one, the women's grips faltered, dizziness overtaking them as the strength drained from their bodies with their blood. And the spell they had completed rose up from the pool of molten metal and cracked gems and sank into the earth, making its way down to the Wellspring, the source of all magic. And changing everything.

CHAPTER THREE

Alys spent the whole day waiting for the momentous event her mother had predicted, but the afternoon and the evening were unremarkable. Jinnell continued to sulk about having to spend the day at home, complaining bitterly of the harbor smell. Either her daughter had a hound's nose, or she was just complaining on general principle; the manor house was well insulated from the harbor breezes, and each room held a vase of sweetlace flowers that filled the air with their scent. Corlin was equally sullen, bored with his lessons and taking his cues from his sister. Alys's tension did little to soothe either of her children.

By the time Alys headed up to her bedroom for the night, she'd halfway convinced herself her mother's warnings had been overwrought. She had just sat down at her dressing table so her maid, Honor, could begin the long process of releasing her hair from its carefully arranged braids when the floor seemed to shudder beneath her. A mild, brief pulse that was not entirely unfamiliar. The earth did seem to have a tendency to shake once in a while in Aaltah, though it was never anything serious. Once or twice in her lifetime, Alysoon had felt a quake strong enough to knock over an unsteady bottle or glass, but nothing worse than that.

Alys met Honor's eyes in the mirror. "Well, that was exciting," Alys said. The comment was meant to be light and flippant, but thanks to her mother's predictions, Alys's pulse was racing and her entire body tense.

Her maid chuckled and plucked at one of Alys's braids. Unlike Alys, she didn't read any ominous portent in that minor quake and seemed to dismiss it from her mind the moment it was past.

Alys's insistence on reading and studying history meant she was aware of the potential dangers of the shaking earth in ways few women were. There had been no serious quakes in Aaltah for centuries, but Alys had read about one that occurred almost four hundred years ago. That quake had caused the sea to swell and flood the entire Harbor District. Thousands had died, and it had taken decades to rebuild all that was lost.

The earth shook again, a little harder this time, rattling the perfume bottles on Alys's dressing table and causing Honor to sway and almost fall. The maid laughed again when the shaking subsided.

"Enough excitement for one night," Honor said with a cluck of her tongue, reproving the earth as though it were an ill-mannered child.

Alys's chest felt tight, her hands cold and clammy. Surely she was reading too much into this ordinary occurrence. But her heart insisted on pounding, and she was almost holding her breath as she willed the earth to do as it was told and be still.

The next quake brought a portrait crashing down from the wall and spilled three tall bottles of perfume. And it didn't stop there. Honor tottered sideways and grabbed on to Alys's shoulders to support herself.

"Pardon, my lady!" she cried, but she didn't let go.

"Sit down!" Alys barked at her as she braced herself against the dressing table, her spindly chair rocking precariously. The spilled perfumes formed a waterfall over the edge of the table, the sweet, delicate scents overpowering. Alys sneezed and grabbed for a bottle, hoping to recap it, but it rolled off the edge of the table and shattered.

Letting go of the table to reach for the bottle proved to be a mistake. Alys's chair tipped sideways, and the legs skidded, sending her tumbling to the floor on top of her poor maid. Honor stifled a cry of pain, and Alys rolled off her, staying on the floor and grabbing hold of the other woman's hand as the world continued to shake.

Outside her door, she could hear the rest of the servants calling to one another, and she heard ominous clatters and bangs. Something fell over with a shriek of breaking glass.

"The children," Alys gasped, trying to get to her feet, but the earth was shaking too hard, and she quickly stumbled and went down.

Alys had never felt anything like this before. A pair of luminants, set into the wall with heavy iron sconces, dropped to the floor, the glass shattering and releasing the trapped elements, snuffing the light. And still the earth shook and bucked beneath them. From all around came the sound of shouts and thuds and bangs. Blind in the darkness, Alys reached for where her maid had fallen and touched a shoulder.

"We have to get out," she shouted, fearing the house might collapse. How they would make it down two flights of stairs to the ground floor and an exit, she wasn't sure, but better to try than to cower uselessly on the floor.

"Go!" Honor cried. "I'm right behind you."

Knowing she could never stay on her feet, Alys crawled on all fours, hampered by the three layers of skirts and long trailing sleeves of her evening gown. She wished she'd dispensed with the formality of dressing for dinner after Sylnin had died, but old habits were hard to break. She looked over her shoulder, checking on Honor, but could see nothing in the oppressive darkness. She just had to hope the maid was following. Under her breath, she prayed that

Jinnell and Corlin had fled from their rooms on the floor below and were on their way to the relative safety of the outdoors.

Groping blindly in the dark, Alys bumped into a wall and felt her way along it until she reached the doorway. She fumbled for the knob, her fingers finding it then slipping off as an especially hard lurch pitched her to the side.

An earsplitting shriek rent the air, followed by an even louder series of bangs and crashes so strong she could feel them shaking the floor even through the movement of the quake. More frantic screams and shouts from outside the closed door, and behind her Honor cried out, "What was that?"

Alys had no answer, though she was sure it was the sound of something huge collapsing. She was just glad her own house was still standing, though she had little confidence it could withstand much more shaking. Grimly, gritting her teeth, she reached for the doorknob again, this time getting a firm grip and yanking it open.

There was no light in the hallway outside, and as Alys crawled, her hands encountered jagged shards of glass from more broken luminants. She called a warning to Honor over her shoulder, but it wasn't possible to be particularly careful. Alys winced as a sliver of glass cut into her palm. She gathered her long trailing sleeves and wrapped them around her hands, giving herself as much protection as possible as she continued to push forward, sweeping the glass aside to create a path.

It was hard to stay oriented in the darkness, but Alys kept moving in what she felt certain was the direction of the staircase.

The earth shuddered to a stop, the sudden stillness almost as unnerving as the shaking. The household was still filled with the sound of shouting voices, with the crunching of broken glass underfoot and the banging of doors. From somewhere down below, a child was wailing at the top of his lungs, but he was too young to be Corlin. The cook's apprentice, Alys guessed, and while she hoped the boy was unharmed, she was glad the voice wasn't her son's.

She yelled out her children's names, but doubted they would hear over all the other voices even if they were nearby.

"Are you all right, Honor?" she called, her whole body tense as she waited for the shaking to start again.

"Yes, my lady. And you?"

Alys winced as her cut hand began to throb to the beat of her heart. "I think so."

Somewhere below, on the second floor, a luminant was lit, and Alys was almost surprised to find they hadn't all been destroyed. The light was feeble and far away, but at least it was enough to help orient her. She looked around and found that her long, torturous crawl had taken her little more than a body's length from her bedroom door and that she'd been crawling straight toward the edge of the hallway, where a banister used to be. All that was left of it were a few nails that had been ripped out when it fell over the edge, no doubt landing in the foyer two stories below.

The light got brighter, and Alys saw her steward, Mica, rushing toward the stairs, eyes searching the balcony above, holding a brightly glowing luminant as he picked his way through glass and other debris.

"Lady Alysoon!" he shouted, and Alys realized he couldn't see her, blinded by the light he held in his hands.

"I'm here!" she responded. "And I'm all right. Where are the children?"

He breathed a visible sigh of relief as he started up the stairs, taking them two at a time until he came upon a large painting that had fallen from the wall and blocked the way.

"They're outside and safe," he said, and Alys's heart rate finally started to calm.

"Is anyone hurt?" she asked, finally trusting that the quake was over and climbing shakily to her feet.

Mica worked his way around the fallen painting and made it to the head of the stairs. Alys shook her head in amazement at the damage. There was not a luminant left on the walls or ceiling, and every tall piece of furniture had fallen down. But at least it was all superficial damage, as far as she could see. No ominous cracks in the walls, no dust raining from the ceiling. *Something* large had collapsed and made that horrible noise, but it wasn't her house.

She didn't have to be told that the people of the Harbor District had not fared so well. The crowded streets and ramshackle buildings, many decades past their prime, could not have withstood the force of that quake. She prayed history would not repeat itself and bring a wave that would swamp the district—and destroy the ragtag flotilla.

"I haven't seen anyone seriously injured," Mica responded, frowning at her bloodstained sleeve. "Except, perhaps, you."

She waved off his concern. "I'm fine. Just a little cut." A cut that throbbed uncomfortably. She wondered if it was still bleeding but didn't want to unwrap her sleeve to see. She'd worry about getting it properly bandaged once she'd had a chance to assess the damage.

With Mica's help—and with the light of his single luminant—Alys made her way down the stairs. Honor followed Alys down to the second floor and then veered off, heading for a huddled group of housemaids who looked lost and frightened. One girl held a lit candle, and the others were practically clinging to that small circle of light. Honor technically had no authority over the housemaids—they were under the housekeeper's purview—but she exuded calm and confidence, and Alys could see the girls start to relax the moment she took charge.

On the first floor, she found several footmen beginning to clear the debris in the light of a hastily lit candelabra fitted with candles. All looked up when she passed, ready to drop everything if she issued new orders, but she saw no reason to interrupt them.

She stepped outside to the welcome sight of her children, sitting together on a bench in the garden, a lit luminant at their feet. Corlin was dressed in his nightclothes, his hair tousled. His feet were up on the bench, his arms wrapped around his knees. For once, he and his sister weren't bickering. Jinnell, still dressed although her hair was down for the night, had one arm draped around her little brother's shoulders, offering silent comfort though her own eyes were wide and shocked-looking and there were tear tracks on her cheeks.

Jinnell spotted Alys first, leaping to her feet with a cry of sheer joy and throwing herself into her mother's arms. Alys hugged her tight, her own eyes now stinging with tears as she wondered how she could ever force herself to let go. Corlin, always more reserved than his boisterous sister, hovered just out of arm's reach.

"Are you all right, Mama?" he asked, his eyes locked on her bloodstained sleeve. His lower lip quivered until he bit down on it. A boy was allowed to cry, though only in the direst circumstances. A man was not. And Corlin was anxious to prove himself a man, though the law would consider him a child for four more years.

"I'm fine," she assured him, releasing Jinnell from her embrace. She ached to hug Corlin and tell him everything would be all right, but he was well past allowing such displays of affection. She settled for reaching out and squeezing his shoulder—a gesture he accepted with manly stoicism.

At this time of night, the third level of the Terrace District would usually be silent, but tonight Alys could hear people shouting in all directions. There were very few lights visible in any of the neighboring manors, but mostly the damage didn't look too terrible. There were some downed trees and broken windows, and a few small outbuildings looked like they might need to be torn down. Of course, from this secluded back garden, and with so little light, there was a lot Alys couldn't see. But she kept remembering her mother's ominous warnings and the teachings of history.

"I want to go back inside and get a better view," she told Jinnell and Corlin. "Wait here, and I'll be right back."

Jinnell immediately grabbed her arm. "What if the shaking starts again? Shouldn't we stay outside?"

It was a fair question, and though Alys was familiar enough with history to worry about a swell from the sea, she didn't know how likely the earth was to shake some more. Should she order all the servants out of the house, just in case? She should at least make sure no one was seriously hurt. Mica said he hadn't seen any serious injuries, but she doubted he'd toured the entire house before coming to find her.

Her instincts said the water was a greater threat, and standing outside would not protect them from that. They needed to get to higher ground, just in case. Alys regarded her children, trying to judge whether they were aware of the danger. Corlin was an indifferent student of history, at best, and while Jinnell had had the best education Alys and her husband could provide, she was much more concerned with being ladylike and paid much more attention to subjects deemed more "appropriate" for girls—poetry and music and fashion and etiquette.

Alys's thoughts were interrupted by the arrival of Falcor and two of his men. The honor guardsmen rarely interacted with the family on the grounds of the manor, keeping themselves as unobtrusive as possible per Alys's request, but she wasn't surprised they sought her out in this crisis.

Falcor was carrying a small bag with him, and after giving her a respectful bow, he opened up the bag to reveal salve and bandages.

"Mica said you were hurt, my lady," he said as his men checked on Corlin and Jinnell.

"It's nothing," Alys responded. "We can deal with it later. I need to arrange for a few belongings to be packed. I think we should spend the night at the palace." She made eye contact with the man and willed him both to understand her implication and to refrain from putting it into words in front of the children. The honor guardsmen were all Citadel-trained and certain to know about the centuries-old disaster.

"That would be wise, my lady," he said, holding the eye contact in a meaningful way. "But it will be a long trip and will require a cheval carriage. The risers were destroyed in the quake."

Alys drew in a startled breath, remembering that huge crash. The risers were built into the cliffs and ran beside a long metal track, powered by magic. Those who could afford the fare could make it to the top of the cliffs in about ten minutes, whereas the common folk had to use the long, zigzagging paths on either side of the city. The trip was exhausting for those on foot and not much better for those who traveled by horse and cart. A cheval—which would not tire from the climb and was far more sure-footed than a horse—would shorten the trip, but it would still take the better part of an hour.

"Then we'll take the carriage," she said, about to move off to find Mica, but the guardsman had the temerity to step into her path.

"Let me bandage your wound first," he said. "It will only take a minute, and you wouldn't want to get an infection."

Alys considered arguing, but quickly determined it would only delay her more. Falcor and his men took their orders from the Lord Commander of the Citadel, not Alys. Ordinarily, they would obey her, but not when they thought her safety might be at risk. The cut on her hand wasn't much of a threat in Alys's mind, but thanks to her father's "gift" of an honor guard, it wasn't her choice to make. Gritting her teeth against the injustice of not being allowed to make her own decisions, Alys held out her hand.

Falcor smoothed some salve on the cut, then wrapped it neatly in a clean white bandage. He moved at a gratifyingly brisk pace, but the process felt like it took an eternity. When he was finally satisfied, Alys hurried the children into the house, urging them to change quickly into traveling clothes. She found Honor on her way up to her own room on the third floor and bade the maid follow and help her change.

Servants had lit candles in all the hallways and were busily cleaning up the worst of the mess. Honor grabbed a candle from the hall to light Alys's room, and Alys began stripping off her soiled dress before the door was closed behind her. Honor headed for the wardrobe, but Alys stopped when she passed in front of the window.

In the dark of night, she should have seen nothing more than the occasional flicker of lighted windows in the distance, but her window glowed with flickering orange light. When she looked out, she saw that the Harbor District was on fire. She gripped the cold stone of the windowsill and stared with horror.

It shouldn't have come as much of a surprise. Very few people who lived in the Harbor District could afford luminants, so their lighting was provided almost entirely by fire. How many candles and lanterns had been knocked over as the earth shook? Alys covered her mouth to stifle a sob. From her window at the highest level of the Terrace District, she could see the streets filled with frantic people, small silhouetted figures trying to organize bucket brigades in what was surely a lost cause.

As if that weren't bad enough, the blazing fires illuminated the harbor front, where Alys could see numerous boats mired in land that had been covered in water. Residents of the flotilla were picking their way through the muddy bottom, trying to find paths between the listing, grounded boats that were nearly on top of one another, sometimes being forced to climb over or duck under. And many of those boats were on fire, too.

But the worst news was what that suddenly dry land portended. The surge was coming, and Alys had no idea how long it would take to arrive or how high it would reach. The vast majority of people in the Harbor District had no way of knowing what was coming, having no education in history whatsoever. They should all be running to higher ground, not wasting their time in a futile battle with fires that were beyond controlling.

Honor brought a traveling dress, and Alys almost decided against changing, but the last thing she needed was to be tripped up by her layers of skirts and trailing sleeves, so she allowed Honor to help her out of her evening dress, ripping stitches in her hurry to change.

"Shall I pack a bag for you, my lady?" Honor asked, but Alys shook her head.

"Never mind that. Let's get the children to the carriage."

Just before she left her room, Alys grabbed the little red book her mother had given her and tucked it into a pocket of her traveling dress. She didn't have time to look at it now, but the moment she had some peace and privacy, she intended to feed some Rho into it as the abbess had instructed. She wondered briefly if her mother and the rest of the abigails were safe. The Abbey was right at the harbor's edge and would most definitely suffer if the sea surged. But there was nothing she could do for them right now, and Alys tried to take comfort in the conviction that her mother had known full well what was coming. Surely she would have taken precautions to protect the women in her care.

Jinnell and Corlin both dragged their feet and complained bitterly about their mother's decision to go to the palace.

"It will take *forever* to get there with the risers out," Jinnell said.

"And I don't care if the house is a mess. I'd rather sleep in my own bed."

"And I'd just rather sleep," Corlin added with a dramatic yawn.

Alys didn't want to scare them by explaining her own fears, and she didn't have time for an argument. "We're going, and that's final," she snapped at them, using her fear to create a façade of anger. She'd rather they think her ill-tempered than frightened. "The sooner we get moving, the sooner we'll arrive."

The complaining didn't stop, but at least the children followed when she made her way to the coach-house. Falcor and his two guardsmen were already mounted on sturdy chevals by the front of the building, ready to escort their charges to the safety of the palace. Alys wondered if Falcor's men had balked at riding chevals, which was considered unmanly except in the case of dire need. She was glad her master of the guard wasn't so proud as to insist on riding horses and making the trip four times as long. Alys nodded to them as she bustled Jinnell and Corlin into the coach-house and well-nigh shoved them into the waiting carriage.

"I'll join you in a moment," she told her children, then shut the carriage door on their protests.

Alys could get her children to the guaranteed safety of the cliffs, but when she thought of all the helpless men, women, and children of the Harbor District, none of whom knew what was coming, she realized she couldn't just leave. No doubt there were others—especially soldiers of the Citadel—who would do their best to get people to higher ground, but they would need all the help they could get.

Noble was standing by the cheval's flank, waiting for her to get into the carriage before feeding Rho into the cheval. Alys walked briskly to his side and lowered her voice to just above a whisper.

"I want you to take the children to the palace as fast as you can," she told him.

His brows creased in puzzlement. "What about you, my lady?"

"I'm not going," she said, offering no explanation. "That's why you have to go fast—so that Falcor and his men won't realize I'm not in the carriage."

Noble gaped at her, and she knew a protest was coming. She cut it off before the coachman had time to form words.

"If you value your position, you'll do as you're told." She glared at him to let him know she meant what she said. She hated to be such a shrew—it was not at all her way to threaten her servants' livelihoods—but she didn't have the time or patience to deal with the male insistence on protecting women whether they wanted it or not.

Noble drew back as if slapped. "Yes, my lady," he said, his lips barely moving as his shoulders went stiff with indignation. His eyes filmed over as he opened his Mindseye to find some Rho for the cheval. But instead of activating the cheval, he merely stood there, his face going entirely bloodless and his jaw dropping open.

"What is it?" she asked, holding on to her patience by the thinnest of threads.

He opened and closed his mouth a few times as if struggling to find words. The thread holding Alys's patience broke. "Start the cheval!" she snapped at her coachman, but he seemed incapable of speech or action.

With her sense of urgency too overpowering to ignore, Alys did the unthinkable and opened her Mindseye. At least the children were already in the carriage and couldn't see, and the coachman seemed too shocked to even notice. Her worldly vision blurred behind the riotous colors of the elements. And suddenly, Alys knew exactly what had stolen her coachman's voice.

She had expected to see what she always saw with her Mindseye: a sea of snow-white Rho, peppered with a generous dose of blue-marbled Aal and numerous other elements. But tonight, the sea was no longer snow white.

Alys turned her head left and right and blinked a couple of times, just in case her imagination was running away with her, but no. The most common element, the one that was gathered around her own body and her coachman's, the one that should have been Rho and should have been pure white, was . . . not.

It looked very like Rho and was every bit as plentiful. But instead of being pure white, each mote had a small spot of red in it. There was not a pure-white mote of Rho anywhere.

Alys had no idea what would happen if she touched these red-spotted motes, nor what they would do. But there was no normal Rho in sight, and she needed Rho to activate the cheval and get her children to the safety of the cliffs. She reached out and grabbed the nearest motes and shoved them at the cheval.

The cheval snorted and stomped its hoof, just as it always did when fed Rho. Alys closed her Mindseye and shuddered. The coachman had turned his back on her, too prudish to watch his lady working magic. She hoped that meant he would keep his mouth shut about what he'd seen.

"Get the children to the palace!" she ordered him, and he finally seemed to snap out of his stupor. He climbed shakily up to his perch, eying the cheval with unadulterated suspicion. Alys worried for a moment that he might refuse to drive the coach, but perhaps her sense of urgency had finally gotten through to him. He slapped the reins, and the cheval started forward.

The last thing Alys saw as the coach drove out of the coach-house was her daughter sticking her head out the window and staring back at her in wide-eyed surprise. Jinnell called out something, but Alys couldn't hear over the rattling of the coach. She stepped sideways into a pool of darkness as the honor guardsmen followed the coach. She needn't have bothered hiding, for none of the guardsmen looked back.

Hoping that wasn't the last she would ever see of her children, Alys hurried back to the house to organize the servants and do what she could to get as many people to higher ground as possible.

CHAPTER FOUR

S helvon of Nandel, daughter of the Sovereign Prince of Nandel and future Queen of Aaltah, lay bent over the edge of her bed with three layers of skirts halfway smothering her as she closed her eyes and gripped the bedclothes in white-knuckled fists. Her husband, Crown Prince Delnamal, grunted like a rutting stallion as he thrust into her. In Nandel, tradition held that a man should not lie with a woman while she was pregnant, and while Shelvon had known such was not the custom in Aaltah, she had nonetheless thought herself safe from her husband's attentions. He'd made no secret of the fact that he found her homely. In truth, there seemed to be nothing about her that he found even remotely appealing, so she'd expected to have to endure him in her bed only as necessary to create the requisite male heirs. And yet here she was, three months pregnant with a child the midwife assured them was a boy, with her husband making that disgusting grunting noise as he pleasured himself with her body.

Shelvon bit back a cry of pain at an especially hard and inexpert thrust. Delnamal didn't go out of his way to hurt her—a pleasant surprise, considering his generally unpleasant nature—but he saw no need to be gentle, either. And at thirty-one years old, he had both the stamina and the self-control to make each coupling last exactly as long as he liked.

With a shout of triumph, Delnamal climaxed, and Shelvon let out a quiet sigh of relief even as he continued to pump into her. It was almost over.

He all but collapsed on top of her, breathing heavily and pressing her face deeper into the feather bed as his weight held her skirts closer over her head. Her eyes sprang open in alarm as she tried to take a breath and could find no air. Luckily, Delnamal's ability to pretend she was the woman he really wanted faded within seconds of climax. Once he remembered who was beneath him, whose face was hidden by the cascade of skirts, he pulled away with alacrity.

Shelvon sucked in a much-needed breath, but didn't move from her ignominious position. When she'd first married Delnamal, she'd been ashamed of her nudity and had always hurried to cover herself. It was especially humiliating that he always took her from behind, hiding her face and throwing up her skirts to cover the blond hair that was a constant reminder of who she was. Holding still with her buttocks bared to the world took an effort of will, even after almost a year of marriage, but she'd learned early that her husband grew surly if she attempted to protect what was left of her dignity. He was bad enough cheerful; surly, he was intolerable. He didn't have to raise a hand to her to make her life miserable.

Still panting, Delnamal patted one bare cheek.

"That was nice," he said in a husky voice. She heard the sound of him setting his clothes to rights and wished she could do the same. Her fingers dug deeper into the bedclothes, and she clenched her jaws tight, afraid one of her scathing thoughts would escape her mouth if she wasn't careful. Did he think his words somehow flattering? Did he think the pat was comforting, or tender, or welcome? Did he know that he spoke to her with the same tone he used with his dogs?

Rage boiled in Shelvon's belly—rage that she had no right to feel. Her marriage was far from a picture of bliss. Her husband hated her for not being the woman he loved. Her future people looked down their noses at her for being a Nandel "barbarian" with odd blond hair and a guttural accent that no amount of training and practicing could tame. But she would be a queen, and someday her son would be the king, both of them living a life of luxury that would not have been possible in Nandel, where austerity was a way of life even for the royal family. And at least in Aaltah, she was allowed to make some of her own decisions instead of having every aspect of her life controlled by her closest male relative.

How many women in Seven Wells would kill to be in my position? Shelvon wondered as the door closed behind her husband, and she could finally shove her skirts down and rise.

For the thousandth time, Shelvon reminded herself how very lucky she was to have a husband like Delnamal. And yet as she began unlacing the front of her gown, she found her hands were shaking. She knew she should call for her lady's maid to help her undress for bed, but she wanted a little more time to regain her dignity before she had to face anyone. Even a maid. Besides, in Nandel, even women of the royal family dressed themselves and considered women of the other kingdoms and principalities decadent for needing help.

The front lacings came loose obediently, but the bodice was pinned into place, its boning restrictive enough that she couldn't reach all the pins. She gave an unladylike grunt of frustration. The reason women of Nandel didn't need lady's maids was that their clothing had only two layers, with all lacings and fastenings at the front or sides, where they could easily be reached.

Giving up on the gown, the bodice flopping loose in front of her but still attached at the sides, Shelvon sat heavily on the edge of the bed and grabbed a bedpost. She couldn't get out of the gown herself, but she couldn't bear to call in her maid just yet. Not while her hands were still unsteady. Not when the room still smelled of sex.

The bed quivered beneath her, and at first Shelvon thought it was her own body that created the shaking. Then a couple of heartbeats later, it happened again, and she heard the bottles on her dressing table rattle.

And then it began in earnest. Born and raised in Nandel, Shelvon had never experienced an earthquake before, though she had heard they occurred periodically in Aaltah. Everyone had assured her they were harmless, just a little shaking that quickly went away with no harm done. Either everyone had lied, trusting that an uneducated barbarian such as she would not know the difference, or this quake was unusually strong.

Shelvon gripped the bedpost as the shaking grew stronger. From outside her door, she heard distant shouts and cries as luminants and other glassware began falling and breaking. It seemed she wasn't the only one the force of this quake had taken by surprise. She closed her eyes and held on as all around her things crashed to the floor and the world shook so hard she felt her own bones might shatter with the force of it. An iron chandelier that hung from her ceiling broke free, hitting the floor with a loud bang and smashing the dozen or so luminants it held.

Had the chandelier fallen a hand's-breadth to the right, Shelvon would have been crushed beneath it. Broken glass pattered against her skirts, but for once she was glad for all the thick layers, as nothing seemed to break the skin. The room was cast into darkness, and still Shelvon held on. She wondered if someone would come to check on her after hearing the crash, but her door remained closed.

The quake eventually petered out. Shelvon could tell from all the cries and shouts that the entire palace was in a state of panic, and yet it still stung that not one person came to look in on her. Her husband was certainly now surrounded by servants and guards, who no doubt shielded him with their bodies, but no one came running to help his pregnant wife. She'd weathered the quake by herself, feeling more alone than she'd ever felt in her life.

Even when it was over, no one immediately came to check on her. She continued to cling to the bedpost, not knowing whether the shaking would start again, her heart still pounding, her hands wet and clammy with sweat.

If she'd been injured, they'd have been too late, but eventually a couple of maids opened her door, at which point a virtual flood of servants and guards and healers descended on her. In the throng was the midwife, and Shelvon realized the sudden outpouring of care had nothing to do with her and everything to do with the child she carried. Her maid gave her body a cursory glance to make sure she wasn't bleeding and had no obvious broken bones, but she immediately gave way to the red-robed midwife, on loan from the Abbey until the child was delivered. The midwife's eyes filmed over, and Shelvon looked away. In Nandel, even the women of the Abbey were forbidden to practice magic. Shelvon couldn't get used to seeing a woman with her Mindseye open, though perhaps by the time her baby was born she would finally stop feeling so ill at ease. The midwife proclaimed the baby unharmed by the stress of the earthquake, much to the relief of the mingled ladies.

A handful of minutes after the midwife finished with her, Shelvon was alone again in her room with a hastily lit candelabra sitting on a bedside table and the worst of the glass and debris swept into a corner. It was then that she finally allowed herself to cry. She would never admit it out loud to anyone, but she would have been far from heartbroken if the midwife had reached a different conclusion. Producing an heir was her single purpose in life, and Shelvon knew she should want this child more than she wanted anything at all. And yet . . .

The pregnancy hadn't kept her husband from her bed as she'd hoped, nor had it made him love her—or even *like* her. All it had done was make her violently ill every morning and emphasize how expendable and unimportant she herself was to everyone. Even her servants.

Sinking deeper into a pool of self-pity—and not caring because there was no one around to see her and scold her—Shelvon let the tears fall unheeded. Until a sudden, sharp pain stabbed through her belly and her shrill cry brought her lady's maid running.

———

Alysoon fell into her bed exhausted, and yet she knew she would not sleep. Not after the horrors of this interminable night.

She'd done what she could to help the people of the Harbor District. Most of the nobles from the Terrace District had raced for the cliffs, only a few of the men staying behind to try to evacuate those who were in the most danger of being flooded. She'd flouted all conventions of womanly behavior by mounting her husband's horse and organizing flustered servants—both her own and those of her neighbors—urging them to help bring the commoners of the Harbor District to safety.

Falcor had eventually noticed she was not in the carriage and raced back to the manor, prepared to carry her to the palace against her will if necessary, but he was a man with a good heart. His duty to his king was to get Alys to safety, whatever it took, but his duty as a human being was to help with the evacuation. He'd chosen his duty as a human being, though he would surely face the wrath of the king if word of his actions reached the palace.

Alys had no idea how many were left in the Harbor District when the surge came. The Terrace District was peppered with clusters of commoners in various states of shock and dismay. The soldiers of the Citadel had done their best to drive people like cattle to higher ground, ruthlessly leaving the wounded and missing behind in their effort to get as many people to safety as possible. Many brave men had died, still trying to save others when the surge finally came, sweeping away boats and buildings as if they were twigs in a stream.

The water rose and rose and rose, filled with screaming, flailing people, as well as the bodies of the dead. It rose so high that water spilled over onto the first level of the Terrace District at the very height of the surge, flooding every expensive home and dragging a few more exhausted stragglers out to sea when it finally began to recede again.

Certainly hundreds had lost their lives this night, probably thousands. And though she knew she'd done her part and saved as many as she could, the weight of all those deaths sat heavily on Alys's shoulders. She lay down on her bed fully clothed, not even bothering to dowse the luminant Honor had put in her room. She stared at the ceiling and tried not to think, tried not to let the images of tonight's terror haunt her, but it was an impossible task. She turned over onto her side and felt the bulge in the pocket of her torn and soiled traveling dress.

Happy for the distraction, Alys sat up and pulled the book her mother had given her out of her pocket. Her nose wrinkled in instinctive distaste when she saw again the gaudy red cover and the overwrought title. She opened her Mindseye, staring at the book and still seeing no evidence that it was a spell vessel. She plucked three motes of Rho from the air around her, trying not to be distracted by the disturbing red dot. She pushed the three motes into the book, expecting it to suddenly glow with elements, but all she could see were the three motes of Rho she'd put there.

Shaking her head, she poked at the book as if that would somehow make something happen. With her Mindseye open and all the elements filling the air, she could barely make out the book's contours with her physical sight. Reluctantly, she closed her Mindseye. In her hand was the same tawdry red book of love poetry, unchanged by the influx of Rho. Alys wondered if her mother had been playing a trick on her, or if old age and austerity had begun whittling away at her mind.

So desperate was she for distraction that Alys actually cracked the book open, intending to read as much of the poetry as she could stomach. But her jaw dropped open when she turned to the first page.

When she'd opened the book in the Abbey, the first page had contained an illustration, a drawing of a woman smiling coyly as an absurdly lovestruck man gazed at her and offered her a single flower. Now, there was a small painted circle, white with a spot of red in it, that was clearly meant to represent the changed version of Rho Alys had seen with her Mindseye. And below that painted circle was a handwritten letter that began *My dearest Alysoon.*

Alys's heart beat erratically, her exhaustion all but forgotten.

This book was completely impossible. While she had no education in using magic, she'd been surrounded by magic items all her life. She couldn't say what made a luminant light up, or what made a cheval come to simulated life with a few motes of Rho, but she knew what they did. Just as she knew that the risers worked—or had before the earthquake had destroyed them. She knew of battle-field magic and death curses and women's minor magics—but she had never heard of anything remotely like the magic in this book. Magic that made the book look unmagical—even now, when its spell was active.

Then she read the first line of the letter.

By the time you read this, I will be dead.

Alys gasped and covered her mouth, tears springing to her eyes. She wanted to throw the book across the room, to deny its message, or at least pretend to disbelieve it.

Instead, she kept reading, finding one shock after another. She'd had a half-sister and a niece she'd never known existed, and they were dead along with her mother. All three of them took their own lives to cast a spell Alysoon would have said with complete certainty was impossible—except she'd seen the changed motes of Rho. *With the change in Rho,* her mother wrote,

> *women will for the first time have a degree of control over their own lives. From now on, no woman will conceive or carry a child unless she wishes to of her own free will. This is women's magic, and it is subtle. The spell will know the difference between true free will and coercion.*

"Impossible," Alys muttered under her breath, shaking her head. And yet even as she said it, she found herself believing it wasn't so impossible, after all.

> *The change we three have made is based in the Wellspring itself, and it will affect all the world. It's likely that such a*

disruption of the Wellspring will cause other changes, ones
we could not anticipate, but we believe unequivocally that
with time, the lives of women everywhere will be greatly im-
proved.

How could a spell affect the Wellspring itself? And how could casting a spell on the Wellspring bring anything but disaster?

Had the earthquake and the flood been an example of those "other changes" the spell might cause? Or was there more to come?

The men of this world are going to do everything they can
to reverse what we have done, but rest assured that it is
not possible. The spell is a culmination of generations of
work. Myself, Nadeen, and Vondeen are the only ones
who know what we've done and how we've done it, and
the knowledge dies with us. Which brings me to you, dear-
est daughter.

You will have inherited some of the magical abilities
that were bred into my blood. Not enough to reverse the
spell, but enough to make you vulnerable. Your father
will protect you, but he will not live forever, and the
crown prince will not be so forgiving. You, your brother,
and your family are all in danger, and for that I am
deeply sorry. My best hope of protecting you is through this
book, which you must keep hidden at all costs.

Each time you put Rho into the book, a magic lesson
will appear in these pages. I have tailored these lessons to
the abilities I know you have and the elements I know
you are capable of seeing. Read and absorb everything
carefully—the book will not present a new lesson until
you have mastered the current one.

I wish I could say with certainty that the magic you
will learn from this book will be enough to protect you. I
cannot control what my foresight allows me to see, and
I've had no glimpse of your future nor Tynthanal's. Take
care of your brother as best as you are able—and as best

*as he will allow. You are both more precious to me than I
can possibly say.*

Alys closed her eyes, fighting a wave of dizzying panic. Once
Delnamal found out the spell had been engineered by Alys's mother
and two descendants from the same bloodline, he would want her
and her brother and her children dead. More than he did already,
that is. Thanks to the divorce, neither she nor Tynthanal was legitimately in the line of succession, but their half-brother had always
seen them as a threat to his future throne—and as competitors for
their father's love. And now he would have a legitimate-sounding
reason to call for them to be thrown in the dungeon, at the very
least.

What magic could her mother possibly teach her through this
book that would protect her if the crown prince wanted her dead?
It seemed ridiculous to think Alys could protect herself, much less
herself and her children and her brother.

Her head suddenly pounding, she closed the book and closed
her eyes. She couldn't even begin to understand how her life—and
the lives of so many others—had changed so drastically over the
course of a single night.

CHAPTER FIVE

Princess Ellinsoltah groaned, then coughed and tried to gasp.
The weight of the man lying on top of her pressed the air out of her lungs, and she pushed on his chest, hoping to move him. He didn't budge.

She coughed again, breathing in clouds of dust from the settling debris, blinking against the darkness. Her whole body ached, and her mind felt sluggish as she tried to make sense of what had just happened.

Moments before, she'd been delicately sipping a glass of wine, dreading the inevitable conclusion of the intimate family dinner. The king—her grandfather—planned for the dinner to end with the announcement of her betrothal. The end of life as she knew it—though her father would insist she was being melodramatic. Perhaps if *he* were the one who had to upend his life and move to the dismal principality of Nandel to marry someone he couldn't stand, all for the good of a stupid trade agreement, he would see things her way.

She pushed harder on the body that held her pinned, her heart pounding as she tried to struggle out from under him. Around her, she heard someone moaning softly, and the occasional patter as loose bits of debris shifted.

Never had Ellin struggled as mightily to play the role of the dutiful daughter and loyal subject of the king than during the endless hours of that engagement dinner. Beside her, Zarsha of Nandel—her intended—had been his usual genial self, his clever tongue ever quick with the witty rejoinder that everyone but Ellin found so charming. He'd been courting her—despite his certain knowledge that she had no say in the marriage arrangement—for two months, and the only thing she truly knew about him was that he was an expert courtier, who always played to his audience and never revealed the smallest hint of what was truly behind the multitude of masks he wore. Not until they were married and living in Nandel—where she would have no more rights than his horses—would she see what truly lay behind those masks. But one did not wear such masks if one did not have something truly dreadful to hide.

The dinner had been drawing to its end when the earth had started to shake. Earthquakes were rare in the Kingdom of Aaltah, but they were unheard of in the Kingdom of Rhozinolm, so at first everyone was confused by the shaking. When it had grown stronger, more than one person at the table had pushed his or her chair back and stood indecisively on the swaying balcony with the lovely view of the palace grounds. Some laughed nervously and grabbed glasses that were about to topple, but Zarsha—for once—had not been amused.

"We should get inside," he said, pulling back Ellin's chair with her still in it. He wasn't even looking at her, but was instead staring at the columns that bordered the balcony—and held up the roof. Ellin followed his gaze and realized the columns were bowing and bending in ominous ways.

"Everyone keep your seats!" the king demanded, and the family was so used to following his orders that they all leapt to comply.

But Zarsha was not yet part of the family, and Ellin doubted he was much in the habit of following orders anyway. For all his skill at ingratiating himself to others, there was a degree of arrogance in him that Ellin thought might be a glimpse of his true self. He always thought himself the cleverest person in the room. To be fair, he usually was right, but Ellin thought a touch of humility would do him good.

"This balcony was not meant to withstand earthquakes," Zarsha shouted. He had the audacity to grab Ellin's arm and bodily pull her to her feet, shoving her chair out of the way and dragging her toward the nearest door. Perhaps a prelude to how he would treat her when he no longer felt obliged to follow Rhozinolm custom and acknowledge women as fellow human beings rather than possessions. He'd shown a great deal more courtesy to women than had other Nandel-born men Ellin had encountered, but she had no doubt that was just another one of his masks.

There was a deep, groaning sound, followed by a sharp crack. The earth continued to buck and writhe, and Ellin let out a gasp as she felt the angle of the floor beneath her feet change. Their dinner was being held on the upper of two balconies, and the crack they'd all heard came from the lower level.

"Hurry!" Zarsha shouted, shoving her toward the door.

The rest of the diners hastily decided Zarsha's was the correct approach and started struggling to their feet. Ellin tried to pull free of Zarsha's grip when she heard her mother cry out in pain as one of the luminants from the ceiling fell and struck her a glancing blow on the shoulder.

And then there was another sharp crack from much closer.

Zarsha plowed into Ellin, shoving her toward the door as the entire balcony lurched beneath them. Ellin's heels caught on something and she toppled backward. Everyone was screaming now—cries of terror and pain as the floor buckled and cracked and ultimately fell. From her vantage point on the floor, Ellin could see her husband-to-be cast one longing glance at the door. But instead of running for safety, he threw himself down on top of her, protecting her with his body as everything around them crumbled.

Ellin's confused sense of time couldn't decide whether that had all happened just a few heartbeats ago or whether she'd been lying dazed for hours.

But the shaking had finally stopped, and Ellin was pleasantly surprised to find herself alive, though she wasn't sure how long that would last if she couldn't get Zarsha off her. It was pitch-dark, and she couldn't tell if he was breathing, but he certainly wasn't moving. The pressure of his body on top of hers kept her from taking a full breath, and the drifting clouds of dust meant every breath she managed caused her to cough out more air than she took in.

To her immense relief, Zarsha shifted and groaned. She pushed on him some more, and he finally moved to the side just enough to let her draw in a deep breath. Another spasm of coughing followed, her ribs screaming in protest at the sharp movements.

There were no lit luminants anywhere in sight, but there was a full moon, and Ellin's eyes were beginning to adjust to the darkness. She pushed up onto her elbows—the most movement she could manage with Zarsha still lying half on top of her—and looked around.

All that was left of the balcony were a few feeble wooden beams, and most of those were broken. Ellin and Zarsha were lying on one of those beams right where it joined the outer wall of the palace at the doorway. The extra support of the sturdy wall had preserved a few floorboards around the beam and kept Ellin and Zarsha from crashing down to the floor below, though they were both covered in dust and glass shards and splintered wood. Zarsha was bleeding heavily from a gash on the back of his head. He was the only person in her field of vision.

"Mama!" she called. "Papa!"

But there was no answer.

She tried to crawl to the edge of the floor, but Zarsha had regained his senses and held her back. "It's not safe," he said in a raspy, cough-roughened voice.

Almost everyone she knew and loved had been on that balcony with her. Her mother, her father, her grandfather, her uncle. She let out an incoherent cry of rage and grief and fear.

Maybe they were all right, she told herself. The fall hadn't been from any great height, after all. They would be injured, certainly, and they were probably too disoriented to respond to her cries. But surely they weren't *dead*.

"Mama!" she screamed again, desperate to hear her mother answer back. Lights were flickering around the edges of her vision now, servants and palace guards with hastily lit candles and torches converging on the ruined balcony and calling out urgently in search of survivors.

Somehow, Ellin ended up wrapped in Zarsha's arms, sobbing against the dirty and torn silk at his shoulder as he made soothing sounds and rocked her. She was in too much pain, both emotional and physical, to care that she was taking comfort in the arms of a man she despised.

Ellin felt numb in body and mind. The numbness was caused at least in part by the potion the healer had bullied her into drinking. As promised, it had soothed her raw throat and eased the pain in her ribs, but she'd barely drunk a quarter of it before her head had started swimming. She poured the rest out while the healer wasn't looking, having no wish to fall into oblivion until she'd received word about the rest of her family. She'd demanded information from no fewer than five people, and no one had been able—or willing—to tell her anything.

To get out from under the watchful eye of the healer, Ellin had retreated to her bedchamber, swaying on her feet as though the healing potion were in full effect. The healer looked smugly satisfied as Ellin leaned on her ladies and allowed them to guide her to her rooms. But when the ladies tried to undress her and put her to bed, she stopped them and ordered them out.

It was well past midnight by now, and Ellin was more exhausted than she could say, but she refused to go to sleep. While no one she had yet encountered had been willing to tell her anything, she knew there was one person who was not afraid to tell her the truth, even when the truth was unpalatable. She spent a few minutes in front of a mirror, brushing off the worst of the dirt and debris that was ground into her skin and clothes. There was a swath of Zarsha's blood in her hair, but she cut off the pink hair ribbons that showed the stain, and the rest of it was barely visible against the black braids and coils. She still looked a mess, but at least she could roam the halls without everyone stopping her to see if she was injured.

She slipped into the hallway, trying to decide where best to look for Graesan Rah-Brondar, her master of the guard. He'd been off duty tonight because of the family dinner and the presence of the king's honor guard, but she was sure he'd have joined the search for survivors in the rubble of the collapsed balconies. If any of her family still lived, he would know.

She'd taken no more than a dozen steps from her doorway when he turned the corner at the opposite end of the hall. Her throat caught at the sight of him, and it was all she could do not to fling herself into his arms. Not until she saw him did she realize how frightened she had been that he, too, might have come to harm.

Graesan was everything her intended was not. Loyal, genuine, kind, and easy to talk to. While Zarsha was quick with the easy quip and empty, shallow banter, Graesan actually listened to—and cared about—what other people said. She'd developed what she'd thought of as a teenage crush on him when he'd first joined her honor guard. But that was five years ago now, and the "crush" showed no sign of fading away with maturity.

Objectively, Zarsha was the more classically handsome of the two. His blue eyes, which forever marked his Nandel origins, were a little off-putting, but his high cheekbones, his arrow-straight nose, and his full lips carved out a beautifully symmetrical face, and his tall frame and nicely muscled body made nearly every woman in the kingdom watch him admiringly when he walked past. But it was Graesan's slightly hawkish nose and his lean, wiry build that made Ellin's pulse race, and if she could choose any man in the world to be hers, she would choose him.

Graesan gave her a formal bow as she hurried to close the distance between them. She wanted so badly to reach out and touch him, to reassure herself that he was unhurt. His clothing was filthy, his hands covered in dust and scratches, his nails ripped and ragged. Her guess had been right; he'd been digging through the rubble.

"Are you all right, Your Highness?" he asked when he rose from his bow, his eyes scanning up and down her body in a way that would not be considered strictly proper. There was too much fear, too much genuine concern in those eyes. Usually, he was more careful and reserved—if anyone guessed they had feelings for each other, he would be summarily dismissed, no matter how proper their outward behavior. But unlike Zarsha, he had no aptitude for subterfuge, and he could not hide his feelings at a time like this.

"I'm fine," she said. "Nothing worse than a few bruises, which the healer has already taken care of." Zarsha's injuries had been far more serious, but he'd been conscious and alert when the healers had separated them, and she presumed he wasn't in mortal danger. It occurred to her that if he hadn't dragged her toward the doorway and then shielded her with his own body, she might be dead right now.

Was it possible she owed Zarsha her life? Ellin shuddered, thinking about how a man like him might take advantage of such a perceived obligation.

Then she shook off thoughts of her injured husband-to-be and met Graesan's eyes as she steeled herself for the question she had to ask, no matter how badly she dreaded the answer.

"My family?" she asked in the barest ghost of a whisper, her eyes already stinging with tears. Instinct told her that if there was good news to be had, her repeated questions earlier would not have been so roundly ignored.

Graesan winced in sympathy, his hands twitching toward her as though wanting to offer her physical comfort. "You and Zarsha of Nandel are the only survivors from that balcony."

She covered her mouth as a half-gasp, half-sob escaped her. "My father?" she choked out. "My mother? My uncle? The king?"

Graesan shook his head. "I'm sorry, Your Highness," he said, and she heard genuine sorrow in his voice. He swallowed hard, struggling against emotions his fellow guardsmen would almost certainly mock him for letting show. "The tragedy is . . . unimaginable."

Tears flowed freely down Ellin's cheeks, and she leaned against a wall for support as her knees threatened to buckle. Her relationship with her father and her grandfather had been strained—and that was putting it mildly—ever since they had decided to ship her off to Nandel in a marriage she'd made no secret of objecting to, but to have lost them both, as well as her mother and her uncle, in one night . . .

The pain stole her breath and made the floor feel unsteady beneath her feet once more. She was utterly alone in the world now, and the desolation of that knowledge was unbearable. Graesan finally set aside concern for propriety, taking both her hands in his and squeezing, lending what support he could. She wished he would take her in his arms, wished she could hide her head against his shoulder and sob out the renewed burst of pain as she'd done with Zarsha. But Zarsha was her intended husband and her social equal, and Graesan was not. He would face censure even for holding her hands if anyone were to see them. Certainly he could not afford an embrace.

Clinging to the hands that were her only lifeline, Ellin searched for the strength she so desperately needed to help her endure the agony.

CHAPTER SIX

The last Alysoon had heard, the death toll of last night's devastating quake and flood had reached two thousand, with thousands more missing or wounded. The Harbor District was in shambles, its displaced survivors homeless and penniless and lost. Rescuers were still searching through the wreckage, and soldiers were doing their best to discourage scavengers, but it would be a long time before true order was restored.

The Terrace District had fared better, with only the lowest level experiencing any flooding, and few homes taking substantial damage beyond broken windows and toppled furniture. Alys's manor house would be livable after the servants had had a few hours to clear out the most vital rooms, and she planned to send for the children as soon as that work was complete. No doubt the palace would be more comfortable, but she greatly preferred her own home over enforced proximity to her father and half-brother.

She had meant to spend a few hours with her mother's book

while the servants continued the cleanup, but the peremptory tone of the royal summons that appeared just after breakfast made it clear she was expected to drop everything and come at once. Under ordinary circumstances, Alys would have delayed just because she could, but her mother's ominous warnings still rang in her ears, and antagonizing her father for no reason would not be wise.

Reluctantly, she'd left the book behind and set out on the long and uncomfortable journey up the zigzagging road to the top of the cliffs. The palace was an enormous walled complex built around Aaltah's Well—the heart of the city of Aalwell, indeed of the Kingdom of Aaltah itself. While the palace had originally been designed as a fortress meant to protect the Well, each successive king had adorned it and added on to it until over the centuries it became a virtual city all by itself.

Alys was not surprised to find the royal palace showing few signs of last night's devastation. There were fewer luminants in the halls than usual, and the rooms all looked comparatively sparse from the removal of glass-fronted cabinets and breakable ornaments. A marble bust of King Aaltyn's grandfather was conspicuously missing from the top of the grand staircase, and the crackled floor tiles below its pedestal suggested its likely fate. But she doubted she would have recognized these differences if she weren't intimately familiar with the palace.

The entire palace was teeming with carpenters and stonemasons and maids and footmen, all industriously setting things to rights. Alys suspected that within a week, the palace would be fully restored to its usual grandeur. In a better, fairer world, all those carpenters and stonemasons and servants would be down in the Harbor District, trying to help those who were in desperate need, but Alys was under no illusions as to the priorities of the Crown and the aristocracy.

She was escorted to the royal living quarters, and then deposited in a sitting room and left to wait. And wait. And wait.

After what she judged to be at least an hour, she'd attempted to leave the sitting room only to be blocked by one of the palace guards stationed outside the door.

"His Majesty has requested that you remain here, my lady," the guard said apologetically.

"I've been remaining here for over an hour," she said. "I was going to go and check in on my children." *Which I would have done when I first arrived if I hadn't been led to believe the king was waiting for me.* "I'll be right back."

But the guard remained planted in the doorway. "I'm sorry, my lady." He shifted in apparent discomfort. "I have my orders."

Alys suppressed a shiver of unease. The tone of the summons, the long wait, and the guard's refusal to let her leave the sitting room painted the picture of an angry king. Her father had always had a temper, but rarely had she found it directed toward her. Perhaps he'd heard that she'd spent the night on horseback, trying to help the rescue efforts. Her behavior had been improper and unladylike, to be sure, and she'd expected him to be irritated by it. But not actually *angry.* He might not approve of some of her more mannish ways, but he'd tolerated them even when she'd been living under his roof and he'd had the ability to curb her behavior.

Returning to the uncomfortable sofa in front of the cheerfully crackling fire, she chewed her lip and stared into the flames. Her mother's letter had warned her of danger to come, but surely that danger wouldn't come from her own father. He couldn't even know that her mother had been responsible for last night's disaster and the change in Rho. He couldn't yet know what that change signified.

When she'd been waiting for at least two hours, a guard finally came to fetch her and said His Majesty was ready to see her. She half expected to be led to the formal audience chamber for some kind of official reprimand, but she was taken instead to yet another sitting room and told to wait once again. This might not be a formal audience, but it was not a casual meeting between father and daughter, either. His tactics were making that abundantly clear.

This time, she had to wait only a few minutes before the door opened and her father strode in.

At seventy-two, King Aaltyn II was well past his prime, but a stranger seeing him would never have guessed his age. Tall and barrel-chested, with the straight back and the salt-and-pepper hair of a much younger man, he exuded strength and authority. He was dressed today in a quilted royal purple doublet with fine gold embroidery. A rich velvet cape draped over his shoulders and attached across his chest with an enormous sapphire brooch. Alys didn't need Mindsight to know that brooch was a powerful magic item, though it was not one she'd seen her father wear before. Atop the king's head sat a thin gold circlet peppered with more sapphires, and that magic item she *did* recognize. With the addition of a few motes of Rho, the circlet could create an invisible shield all around the king's body.

That he was wearing the circlet in the palace, in the privacy of the royal residence, did not bode well for his state of mind. Nor did the coldness in his hazel eyes or his straight, thin lips.

Alys quickly rose from the sofa and gave a deep curtsy when ordinarily she'd give no more than a token bob.

"What do you know about this?" the king demanded, thrusting a small sheet of parchment in her face.

She gave him a worried, puzzled look as she took the parchment. "What is it?" she asked, frowning at the parchment, which had clearly once been tightly rolled and wished to return to its natural state. She made the assumption that it had been delivered by a flier.

Her father didn't answer, merely glaring at her from under heavy brows. She forced the little roll open and saw several paragraphs of tidy but heavily slanted handwriting that she recognized as her mother's.

The message was as concise as it was devastating. The abbess laid out what she, her daughter, and her granddaughter had done, and how the changed Rho would affect the lives of women everywhere. She also claimed that the only people who could understand the spell well enough to have a chance of undoing it had died in its casting. Finally, she said she'd sent similar messages by flier to the kingdoms of Rhozinolm and Khalpar, as well as to each of the four principalities, so that everyone would know what the changed appearance of Rho meant.

"Well?" the king demanded before Alys had reached the end of the message. Not that she needed to read every word to understand his anger.

"Well what?" she asked, then immediately regretted the quick and easy rejoinder. Right now, she was speaking to King Aaltyn, not to her father, and a wise woman would choose her words carefully. "I didn't know about it, if that's what you're asking," she hastened to say.

"You don't look surprised!" he snapped, his eyes flashing as he glared at her so fiercely she had to fight the temptation to take a step backward.

Alys cursed herself for not thinking things through. She'd had hours of traveling and waiting, and instead of using that time to think about what the king's summons meant and how she should respond, she'd assumed it had something to do with her unladylike behavior and given her position little thought. Her father would know perfectly well she'd been to the Abbey yesterday, and it wasn't unreasonable for him to think her mother might have warned her what was going to happen—or at least said goodbye.

If her mother *had* warned her, Alys could be charged with treason for not passing that warning on to the king. And if she *hadn't* warned her, then Alys should have been visibly shocked by the contents of that letter.

Telling her father about the spell book and its hidden message was out of the question, so Alys had to think quickly to escape the trap she had blindly stepped in.

"Mama was acting strange when I saw her yesterday," she said, forcing herself to meet her father's angry gaze and hoping she looked completely innocent and honest. "I kept asking her what was wrong, and she kept telling me it was nothing, but . . . Well, I could tell it wasn't nothing. I had the uncomfortable feeling that she was saying goodbye, but I told myself it was my imagination. Then the earthquake happened."

Alys shuddered and hugged herself as images of last night's chaos forced themselves into her mind. The sound of the rushing water rending and tearing as it destroyed everything in its path would echo in her nightmares for years to come, punctuated by the screams of those being dragged out to sea and the sobs of those who were left behind.

"I didn't think the earthquake had anything to do with Mama, but then when everyone kept telling me that Rho had changed . . ." She let her voice trail off.

The king was still glaring at her, his chin still jutting out in a way that said his jaws were tightly clenched with fury. It took every scrap of Alys's will not to break eye contact like a frightened—and guilty—child.

"I had no idea what was going to happen," she finished firmly. "Do you honestly think I would have kept quiet if I had?"

"You were always your mother's creature," he said, and she flinched at the bitterness in his voice.

"I loved my mother." Her throat tightened and her eyes began to sting as the weight of loss settled on her shoulders. "But I would not have let her do this had I known."

Which was why her mother had settled for those cryptic, useless warnings, she realized. Maybe the change that was made to Rho would genuinely improve the lot of women everywhere—Alys regarded that claim with a heavy dose of skepticism—but the loss of life had been intolerable. If Alys had had any inkling of what her mother was up to, she *would* have found some way to stop it—even if it meant betraying her mother by telling her father.

"Please believe me, Papa," she begged, and was relieved to see a hint of softening at the corners of his eyes and lips. He might not be wholly convinced, but she had at least succeeded in planting doubt of her guilt in his mind.

She glanced again at the scroll in her hand, her mind hardly able to encompass the enormity of what her mother had done. Not only had she cast the terrible spell, she had sent out fliers to make sure the whole world knew about it.

"Everyone's going to blame us for this," she said, shaking her head.

Her father let out a heavy sigh. "Thanks to your mother shouting her guilt from the rooftops, of course they will. And rightly so."

"All of Aaltah isn't to blame for one woman's acts."

Her father laughed briefly. "I did not raise a naïve daughter."

"It wasn't for lack of trying," she retorted. She wouldn't say she felt completely at ease with him yet, but she no longer felt like she was talking to a dangerous stranger. He gave her a reproachful look, but didn't otherwise scold.

"Shelvon lost her baby last night." Her father pointed at the message she still held. "Delnamal saw that message before it reached me."

Alys grimaced. She barely knew her half-brother's wife, but she knew Delnamal much better than she'd have wished. Perhaps Shelvon lost the baby due to nothing more than the stress of last night's earthquake, but many would assume she'd lost it due to the spell. No one would want to suggest out loud that a woman might not wish to bear the crown prince's baby, but no one seeing the two of them together would mistake theirs for a happy marriage.

"Is Shelvon all right?" she asked. For all his faults, Alys had never known her half-brother to hit a woman, but if he blamed his wife for losing the baby, she wouldn't put it past him.

"The midwife assures us she will make a full recovery and that there's no reason she shouldn't be able to carry her next child to term."

It was on the tip of Alys's tongue to point out that wasn't what she'd meant, but the quelling look on her father's face convinced her to keep the thought to herself. She wasn't sure if he was blind to all his heir's faults or if he merely refused to acknowledge them, but he was highly sensitive to anything Alys said that could be perceived as critical. Rarely did knowing that stop Alys from criticizing, but rousing the king's temper a second time seemed ill-advised.

"Delnamal wants me to arrest you on suspicion of treason," the king said, and Alys's heart skipped a beat, though the accusation was hardly a surprise.

Her mother had warned her, and Delnamal had always hated her anyway. Practically all his life, he'd tried to drive a wedge between his father and both his half-siblings. As a teenager and a young woman, Alys had tried to win him over with kindness, but she had eventually realized his hatred and jealousy ran too deep to be conquered. Since then, her defenses had turned to avoidance when possible, chilly courtesy when not.

"Is that why you summoned me?" she asked in a ghostly whisper. She was sure all blood had drained from her face, and suddenly the tone of the summons and her father's anger when he'd entered the room took on new meaning.

"Of course not," he said, but she wasn't sure she believed him.

It was hard to imagine her father ordering her arrest, throwing her into some dungeon and putting her life in danger. But then she doubted her mother had ever imagined her loving husband divorcing her, banishing her to the Abbey, and publicly disinheriting their children. He'd told Alys time after time that in denying her his name, he was not denying her his love. But he was the only one who believed he could possibly love Alysoon Rai-Brynna as much as he'd loved Alysoon Rah-Aaltyn.

"I knew you couldn't have been part of this," the king said, apparently forgetting that he'd entered the room in a rage and all but accused her of just that. "However, Delnamal won't be the only one who suspects you. You were right to send the children here last night. And you should have come yourself. You will be safe here."

"I'll be perfectly safe in my own house," Alys said firmly. Which was far more diplomatic than what she wanted to say, that she would be far safer putting as much distance as possible between herself and her half-brother.

"Not without a husband you won't!"

"I have an honor guard, Papa. And a houseful of servants." She tried to imagine how her late husband could possibly have protected her against any attackers who might blame her for her mother's spell, and it almost made her laugh. Sylnin had been a dear, sweet man and a better husband than she ever could have hoped for, but he'd been far more philosopher than soldier. Their thirteen-year-old son could have bested him in a wrestling match.

"And *here* you would have them along with the entire palace guard."

Alys hoped her father was truly thinking only of her protection. It was also possible he wanted to keep her close so that he could keep an eye on her.

"I'm sure neither Delnamal nor Shelvon would be happy to see me wandering the hallway."

"It isn't their decision to make."

"No. It's mine. And I would like to take my children home so we can all return to something resembling normal as soon as possible."

Alys held her breath as her father thought it over. Where she lived was her decision now that she was a widow—and would continue to be so until she remarried or until Corlin came of age—but if the king really did suspect her of conspiring with her mother, he could force her to stay. He might not want to throw her in a dungeon as Delnamal would prefer, but he could put her under house arrest of a sort. It would destroy her reputation and put her in exactly the kind of danger he'd said he wanted to protect her from, but he could do it.

The king heaved a sigh and shook his head. "You are as stubborn and reckless as always. I will send additional men for your honor guard. Neither you nor your children may leave the house without at least three men until things settle down."

Alys bit down hard on the urge to argue.

CHAPTER SEVEN

Ellin had spent most of the day in a numbing haze, trying to come to terms with everything that had happened. Occasionally, the numbness deserted her and she wept. It was likely that she'd never have been able to repair her relationship with her father after he'd agreed to marry her off to Zarsha of Nandel, but now she'd never have the chance to try. To have lost so many people all in one day was just . . . Well, she didn't have the words to fully express all she felt.

In the immediate aftermath of the tragedy, she had not given any thought to what all those deaths meant to anyone but herself; however in the cold light of the next morning, it had occurred to her that not only had the king died, but both his heirs had died also.

Once or twice, she'd allowed herself a passing worry about the future of the kingdom with no clear heir to the throne, but mostly she'd been too sunk in her own misery to give the situation any significant thought. She'd tried to think as little as possible as the

interminable day brought a constant wave of well-wishers and condolences that she could barely tolerate.

Late in the afternoon, she received a visit from Semsulin Rah-
Lomlys, the lord chancellor and head of the royal council. Fifty
years old, with steel-gray hair, a hawkish nose, a razor-sharp mind,
and an even sharper tongue, Semsulin somehow managed to arouse
an equal quantity of dislike and respect in everyone who knew him.
Well, in *almost* everyone. Ellin couldn't manage much in the way of
respect, for she knew it was the lord chancellor who had first suggested marrying her to Zarsha of Nandel. He'd known her since
she was born, and had a daughter of his own, and yet he'd thought
nothing of shipping her off to a principality where she would have
few—if any—rights beyond what her husband granted her. She understood that the trade agreements were important—Rhozinolm
got almost all its iron from those agreements, and a large percentage of its gemstones, which were necessary not just for adornment
but for use in magic items, as gemstones could hold a large number
of elements. But she was certain there could have been some way to
renew those agreements without forcing her to marry Zarsha, if
only Semsulin and the king would have worked harder at it. She
would never forgive him for planting that idea in her grandfather's
ear, and he was the last person she wanted to hear condolences
from. Unfortunately, simple manners insisted she receive him.

He was shown into the parlor, which had seen a steady influx of
visitors for whom she had forced a façade of strength and stoicism
throughout the day. Seeing him and remembering the wedge he
had driven between her and her father—a wedge she would never
be able to repair—it was all she could do not to burst out in tears.
She had allowed him as much courtesy as she could muster by not
turning him away. True warmth and welcome were beyond her.

"Lord Chancellor," she said in chilly greeting. She made no attempt to temper the frost in her voice. It wasn't as if he didn't know
how she felt about him.

"Your Highness," he said, bowing elegantly. Although he was
impeccably dressed and groomed as always, there was a tightness

around his eyes that suggested he was grieving, and his shoulders had an unaccustomed slump to them.

Ellin braced herself against the onslaught of grief he was about to trigger with his sympathy. He met her eyes boldly in a way others today had been reluctant to do, as if her grief might burn holes in them if they gazed upon it too closely.

"I'd tell you how sorry I am for your loss, but I know you don't want to hear that from me."

Ellin blinked. She'd have liked to answer with some appropriately cutting remark, but none came to mind. "Then why . . . ?" she started, but words failed her. She'd been so certain she knew what he was going to say that she seemed incapable of adjusting to the reality. She was not usually so slow-witted, but grief and lack of sleep had slowed her both in body and in mind.

"Why am I here?" he finished for her. She nodded, suddenly certain she was not going to like the answer. "I can't imagine how you must be feeling right now, and I swear I would not be coming to you like this if it weren't important."

Her whole world, her whole life, had crumbled into ashes last night. "What could possibly be so important that you had to bring it to me today of all days?" she asked with some heat. "I want nothing more than to be left alone."

Semsulin bowed his head. "I know. And I would honor your request if I didn't feel it was critical that we talk immediately." He gave her a shrewd look. "Besides, I suspect you already know what brings me."

She squirmed in her seat. All day long, she'd been shunting thoughts of the succession aside, reminding herself time and time again that it was none of her business. But to what else could Semsulin possibly be referring?

"The succession is none of my concern," she said. "I presume the royal council will honor Lord Kailindar's claim to the throne."

Kailindar Rai-Chantah was the late king's illegitimate son by his favorite mistress. While not technically in the line of succession, he was the late king's closest surviving male relative, and though the

king had never married Kailindar's mother, he had nonetheless acknowledged Kailindar as his son. It was not unheard of for an acknowledged illegitimate son to take the throne when no legitimate
heir presented himself.

The succession would have been irregular, but nothing to consider a crisis, if it weren't for the late king's second-closest surviving
male relative, his illegitimate grandson, Tamzin Rai-Mailee. Tamzin
was everything Kailindar was not. Young. Handsome. Personable.
And a veritable hero of the people after his role in wiping out an
enclave of bandits who'd been terrorizing the outer provinces. He
and Kailindar also harbored a violent hatred for each other. If the
council put Kailindar on the throne, it was highly unlikely Tamzin
would hold still for it. And with his widespread popularity and legendary ability in battle, he could easily muster a significant army.

"If the crown goes to Lord Kailindar, there will be war," Semsulin said. The lord chancellor was not one to mince words.

Ellin had no doubt he was right. She'd known Lord Tamzin since
childhood, though he was ten years older than she. Behind his easy
charm and good looks, he was one of the most petty, vengeful men
she'd ever known, and she'd never heard of him letting go of a
grudge. She'd also heard plenty of whispers—which his adoring fans
conveniently ignored—that his defeat of the bandits had not been so
heroic as he claimed. Not a single bandit had survived to be put on
trial, and while he and his small band of men swore they'd been killed
because they had refused to surrender, it was hard to believe every
last one—some of them were no older than twelve—had been stubborn and stupid enough to fight to the death. There'd also been
rumors that before freeing the kidnapped women Tamzin had supposedly been fighting to save, he'd let his men rape them as spoils of
war on the theory that they were already ruined anyway so it didn't
matter. It was a rumor Ellin had no trouble believing based on her
opinion of Tamzin's character. His mask was as pretty as Zarsha's, but
once she'd glimpsed what was behind it, it could never fool her again.

"Well Kailindar certainly isn't going to step aside for Tamzin,"
she responded with a sinking heart.

"No indeed. He would only step aside for a legitimate heir."

She frowned. "But there *is* no legitimate heir."

Semsulin said nothing, merely looked at her and raised his eyebrows.

"Surely you don't mean *me*!" she sputtered. Admittedly, every time she'd started thinking about the succession, she'd forced her thoughts to turn aside, but she had never even flirted with the idea of taking the throne herself. "In case you haven't noticed, I'm a woman."

The corners of Semsulin's eyes crinkled with what looked like genuine humor. "I had my suspicions." He quickly sobered. "You would not be the first woman to sit on the throne of Rhozinolm."

Ellin swallowed hard and made her way to the nearest chair. Her wobbly knees threatened to collapse beneath her, and it was all she could do to sit gracefully and with an air of control. "But that was centuries ago," she breathed. "And Queen Shazinzal took the throne because there was no male heir to be found and we were at war."

Semsulin nodded sagely. "And you will take the throne to *prevent* a war. Lord Kailindar and Lord Tamzin would take up arms each against the other, but they are far less likely to take up arms against *you*."

She thought that might be true about her uncle Kailindar. His hatred of Tamzin was legendary, but in all other ways he seemed a steady and reasonable man. He was not without ambition, but he was hardly power-mad. He would not want to put the kingdom through a war as long as he didn't have to stomach bending a knee to Tamzin.

Tamzin, on the other hand, made no secret of his desire for power and his lack of interest in anyone but himself. She imagined his first thought on learning of the deaths of the king and his heirs was that the crown would look most excellent resting on his own head. The best interests of the kingdom were unlikely to be of much concern to him.

Semsulin read her doubts easily. "A bastard heir raising an army to challenge the claim of another bastard is one thing. But you are the legitimate heir to the throne—our new Queen Shazinzal. It will be much harder to raise an army against a legitimate heir, especially when there's a clear precedent. Tamzin is bold and he is arrogant, but he is not stupid."

Ellin nodded absently. Queen Shazinzal was one of the most beloved monarchs Rhozinolm had ever known. She'd been on the throne when Rhozinolm finally won one of its many long and costly wars against Aaltah, which earned her a great deal of good will. And after the war, she'd promptly married one of the royal dukes and ceded the throne to her husband. In total, her reign had lasted less than two years. Ellin doubted history would have been so kind to the sovereign queen had she attempted to remain on the throne, nor did she think her own ascension to that throne would be met with such wholehearted support.

"Of course," Semsulin continued, "if you were to take the throne, marriage with Zarsha of Nandel would no longer be an option." There was an unpleasant gleam in his eyes—the gleam of a man who knew exactly how to get what he wanted and did not for a moment scruple to play with the lives of others.

Ellin's heart nearly skipped a beat. Of course she couldn't marry Zarsha if she became queen. Like Queen Shazinzal before her, she would be expected to cede her throne to her husband when she married. Which meant she could not marry a foreigner, for no foreigner could ever be accepted as king.

"It is for the good of all that I ask you to take the throne," Semsulin said. "To stop a war, and to escape a fate I know you did not wish for yourself."

She glared at him. "A fate I would never have faced had you not whispered in the king's ear!"

The lord chancellor snorted. "You truly think the king needed *me* to suggest a marriage with Nandel? He'd had his eye on those trade agreements for nearly a decade, and he knew exactly how best to assure they were renewed on favorable terms. You were bound for Nandel since you were a child, whether you knew it or not."

Ellin gripped both arms of the chair she was sitting in and fought—no doubt in vain—to keep her feelings off her face.

How easy it had been to blame Semsulin for suggesting the despised marriage. She owed him no family loyalty and had never liked him. Her father had assured her the marriage was the lord chancellor's idea, though he had also assured her—with much feigned sympathy—that both he and the king agreed it was best for the kingdom. It was her duty as a daughter of Rhozinolm and a member of the royal family to marry for political advantage. An "unfortunate reality of life" her father had called it.

Ellin's eyes were stinging, and she prayed that she wouldn't start crying in front of the odious man. She reminded herself that he might be lying, trying to ingratiate himself to the woman he intended to put on the throne and distance himself from the machinations that had doomed her to a marriage bound for misery and disaster.

"It was you," she whispered, barely able to force any sound from her throat.

Semsulin grabbed a nearby chair and dragged it closer so he could sit an arm's length away from her. It was a breach of propriety when she hadn't offered him a seat, but her emotions were too out of control to let her rebuke his behavior without the risk of a humiliating breakdown.

"If the king had been so thick he needed my prompting, then I would have suggested it," Semsulin said. "But, Your Highness . . . Your Majesty, King Linolm was a shrewd man and wise, and he was cognizant that his first duty would always be to the kingdom. Not to his family. Not even to himself. It is the only appropriate attitude for a sovereign, and it is one you yourself will have to adopt when you take the throne.

"We will have to find a new way to motivate Nandel to renew the trade agreements now that we no longer can offer your hand in marriage. That will not be easy, especially not when the prince's daughter is married to the heir to the throne of Aaltah. We needed a royal marriage to cement the alliance, and now we can't have one."

Ellin's head was spinning again. "I lost my whole family less than a day ago," she rasped, shaking her head. "You're telling me I have to take the throne myself to stop a war. And you want me to tackle a sensitive political issue that yourself, the king, and the entire royal council couldn't solve without using my marriage as a tool."

He leaned forward, and if she didn't know him too coldhearted to experience such human emotions, she would have labeled the look on his face as sympathy. "I'm not suggesting you solve it immediately. It's urgent, to be sure, but we still have a year before the old agreements expire. I merely wish you to understand the challenges you will face when you take the throne. There are certainly others, but I won't burden you with them now."

"I haven't said yes yet, you know." For all the power of the lord chancellor and the royal council, they could not put her on the throne without her consent.

"But you will," he said with absolute confidence. "You were willing to marry Zarsha for the good of the kingdom. That tells me all I need to know about your character and sense of duty."

Her fists clenched, and she glared at him. "It shows you I feared being sent to the Abbey of the Unwanted more than I feared marrying that insufferable bastard and living as a barbarian in the mountains."

He shrugged as if the distinction were insignificant. "I trust that you will fear our kingdom being torn apart by war more than you fear the burdens of the crown."

He stood and returned his chair to its original position, lining up the chair legs with the faint impressions they had made in the carpet beneath.

"I will leave you with your thoughts," he said. "Send for me if you need me. If I don't hear from you, I will be back tomorrow to discuss your decision. We cannot leave the throne empty for a moment longer than necessary. You can be certain both Kailindar and Tamzin will be coming to the capital the moment they hear the news, and we should have you in place before either arrives."

He bowed and left the room, and Ellin wondered when she would awaken from this all-too-vivid nightmare.

Alys planned to return home from the meeting with her father as soon as humanly possible and was making her way through the palace halls to gather her children when into her path stepped the man she least wanted to see. She came to a wary stop just out of his reach and eyed him with what she hoped looked like cool aplomb.

Delnamal Rah-Aaltyn, the Crown Prince of Aaltah, was eleven years Alys's junior. He'd been eight years old when she'd left home to marry, and already well on his way to being thoroughly disagreeable. He bore a striking resemblance to his mother, Queen Xanvin, with his round, dimpled face, his slightly upturned nose, and his unfortunately diminutive stature. The queen, however, possessed a level of grace, humility, and dignity her son could never hope to match. Alys couldn't say she was fond of the woman who had supplanted her mother, but she at least respected her. She could not say the same of the crown prince.

Delnamal's lip rose in a sneer of distaste. Alys wished she'd chosen a different path to the children's rooms. Her emotions were still raw after everything that had happened, and she wasn't sure she trusted herself to hold her tongue when Delnamal inevitably managed to get under her skin.

"I see you're not in shackles," he said, shaking his head wonderingly. "Pity."

Alys clenched her teeth and reminded herself that silence was always her wisest option. He had an impressive ability to turn even the most harmless pleasantry into fuel to kindle his temper. A dutiful sister might be expected to give him condolences for the loss of his heir-to-be, despite his scathing words. However Alys could clearly see the opening such condolences would give him, so instead she said nothing.

"I suppose this means you managed to convince Father of your innocence," her half-brother continued. "I can't say I'm surprised, though I had hoped he would finally see sense about you."

He took a step closer. Alys debated whether to step backward to try to maintain a safe distance. Showing fear—or even discomfort—

in front of a bully was rarely a good idea, but her survival instincts insisted that staying out of his reach was important.

Reminding herself that Delnamal was more of an emotional bully than a physical one, Alys forced herself to hold her ground. When he glared at her, she held his gaze, refusing to look away as if she were guilty of something.

"How long have you known what your mother was planning?" he asked. He was now close enough that she could smell onions on his breath. Perhaps he felt a man of his rank needn't abide by court etiquette, which suggested using a minty mouth rinse after each meal. Then again, his straining doublet told the tale of a man who did not confine his eating to meal times.

Alys surreptitiously scanned the hallway, wondering if there were any witnesses around who might inspire Delnamal to keep his temper in check, but she saw only servants. He wouldn't care if he made an ass of himself in front of servants, considering them as background scenery rather than people.

Alys stepped to the side, hoping to slip past him without a word, but he was expecting the move and blocked her path once more.

"I asked you a question, sister mine."

His eyes bored into her, and he leaned ever so slightly forward into her space. He was no taller than she, but his weight made him an imposing figure nonetheless. Despite her assurances to herself that she was in no physical danger from her half-brother, he was easily large and angry enough to intimidate her.

"You have no interest in my answer," she said, "so there's no point in demanding one. Now let me pass."

She tried another side step, only to be blocked again.

"You think that because you can fool Father, you can fool *me*," he snarled. "Well you're wrong!"

Alys rolled her eyes dramatically. All well and good to tell herself to stay silent, but it seemed Delnamal had no intention of allowing it. "Just because you would like me to be guilty of something doesn't mean I am. Not that I expect you to understand such a subtle distinction."

Her barbed words missed their mark, for Delnamal showed no

signs of having heard the insult. "Mark my words, I will see you executed as a traitor for what you've done."

Alys hoped she kept her expression impassive and unconcerned while a chill traveled down her spine. "I have done *nothing*," she insisted. Not that her insistence would mean anything to Delnamal, not when he'd already tried and convicted her in his mind. Without needing a shred of evidence save his own personal dislike of her.

"Father won't always be here to protect you," Delnamal said, deepening the chill at her center. "If I were you, I would pack up my family and leave Aaltah. You are still a reasonably attractive catch for some petty lordling in some backwater principality. Find a new husband as far away from here as possible. That is the only way you can escape the fate you so richly deserve."

Alys was speechless. She had given no thought to the possibility of remarrying, and if she had, it certainly wouldn't have been as a means to escape her homeland. "I have done nothing wrong," she said again, knowing it was futile. "I have no intentions of fleeing like a criminal."

"I hear Waldmir of Nandel is on the hunt for a new bride once more."

She suppressed a shudder. The Sovereign Prince of Nandel was famous throughout Seven Wells for marrying young and beautiful noblewomen and then discarding them when they failed to provide him the male heir he so desperately wanted. He'd already sent three wives to the dismal Abbey of Nandel in disgrace after divorcing them, and a fourth had met with the headsman's ax. With his history, no woman in her right mind would willingly marry him, and since he'd already ruined or killed four wives without any fear of potential political repercussions, even the most ambitious family would hesitate to hand a daughter over to him.

Of course, since Sovereign Prince Waldmir preferred his wives young, beautiful, and virginal, he would hardly be interested in a forty-two-year-old mother of two like Alys. "I will send him a proposal of marriage the moment I return home," she said with scorn dripping from her every word.

Delnamal raised his eyebrows in mock surprise. "Oh, did you

think I meant to suggest *you* would make a suitable bride for such a great prince?" He snorted derisively. "I would never insult him by offering him a withered old hag. No, I had in mind your lovely daughter."

The blood drained from Alys's face, and no amount of court-trained self-control could hide the horror his words provoked.

"Jinnell is a lovely, nubile young thing," Delnamal continued, his nostrils flaring as if he could smell her fear. "A king's grand-daughter, and born within the sanctity of marriage even if her mother was not. She is exactly the kind of bride Prince Waldmir desires, don't you think?"

Alys fought off a chill. She had learned to live with Delnamal's hatred of her, and she'd known in a distant way that some of that hatred would spill over onto her children. But somehow she hadn't dreamed even he would be cruel enough to threaten his own niece with a marriage to Prince Waldmir.

"The king would never approve such a match," Alys said. She was certain that was so, and yet she couldn't stop the quaver in her voice. Just the thought of her daughter in that horrible man's clutches was enough to make her sick.

Delnamal shrugged casually. "Not today, I'll grant you. But thanks to you and your bitch mother, my wife has lost our baby. It is possible that thrice-damned spell will prevent her from providing me with an heir, in which case I'll need to find another wife—and another marital tie with Nandel. I could rid myself of her right now did we not need our trade agreements, you understand."

Alys swallowed hard. "Then perhaps you might try being kind to your wife. If I understand my mother's spell correctly, Shelvon might be willing to give you that heir if you treated her like a cher-ished human being instead of like a dog that has soiled your rug."

"I believe you are missing the point of this conversation," he growled. "How I treat my wife is none of your concern. But if she does not quicken again soon, the king will have to consider alterna-tive ways to strengthen our ties to Nandel, and your daughter's hand would make an effective inducement."

"He would never do that to Jinnell!" she insisted. "He loves her."

"Rumor has it he loved your mother once. But when it became necessary to form an alliance with Khalpar by any means necessary, he did not hesitate to divorce her and disown her children so he could marry my mother. As Father has always said, a king rules for the good of his kingdom above all else. And Father is a good king."

Alys couldn't force a sound past her tightened throat. Delnamal had spoken nothing but the truth. She remembered her mother explaining the impending divorce to her while weeping uncontrollably. Her mother must have hated the king for his heartless decision, and yet she'd tried to justify it to Alys, tried to convince her that he was doing the right thing for the kingdom. Even when Alys had finally grown old enough to understand the reasoning behind her father's decision, she'd never understood how a supposedly good man could divorce the woman he loved and condemn her to a life of privation, shame, and whoredom.

Could he be heartless enough to send his beloved granddaughter to marry a monster? Alys feared the answer more than she could say. And she hated that she was giving Delnamal such a satisfying reaction, feeding his appetite for cruelty, but how else could a mother react?

Having successfully struck fear into Alys's heart, Delnamal finally allowed her to pass. She clasped her shaking hands together as she hurried to find her children and remove them from the poisonous atmosphere of the palace.

Delnamal had admitted that their father wouldn't be willing to sell Jinnell to the Sovereign Prince of Nandel just now. He still had every reason to believe that Shelvon would produce the required heir, and therefore would feel no urgent need to shore up ties to Nandel.

The moment she returned home, Alys would begin in earnest the search for a suitable husband for her daughter. The faster Jinnell was married—preferably far away from Aaltah and her uncle's reach—the safer she would be.

CHAPTER EIGHT

"Lord Zarsha of Nandel is here to see you, Your Highness," Ellin's steward announced just as she had finally given up pushing food around her dinner plate. She had had all her meals served to her in her rooms today, unable to face more people than absolutely necessary. She'd eaten a few bites for breakfast, and maybe a third of her lunch, but after her meeting with Semsulin, eating more than a mouthful of dinner was beyond her. And a visit from Zarsha would not improve her appetite.

"Shall I send him away?"

Ellin sighed and pushed her plate away. Whatever her feelings about him, Zarsha had likely saved her life last night, and he'd been hurt in the process. She would have expected such danger to strip away his masks and reveal the ugliness she was convinced lay beneath, and yet he had acted selflessly and without thought for his own safety. Sending him away seemed . . . churlish. Or maybe just childish.

"I'll meet him in my sitting room," she said. "I'll be there momentarily."

"Very well, Your Highness," her steward said, bowing.

Ellin pushed back her chair and took a moment to examine herself in the mirror. Though she'd barely eaten, she checked to make sure there was no food stuck between her teeth and adjusted the brooch that held a soft black brocade shawl around her shoulders. Her ladies were hard at work putting together a mourning wardrobe for her, but so far the shawl was the only piece of black she owned. She used it to cover the dark purple bodice with silver embroidery that was far too festive for the occasion, and instead of wearing an evening gown, she wore a utilitarian gray wool traveling skirt that was too warm for the temperate autumn weather. She dabbed away a sheen of perspiration on her forehead and considered removing the shawl altogether. She doubted Zarsha would be offended.

But in the end, she opted to keep the shawl despite the heat. Zarsha might not be offended by her lack of mourning attire, but she was unwilling to disrespect the dead.

Zarsha had his back turned, examining the titles on a shelf of books, when Ellin entered the sitting room. He wore what for a man of Nandel equated to evening attire: a granite-gray doublet over black breeches. A belt of earthy green brocade was the only nod to color, and a large gold signet ring was his only adornment.

He turned to face her when he heard her footsteps. A barber had shorn away most of his blond hair—no doubt so that a healer could have better access to the gash on his head—and his face looked even more severe and angular without the softening of his habitually untidy locks. She had always found the blue of his eyes cold, but the sympathy in them this evening made him look much more approachable.

He bowed. "I can't tell you how sorry I am for your loss, Your Highness," he said as he rose.

A lump instantly formed in Ellin's throat, as it did every time someone expressed condolences. She wasn't sure she'd fully absorbed the loss yet, because every time someone mentioned it, it was like being slapped in the face with reality. She swallowed hard.

"Thank you, my lord," she forced out past the lump. "And thank you for what you did last night. You might very well have saved my life."

She expected the arrogant ass to preen at this mention of his heroics, but he surprised her by waving off her thanks.

"I did nothing special. And if I'd acted sooner, or more wisely . . ." His voice trailed off and he shook his head, his eyes downcast.

Ellin remembered the king bellowing for everyone to remain in their seats while Zarsha tried to urge them to flee into the building. "There was nothing you could have done."

"I should have tried harder."

Ellin was surprised to find herself sympathizing with Zarsha, which was an entirely new sensation. It was possible he was continuing his long tradition of putting on a performance to suit his audience, but rarely had those performances included any hint of vulnerability. It struck her that while she had always thought that, like her loathsome cousin Tamzin, Zarsha's charming demeanor and handsome face hid a rotten heart, she had never actually seen any evidence to support the idea. Tamzin let slip the occasional glimpse behind the veneer—Ellin couldn't understand how no one else seemed to notice—but with Zarsha, she had merely *assumed* the ugliness was there.

"You saved *me*," she reminded him. And she was going to reward him by going back on the marriage agreement he had reached with her father. She'd led Semsulin to believe she was still mulling over the question of whether to take the throne, but in truth she knew it was the only reasonable decision she could make. She could never live with herself if she refused the crown and thereby gave Kailindar and Tamzin an excuse to start a war. She was ill-prepared to lead a kingdom, and she harbored no illusion that hers would be an easy rule. Her uncle and cousin might not immediately march on the capital to wrest the crown from her head, but she imagined they might both be on the lookout for an opportunity. Especially Tamzin. Every step she took, every word she uttered would be under the utmost scrutiny, and a single mistake could lead to disaster.

Zarsha acknowledged her words with a dip of his chin. "More than nothing, I'll grant you, but less than I should have." He moved a little closer and looked her up and down. "You are unhurt?"

"I'm fine. And you?" She peered at the place on his head that had been bleeding so copiously the night before. There was an angry red line visible beneath the thin fuzz of blond hair, but the healer had obviously done a fine job closing the wound.

Zarsha reached up and touched his head, fingering what would be a long scar when it had finished healing. "I owe my life to your healers," he said. "I'm told my skull was cracked and there was bleeding in my brain."

Ellin gasped. She had blithely assumed that because he had regained consciousness by the time they were pulled from the rubble, he hadn't been that badly hurt. She'd practically dismissed him from her thoughts and hadn't even had the decency to ask after his health this whole day. Her callousness shamed her.

"I'm so sorry," she murmured. "I had no idea."

He shrugged as if it hardly mattered. "You've nothing to apologize for. Your healers took good care of me, and I'm told a man looks better with a few battle scars." He gave her a crooked smile and stroked the line on his skull.

This was just the tone of flippant amusement that had never failed to rub her nerves the wrong way over the last few weeks of his visit here in Rhozinolm, but for some reason she found herself returning his smile—and not having to force it. The smile quickly faded as she imagined telling him she would not abide by the marriage agreement. She could leave it to Semsulin, but after all the effort Zarsha had put into courting her, the least she could do was deliver the bad news personally.

Zarsha sobered just as quickly, the smile fading from his lips as some grim emotion clouded his eyes. "Coming so close to death . . ." He shook his head. "It changes you. Changes how you look at the world."

Ellin knew she had come close to death last night as well, though not as close as Zarsha. She had no sense that it had changed the way she looked at the world. In fact, her mind could barely grasp how close she had come to dying along with the rest of the royal family.

"May I sit?" Zarsha asked.

"Forgive my manners," she said, waving him toward a comfortable armchair by the fireplace and taking a seat across from him on a tufted velvet settee. She should have told the servants not to light a fire tonight when she was draped in a heavy shawl and wearing a wool skirt, but her mind had been elsewhere and it had never occurred to her that she'd find herself sitting in front of that fire. Perspiration gathered under her arms and below her breasts.

Zarsha sat, and the flickering light of the fire carved interesting shadows into the angles of his face. He really was quite nice to look at, even in his decidedly drab dinner ensemble and with his now unfashionably short hair. Surely he would have no trouble finding a suitable bride, one who would find his good looks, good connections, and good humor appealing enough to brave the wilds of Nandel. In fact, Ellin should put some serious effort into finding an alternative marriage for him. She was the only eligible woman of the immediate royal family, but perhaps marriage with another noble house would be enough to help induce Sovereign Prince Waldmir to renew the trade agreements.

"As I was saying," Zarsha said, "almost dying has changed my outlook on life." He met her eyes, and there was something in his gaze that trapped her so that she could not look away. "I know you have always been against our marriage."

She flinched and finally broke his gaze. She had tried her best to play the part of the dutiful daughter, to keep her objections to the marriage between herself and her father. She had bitten her tongue more times than she could count to stop herself from sniping at the man she'd been destined to marry, and she'd laughed—or at least smiled—at many a joke she didn't find the least amusing. But she couldn't say it was a great surprise to find she hadn't hidden her feelings as well as she'd hoped.

"It's all right," Zarsha hastened to say. "I assure you my ego can handle the blow."

For all her embarrassment, she felt her lips tip up into a smile. "Are you certain? I was always under the impression you were rather protective of it."

It was just the kind of cutting remark she'd often stopped herself from saying, but far from being offended, Zarsha laughed with what sounded like genuine humor. "It's true, I am, but then I've got such a lot of it that I will hardly miss the small gouges your disdain puts in it."

She tilted her head to the side and regarded him with no small amount of curiosity. She'd expected him to puff up with indignation at the suggestion that he was egotistical, and here he was not only agreeing with her assessment, but poking fun at himself. He grinned at the surprise on her face.

"I am well aware of my flaws, Princess, and am not afraid to face them. Most women seem to find me charming, but I know you are not among them."

Ellin squirmed and looked away. She was not as comfortable acknowledging her own flaws. And if she were being perfectly honest with herself, it was hard to say how much of her dislike for Zarsha was genuine, and how much was merely a general anger that he was not the man she wished to marry. Not that she'd ever thought she could marry Graesan. Bad enough that he was illegitimate despite his father having gifted him with his name. But his mother had been a lowly maid, and his father's support and name would never be enough to overcome such a birth. He had ascended as far as he could when he became her master of the guard, and when he married, his bride would be of the lowest orders of nobility. Certainly not a princess royal.

"What I'm leading up to here is that I will not hold you to the agreement your father signed," Zarsha said.

Ellin's jaw dropped in a most unladylike fashion. She hadn't known where this conversation was going, but she certainly hadn't expected it to be *here*. "Excuse me?"

"That's what my brush with death made clear to me," he said. "I don't want to marry a woman who doesn't want to marry me."

Ellin opened and closed her mouth a few times, stunned. She'd been dreading telling Zarsha that circumstances had changed such that she couldn't honor the marriage agreement. Not because she feared hurting his feelings—as smooth and facile as he was, he had never tried to pretend he was madly in love with her. His courtship had less of a sense of romance and more that of a business transaction. But she feared that like Tamzin, his true character would peek out when he was thwarted. And now, rather than turning on her, he had offered her a release from their engagement without any prompting from her. She was beginning to wonder if maybe, just maybe, she'd been unfair in her assessment of his character.

"I don't know what to say," she admitted.

He flashed her another crooked grin. "All I ask is that you refrain from bursting into joyous song. Beyond that, you may say whatever you like or nothing at all."

She laughed, feeling like a tremendous weight had been lifted from her shoulders. It was really true. She didn't have to marry him and live in Nandel, after all. She didn't even have to accept the crown to escape the fate that she had so dreaded. Zarsha had given her an easy way out.

"Thank you," she said, the words feeling distinctly inadequate. Freedom from the marriage contract hardly spelled an end to her troubles, for she would have to marry as soon as possible after her mourning period was finished, and she doubted she would find *any* man pleasing when her heart had already been given to Graesan. But at least she wouldn't have to upend her life and move to Nandel, where she would be considered little better than her husband's property.

"Well, now, don't be *too* grateful just yet. I still have every intention of winning you over."

"What?"

"We are a good match, you and I, for any number of reasons. I would like a chance to convince you of that without your family forcing your hand."

So, he wasn't entirely setting her free, after all. But since she had no intention of letting her kingdom devolve into war because she was afraid of taking the throne, a marriage with Zarsha would always be out of the question. Semsulin would no doubt expect her to announce her intention to take the throne to him and the royal council before informing anyone else—especially a foreigner—but she saw no reason to allow Zarsha to keep believing there was a chance.

"I'm afraid a match between us will be impossible now," she told him. "You see, I am the only legitimate heir to the throne."

He smiled. "I am aware of that."

She blinked. "You are? But . . ."

"Dearest Ellin, ours was always intended to be a political match. I would hardly come to Rhozinolm without a clear understanding of the political climate. Which means I am aware of the line of succession and what last night's tragedy means. You are the only person who can claim the throne without causing an immediate war."

Ellin wondered if she was the only person in the kingdom who hadn't grasped that fact from the beginning. Then again, she had lost her whole family the night before and had herself escaped a brush with death. It was no great surprise that her mind had not leapt to examine the political ramifications in the immediate aftermath. When she became queen, she would have to develop a habit of strategic thinking.

"If you know I will be taking the throne, then you know I cannot marry you."

He sat back casually in his chair, not in the least perturbed by her logical objection. "I know there will be pressure for you to marry within your own kingdom. But I also know your kingdom is badly in need of the trade agreements Nandel can offer and that the best way to secure them is by marriage."

"But not by *my* marriage," she argued. "When I marry, my husband will become the king, and neither the royal council nor the people would accept a Nandel-born king. I will make it one of my highest priorities to secure another—"

"You do understand the late king and your father would never have agreed to this arrangement if there were another way to secure the trade agreement. There are few fathers outside of our own prin-

cipality who would be overjoyed to send their daughters into Nandel. I'm not unaware of the disadvantages of my homeland for the
fairer sex."

"Surely there must be *some* other way. The agreement is beneficial to both Rhozinolm and Nandel, after all."

Zarsha nodded. "Ten years ago when the original agreement was
signed, it certainly was. But then ten years ago, the prince's daughter was not married to the heir to the throne of Aaltah. So you see
we already have a buyer for as much iron and as many gems as our
principality can produce. There's little inducement for us to continue reserving some of our product for trade with Rhozinolm.
Only a marriage of the highest order could possibly lead the sovereign prince to consider renewing the trade agreements under the
current generous terms."

Ellin's heart sank. She hadn't even taken the throne yet, and already she saw the seeds of her destruction taking root. If she
couldn't secure those trade agreements, her rivals could seize on
that failure to challenge her rule.

"Because you are to be queen," Zarsha said, "ours obviously
cannot be a conventional marriage, and you cannot live in Nandel.
But I can live here. I've found myself quite fond of life in Rhozinolm
and am less eager than you might think to return to my homeland."

There was a faintly ironic grin on his lips. Ellin supposed it wasn't
any great surprise that someone who had grown up in the harsh and
forbidding land of Nandel might be seduced by the comparatively
free and easy ways of the court in Rhozinolm, although most Nandelites she'd known were more apt to sneer than be seduced.

"Be that as it may," she said, "I'm sure you understand that the
people would never accept a foreigner as their king."

He nodded. "Especially not a foreigner who hails from Nandel,"
he agreed. "We would have to create a situation wherein I would be
named your prince consort instead of king."

"You must be joking," Ellin said, although she could clearly see
that he was not. "I may not be an expert in law, but I know it is not
legal for a woman to reign as sovereign in any permanent capacity.

Rhozinolm must have a king, and if I don't provide one by marriage, there are two eager claimants waiting in the wings."

Zarsha shrugged. "Then if we are to marry, we will have to change the law."

She shook her head wonderingly. "That is impossible."

"I think you'll find it surprising how many things are possible when you wear a crown on your head. And because you have a year of mourning before you will be expected to marry, we shall have time to make a great number of seemingly small and harmless changes that will eventually lead to the outcome we desire."

"*You* desire, you mean," she retorted. She should have known it was too good to be true when he'd offered her that tantalizing glimpse of freedom.

"I meant what I said. I don't want to marry you if you don't want me. But while I don't expect time to cause you to love or even desire me, it's not impossible to imagine it might cause you to desire our marriage."

He rose from his chair, but Ellin remained seated, wondering how her life had become so complicated so suddenly.

"Take some time to investigate the possibilities," he said. "You are far more clever than most people realize, and perhaps you will be able to find a solution that escaped your father and King Linolm. If you do, then I will speak no more of our marriage or of the steps we should take to make it possible."

He stepped forward, and before she had a hint of what he meant to do, he had put his hand on her shoulder in a most familiar manner and given her a firm squeeze. The expression on his face told her the gesture was meant to be comforting, and he let go immediately when she tensed under his touch.

"Whatever you choose, I can be your friend," he said. "I suspect you will find true friends exceedingly rare once you take the throne, so do take advantage of those you have."

Ellin could think of no clever reply as Zarsha bowed low and then left the room.

CHAPTER NINE

After leaving his traitorous half-sister to sputter helplessly—and, he hoped, to plan a hasty flight to the farthest reaches of the land—Delnamal intended to retreat to his chambers and drink himself into blessed oblivion. Since the quake the night before, he'd darted from one crisis to another, barely having a chance to eat, much less take a quiet moment to absorb his loss. Not that he *wanted* to absorb it, mind you. He'd much prefer to pretend he still had an heir on the way, that his marriage to Shelvon of Nandel served some purpose other than to torture him.

To torture them both, he mentally amended. He was under no illusion that Shelvon was any happier with their marriage than he, but though he tried, he couldn't seem to find any true sympathy in his heart. A woman that homely, meek, and frigid had no hope of finding happiness in marriage, so it was hardly his fault she was miserable.

But thanks to his father's whore of a first wife, Delnamal's heir was no more. And thanks to the vital trade agreements with Nandel, he was stuck with Shelvon whether she produced an heir or not. Prince Waldmir hardly seemed to be a doting father, but there was no doubt he would take it poorly if Delnamal divorced his daughter. Never mind that Waldmir himself had divorced and even executed wives who failed to provide heirs.

The injustice of it all made Delnamal want to scream, but drinking himself unconscious in the privacy of his own rooms was the next best thing.

Unfortunately, the world was conspiring against him, and it seemed every time he turned a corner he ran into someone who had urgent need to speak with him. And when he thought he was finally in the clear, he discovered an ambush awaiting him in his sitting room.

Queen Xanvin had the regal bearing and steely backbone her daughter-in-law so badly lacked, and she commanded a great deal of respect from the nobility of Aaltah despite her foreign ways and her unfashionably devout nature. The people of Aaltah were content to harbor their love of the Creator and the Mother in their hearts without having to make the grand show of it that was typical in his mother's homeland of Khalpar. Delnamal had heard that when his mother first came to Aaltah, people had been taken aback by her fervor and compared her unfavorably to their previous queen. She had won them over long before Delnamal was old enough to notice any tension, though she had not succeeded in making religion fashionable in her adopted land.

The queen carried a Devotional with her at all times, either a full-size copy tucked in a discreet pocket or reticule, or a miniature that hung from a chain that circled her waist. She abhorred idleness, and whenever she had a spare moment, out came the Devotional.

She was, of course, reading it while she sat in wait for her son, her attention focused so strongly on the page that she seemed at first not to have noticed her quarry enter the room. Delnamal could not fathom how she could read those same words over, and over, and over again without her eyes glazing. He had no doubt she could recite the entire tome by heart, and yet she read with intense concentration, as if it were all new to her. He could hardly credit that concentration as genuine, and yet it seemed impossible that she would keep up the pretense for year after year after year.

Eventually, the queen blinked and became aware of Delnamal's presence. She closed her Devotional and stroked its worn cover lovingly before laying it on the table beside her. She stood and held her hands out to him.

Delnamal suppressed a sigh and took his mother's hands, pressing a kiss on each of her cheeks. She had already expressed her sorrow at his loss that morning, so he wasn't sure why she was here. Certainly it was not because she thought he needed a mother's comfort. He had never thought of the child in Shelvon's belly as an actual human being, and he hardly could claim he'd looked forward to having an infant in his household. Many a father—including his own—had assured him that once he held his child, he would instantly fall in love with it, but secretly, he had doubted it. He failed to see the attraction of a squalling infant. All he felt at the loss of his heir was anger, not sorrow.

Not that he would say as much to his mother. While she had failed to instill in him her religious fervor, he knew enough about the Creator and the Mother to know loving his own child—even before it was born—was considered a cornerstone of the faith. She would be scandalized to know the ambivalence with which he had faced fatherhood, and he could only imagine the choice words she would have for him.

"You have not been to see Shelvon today," his mother said, fixing him with the kind of reproving stare only a mother could manage.

And here he'd thought he could escape a scolding by keeping his feelings to himself. "The day has been madness. Have you any idea how many crises I've had to deal with?"

The queen arched a brow at him. "And yet you do not seem to be dealing with a crisis at this precise moment."

He made a growling sound of frustration, but more at himself than at her. He'd walked right into that reproof, and truly he had no acceptable excuse for not seeing his wife. It was his duty as a husband to console her, as he'd been assured she was devastated by the loss. He wondered how long everyone would remain sympathetic to the woman when they discovered the reason behind her miscarriage. He and the king had both agreed it would be pointless to try to make a secret of the spell that had been cast—they had no reason to doubt the abbess's claim that she'd sent fliers throughout Seven Wells to spread the news—but they weren't in any hurry to get the word out. The men of Aaltah had to keep their minds on recovering from the disastrous earthquake and repairing what damage they could instead of worrying about some twisted women's conspiracy.

Delnamal regarded the queen carefully, trying to gauge from the look on her face whether she knew the cause of Shelvon's miscarriage or whether she thought it was simple misfortune.

"You are the crown prince, my son," she said, still in that reproving tone he knew so well. "People observe and judge your every move. Don't think no one has noticed you have not even inquired after the health of your wife. When people begin to learn exactly what happened last night, they will note your lack of husbandly devotion and come to the immediate conclusion that Shelvon did not wish to carry your child."

The corner of his eye twitched, and his hands closed into fists. So, his mother knew about the spell—and what Shelvon's miscarriage meant.

"They'll think that no matter what," he said, dropping heavily into the nearest chair. If he played the concerned husband and went to Shelvon's bedside, he might not be able to stop himself from strangling her. Her failure to do her duty as a wife would make him the butt of many a jest. No one would dare mock him to his face—if they did, they would quickly be made to regret it—but he would know it was happening behind his back, that people would take it as evidence of his own shortcomings as a man. It was intolerable!

"They'll speculate, I'll grant you. But a miscarriage in the wake of a traumatic event is hardly exceptional or unexpected. If you show every sign that Shelvon's miscarriage is a devastating loss to you both, people will be less likely to believe it was caused by the spell."

"That's women's logic," he scoffed. "People will believe whatever they find the most entertaining. It wouldn't matter if she'd lost the baby when falling down a flight of stairs. They will all lay the responsibility at my feet."

Although the queen had eventually won over her people, Delnamal was under no illusion that her popularity extended to him. He might be the heir to the throne, but in moments of honesty he had to admit to himself that he was the least favorite of King Aaltyn's children. The bastard Tynthanal—the handsome and charismatic soldier who had every reason to expect he would be the next Lord Commander of the Citadel—was unquestionably the people's favorite. As crown prince, Delnamal was nominally the top military authority in the land, but he hoped never to have to give a command that contradicted his half-brother's, as he could not swear that the men would obey him. And then there was the "tragic" figure of Alysoon, whose devotion to her disgraced mother had endeared her to softhearted—and soft*headed*—people everywhere. Delnamal ranked a distant third in the hearts of his people, and in the heart of his own father. How delicious many of them would find it that his wife was humiliating him for all to see.

"I don't deny there will be talk," his mother said. "But the easiest way to quiet it is to beget another heir as soon as possible, and neglecting your wife after her ordeal is a poor start."

Delnamal ground his teeth and crossed his arms over his chest. "My relationship with my wife is my own affair and hardly something I wish to discuss with my mother."

He was not entirely surprised that the queen ignored his wishes. "You *have* no relationship with your wife. That is the problem. One you could work around when you had no need of her cooperation. That has changed, and you had best recognize it immediately."

Delnamal felt his lip curling in disdain and tried to keep the expression from growing into a full-out scowl. He could hardly stomach being in the same room with Shelvon for as long as it took to plant his seed, and he certainly had no interest in *talking* to a woman so dull she would bore a stone wall. He had married her and destroyed his own chances for happiness for the good of the kingdom, but he was damned if he was going to woo her.

"I will not go down on my knees and beg my own wife to grant me a child, if that's what you're suggesting," he growled. "I will make it clear that if she does not do her duty, she is bound for the Abbey and to hell with the trade agreements!"

The queen stroked the cover of her Devotional as if soothing the damn book over the sacrilege he had voiced. Rage at the injustice of it all burned in his blood and made him want to break something. He'd sacrificed *everything* to marry that pallid, bloodless bitch, and she had repaid him in the foulest manner. No doubt she was even now reclining smugly in her sickbed, laughing at him and congratulating herself on her victory.

"Have caution, my son," the queen said in a gentle voice that only grated on him. "You cannot be seen to endanger those trade agreements. Rebuilding all that was lost will drain the treasury to the breaking point, and those who have been bankrupted or displaced by the disaster will look to the royal family for leadership and support. Tynthanal is already being heralded as a hero for leading his men into the Harbor District last night and saving many lives. If you give the people reason to hate you while they love him . . ." She shrugged delicately.

"If there were any justice in this world, that man would be in a dungeon right now!" Delnamal snapped.

She arched one eyebrow. "Whatever for? I know you suspect Alysoon of collusion, but surely not Tynthanal."

"Why not?" he demanded. "He's as much the witch's child as Alysoon is."

"And yet he calls *me* Mother. I've known him for a very long time, my son, and he has never shown any sign of attachment to the woman who bore him."

"That doesn't mean there wasn't any attachment. And even if there *wasn't*, his blood is tainted. That woman was an abomination, and the world would be a better and safer place if her get were all destroyed."

Queen Xanvin shook her head and gave him a reproachful look. "You are too full of anger to see what is right before your eyes. Neither Alysoon nor Tynthanal should be of any concern to you. It is you who will inherit the throne—unless you work long and hard at sabotaging yourself. Say, for example, by insulting the Sovereign Prince of Nandel by divorcing his daughter and plunging the kingdom into an economic crisis."

"I will describe to her exactly what it will be like to work the pavilion at the Abbey," he said with a snarl. "I will describe the perversions she will be forced to endure day after day, night after night, year after year. Perhaps that will motivate her to do her fucking duty."

His mother flinched at his language, but he was too angry to take it back.

"Perhaps you should read the abbess's message again," the queen said. "I don't think any form of coercion will obtain the results you desire."

"I remember what it said! And if you think I'm going to take the witch's word for it, you're a fool."

"Delnamal—"

"Enough!" he shouted, once again causing his mother to flinch. She was not deserving of his rage, and he knew that she meant well. That didn't mean he had to listen to her. "Shelvon is my wife, and I will treat her as I see fit. She will bear me the heir I am owed, or she will rue the day she was born."

His mother rose to her feet and held her chin high, glaring at him with maternal fire in her eyes. "If you want an heir—and an end to the whispers that we both know will spring up—you will treat that woman with the care and respect a wife deserves. That may not be enough when you harbor such hatred in your heart, but it is much more likely to work than heaping even more abuse on her."

She held up her hand to halt the tirade he prepared to release. "I've said all I mean to say on the subject. For now."

Delnamal watched through narrowed eyes as she made her stately, dignified exit. Just before she stepped out the door, he grabbed hold of her arm and jerked her toward him, causing her to gasp in surprise. Her eyes widened as he glared at her.

"Don't ever forget, Mother," he growled, giving her a light shake. "Someday, I will be king, and you will be naught but a dowager. If you wish to continue living like a queen till the end of your days, you had best learn to keep your opinions to yourself. If I ever wish to hear your advice, I will let you know."

He wasn't sure whether he was satisfied or appalled to see the flash of fear in his mother's eyes.

"So, what is it you want to talk about, Mama?" Jinnell asked as she spread her skirts and took a seat on the settee by the fire.

Alys double-checked to make certain she'd locked the sitting room door. Her heartbeat felt strangely erratic, her stays too tight. Every protective instinct in her body cringed at the thought of having this conversation with her daughter. She'd already put it off for two days as she and her children returned to the manor and tried to restore a semblance of a normal life, but Delnamal's threat continued to echo in Alys's head, and she had no doubt that he'd been entirely serious. It was vital that she find a husband for Jinnell as soon as possible, and she had never subscribed to the notion that girls should be kept in blissful ignorance. She had long ago educated her daughter about both the joys and the burdens of womanhood, and it was now time to explain the dangers.

Alys took her own seat by the fire and wrapped her shawl more tightly around her shoulders. Jinnell's worried eyes said she'd already seen her mother's unease. She folded her hands in her lap, but the fingers kept moving restlessly and she bit her lip.

"What is it, Mama? What's wrong?"

"You know that your uncle Delnamal has never been overly fond of our family," Alys began.

Jinnell snorted. "That he hates us, you mean. Yes, I am aware."

Of course she was. Delnamal was hardly subtle about it. Jinnell was in many ways a typical—if spoiled—teenage girl, and she was very mindful of what others thought of her. Not that her uncle's dislike had ever seemed to trouble her, but she could not be oblivious to it.

Alys tried to think of a delicate way to explain the situation without alarming her daughter any more than necessary, but Jinnell was perhaps a little more perceptive than she'd realized.

"He blames us for Grandmother's spell, doesn't he?" she asked.

Alys grimaced. "I ran into him at the palace, and he was . . . very put out." If she were being as honest as she should, she would tell Jinnell about Delnamal's attempt to have them all thrown in the dungeon. But she hoped she could be forgiven for keeping the worst of it to herself, for though she believed Jinnell had a right—and maybe even a need—to know the danger, she could not bring herself to terrify the girl. At least not any more than was absolutely necessary.

"I have never known him *not* to be put out," Jinnell countered.

"This was different." Alys suppressed a shiver as she remembered the hatred that had shone in her half-brother's eyes. She disliked him intensely, and had, ever since he was old enough to have a recognizable personality, but she'd never hated him the way he hated her and her brother. "He was . . . beside himself."

"Grandfather would never let him do anything to us," Jinnell said, but there was a faint quaver in her voice that said she was not fully convinced.

"You are the granddaughter of a king and of marriageable age. You may not be of his legitimate family, but your marriage can still be used for political gain. If Shelvon fails to produce an heir, then there may be a need to strengthen the ties between Aaltah and Nandel."

The color leached out of Jinnell's face. Alys had thought she'd have to explain the situation in great detail before her daughter would see the threat—Jinnell was hardly what she thought of as a strategic thinker—but it seemed she'd underestimated her.

"Grandfather would not sell me to Nandel," Jinnell said with no conviction whatsoever. Her eyes glistened with tears, though she blinked rapidly to hold them at bay.

"There's no telling what he would do if he felt desperate enough." Alys reached out to touch her daughter's arm. "But he's nothing like desperate right now. There's a chance there was nothing magical about Shelvon's miscarriage. Perhaps we'll soon have happy news once more." Not that Alys truly believed what she was saying. She did not have to have a close personal relationship with her sister-in-law to know that the woman was miserable. If the abbess's spell really worked as she'd explained, then it seemed highly unlikely Shelvon would produce an heir anytime soon, if at all.

"You don't believe that." Jinnell dabbed delicately at the corners of her eyes, but aside from her pallor and the shimmer of tears, she was taking the news remarkably well.

Alys shrugged one shoulder. "Whether I believe it or not, it is still possible. And as long as the marriage might still produce an heir, there's no need to marry you to someone in Nandel."

Jinnell's eyes locked with hers. "You mean Prince Waldmir, don't you? Not just *someone in Nandel*."

Alys blinked. Once more, her daughter's perspicacity surprised her. Because her mother was considered illegitimate and her father was only a baron with moderate holdings, Jinnell had never had to face the prospect of a marriage of state. She had trusted her parents to find her a husband who would make her happy, unlike many girls her age who looked upon their future marriage arrangements with a combination of excitement and dread. "It doesn't matter. The point is we must find you a husband sooner rather than later. If you are married, then you won't have to worry."

Jinnell shifted on the settee, staring at the fire as her brows drew together in thought. Alys had expected a torrent of tears at best, blind panic at worst. Her daughter had always had a flair for the dramatic, and this quiet, thoughtful acceptance was unlike her.

"If Delnamal is already whispering in the king's ear," Jinnell mused, her eyes still distant, "then he may be reluctant to approve my marriage if he believes he could one day have need of me."

"One benefit of my illegitimacy is that you do not need the king's approval to marry," Alys reminded her.

Jinnell turned back to face her. All traces of tears were gone, and there was nothing but calm calculation in her eyes. "I may not *legally* require it," she said, "but we both know what is expected."

Alys was temporarily at a loss for words. Where was the carefree little girl she'd raised? The naïve child who would be devastated at this threat to the storybook life she'd had every right to expect? Alys wondered if recent events had had a profound effect on Jinnell's psyche or if perhaps she herself had been willfully blind. Her little girl was not a child anymore.

"I can't marry without the king's permission," Jinnell said firmly. "No man would risk taking me under those circumstances, and even if we could find one who would, it would leave you and Corlin in an impossible situation."

A small, aching lump formed in Alys's throat, and she feared it might be she who would break down and cry. "I will find a way to protect you," she promised her daughter. "I will find a husband your grandfather will accept, and I will do it before he's willing to entertain the possibility of Nandel. I promise."

But Jinnell shook her head. "You can't promise that, Mama." She rose from the settee and came to kneel at her mother's feet, taking her hand in a comforting grip. "I know you will try, but it is the king who will make the final decision, and you cannot speak for him."

Alys squeezed her daughter's hands, looking down into that calm face and barely recognizing her. This was the same girl who just a few days ago had whined when Alys had declined to take her shopping. "I *will* find a way," she promised once more, willing Jinnell to believe her. And wishing she didn't share Jinnell's doubts.

Jinnell sighed. "I am neither as frivolous nor as fragile as you think me, Mama. If Delnamal convinces the king to consider wedding me to Prince Waldmir, I will find a way to change his mind. And if I can't get Grandfather to change his mind, I'll convince the prince he doesn't want me."

Once again, Alys was rendered speechless. She remembered having made similar promises to herself when it was time for her own marriage to be arranged and she'd been terrified of whom her father would choose for her. Her mind had been full of plans for how to avoid a terrible marriage—to the point that she'd even researched poisons—but it turned out she had needed none of them. She had fallen for Sylnin the moment she'd met him, and had had the rarest of opportunities to marry for love. How could she not want the same kind of marriage for her own daughter?

Alys looked down at her daughter in amazement as she realized what Jinnell's calm acceptance signified. "Nothing I've told you has come as a surprise, has it?"

Jinnell smiled faintly and shook her head. "What exactly do you think my friends and I talk about when we're together?"

"Gowns and gossip," Alys replied quickly, because it seemed anytime she caught a snippet of conversation those were the topics at hand.

Jinnell giggled, sounding more like herself for a moment. "Well, that too, of course. But we've been talking about our marriage prospects for *years* now. And we've each plotted out how we would escape from the worst possibilities. Prince Waldmir being the worst of the worst."

"But you had no reason to believe I would marry you off to someone you didn't care for!"

Jinnell gave her a knowing look. "You're the only one in this family who did not see this coming. Not Prince Waldmir, but a diplomatic arrangement. Papa warned me long ago that he might not be allowed to choose my husband if there were still alliances that needed to be made."

Alys closed her eyes. One shock after another. Sylnin had never once mentioned to her the possibility that the choice might not be in their hands. And yet he had discussed it with Jinnell. If he weren't already dead, Alys might have been tempted to kill him.

Her heart squeezed tight in her chest, and grief shot through her in a startling bolt. It was more than a year since he'd died, and grief was no longer her constant companion, but it tended to sneak up on her at inopportune moments. She couldn't afford it now, when she had to be strong for Jinnell.

She opened her eyes, and love for the daughter who knelt before her swept the grief to the side. It was her duty as a mother—and it was her duty to her husband's memory—to keep their daughter safe. Delnamal would do his best to make her fail, and all she could do was arm Jinnell to the best of her ability.

"My mother left me a book," she said, pulling the little red book of magic lessons from her reticule.

CHAPTER TEN

Delnamal's horse tossed its head so hard he almost lost his grip on the reins. "Damnable beast," he growled under his breath as the impossible animal skittered sideways to avoid the Creator only knew what invisible obstacle lay in its path. Bad enough that he had to endure the revolting stench of the Harbor District, but the muddy, debris-strewn streets were impassable by carriage so he'd had no choice but to carry out his inspection tour on horseback. How he wished it were socially acceptable for a man to ride a placid and predictable cheval instead. But only women, children, and old men could ride a cheval without being ridiculed.

He flicked a glance sideways, making sure his honor guardsmen weren't laughing at his poor horsemanship. The way they all studiously avoided meeting his gaze suggested that while they hadn't the temerity to laugh out loud, there would be snickering jests in the barracks tonight.

He had put off his inspection tour for as long as the king would allow, hoping that at least the risers would be repaired by the time he had to make his way down the cliffs. But it seemed the risers would take up to a week to be declared safe for human use once more, and eventually he'd had no choice but to face the excruciating journey.

The damage was worse than he could possibly have imagined. Whole blocks of buildings had been completely destroyed and swept out to sea, and most of the buildings still standing would have to come down and be rebuilt. A few thoroughfares had been cleared so that workers could traverse the district on foot or horseback, but debris still clogged all but the largest streets. There were countless bodies trapped in the rubble, and everything was waterlogged, breeding mold and mildew that had already become a public health hazard.

And the stench! Delnamal had thought the Harbor District revolting before the flood, but it was now intolerable. He felt ridiculous riding around with a kerchief over the lower half of his face like some storybook masked bandit, but the grand magus had insisted it was a necessary precaution. The Academy had no spells to treat disease—such things were ordinarily in the realm of women's magic, though women's potions and spells did not prevent disease and merely eased symptoms—but there was a modified version of a shield spell that seemed to provide at least some protection. The Academy was putting out spelled kerchiefs as fast as it could, hoping to stave off an epidemic, but Delnamal noted as he toured what streets he could that the vast majority of the workers still combing through the rubble had no such protection. The kerchiefs were not inexpensive, for to hold all the elements necessary for the spells, they had to include metallic threads. He looked over his shoulder at Melcor, his secretary, who rode at a discreet distance behind him.

"We must encourage the Academy to produce kerchiefs faster."

His secretary rarely expressed any of his own opinions—presuming he had them—but when the man did not hurry to jot down a note, Delnamal knew an inconvenient opinion was on its way.

"They are working day and night, Your Highness. They cannot—"

"I've seen perhaps twenty people wearing kerchiefs so far today," Delnamal interrupted. "They must work harder."

"Most of the kerchiefs have been purchased by residents of the Terrace District."

Of course they had. Those nobles who did not have other homes above the cliffs—or friends above the cliffs who would give them shelter until the worst of the cleanup was completed—naturally wanted protection from the ill winds that might blow in from the Harbor District. He could hardly blame them—he wasn't about to give up his own kerchief, after all—but it was deplorably selfish not to protect those who were in the greatest danger.

"We must pay a visit to the Academy first thing tomorrow morning," he said. "I will put an end to the sale of kerchiefs and demand they be given to the workers."

He didn't have to see his secretary's face to imagine the expression. The grand magus and his stable of crafters would not appreciate being ordered to work for free, and Delnamal didn't have the authority to force them. He hoped a sense of civic duty and basic humanity might persuade the grand magus to see things his way, but if not, he might find himself forced to purchase the kerchiefs himself if he wished to protect the workers.

Having seen enough of the decimated district, Delnamal and his men made their way to the harbor front. There were two more stops in his inspection tour, one at each end of the harbor. First was the Abbey. Advance reports had told him the sturdy stone walls had held up against the flood, though the interior had been gutted. The abigails had ridden out the flood on the Abbey's top floor, crammed into a pair of rooms that were the abbess's living quarters. Except for the miserable witches who had cast the spell that killed so many, the women of the Abbey had all survived. Delnamal meant to make each and every one of them regret it.

It was a nasty, difficult slog to traverse what had once been the busy thoroughfare of Front Street. A narrow path had been cleared

in the midst of the wreckage, but there was no clearing the squelching mud that coated everything. Mud splattered the horses' coats
and stained the riders' boots and breeches, and Delnamal was in
constant battle against his balky, stubborn horse. He prayed the
damned beast wouldn't panic at some imagined danger and carry
him off at a blind gallop. He could only imagine the talk that would
circulate through the barracks and the palace if his men had to run
him down to control his horse.

Delnamal had never once set foot in the Abbey, though he suspected he was one of the few men of his entourage not to have indulged. But being the crown prince, he saw no reason to throw
away good money for favors any number of women—common and
noble alike—would happily grant him. He suspected even Lady
Oona, whom he'd loved since they were both teenagers, would
happily grant him access to her bed despite their inconvenient marriages to other people, were he willing to break his own marriage
vows. But however distasteful he found Shelvon, she was his wife,
and he had vowed to share his bed with no other. No matter how
painful the keeping of that vow became.

He'd heard many a tale of the Women's Market and of the grand
pavilion that was its most profitable venture, but when he and his
men passed through the gates, the scene that met his eyes was like
nothing he'd ever heard described.

The courtyard that had once been a market was bustling, as he
imagined it had been for every day of its existence, but not for the
usual reasons. Women in stained and torn red robes were steadily
streaming in and out of the main building, carrying armfuls of
soaked, muddy debris and piling it in stacks along the outer walls.
A few equally dirty and ragged men roamed about with blind white
eyes, reaching out to pluck elements from the air to activate various
magic items. Women passing by picked up the activated magic items
and carried them to cracks in the Abbey's walls and foundation,
using the contained spells to make repairs.

Activity halted when the crown prince and his entourage entered
the courtyard. Those who'd had their Mindseye open quickly closed

it. Women who'd been about to enter the courtyard with armloads
of rubbish quickly ducked back inside, and those who were in the
courtyard froze in their tracks. Eyes that had moments before been
dull with exhaustion and hard labor were suddenly wide and wary.
With good reason. Only a naïve fool would believe the women of
this abbey had all been ignorant of what their abbess and her ac-
complices were up to, and one way or another, Delnamal intended
to extract the truth out of the traitorous wretches.

Several of his men dismounted, fingering their swords and making sure there was no room for anyone to duck past them and out
the gate. Delnamal looked at the churned, muddy earth of the
courtyard and decided to stay on his horse.

"Who is in charge here?" he demanded. The women all looked
to one another, none daring to speak. The most timid among them
were edging back toward the building's main entrance as if taking
themselves out of his sight might protect them from his wrath. "No
one move!" he barked, glaring at a young girl with an unsightly
blotched face who had one foot in the doorway. Reluctantly, she
turned back to face the courtyard. Her gaze remained riveted to the
ground before her feet, and she was clearly petrified. Delnamal
spurred his horse forward until he was practically on top of the girl.
Up close, he saw that beneath the dirt and the hideous birthmark,
she was a pretty little thing.

"Tell me who is in charge, or I shall have you whipped right here
in this very courtyard in front of everyone!"

The girl swayed on her feet, and Delnamal thought perhaps she
was about to faint in terror. Belatedly, he realized he should not
have selected the most frightened-looking woman in his sight if he
wished to obtain information.

"I am in charge," called a voice from within the Abbey proper.
Hurried footsteps echoed within the stone hallway and soon an
older woman emerged from the darkness, gently pushing the frightened girl to the side.

When she came into the light, Delnamal saw the woman who
claimed to be in charge was at least seventy-five years old. Her back

was crooked with age, her hands gnarled with what he guessed was
arthritis, but the mud and water that spotted her robes and her
wimple declared she did not consider herself past the age of physical
labor. He winced as she dipped a shallow curtsy that looked like it
might turn into an inelegant sprawl, but she kept her faulty balance.

"Forgive me, Your Highness," said the crone. "I do not move as
fast as once I did, and I was in the back when you arrived."

"You are the new abbess?"

She kept her head respectfully bowed as her shoulders rose in a
shrug. "That has yet to be officially determined. I am the most senior, therefore—"

"Fetch me the next two candidates for the position."

The women in the courtyard began to murmur to one another,
but a sharp glance from Delnamal shut them all up.

The would-be abbess sent the girl with the marked face into the
Abbey. She quickly returned with two more old women. One
walked with the aid of a cane, and yet still the girl had to steady her
with a hand on her arm. Delnamal shook his head at the thought of
any of these crones being in charge of anything.

Delnamal gestured his men forward. "Arrest them. All of them."

The murmurs in the courtyard were louder this time, and they
did not immediately die down at Delnamal's glare. His men obeyed
promptly, seizing each of the would-be abbesses and slapping man-
acles on their wrists. The old woman with the cane lost her balance
when the cane was torn from her grip. The guardsman who had
shackled her flicked a brief glance toward Delnamal as if worried
he disapproved. When Delnamal showed no sign of displeasure, the
man grabbed the old woman's arm and dragged her through the
mud. She cried out in pain and distress.

The three women were all yammering at once, but Delnamal
had no interest in their pleas and excuses. Many of the remaining
abigails dissolved into tears, clutching one another's hands and
huddling together for comfort. Delnamal spurred his horse into a
high-stepping walk, circling the courtyard and examining the tat-
tered women and thinking about how best to reassert the authority

of the Crown. The trade minister had clearly allowed them too much autonomy and put too much power into the hands of the abbess. It was time to remind them what it meant to be Unwanted.

"You!" he said, pointing at one of the women who hadn't the good sense to weep. "And you, and you." He pointed out each woman, young or old, who seemed not to be fully cowed by the arrest of the three crones. He picked five in all, noting that several of them raised their chins proudly rather than cowering as they ought. He'd taken care to choose the most unlovely of them, women who had most likely been homely enough to escape working the pavilion. "You will service my men in any way they desire until they are fully sated. Free of charge, naturally."

The chorus of gasps and protests from the assembled abigails— even the three arrested women—was music to his ears. Perhaps they were finally understanding that defying the Crown had consequences. Delnamal looked over his shoulder at his entourage, twenty men strong. Some looked at the selected women with obvious distaste, but the more junior guardsmen—whose wages did not allow them to visit the pavilion—were not so picky. At his signal, they advanced on the chosen women. One of the women tried to run away, but a guardsman easily ran her down, shoving her face-first into the mud.

The courtyard echoed with screams and sobs, but any woman who tried to protest or interfere was beaten back with fists or feet, and most were too terrified to take action at all. A few of his men decided not to restrict themselves to the women Delnamal had chosen. Melcor was eying a buxom beauty with deliciously pouty lips. He raised an inquiring eyebrow at Delnamal, who saw no reason any abigail should deny her services to any of his men. He lowered his head in a small nod, and Melcor leapt on the girl, who let out a cry of pain when he grabbed a handful of wimple and hair.

Delnamal stayed on his horse, monitoring the activity in the courtyard. He had no inclination to partake himself—even were he willing to abandon his vows, he had no interest in screwing a woman who was not exclusively his—but he likewise had no inclination to stop his men from indulging. He only intervened when one of the men grabbed a girl in the gray robes of a novice. She looked to be on the cusp of womanhood, and would probably don the red robes within the next year or two, but she was not there yet.

"Leave her!" he barked at the man, who threw the child into a mud puddle in disgust. The screams and cries of the abigails did not trouble Delnamal's conscience, but the novice's terrified sobs made him squirm in his saddle. If it would not have made him look weak in front of his men, he might have dismounted and tried to comfort the poor child. He was not a monster, after all.

He allowed his men to enjoy their sport for about half an hour, but they had another important stop to make before the day was over, so he had to call a halt. The courtyard was littered with torn red robes that had been trampled into the mud and shat on by the horses. Naked women coated in mud curled their bodies into protective balls, awaiting their next assault, and those who had not been touched were too frightened to come to their aid.

"Let this be a warning to you all!" Delnamal bellowed, wondering if all the crying women had enough wits to hear him through their distress. "The Crown will not be defied. You will undo the spell that you unleashed upon the world, or you will all be declared traitors to the Crown."

Hearing in his words an indication that the Abbey's violation was over—at least for now—several of the abigails ran to their fallen comrades, covering their bodies with whatever filthy scraps of fabric they could salvage. Delnamal looked from one bruised and battered woman to another, then chose one whose bloody nose was crooked and broken and whose breasts were covered with bite marks. She was old enough to carry an aura of authority and battered enough to have learned her place.

"You," Delnamal said, pointing at her. "What is your name?"

The woman's lips moved, but no sound came out. The abigail with the birthmark put her arm around the older woman's shoulders and answered for her without meeting Delnamal's gaze.

"She is Chanlix Rai-Chanwynne, Your Highness."

Delnamal could not have cared less what the woman's name was save for the need to enter it in a record book somewhere. "You are the new abbess. And if your Abbey fails to reverse the spell, you will be the first of many to pay. Is that understood?"

The new abbess cringed in the mud, but she managed a nod.

Satisfied that the Abbey had been suitably punished for whatever role it had played in the casting of the abominable curse, Delnamal gathered his men, ordering several of them to take the arrested women to the dungeon. The other men would accompany him to his next stop. One he did not anticipate would be anywhere near as satisfying.

Chanlix Rai-Chanwynne spat out a mouthful of blood as she watched the prince and his men exit the Abbey. Blood continued to drip down the back of her throat, and her right eye was well on its way to swelling shut. The fiery burn between her legs made the thought of getting to her feet and moving daunting, but better to hurt more than to remain lying here in the cold mud. Besides, if she was to take the prince at his word, she was now the abbess and responsible for all the groaning, crying women in the courtyard.

"I'm all right, Maidel," she told the frightened young abigail with the stained face. The girl was crying and shaking, and Chanlix thanked the Mother that the soldiers had let her be. Maidel thought of that mark on her face as a source of shame and misery, but in this instance it had saved her the horror that had befallen the prettiest of the abigails. And the older women the prince had ordered his men to defile.

Maidel's teeth chattered as she tried to pull herself together, and the worry in her eyes clearly stated she did not believe her abbess's claim.

Chanlix spat again. There was less blood this time. "Help me up," she said, taking the younger woman's hand and bracing herself for pain. "We will need to heal as many injuries as we can before we go back to work." The flood had devastated the Abbey's supply of

healing potions and magic items, but a small store of them had survived. It would not be enough—the healing potions produced at
the Abbey were meant to ease pain and heal only minor injuries,
and Chanlix could easily see that many women were hurt beyond
the potions' abilities to fix. Broken bones and internal injuries
would require men's healing spells, and though the Abbey had
some of those in its possession, they would have to compensate the
Crown for any they used, which they hadn't the funds to do.

Maidel draped the abbess's arm around her shoulders and helped
her slowly rise to her feet. Chanlix couldn't suppress a gasp of pain,
and she swayed dizzily, afraid she was going to take both of them
back down into the mud. All around the courtyard, the uninjured
abigails were helping their sisters as best they could, covering them
with rags and blankets and gathering them into hugs.

"Let's get everyone together in the dining hall," Chanlix said.
She'd have liked to pass the word personally to each and every
woman in the courtyard, but with her spinning head and blurred
vision, she was not up to the task.

One of the men who'd been helping with repairs came and
scooped her up into his arms without being asked. She didn't know
his name. She would have requested that he put her down—despite
her doubts that her feet would stay firmly under her—except that
when she tried to speak, she practically choked on a mouthful of
blood. Her anonymous benefactor murmured soothing words to
her as she coughed blood onto his mud-stained shirt. He carried
her to the dining hall and set her down gently on the edge of a
water-stained bench. The room swayed and wavered before her
eyes, then went dark.

When Chanlix regained consciousness, she had no idea how
much time had passed. The dining hall was now full of chattering
women, all clothed once more. She herself was still naked, but
someone had laid her down on her back on the bench and covered
her with a warm, dry blanket. Her vision was clear once more, and
the world did not seem to waver and buck. Nor did her head throb
in time to the beat of her heart.

With a sigh of relief, Chanlix pushed herself into a sitting position, clutching the blanket around her. The gathered abigails did not notice at first, for they were all busily talking to one another. Along with the residual notes of pain and terror and anger, Chanlix detected a degree of excitement in the talk and wondered what she had missed.

Finally, Maidel, who was sitting quietly on the floor by Chanlix's side, noticed the abbess was awake.

"How are you feeling?" the girl asked, offering a warm and comforting touch on the hand.

Chanlix reached up and felt her head, not surprised to find it wrapped in a turban. There was no explanation for her clearheadedness save for magic. Her questing fingers found the telltale bumps of beads and gems, each of which would be infused with a healing spell of the sort the women of the Abbey could not produce. The only reason such powerful magic items were in the Abbey's possession was so that the abigails could sew them into garments for sale at the market.

Freeing her hand from Maidel's, Chanlix removed the turban. The fabric had been badly damaged by the flood waters, but water could not harm the beads, and they could have been salvaged and sewn anew. Certainly that was the Abbey's obligation under the law. Most magic items could be used repeatedly simply by reactivating their spells, but men's healing magics were one of the few kinds of magic that consumed the elements that went into their spells. The gems on the turban would have to be returned to the Academy and new spells added before they could be used again.

Maidel raised her chin. "It seems that all of our market wares were lost in the flood," she said, her eyes gone steely and cold.

Chanlix stroked the fine silk fabric. Now she understood why the women in the dining hall seemed in such good health even after the abuses they had suffered. Obviously the prince and his men hadn't bothered to take inventory of the Abbey, and considering the level of damage throughout the Harbor District, it would not surprise anyone to learn the Abbey's precious magic items were missing or destroyed. However, it was a dangerous game. Chanlix didn't imagine any of the abigails would report the truth, but she was also sure the prince was not finished with them. Hiding the emptied spell vessels would be one of the highest priorities as soon as they got back to work.

Perhaps it was the act of communal defiance that had added the undertone of excitement to the room. Chanlix couldn't think of any other reason why the women weren't still reeling in the aftermath of the prince's visit.

"Has something happened while I was . . . recovering?" she asked.

Maidel's eyes lit with ferocity of a sort Chanlix would never have expected on the girl's face. Maidel was usually painfully shy and deferential, unsure of her own value. "Open your Mindseye. You'll see."

Chanlix frowned briefly, having no idea what Maidel could possibly mean. But she did as the girl suggested, opening her Mindseye and letting her worldly vision fade.

Chanlix was almost getting used to seeing all those red-spotted motes of Rho in the air, though she suspected it would be at least a few more days before the strangeness of it stopped feeling like such a shock to the system. The room was filled with Rho and Aal, with a smattering of Tah and Von and a few other single motes. But as Chanlix swept her Mindseye over the length and breadth of the room, her mouth dropped slowly open and her breath caught in her throat.

"That's impossible," she whispered.

"It's Kai," Maidel responded. "It must be."

Chanlix shook her head. "Impossible," she said again.

Kai was a masculine element. Only visible to men—and powerful men, at that—and only generated by a violent, bloody death. It was the most powerful of all elements, and the terror of the battlefield. A mortally wounded man could use his Kai to cast spells of devastation. But only the dying man himself could use his Kai, and there was a great deal of battlefield magic meant to prevent the kinds of slow death that could produce usable Kai.

Chanlix closed her Mindseye once more, looking around the room just to make sure there weren't a bunch of dead men within the walls of the dining hall. But even if there had been, it wouldn't have explained why she could suddenly see a masculine element. Yet there were no men of any kind in the room.

"Look again," Maidel urged. "Look where the Kai appears."

Chanlix frowned at the girl once more. "Can you see it?" Maidel had many sterling qualities, but her magical talent was negligible. There was no official ranking or testing of women's magical abilities, but if there were, Maidel would rank as a Novice, capable of seeing only five elements. In all likelihood, a man ranked lower than Prime would not see Kai, and even many Prime men couldn't see it, as ranks were assigned based on the *number* of elements a man could see, not *which* elements.

Maidel nodded. Chanlix refrained from saying "impossible" yet again, tempted though she was. One more time, she opened her Mindseye and looked around the room. And there was the Kai, maybe eight or ten motes spread throughout the room.

"Look above your head," Maidel said, and Chanlix did.

She gasped yet again, reaching up to touch the jagged black, red, and white mote that hung in the air above her. It felt like a crystal that had been sitting out in the snow, so cold her hand jerked away at first touch. Then she closed her fingers around it and dragged it down to eye level, turning it this way and that.

She had never seen a mote of Kai in her life, but she had seen pictures of it in the *Book of Elements*, several copies of which resided in the Abbey's library. It was traditionally pictured in solid black, though the color and form were supposedly different for each person. But no other element was crystalline in structure.

Chanlix closed her Mindseye, because with it open, her physical vision was too obscured to make out the faces of the other women to whom motes of Kai clung. But when her physical vision became clear once more, so too did the nature of the black, red, and white Kai.

The motes clung only to the women who'd been brutalized in the courtyard.

"We've been talking about it ever since we first saw it," Maidel said. "The men beat Gruneen to within an inch of her life, but she was not raped, and she does not have Kai. And there are several who have lain with men willingly since the spell was cast, and they do not have Kai. Only those women who were taken by force have it. And we all—even the weakest of us—can see it."

The implications made Chanlix's head spin, and not because of any concussion. If this was true, and if this was not just an isolated incident . . .

"There was nothing in Mother Brynna's letter that spoke of this," Chanlix murmured. Every woman in the Abbey had read Brynna's explanation of what she had done, as well as the dire warnings and the heartfelt apologies for the price they would pay for her crime.

"But she did say there were likely to be unintended consequences," Maidel reminded her. "Surely this is one of them." Her eyes were practically glowing with excitement, and Chanlix couldn't blame her.

If the women's Kai had all the same properties and powers as that the men produced, it could serve as a very strong disincentive for men to commit rape. But Chanlix was forty-three, and she'd seen more ugliness in the world than young Maidel could ever imagine. The Kai motes hovering in the room would give the violated women a powerful weapon for revenge, and it would make many men think twice before taking an unwilling woman. But the worst of them—men like the crown prince, for example—would not see the Kai as a reason not to rape a woman.

They would see raping a woman as a way to produce Kai—and because the woman didn't have to die to produce it, she could then be forced to use it to the man's advantage.

Chanlix did not immediately give voice to her concern, because she wanted a little more time to think about it. But before the day was out, she would gather the violated abigails in her office and discuss the critical importance of keeping their discovery secret.

CHAPTER ELEVEN

Delnamal was hard-pressed to say which of his half-siblings he hated the most. Alysoon was a harpy of a woman who had never shown any sign of knowing her place, and he couldn't be in her presence for more than a handful of minutes without wanting to stuff a gag in her mouth. But despite her delusions of grandeur, she was just an ordinary noblewoman, the widow of a minor lordling whose only possible appeal had been his fortune. Tynthanal was a different story.

If there were any justice in the world, the man who had been crown prince for the first six years of his life would have retired to genteel obscurity when he was declared illegitimate. It was hardly rare for kings to have illegitimate sons scattered around, and though those sons—the ones who were acknowledged and had mothers of consequence, at least—enjoyed a certain level of prestige, they were rarely so steadfastly in the public eye as Tynthanal Rai-Brynna. And never were they so gifted with unfair advantages.

At thirty-five years old, Tynthanal had become the youngest man ever to attain the rank of lieutenant commander at the Citadel, the heart and soul of Aaltah's military. Now at thirty-nine years old, it was widely believed that he would eventually be named the lord commander and take a seat on the royal council. Every night, Delnamal prayed for the health and stamina of the current commander. He was the most disloyal of sons for even allowing the thought to enter his head, but if the current commander could outlast the current king, then it would be Delnamal's privilege and duty to name the next commander. And he would rather name his horse to the post than his half-brother.

As a lieutenant commander in a time of peace, Tynthanal should have spent most of his days behind a desk, with occasional forays out to inspect his troops and remind them of his existence. Any self-respecting officer of his age should possess an expanding middle and a retreating hairline, but no, not Tynthanal. The bastard was as lean and well-muscled as any twenty-year-old, and not only did he possess a full head of raven locks, there was not a strand of gray to be found. Delnamal was eight years younger and already had streaks of gray in his thinning brown hair. Not to mention the paunch that had defied his every attempt to lose it. His valet had just this morning suggested it was time to consider putting some discreet stays under his doublet, but Delnamal would be damned before he'd resort to wearing women's undergarments, no matter how well-hidden—or how commonly used at court—they might be.

When Delnamal and his men passed through the front gates of the Citadel, he was instantly impressed by how well the ancient military complex had held up to the flood waters. The last time Delnamal had set foot inside, there had been any number of small wooden outbuildings within the complex, and it looked as if all of those had been swept away. But the stone walls appeared none the worse for wear save for the occasional water stain, and while there was certainly still repair work being done, the soldiers appeared to have for the most part resumed at least some of their normal routine. There were marksmen taking target practice with their longbows and crossbows on one side of the entrance, and on the other, men were standing in orderly circles to watch one another spar while a trainer bellowed critiques of each man's performance.

Delnamal only noticed how tightly his fists had closed on the reins when his horse tossed its head and started doing its annoying, side-stepping dance for the thousandth time that day. And he was tired enough from the agonizingly long day on horseback that he didn't immediately recognize what had caused his whole body to clench. Until he glanced around at his men to make sure no one was laughing at his horsemanship and found they were all watching one of those sparring circles with rapt attention.

Delnamal gritted his teeth and held back a curse. Of course his preening ass of a half-brother would arrange to be showing off his skills in one of those sparring circles when Delnamal and his men arrived. There was no doubt they had been seen long before they reached the gates, and Tynthanal would welcome any excuse to make himself feel superior to the man who would be king.

The air was crisp with the bite of autumn, but the chill had not discouraged Tynthanal from removing his jacket and shirt. His nut-brown skin gleamed with sweat in the sunlight, and every muscle in his back, chest, and arms stood out in sharp contrast, dancing lithely with his every move. His sparring partner was half a head taller, at least a decade younger, and every bit as chiseled. A man in his prime, who moved with the practiced ease of an expert swordsman. Someone who by all rights should make easy work of Delnamal's middle-aged half-brother.

The other sparring circles were breaking up as men began to notice their lieutenant commander putting on a show. Men murmured and nodded approval, gathering around, making a wider circle so that more of them could see. Tynthanal was grinning broadly, eyes glowing with a combination of focus and pleasure as he danced and parried a couple of blows from his opponent's sword. Delnamal himself was as unskilled a swordsman as he was a rider, but sparring had been a routine part of his education as a prince, and he knew from way too much personal experience how much it hurt to be hit with those sparring swords despite their blunted edges.

Circling each other, making the occasional exploratory jab, the two men traded insults and taunts, although the smiles on both their faces revealed that the insults had no teeth. Delnamal was sorely tempted to spur his horse forward and break into the circle, interrupting the show he was sure was being put on entirely for his benefit. If he weren't worried that his horse would refuse him, he might have given in to his urges.

Tynthanal surged forward, swinging his sword as if it weighed no more than a teacup and slipping under his opponent's guard. At the last second, with almost superhuman reflexes, Tynthanal slowed his swing so that when his blade hit his opponent's ribs, the force was enough to knock the larger man to the ground but not so hard as to break any bones.

The gathered soldiers burst into cheers, shouting congratulations to the winner and a combination of encouragement and jeers to the loser. Delnamal felt blood rising in his face as he noticed the smiles and nods of approval among his own men. And though he immediately hated himself for it, he dreamed of the day the king would die and leave his bastard son unprotected.

Tynthanal offered his vanquished foe a hand up, a picture of charming sportsmanship. Delnamal's lip curled in distaste as his half-brother retrieved his shirt and jacket, covering his gleaming chest. It was, of course, ridiculous for Delnamal to be jealous. Tynthanal had enviably good looks, was disgustingly skilled with the sword, and had tested as an Adept—the highest possible magical rank—though he had chosen a life at the Citadel rather than the Academy. But for all those advantages, he was still a bastard who owned no land and made his home in a military barracks. Even if he became the lord commander—a rare honor for a bastard—he would always be Delnamal's social and political inferior. And when he became king, Delnamal would have the power to make his half-brother's life a living hell.

Fully clothed once more, looking barely winded after his efforts,

Tynthanal commanded his men to resume their training as he crossed the field toward Delnamal and his entourage. Simple politeness would have Delnamal dismount to greet his brother. However, even if Delnamal were inclined to be polite, he had never in his life spent so many hours on horseback. He wasn't certain his legs would hold him if he dismounted, and he *was* certain getting back on the horse afterward would be an epic struggle and a source of amusement for all who witnessed it.

"Greetings, brother!" Tynthanal called as he approached, smiling broadly as if delighted to see him.

Delnamal ground his teeth at the informal address. If the king's bastard had any respect, he'd have addressed Delnamal as Your Highness, as was appropriate. Even his own wife and mother addressed him as Your Highness in front of others. But Tynthanal, damn him, never tired of rubbing Delnamal's face in their unfortunate blood tie.

Delnamal forced a grimace of a smile, knowing that if he rebuked Tynthanal's informal address, he would look both petty and pretentious. "You're getting old and slow, brother. Your opponent almost had you."

Internally, Delnamal cursed himself for the feeble insult. No one who'd seen that performance could accuse Tynthanal of being either old or slow, nor had he come close to losing. And yet somehow when he was in Tynthanal's presence, Delnamal never seemed able to control his own tongue. The need to put the bastard in his place was so strong that he had to speak out, even knowing he was making himself look like an idiot.

"Perhaps you'd care to school me, little brother?" Tynthanal asked pleasantly. His eyes twinkled with amusement as he took hold of the horse's bridle—presumably to hold the animal still while Delnamal dismounted. "I'm sure after a grueling inspection tour you would be happy for the opportunity to stretch your legs."

Delnamal would have loved to kick the smirk off his half-brother's face. Clearly the bastard knew exactly why Delnamal had chosen not to dismount. And of course the thought of Delnamal stepping into a sparring circle was ridiculous. Delnamal hadn't handled any but a ceremonial sword since he'd turned seventeen and finally escaped the tyranny of his tutors.

"I've no time for horseplay," Delnamal snapped, fully aware that his brother had merely stepped into the opening he himself had made. "I'm here to inspect the Citadel and wish to return to the palace before dark. Let us get on with it. Where is the lord commander?"

Tynthanal made a regretful face, but there was still plenty of good humor sparkling in his eyes. "I'm afraid you've missed him. He did not know that you were coming, so he left at noon to deliver a full damage report to the palace. But I can take you on a tour of inspection if you'd like to view the damage yourself."

Delnamal could feel the heat of blood in his cheeks and knew it was creating a visible flush, but there was nothing he could do to hold it back. "I sent a flier this morning!" he snapped, but it was a lie. With the risers out, the lord commander had been excused from attending the daily meetings of the royal council, and it had never occurred to Delnamal that the man would undertake the long journey on horseback to deliver a report in person.

Tynthanal shrugged. "Apparently it did not arrive, or I'm sure the lord commander would have been here to greet you."

The heat in Delnamal's cheeks increased. Every word that left his mouth did further damage. It was certainly possible for fliers to be fatally damaged in transit, but the likelihood of that happening on the short flight from the palace to the Citadel was less than slim. Everyone saw the lie for what it was.

Delnamal was not a stupid man, but something about his half-brother caused his mind and his mouth to malfunction. If he didn't know better, he would swear Tynthanal had invented some kind of spell to turn his half-brother's brain to mush. Perhaps he'd developed his magical skills more than he'd let on. But of course that supposition was ridiculous. Delnamal was of only Medial rank in magic, but he'd had enough education to know what magic was capable of doing and what it wasn't. Mind control was not possible.

If the lord commander was already presenting his report at the palace, then there was absolutely no reason for Delnamal to perform the tedious tour of inspection himself. He was not disappointed to be spared the inconvenience, but he could not bear to let Tynthanal show off his swordsmanship, humiliate him, and then all but call him a liar in front of his men without striking a blow of his own. So far, his every attempt to put the bastard in his place had failed, and Delnamal scoured his brain for some way to leave his mark and knock that smirk off Tynthanal's face.

He began speaking before a plan had fully formed in his mind, because if he sat atop his horse and thought about it too long, it would be clear to everyone that he was once again lying.

"I have no need for an inspection tour," he said. "I'm sure the lord commander will provide a thorough report. However, that is not the only reason I came to the Citadel."

Tynthanal quirked a curious eyebrow and gazed up at him with an expression of polite interest. As if he already knew Delnamal was improvising and was happy to let him dig as deep a hole as possible.

Delnamal knew a brief moment of panic as he searched desperately for something to say. Then inspiration struck.

"The king, in his great generosity of spirit, has for the time being decided not to hold all the women of the Abbey responsible for your mother's crime." He had the unique pleasure of seeing the faintest twitch in the muscles of Tynthanal's jaw. From all accounts, the man had had no contact with his mother since she'd entered the Abbey when he was six years old, but he was still her son, and it was satisfying to remind him—and everyone who so admired him—of his blood relation with the witch who'd cursed the Wellspring.

"The three most senior abigails have been arrested and will be forcefully questioned as to the Abbey's involvement with this abomination. We cannot be certain the remaining women aren't traitors, and they must not be allowed to flee justice. The king commands that you personally lead a garrison to maintain the security of the Abbey and make sure none of its inhabitants leave until we've gotten to the bottom of their heinous conspiracy."

He met his half-brother's eyes, and for the first time since he'd entered the Citadel, he felt the tiniest hint of a smile tugging at the corners of his mouth. The king had, of course, made no such command, a fact which Tynthanal no doubt deduced immediately. However, guarding the Abbey when the loyalty of its inhabitants was so much in doubt was a more than reasonable idea, and both men knew that the king would never make a liar of his heir. He might offer Delnamal a mild rebuke in private, but he would publicly confirm he had given the order.

Tynthanal was better than his half-brother at hiding his emotions. His smirk did not fade, and his body language did not change. Nonetheless, there was an angry spark in his eyes that said he'd been bested and he knew it. Delnamal felt a warm glow of satisfaction in his chest, his good humor almost restored despite the infernal pain in his legs and seat from the long day on horseback.

"I know serving as a glorified prison guard is beneath the dignity of a lieutenant commander," Delnamal said with feigned commiseration, "but the king would trust this vital duty to none less."

Tynthanal managed a wry smile, covering the surge of anger with his trademark humor. "I am as always honored by His Majesty's command and his trust in me."

Delnamal suppressed a snort. Not a man in earshot would mistake this command for an honor. And though Tynthanal was probably not the only one who recognized the questionable provenance of the command, no one would dare challenge it.

Knowing well that where Tynthanal was concerned, he had best take his minor victory and run, Delnamal made his stately exit.

Exhausted in body and mind, Ellin made her way through the palace halls toward the royal apartments she'd moved into a few days before. She longed for her old, familiar bed, and for the luxury of a quiet night spent in lovely idleness. However, it had already become abundantly clear that she had a lot to learn about the governance of a kingdom, and after a long and grueling day of appointments and audiences, she meant to spend the next few hours before bed study-ing statecraft and the convoluted laws of Rhozinolm. A daunting task, but at least one she could carry out in solitude, out from under the scrutiny that was a sovereign's constant companion.

Her dressing room was within her line of sight when she turned to dismiss her honor guard for the night. She let out a silent sigh when she saw the look on Graesan's face and realized her work was not yet over, after all.

"What is it?" she asked.

Graesan bowed, though it was hardly necessary under the cir-cumstances. "If you have a moment to spare, Your Majesty, we should review your itinerary for tomorrow."

She tried not to make a face, although she'd spent the last week attempting *not* to think about the ordeal of the state funeral that she would face the next day. Never had the people of Rhozinolm said farewell to so many members of the royal family on the same day, and she wasn't sure how she would survive the endless proces-sion and ceremony under constant, very public scrutiny while try-ing to maintain some semblance of dignity. Genteel tears were to be expected, but a sovereign queen must under no circumstances be allowed to sob out her grief for all to see. Even now, a hard, painful lump was forming in her throat.

"Yes, of course," she rasped, then gestured Graesan into a small public parlor just down the hall. She turned to the other guards. "You may leave me. I plan to retire as soon as the captain and I have finished."

The men bowed and withdrew, taking up stations just outside the entrance to the residential wing.

Inside the parlor, a fire was crackling merrily. A chandelier of luminants that had been damaged during the earthquake was now fully repaired, each luminant lit and throwing back the shadows. Ellin eyed the low sofa in front of the fireplace, but as Graesan was not allowed to sit in her presence, she chose a high-backed chair at a small circular table instead.

Graesan laid a paper on the table in front of her, and she peered at it to see the route the funeral procession would travel on the following day. Her heart sank when she got a good look at how it wound through the streets in a tortuously twisted course that would take hours to traverse.

"Lord Semsulin has suggested that you ride the king's horse for the procession," Graesan said.

She looked at him with some alarm. She had never ridden anything but a cheval her entire life. The people were unlikely to be offended at the sight of a woman riding a horse when that woman was their sovereign queen, but tomorrow would be hard enough without having to face the fear of falling off a horse in front of everyone.

"We can put a calming spell on the saddle to keep the beast placid," Graesan continued. "However, for security reasons, I recommend a carriage instead. While it might not look as . . . kingly . . . it has more powerful protections built in and would allow the honor guard to give you a little more space."

Ellin allowed herself a small smile even as tears filmed her eyes. Graesan knew well how little she liked feeling crowded. She had had an honor guard for as long as she could remember, and she was never out in public without them. However, now that she was queen, the guard had trebled in size, and it felt like she was constantly surrounded.

"It will have to be an open carriage," she said, because the point of the procession was not just that the people be allowed to see their fallen royal family, but to see their new queen as well.

Graesan nodded. "Naturally. But even an open carriage can be warded so that you need have only two men in front and two behind."

Her smile grew a little wider as she looked up into Graesan's eyes. "I presume that as far as Lord Semsulin is concerned, this was my idea and not yours."

Graesan's eyes sparkled, and his lips twitched. "It would be convenient if he were to believe that."

She laughed briefly, then impulsively reached out and gave his arm an affectionate squeeze. His eyes widened, and he shot a brief glance at the open door. He did not, however, make any attempt to avoid her touch.

"If I were a king," she said, "and you were a maid, no one would think twice to see me touching your arm." *Or touching you anywhere else, for that matter,* she thought.

Graesan covered her hand with one of his, the unexpected touch causing her to shiver deliciously. "But you are not a king," he said with obvious regret, "and I am not a maid." Gently, he pushed her hand away, but she could see by the darkening of his eyes that it took some effort.

Ellin had never doubted that Graesan wanted her as badly as she wanted him. While he had never challenged the bounds of propriety, he was too open and honest by nature to fully hide his feelings in her presence. He was a balm against all the scheming and dissembling of the court, and she never had to parse his words for hidden meanings. She could see his affection in his eyes, hear it in the tone of his voice when they spoke privately. He had always needed to be circumspect, and now that she was more in the public eye than ever, he would have to work even harder to keep his distance.

"I feel so alone," she whispered, suddenly on the verge of tears. Wanting Graesan and not being allowed to have him had always been an ache inside her, but now that her life was so irrevocably altered, her whole family gone and the weight of a kingdom on her shoulders, the ache had grown into a sharper, deeper pain.

"You are *not* alone," Graesan said, and his whole body seemed to lean into her. She almost thought he was going to throw off all rules of propriety and put his arms around her. She was fairly certain she would have let him.

Graesan swallowed hard and rocked back on his heels, resisting whatever impulse had moved him into her personal space. "No matter what happens," he said hoarsely, "you will always have . . . people who love you. Not just people who love their queen—people who love *you.*"

She stared up at him, her palms suddenly damp as her hands clasped together in her lap to stop herself from reaching out to him. How glorious would it feel to be wrapped up in his arms, to drink in the warmth of his affection—had he really just declared his love for her in that roundabout way?—and hear the beating of his heart as her head rested against his chest. His warmth would chase away the chill of fear and loss and loneliness that had taken up permanent residence inside her.

"I had best return to my duties," Graesan said abruptly, his eyes shifting away from her. "Tomorrow will be a grueling day, and you must have your rest." He bowed low. "If there is nothing else, Your Majesty?"

She drew in first one deep breath, then another. Graesan was right, and they were tempting fate by staying too long in each other's company in the illusory privacy of the parlor. She trusted Graesan to control himself, and she knew he would never risk damaging her reputation by giving in to his desires—it was her own willpower she doubted. As desperately as she wanted him to stay, it was time for him to go.

"Thank you, Captain. That will be all."

He hesitated for a moment, as if there was something else he wished to say. Whatever it was, he kept it to himself, and with one more bow, he retreated.

CHAPTER TWELVE

Some would say that she was being overly cautious, but Alys had no intention of learning magic while there was any danger of being seen. She trusted the household staff implicitly, but that was not a reason to take foolish risks. Not when Delnamal was in search of an excuse to condemn her entire family for their relationship to the women who had changed the world. She cracked open her daughter's door to find Jinnell pacing the room, hands outstretched before her. Her heart thudded against her breastbone, and she could barely draw a full breath as she hastily stepped inside and closed the door behind her.

"Jinnell Rah-Sylnin!" she hissed, though she wanted to scream it. "What do you think you're doing?"

Jinnell jumped and turned toward her mother's voice. Her milky white eyes said she could see very little of the physical world—hence not having noticed her mother entering the room—and spoke quite clearly to what she'd been doing. The film cleared as she closed her Mindseye and blinked to restore her worldly vision.

Jinnell raised her chin and met her mother's eyes with stubborn pride. "You promised we would learn magic together. Yet we have not cracked open Grandmother's book. I thought I'd see what I could learn on my own."

Alys suppressed a groan, wanting to shake some sense into her daughter. "If someone other than me had walked in—"

Jinnell rolled her eyes. "No one except you would walk into my bedroom at this time of night. Not without knocking first, at least."

That was, of course, why Alys had chosen to hold their first magic lesson when the entire household was supposedly asleep. Both she and her daughter were dressed for bed in shapeless—but wonderfully comfortable—white nightdresses, their hair confined to single long braids down their backs.

"That isn't the point!" Alys snapped.

Jinnell arched an eyebrow. Under other circumstances, Alys might have laughed, for she knew precisely where her daughter had learned that particular expression. "Forgive me, Mama. What is your point precisely?"

What an infuriating, cheeky child!

Alys reined in her temper—temper that was fueled entirely by fear—and took a couple of deep breaths to calm her racing heart. When next she spoke, her voice came out sounding considerably calmer.

"My point, Jinnell, is that unless my mother's spell had effects of which I am not yet aware, you do not have a penis." She had the satisfaction of seeing her daughter's eyes widen with shock and her mouth drop open. "Without one, being caught practicing magic could land you in the Abbey for the rest of your life. When the consequences are so dire, one must take every imaginable precaution, no matter how unnecessary it might seem. If we take only the precautions we think necessary, we will be caught."

Jinnell looked as if she were going to argue, then thought better of it and sighed. "You're right, Mama." She frowned. "Why are you coming into my room without knocking in the middle of the night anyway?"

Alys couldn't help the little smile that tugged at her lips. It showed how distracted Jinnell had been that it had taken her this long to ask that question. Alys reached into the pocket of her dressing gown and pulled out her mother's book. "Why, to start learning magic, of course."

Jinnell grunted and threw up her hands. "Oh! You are impossible."

"I believe that's my line. Save it for when you have a child of your own." Turning her back on her daughter, she withdrew a key from her dressing gown pocket and locked the bedroom door. It was considered highly improper for an unmarried girl to lock her bedroom door—the assumption being that the locked door signified she was doing something she ought not—but Alys's presence would erase any suggestion of impropriety.

"Let us sit where we can both see the book clearly," she said when the door was secure, gesturing to the tufted velvet settee at the foot of Jinnell's bed.

Jinnell hurried to her seat, eyes alight with excitement. For a girl who'd shown little interest in being educated beyond the minimum requirements for a noblewoman, she seemed surprisingly eager for their lessons to begin. And once again, Alys was struck by the sense that she didn't know her daughter as well as she'd thought. She had never thought Jinnell was stupid, but she had to admit to herself that she'd considered the girl shallow, perhaps even a bit vapid.

"Considering you were worried my visits to the Abbey were a blight on your reputation, you seem surprisingly open to delving into magic," Alys said as she sat by her daughter's side.

A touch of color appeared in each of Jinnell's cheeks, and she fidgeted. "I've always been fascinated by magic," she admitted. "I know it's not proper, but . . . well . . ." She shrugged.

Alys was struck by a startling certainty. "Tonight wasn't the first time you'd played with Mindsight, was it?"

Jinnell gave her a sheepish grin. "Not exactly," she said. "I thought that as long as everyone believed I was painfully proper, no one would ever suspect."

Alys shook her head. If she thought too much about the risks her daughter had been taking for who knew how long, she might run screaming from the room. It was best she try to forget about it and move forward.

Opening her Mindseye, Alys found several motes of Rho and fed three of them into the book. Then she closed her Mindseye once more so she could see the book. She opened it to the first page, which had once held the letter from her mother. That letter was gone, replaced with new text.

Lesson One

Before you can work with magic, you must become proficient at identifying the elements. Open your Mindseye and look around you. Pick an element you do not recognize and touch it to the page. The book will identify it for you. The stronger your magical ability, the more different elements you will be able to see. With your bloodlines, you will be extremely gifted and should have no trouble seeing all of the most common elements available near Aaltah's Well.

When you have entered forty elements, the book will test you by showing you a picture of each element you have learned. When you can identify them all, the next lesson can begin.

"Forty elements!" Jinnell wailed, reading along with Alys. "It will take *forever* just to find that many, if we even can!"

Alys blinked and realized she had made an unreasonable assumption when she'd decided to share the magic lessons with Jinnell. She briefly opened her Mindseye once more and glanced around the room. To her Mindseye, the room was like a sea of stars, with an almost countless variety of colors and patterns. She didn't need to count them to know she saw well more than forty different ones.

"How many different elements can you see in this room?" she asked Jinnell.

Jinnell stuck out her lower lip in what was probably an unconscious pout, then opened her Mindseye and looked around. "I don't know," she said with a shrug. "Maybe about twenty-five?"

Her eyes cleared and she met Alys's gaze. "How many can you see, Mama?"

Alys took a deep breath and let it out on a sigh. "A lot more than that."

Jinnell gaped at her. "But, Mama, Corlin tested as Prime level, and as far as I can tell, I can see about as many elements as he can. That puts us both well above average. If you can see a lot more than that . . ." She huffed out a deep breath, shaking her head. "Papa was only Medial level. I should have known what it meant that Corlin and I both seem to be higher level."

Alys shrugged. "How could you know? It's not as if they test women or even acknowledge that our magic has any value. Even if the men of the Academy knew how many elements I could see, they would dismiss my abilities on the grounds that I can see only feminine and neuter elements."

"*Do* you see only feminine and neuter elements?"

"Of course I do," she answered without thinking.

"How do you know? You can't actually identify most of what you see, right?"

Alys frowned, for Jinnell was correct about that. "Well, seeing as I'm a woman, it's safe to assume that I see only feminine and neuter elements, but I suppose we'll find out." She patted the book.

"Even if you don't see the masculine elements, I'll bet you see enough to be labeled an Adept, just like Uncle Tynthanal."

Alys's first instinct was to demur. How could she claim to be an Adept when women were not supposed to be assigned any magical ranking whatsoever? But she had sneaked a few glances at magical texts in her day, and she'd seen that to be labeled as an Adept, a man needed to prove he could see one hundred elements or more. One day when she had visited the Well in the depths of the palace, she'd taken the insane risk of opening her Mindseye and had counted how many different elements she could see spilling from the Well. She'd made it to fifty before confusion took over and she couldn't remember which she'd already counted and which she hadn't. But even in her confusion, she'd felt quite certain she had counted less than half of the elements she could see. Even if many of those elements were feminine and of questionable power, it wasn't such a stretch to label herself as Adept.

"Maybe," Alys finally said, squirming a bit at the prideful admission. "We shall see as I learn to identify the elements. Let us start by identifying those elements that we can both see."

She opened her Mindseye and looked around the room. "Pick an element, and I'll let you know if I see it, too. We can skip Rho, naturally."

"And Aal," Jinnell agreed, pointing at a cluster of Aal motes.

"Yes. Now pick something else. Something you don't recognize."

Jinnell pointed at a purple-pink mote with iridescent hints of silver in it. "Do you see this one?"

Alys nodded. "That's Oon," she said.

"Oh. Right. It seems proper you should be able to see your namesake elements."

"Perhaps, but it's no sure thing."

"How about this one?" Jinnell pointed to a medium-blue mote with a broad stripe of red across its center.

"I can see it," Alys said, "but I don't know what it is."

"Let's find out." Jinnell drew the mote toward the book, then they both had to close their Mindseye to see the result.

Von. F. Soothing, calming. Essential for pain relief spells and sleep spells.

"Oh," Alys and Jinnell said together. The book wasn't just going to tell them the name of the element, but also its gender and use.

"I suppose we'll have to look at Rho and Aal, after all," Alys said.

Jinnell let out a small sigh. "See, I told you this was going to take forever."

Alys shivered, but it was a chill of unease, not cold. They could not move on to the next lesson until they could identify forty elements, and it might take time to find that many that both she and

Jinnell could see. It was still possible that Alys was worrying over nothing, that the sense of urgency that drove her to share her mother's book with Jinnell was all a product of her imagination. But she couldn't shake the feeling that time was not on their side.

"I think perhaps we need to spend more time on this than we might have thought," she told her daughter, hoping she was keeping the anxiety out of her voice. "I'm sorry I waited so long to start. From now on, we should do this every night while the rest of the household sleeps."

Something in her daughter's eyes told her Jinnell had heard the thread of anxiety despite her attempt to hide it. But Jinnell asked no questions. And in contrast to her usual desultory response to the prospect of studying, she made no protest.

There were few places in Aalwell, indeed in all of Aaltah, that Delnamal hated more than the dungeons. He did not like to think of himself as squeamish, and he certainly didn't feel sorry for the wretched creatures who found themselves imprisoned there, but the place oppressed him in ways that made little sense, considering he had no fear of ever occupying such a space himself.

The prison was of modern design, and scrupulously clean. Neither the cells nor the corridors was especially dank or damp, and any vermin that crept in were periodically exterminated. On its surface, even the light-starved dungeon cells where the most unfortunate criminals were entombed were not the storybook pits of despair. Prisoners were provided with straw-tick mattresses, their slops were emptied frequently, and though the temperature was always uncomfortably cool, each prisoner had a single thin blanket to wrap up in for warmth.

It wasn't the physical conditions of captivity in the cells that made the dungeons into a living nightmare. No, the nightmares occurred when the prisoners were dragged out of those cells, and it felt as if the very walls had absorbed decades' worth of screams and terror and misery.

Delnamal shivered as he made his way down the narrow staircase to the dungeon level by the light of a flickering torch. The Crown was not about to waste costly luminants on the wretches in the prison, and despite the basic cleanliness of the place, the walls were stained with soot and scorch marks, and the air smelled faintly of smoke. Then when he came to the bottom of the stairway and stepped into the cell block, the smell of smoke was immediately drowned out by the sharp bite of body odor. The slops might be frequently cleaned, but the prisoners themselves were not.

Delnamal gritted his teeth against a nearly overpowering desire to turn and flee. Surely no one would blame him if he merely allowed the inquisitor to give him a full report of everything he had learned—along with a clinical listing of the methods he'd used to pry out the information—after it was all over. But he knew without having to be told that his father would expect him to have the balls to at least pay a visit and get an in-person report. Certainly King Aaltyn himself had presided over many an interrogation, considering it part of his duty as king. Even knowing that, Delnamal might have turned back, were he not certain his cowardice would immediately invite comparisons to the courage and strength of his half-brother.

Several guards were gathered in the guardroom directly below the staircase, and the inquisitor was there as well. The men were laughing over some jest, the sound echoing through the stone corridors in a direct mockery of the misery that shrouded the place. All leapt to their feet and bowed when Delnamal entered, the laughter dying as if it had not existed. When they quieted, he could hear the faint sound of someone weeping in the distance—a sound far more suited to the environment than laughter.

"What have you learned?" he asked the inquisitor, without much hope of a satisfactory answer.

The inquisitor eyed him warily, no doubt knowing his news would not be pleasing. "I have thoroughly examined all three prisoners, Your Highness," he said. "In my professional opinion, they had no knowledge of the spell that was cast, nor have they any idea how it was accomplished or how it might be reversed."

Delnamal cursed, though it was the answer he'd expected. He'd spoken to the grand magus of the Academy, one of the most magically gifted men he'd ever known, and the man had repeatedly assured him that what the abbess had done was impossible. Regardless of the very obvious evidence that it was, indeed, possible. Expecting three old abigails to know the secrets of the working was unrealistic. And yet he expected it anyway.

"That is not satisfactory," he told the inquisitor.

A hint of worry shone in the inquisitor's eyes, but his voice remained calm. "I can examine them further, of course, and I will if that is your wish. But they are all elderly, and two of them are particularly frail. I fear if I push them any harder, their hearts may not be able to withstand the strain."

Delnamal narrowed his eyes. "Surely you have ways of keeping them alive for questioning." Delnamal knew little of the inquisitor's art, but he did know there were magic items that could repair even potentially fatal injuries.

"I can prevent them from dying of their injuries," the inquisitor agreed. "But I cannot make their bodies young and strong once more, and all three are close to reaching their natural limits."

It was of no consequence to Delnamal if all three of the women expired. They were traitors anyway, whether they admitted it or not. If Delnamal had his way, the Abbey would be razed to the ground and all the women within slaughtered. It was called the Abbey of the Unwanted for a reason, and while some might miss the women's services, it would take little time to rebuild the Abbey and start anew.

Not that Delnamal was going to get his way. The king still considered those wretched women his subjects, and he would not condemn them all even if there were strong evidence to link the three arrested abigails to the crime. Which there wasn't.

"By all rights, their lives should be forfeit," Delnamal said. "If the rigors of your examination should cause one or more to expire, you have my word that you will not be held responsible. They must be made to confess." Delnamal held the inquisitor's gaze, willing the man to understand the full meaning of his words.

The inquisitor's jaw tightened. He was a hard man, with a hard job, but perhaps even he hesitated to torture old women into confessing to a crime he was convinced they did not commit. But whether those particular abigails were guilty or not, Delnamal was sure that damned Abbey was to blame for the Curse that had stolen his heir. And he would find a way to make them pay no matter how reluctant the king might be to condemn them.

The inquisitor swallowed and dropped his gaze to the floor. "I understand, Your Highness," he said with a slight bow of his head. "I will offer the prisoners additional inducement to tell the truth."

CHAPTER THIRTEEN

There was little Shelvon hated more than being dragged to a court party on the arm of the man who made no secret that he despised her. Whenever possible, she demurred, and she'd hoped the miscarriage would be sufficient excuse to shirk her social obligations for at least a few weeks after the earthquake. However, her husband had made it clear that attendance at tonight's ball was not optional. She sat before the mirror in her dressing room and tried to hold still as her maid pinned jeweled ornaments into the netting of her snood. To prepare for a formal occasion here in Aaltah required well over an hour of tedious pinning and prodding and lacing and braiding, and Shelvon wondered if she would ever get used to it all. At home in Nandel, dressing for the evening required nothing more than adding an extra layer of petticoats and choosing a kirtle in a daring shade. Daring in Nandel being considered any color that was not brown or black or gray.

There was a knock on the dressing room door, and Shelvon's

maid put down her pins and went to answer. When she returned to the dressing table, she was beaming. In her hands was a large black velvet box, which she held out reverently to Shelvon.

"This is from your husband," the maid said, looking like she was about to burst with excitement.

Shelvon blinked in surprise. "From Delnamal?" she asked, as if she had more than one husband who could possibly be giving her gifts. But it was so out of character as to be almost shocking. He had given her the traditional jewels on their wedding day, and a decadently soft fur-lined mantle on the day they'd formally announced her pregnancy, but she knew perfectly well it was Queen Xanvin who had selected those gifts—and no doubt it was the queen she had to thank for this impulse, too.

"Well go on. Open it." Her maid was practically bouncing on her heels with excitement. Evidently, she thought this some kind of grand romantic gesture on the prince's part. Shelvon wasn't sure what to make of it herself, but she was certain romance did not enter into the equation.

She opened the box. Inside, she found a necklace and earrings of delicate gold filigree, sparkling with clusters of flowers with ruby centers and diamond petals. Her maid gasped and made a low sound of appreciation.

"They're beautiful!" she said in a voice filled with awe.

Shelvon ran her fingers over the jewels of the necklace. The trailing ends of it would reach to the very bottom of her bodice, and the dangling earrings would brush her shoulders.

"We will have to change your bodice," the maid said speculatively, and Shelvon suppressed a groan. Here she'd thought she was almost done with the ordeal of dressing.

But there was no denying that the stunning necklace would be lost against the embroidered gold brocade bodice she was currently wearing. And that she would have to forgo the assortment of pins and brooches and lace that had already been attached.

"I don't suppose the prince would be happy if I saved this for another occasion," she murmured. Her maid's eyes widened with shock and maybe even horror. Shelvon sighed and gave in to the inevitable.

"What do you advise I change into?" she asked. She had long ago learned that she was always better off wearing what her ladies picked for her instead of making the decision herself. She had no fashion sense whatsoever, at least not any that the court of Aaltah recognized.

Delnamal paced the anteroom impatiently. Ordinarily, he could trust his wife to be painfully punctual, for she'd shown no sign of being capable of adjusting to court time. He would never admit to his mother that he was attempting to take her advice, but though he would be more than happy to set Shelvon aside and find a new wife more to his liking, there was no denying a divorce would cause a diplomatic incident with Nandel. It was possible he could convince his father to offer Jinnell Rah-Sylnin to Prince Waldmir as a bride, and such a marriage might be enough to smooth any ruffled feathers, but Delnamal was well aware that was no sure thing. Despite his lack of enthusiasm for his marriage, maintaining it—and coaxing Shelvon into producing an heir—was the surest way to keep the peace, and he was determined to do his duty.

To that end, he'd sent Shelvon a truly extravagant gift, and he'd even arrived in the anteroom at the appointed hour, instead of fashionably late as was his usual practice. Only to find for the first time ever that Shelvon was not already awaiting him. How like a woman to be so frustratingly contrary.

Delnamal's fingers tapped restlessly against his leg as he paced. His stomach rumbled as a tantalizing whiff of the feast to come floated through the anteroom. For this evening's festivities, he had finally allowed his valet to put some stays under his doublet. How women survived wearing the things day in and day out he could hardly imagine. He felt like he was suffocating, and the bones dug into his flesh like talons. He hoped they would not interfere with his ability to indulge at dinner. The longer he had to wait in this anteroom smelling food, the hungrier he would become.

Delnamal was actually contemplating the unthinkable breach of etiquette of entering the dining hall without his wife on his arm when she finally swept into the room. She curtsied deeply, and when she spoke her voice was barely audible. She was the most softly spoken human being he had ever encountered, though with her unlovely accent and her abysmal conversational skills, he was hardly inclined to complain.

"Forgive me for keeping you waiting, Your Highness," she murmured, or at least that's what he thought she said.

She had certainly not grown any lovelier in the hours since he'd last seen her, but the flash and sparkle of the jewels he had given her were a welcome distraction to the eyes, and her jewel-studded cap and snood kept most of her colorless hair hidden. She would not be a stunning beauty on his arm as he led her into dinner, but at least she would not be an eyesore, either.

"You look lovely this evening, my dear," he said. The words felt awkward in his mouth, and he wondered if he had ever before offered her a compliment. He searched his mind but could come up with no such memory.

If truth be told, he suspected he had spoken more kind words to his hated half-sister than he had ever spoken to his wife, and the realization shamed him. He did not have to love or even like her, but there was no reason he should make their marriage any more miserable than it already was.

"Thank you," she whispered, keeping her head bowed as she reached up to finger the cascade of jewels that hung down the front of her bodice. "I have never set eyes on anything so fine. You honor me."

Delnamal allowed himself a small smile, which she did not see because she was staring so resolutely at the rug beneath her feet. He liked a shy and self-deprecating woman, but Shelvon took the near-groveling to an unpalatable extreme. He had certainly not given her the gift to honor her. Instead, it was an inducement for her to give him what he wanted in return. But even he, with his habitually abrupt manner, knew better than to say that out loud.

"I intend to be a better husband from now on," he said, and

was rewarded by a startled glance up that briefly skimmed his face. Was that a look of hope he detected in those dull, placid eyes of hers?

"You are too good to me," she said, gaze returning to the carpet as she sketched a quick curtsy.

"We both know that's not true." He was almost as surprised by his words as she. He certainly hadn't meant to say any such thing. He had, in fact, barely allowed himself to think it. "I will do better from now on."

Shelvon looked up once more, this time going so far as to meet his eyes. "I will try to do better, too," she said earnestly. Her eyes shimmered suspiciously, and he suffered a brief surge of horror at the thought she might suddenly burst into tears. He was prepared to give her gifts and offer the occasional kind word, but he had no patience for feminine hysterics and had no intention of allowing the woman to weep against his shoulder. Thankfully, Shelvon blinked back the tears and offered him a tremulous smile.

His stomach gurgled loudly, signaling that it had had enough of this evening's marital bliss. It was probably for the best, since he couldn't imagine what else he and his wife had to talk about. He gave her his best, most practiced court smile and offered her his elbow.

"Shall we?"

His gallant offer was rewarded with another shy smile, and Shelvon obediently tucked her hand into the crook of his elbow.

Shelvon could not rightly say she enjoyed that night's feast, but neither did she suffer through it. Both the food and the drink were delicious and decadent, and she had learned through hard experience that she must eat no more than a couple bites of each course lest she spend the latter half of the dinner turning away each platter and receiving offended looks from those around her. It seemed accepting a large plate piled with three days' worth of food and then eating a single bite was considered far more polite than refusing the plate. The waste was appalling—especially when so many of the common folk of the Harbor District were half-starved—but in Aaltah, waste was clearly part and parcel of the royal tradition.

Delnamal wasted far less of his food than Shelvon. Even he couldn't eat everything that was served, but he made a heroic effort, digging into each delicacy with gusto. It seemed that the richer and more decadent the dish, the more he ate, and even with his corpulent frame, she wondered where it all went. She swore she could see him growing fatter as the meal progressed.

She was used to being largely ignored during meals, both by her husband and by the rest of his courtiers. In the early days, people had tried desperately to draw her into polite conversation, and while she'd appreciated the kindness of their efforts, it was a relief when they'd finally given up. She'd been raised to be quiet unless spoken to, to be as unobtrusive as possible in any given situation, and those were lessons she had taken to heart and had so far been unable to abandon. Uncharacteristically, Delnamal had made a couple of attempts to include her in tonight's conversation, asking her the occasional question that required only a brief answer. She would never have thought him capable of such a kindness, nor of having the sensitivity to include her without putting undue pressure on her to prove herself witty and interesting.

It wasn't until the feast was over and the ball had begun that her husband's mood started to sour, and Shelvon knew exactly when the turning point occurred.

There were more people at the ball than there had been at the feast, and an announcement was made when each new person entered the ballroom. The king sat on a thronelike chair on a dais, with the queen on his right and Delnamal and Shelvon on his left. After new guests were announced, they proceeded down the middle of the room to the dais to pay their respects to the royal family. The process was always tedious, and Delnamal was often bored and sleepy after a big meal. It was Shelvon's job as his wife to keep a careful eye on him and make sure he did not embarrass himself by falling asleep.

His head was nodding, and Shelvon was trying to work up the courage to put her hand on his arm to rouse him, when suddenly he jerked, his eyes popping open as he abruptly sat up straighter in his chair. Shelvon had been watching him so carefully she had paid no attention to the announcement of the latest guests, but when she followed Delnamal's gaze, she knew immediately what had roused him.

No one had ever come right out and told Shelvon that her husband was in love with Lady Oona Rah-Wylsem, but sometimes her natural reticence worked to her advantage and people almost forgot she was there. And so over the first few months of her marriage, Shelvon had pieced together what the court considered to be the romantically tragic love story of the crown prince and his childhood sweetheart.

Lady Oona was a noblewoman of middling rank whose father had risen to prominence due to his military prowess in the last war between Aaltah and Rhozinolm—one which had gone so poorly for so long that Aaltah might well have fallen to its most-hated rival had not King Aaltyn married Xanvin and drawn Khalpar into an alliance powerful enough to bring King Linolm to the negotiating table.

Lady Oona and Prince Delnamal had fallen madly in love with each other when they were teenagers, and both had naïvely assumed that one day they would grow up to marry. But while Lady Oona was of noble birth and her father was a noted hero, the family was not a particularly wealthy or prominent one, and there was no particular diplomatic advantage to a match between them.

From what Shelvon had heard, Delnamal had done everything in his power to convince his father to allow him to marry Oona, and the king had shown signs that he might relent. Until Prince Waldmir had offered Shelvon with a healthy trade agreement as a dowry. It had been an offer King Aaltyn could ill afford to turn down with King Linolm still on the throne of Rhozinolm and bad blood continuing to run between them. The iron and gemstones that Nandel provided were vital to the production of weapons and magic that would make Aaltah an unappealing target for King Linolm's ambitions.

Shelvon could almost sympathize with her husband, for love denied was one of life's greatest pains—or at least so she had been led to believe. Having never loved a man, nor having ever had much reason to believe such a love could be hers, she could hardly imagine what it must have felt like. She certainly understood why her husband despised her so much.

Lady Oona was married herself now and was already a mother. But no one seeing the way Delnamal looked at her when she entered the room could doubt that he still loved her as fiercely as he ever had.

Lady Oona and her husband approached the dais, giving the king their curtsy and bow. Oona was a delicate, raven-haired beauty with absurdly large eyes and lush, full lips. For tonight's ball, she wore a deep blue silk skirt set off by a jeweled blue velvet bodice and long slit sleeves with billows of lace puffing out. The ensemble was unusual and stunning, and though the lady was hardly of a rank to steer fashion trends at court, Shelvon had no doubt that the next time there was a ball, there would be more than one lady in attendance with similarly slit sleeves.

Oona's and Delnamal's eyes met for one highly charged second while Oona's husband paid a compliment to the queen as if he didn't notice. But Shelvon doubted there was a person in the room who didn't catch the flash of longing and desire that sparked between the crown prince and the woman who could never be his. And when Oona and her husband ceded their place to the next couple who wished to pay their respects, Shelvon could already sense how the prince's mood had changed.

Shelvon wished with all her heart that her husband would simply take Lady Oona as his mistress and have done with it. How the woman could gaze upon Delnamal—with his doublet straining across his middle and his face set in a perpetually petulant expression—with such longing was a mystery, but she would clearly be happy to share his bed. Her skinny nobody of a husband was in no position to complain, and if Delnamal could actually have the woman he wanted in his bed, then perhaps tonight's careful cordiality could become their normal life.

But for all of Delnamal's considerable faults, he had the one shining—and highly inconvenient—virtue: fidelity. Shelvon was certain she had Queen Xanvin to thank for her husband's unusual devotion. The woman had failed to make her son pious, and yet she had nevertheless convinced him that the vows of matrimony were to be obeyed. Shelvon doubted those vows had so much weight even in the queen's homeland, and yet her son stubbornly clung to them. If she'd had the courage to speak of such things, Shelvon would have encouraged her husband to act on his desires with her blessing.

Shelvon was not surprised when Delnamal abruptly left the ball before it was even half over. Nor was she surprised that he was waiting for her in her bedchamber when she entered hours later. He didn't even give her ladies a chance to undress her before he ordered them out and pushed her to her hands and knees—a position that was torturous in her tightly laced bodice.

It was her duty as his wife to provide him with pleasure, and so she offered no resistance and swallowed her complaints even as he tore her skirts and petticoats shoving them out of the way. Perhaps if she let him know he was hurting her, he would gentle, but she chose to hold her tongue out of a sense of duty—and a sense that it would be over faster this way.

She cried quietly, her nose dripping, her bodice and stays squeezing her ribs so tight she could hardly breathe. She willed her husband's seed to take root, willed her body to give him the heir he expected. But even as she told herself that was exactly what she wanted, her heart insisted on shriveling within her. She had learned from hard experience that her husband would not be any kinder to her if she quickened, and that he would not use her pregnancy as an excuse to finally take the woman he truly wanted. So what was the use?

Shelvon had long ago lost any naïveté she had ever possessed.

She knew that if she did not provide her husband with an heir, he would eventually set her aside and damn the consequences. She would live out the rest of her life in the Abbey, letting any man who bought her degrade and humiliate her at will.

But as her husband grunted and spent himself inside her, his every thrust fueled by anger and hatred, she wasn't sure becoming an abigail would be any worse.

CHAPTER FOURTEEN

Ellin's throat ached with the pain of holding back tears as she sat rigidly straight in her carriage, eyes fixed ahead on the quartet of rose-covered biers, each drawn by a solid black cheval. The scent of the roses carried in the breeze, strong enough to make her eyes water without the additional weight of grief. The streets were lined with mourners, many of whom threw yet more roses into the midst of the procession. The day was sunny and temperate, not at all funereal weather, but the brisk breezes meant the thrown flowers frequently missed their intended targets. If it weren't for the spells contained in Ellin's carriage, she had no doubt she'd have been smacked in the face with a flower more than once.

The procession finally reached the Temple of the Dead, situated on top of the highest hill in the city of Zinolm Well, Rhozinolm's capital. The crowds led up to the base of the hill, where they were held back by a row of soldiers. Only the funeral procession itself was allowed onto the sacred ground. Knowing she would still require a great deal of strength and resolve to get through the rites to follow, Ellin nevertheless relaxed just a little when the crowd dropped away behind her.

Her throat tightened with renewed force when her carriage reached the top of the hill and she caught sight of the enormous funeral pyre that waited in the center of the open-air temple.

The procession came to a halt, and the bodies were ceremoniously lifted one by one, bier and all, onto the wooden platform that would be their final resting place. Ellin waited in the carriage for one of her honor guardsmen to open the door for her and give her a hand down. But it was not an honor guardsman who opened her door and offered her a hand. It was Lord Tamzin.

Both Lord Tamzin and Lord Kailindar had paid her formal visits when they'd arrived at court, and they'd all exchanged condolences over the deaths of their fathers. However, she had been so busy adjusting to her new life—which had so far included nothing that resembled social engagements—that she had had to spend little time in their company. Today, there would be no avoiding either of them.

Knowing it was rude, she nonetheless hesitated for a beat before accepting the hand Tamzin offered. He was dressed all in black, as befitted a man in deep mourning, but he had an ostentatious streak he had never tried to tame. His doublet was studded with tiny black pearls that caught the sunlight, and the cloak that draped his shoulders was lined with glossy black fur that was far too warm for the temperate weather.

Ellin herself had dressed in the strictest mourning, her black gown and headdress unadorned with lace or jewels or even embroidery. Fitting funeral attire for a queen, although the elegance of Tamzin's outfit made her feel frumpy and common. She assured herself that she had looked by far the more dignified and appropriately dressed during the procession, but Tamzin's understated splendor had no doubt drawn many an admiring eye.

She intended to offer her cousin a polite thank-you before moving off without him, but as soon as her feet hit the ground, he put her hand through his elbow as if she could not possibly have any objection to walking arm in arm with him. She gritted her teeth. There was no love lost between them, but it was not worth making a scene at a funeral to refuse his overly friendly—and no doubt purposeful—gesture. With the death of her father, one of the most pressing duties as sovereign was to name the next lord chamberlain, who was the second-ranking member of the royal council, after the lord chancellor. Tradition held that the lord chamberlain should be a member of the royal family, and she had little doubt that both Tamzin and Kailindar wanted the position. She was tense and ready for Tamzin to begin stating his case at this most inappropriate time.

When they arrived at the semicircle of seats before the pyre, Tamzin released her hand and bowed. She regarded him with deep suspicion, but there was no cause to quarrel with anything he had done. She only hoped that her expectation of ulterior motives would prove false.

He waited until she was seated, hovering over her solicitously, then took the seat beside her without awaiting an invitation. She seriously considered objecting to his presumption at sitting next to the queen as if he had some natural born right to it. Only immediate family could legitimately take such a liberty. But with a renewed stab of grief, she remembered that she had no immediate family left, and that Tamzin had more right to that seat than anyone else in attendance.

Lord Kailindar approached the seat on her other side, but he, at least, had the courtesy to wait for an invitation before sitting. She was very much aware of the clash of male egos as her uncle and her cousin glared at each other over her head. She wanted to remind them that they were here to honor their fallen fathers, not to make a public spectacle of their hardly secret enmity.

Ellin took a slow, deep breath in an attempt to soothe her nerves, but the stink of the roses made her sneeze. Both Kailindar and Tamzin offered her a handkerchief, silently vying with each other for the great honor of helping her wipe her nose. Since she was well prepared for tears, she already had a handkerchief of her own tucked discreetly up her sleeve, and so she ignored both offers.

The rows of seats quickly filled, the gathering solemn and nearly silent as the nobility of Rhozinolm continued to grapple with the terrible reality of having lost so many members of the royal family in so short a time. Ellin had been to funerals before, even a royal one with the passing of her grandmother, but never had the silence been so oppressive or the grief so real.

The priests spoke for what felt like an eternity, their words barely penetrating the fog that drifted over Ellin's mind. She could not stop staring at the body of her father, lying so still and pale amidst the red and white roses. Had he lived, she might never have forgiven him for the marriage he had planned to force on her, but she realized, now that it was too late, that she would rather have married Zarsha ten times over than have lost her father.

Finally, the interminable ceremony was over, and it was time for Ellin to do what she had been dreading all day. One of the priests picked up a torch and came to kneel on the floor before Ellin's feet. It was the sovereign's duty and honor to light the funeral pyre, but when the priest knelt, Ellin couldn't force herself to reach out and take the torch from his hand. Her own hands clenched together in her lap, and her vision blurred with tears. She had the unhappy suspicion that her lower lip might be quivering like that of a very young child.

Beside her, Lord Tamzin leaned closer, dropping his voice to something just above a whisper. Ellin might have thought he was attempting to be discreet, except the gathering was so silent that there was no chance of anyone speaking softly enough not to be heard by those nearby.

"Perhaps it would be best to allow me to take this burden from you," Tamzin said.

Ellin swallowed the hard lump in her throat and blinked her eyes rapidly to clear the glaze of tears. Tamzin made it sound as if he was offering a kindness, but she didn't for a moment believe he was trying to spare her the pain and burden of lighting the funeral pyre—he was trying to make her appear weak in front of every person of consequence in Rhozinolm. And cast himself as the gallant gentleman who came to her aid. Out of the corner of her eye, she saw

Kailindar stiffen beside her. Apparently, she wasn't the only one to sense that particular undercurrent. She also wondered if Tamzin thought she was fooled.

"Thank you for your most generous offer, Lord Tamzin," she said, finding the anger was doing an admirable job of chasing away the paralysis of grief. "But the burdens of this duty are mine and mine alone, and I am never one to shirk my duties."

She took the torch from the priest, pleased to see her hand did not shake.

"I'm sure no one here would feel you were shirking your duties if you allowed another to light the pyre," Tamzin pressed. His face and voice were full of gentle concern, and judging by past history, the majority of those seeing this exchange would believe he was genuinely trying to be helpful and supportive.

Ellin locked eyes with her cousin as she gripped the torch. Was she being unjust in thinking she'd heard a subtle threat underlying his words? Those dark, hooded eyes of his bored into her, and she didn't think the hunger she saw there was her imagination. Whether he saw in her his key to the power of the lord chamberlain's office or an impediment to his own ambitions for the throne was yet to be seen. Either way, she had no intention of giving him any reason to think she was weak or vulnerable.

"I appreciate and will fondly remember your kind offer," she said as she rose to her feet. The dread and the grief that had filled her when the priest had first offered the torch faded to the background, and though she still felt them, both her hands and her legs were firm and steady. "But only the rightful sovereign can light the pyre, and so I must once again refuse."

There was a hint of dark amusement in his eyes as he nodded his head respectfully. To her, their bout of verbal sparring seemed a matter of life or death; to Tamzin, it was nothing but a source of amusement, or at least that was what his now relaxed manner suggested. But she would not soon forget that spark of hunger in his eyes, nor could she doubt that they'd been speaking of something other than the lighting of the funeral pyre.

Swallowing hard and holding her chin up high, Ellin stepped to the pyre. Her eyes swept one more time over the family who had once held so prominent a place in her life. She braced against a renewed swell of grief, but she felt next to nothing, her emotions suddenly walled off and inaccessible. She thrust her torch into the pyre and watched it catch instantly. She had never asked, but she suspected the torch was a magic item, spelled to spare her any potential difficulty in getting the fire quickly lit.

The fire blazed hot and bright, the scent of roses quickly obliterated by the billows of smoke that lifted into the sky.

Tradition held that a royal funeral did not come to a close until the funeral pyre had burned itself out, although after the pyre was lit, mourners were free to rise from their seats and move about. Ellin took herself to the opposite side of the fire from Tamzin, and though this was meant to be a time of quiet reflection about the lives of those who had been put to rest, there was no doubt that the jockeying for position in the new royal court had begun. Ellin watched out of the corner of her eye as Tamzin made the rounds, talking softly with each member of her royal council, no doubt to curry favor. Judging by the warm reception he appeared to be getting, he was doing an admirable job.

Lord Kailindar seemed to be doing much the same thing, although with less obvious success. He did not have Tamzin's easy charm, and based on his shadowed eyes, Ellin suspected that unlike his nephew, he was hampered by genuine grief. There was little doubt in her mind that the council would have much preferred to put Tamzin on the throne if they could have found a legal way around Kailindar's stronger claim.

One thing that quickly became clear was that the rich and powerful noblemen of Rhozinolm were a lot more interested in striking up conversations with Tamzin—and to a lesser extent, Kailindar—than with her. Oh, no one was rude, and there was a continual shower of condolences being sent her way. But no one was treating the funeral as an opportunity to ingratiate themselves to their sovereign queen, which let her know exactly how much power they thought she had.

Grimly, she decided that tomorrow she would start scheduling private meetings with each of her councilors. Learning statecraft from books was not enough—she needed to understand each man's role on the council. And make it clear that she meant to rule as a queen, not sit on the throne meekly as the puppet of the royal council.

The flames were continuing their inevitable decline into oblivion when Zarsha appeared at her elbow. She hadn't realized she'd become lost in her thoughts as she stared into the fire until his sudden appearance at her side made her start.

"It is only me, Your Majesty," he said with a smile that showed only the slightest sliver of his teeth. For all his natural good humor, even Zarsha honored the solemnity of the occasion by dimming his usually dazzling smile. "How are you holding up?"

"As well as can be expected, I suppose." She took as deep a breath as the smoky air and her stays would allow. *Soon, the ordeal will be over,* she told herself. Not that tomorrow wasn't likely to be just as unpleasant. She would need to name either Tamzin or Kailindar to the royal council, and either choice had serious drawbacks. She did not relish the thought of having Tamzin present at every council meeting—and whispering in every council member's ear. But neither did she relish overriding her council's wishes. She'd studied enough to know this was one of the few decisions for which she did not require the council's approval, but perhaps it was unwise to start her reign on adversarial footing.

Zarsha dropped his voice, though there was no one standing near enough to overhear them. "You rose admirably to Lord Tamzin's challenge."

She considered feigning ignorance, but there seemed little point when Zarsha had obviously interpreted the interchange the same way she had. She lifted her shoulders in a slight shrug. "This is neither the time nor the place for posturing."

The corner of his mouth twitched and his eyes twinkled, but he suppressed the smile before it fully bloomed. She was almost tempted to smile herself, for the moment the pyre had been lit, every man in attendance had begun posturing and vying for position.

"I'm sure you already know this, but both of them have their eyes on the lord chamberlain's seat."

"And Lord Kailindar may be the only man in attendance who believes it will go to anyone but Lord Tamzin. Yes, I know. Although strangely neither one has yet approached *me* to convince me he deserves the seat, even knowing the decision is ultimately mine."

Zarsha raised his eyebrows, but there was no true surprise in his expression. "It is assumed you will bow to the wisdom of your royal council," he said in a tone that suggested he himself did not make the same assumption. She wondered why not.

"Whom would you appoint, were you in my position?" she asked out of curiosity.

"It would gall me," he answered promptly, "but I would choose Tamzin."

It was her turn to raise her eyebrows, for he did not seem to be as easily seduced by Tamzin's charms as so many others were. "Oh? And why is that?"

"He will be furious if the honor goes to Kailindar, and he will take that fury home with him to nurture and grow where you cannot easily monitor him. I would not want a man with his popularity and power to rabble rouse behind my back. He would be dangerous on the council, but at least you could see the danger and counter it."

"And the same cannot be said of Kailindar?"

Zarsha shook his head. "He will be insulted and sulky, but not so much as Tamzin, and he hasn't Tamzin's persuasive skills. The perceived insult would not be great enough to win people to his side."

She nodded as she looked at the two men in question, one smiling in animated conversation, one dour and stoic as he listened with an air of distraction and did not speak.

"Of course," Zarsha said with another of his small smiles, "I am not the one who would have to sit in council meetings with him and watch credulous fools be blinded by his charms."

She cast a sharp glance his way. "It seems you've formed a remarkably strong opinion of Lord Tamzin on short acquaintance. Have you met before?"

"No. But my father was a diplomat, and I've spent my entire life bouncing from court to court to court. I know his type all too well."

She made a noncommittal noise, thinking his familiarity with courts outside Nandel explained a lot. Like why there was no trace of Mountain Tongue, the unlovely language of Nandel, in his accent. And why he knew the steps to popular court dances when dancing was considered frivolous and common in Nandel. And maybe even why his charm so often struck a false note with her—he was so used to making himself "fit in" with foreign courts that he naturally kept his true self hidden from view.

"When will you be returning home?" she asked, for despite his stated intention to continue courting her, he had no reason to remain in Rhozinolm.

"Eager to be rid of me?"

She gave him a quelling look.

"I am awaiting instructions from my uncle," he said. "He will likely have a new assignment for me now that I am unattached once more."

"You don't sound especially eager to return to Nandel," she ventured. Most of the Nandelites she'd ever met had given her the impression they found Rhozinolm to be a decadent den of iniquity they could not wait to escape.

Zarsha grinned at her with genuine humor, until he remembered he was at a funeral and instantly sobered. "Let's just say that my relationship with my uncle improves with distance. I suspect that if you and I had married, we would have lived in The Keep for at most a year before he decided to post me elsewhere. Thanks to my other rather prolific uncles, I am far enough down the line of succession that my presence at court is not strictly necessary."

Considering how Sovereign Prince Waldmir was reputed to treat those closest to him, she supposed being sent away wasn't much of a hardship for Zarsha, after all.

"And now I suppose I have taken up enough of your time," he said with an almost hurried bow.

She sighed when she spotted both Tamzin and Kailindar heading her way, probably to compete for the honor of handing her into her carriage. She quickly reached out and hooked her arm through Zarsha's elbow.

"You won't mind escorting me to my carriage, will you?" she asked and was grateful when Zarsha played along so smoothly and effortlessly that no one watching would have noticed she initiated the contact herself.

"You do me a great honor, Your Majesty," he said, the slight twinkle in his eye betraying his amusement.

Ellin could only imagine the sour faces Tamzin and Kailindar made behind her back.

CHAPTER FIFTEEN

Chanlix Rai-Chanwynne felt like a fraud. It had been barely ten years since she had spent her days and nights working the pavilion, though happily she was not a great beauty and had never been in great demand. But surely a woman of her age had no business being the abbess. There were a dozen older and more experienced women who were better suited to the job, and yet here she was, occupying the abbess's office and looking out her high window as the Women's Market opened for the first time since the flood.

It was far too early, of course. The Harbor District was still in shambles. There were no inns or taverns or street markets to draw patrons with money to the district, and though the streets were now passable and most of the demolition had been completed, the air was still foul with the scent of rot and mildew and death.

The only people who came to the Harbor District were those who had no other choice, like the soldiers of the Citadel, and those who were tasked with the cleaning and rebuilding that would likely take years to complete. The Abbey itself still required a great deal of cleaning and repairs, but the trade minister had ordered that the abigails drop everything and reopen the market, and Chanlix had no choice but to obey.

The abigails had only been able to cobble together enough magic items and potions to set up five tables, and the women whose job it was to work the pavilion were sitting on the floor in loose clusters, having nothing better to do than talk to one another to pass the time. To no one's surprise, not a single customer had passed through the Abbey's gates, and Chanlix wondered whether she dared defy the trade minister's order and let everyone return to their chores. After all, if a customer were to suddenly appear out of nowhere, she could pull someone aside to serve.

She sighed and shook her head. She might not consider herself worthy of the position of abbess, but it had been thrust upon her, and it was her duty to protect—to the best of her ability—all the women who were under her care and direction. She had already seen what Prince Delnamal could do when he suspected someone had defied him. If she were to defy the trade minister's orders and the prince were to find out, she would put the very lives of her abigails at risk, and that she dared not do.

Just outside the Abbey's gates, easily as bored as the women in the market, was the squadron of soldiers the prince had sent to "guard" the Abbey. Chanlix could only imagine Prince Delnamal had devised this duty as a way to torment his half-brother, Tynthanal. To think that the women of the Abbey required *any* prison guards, much less twenty of them with a lieutenant commander to lead them, was absurd. She had to admit, however, that she was glad the men were under Tynthanal's direction. A leader from the same mold as Delnamal would have used his position to take sore advantage of the women of the Abbey, but there had been not a hint of improper behavior from any of the lieutenant commander's men.

Something glinted in the sun, and Chanlix saw a small bird flying through the sky toward the Abbey from the direction of the cliffs. She frowned and looked more closely, because of course birds didn't glint in the sunlight. The creature continued arrowing toward the Abbey, making a steady descent and traveling in too straight a line to be strictly natural.

The flier dipped when it reached the Abbey's gates and hovered by Tynthanal's shoulder instead of flying into the Abbey's message box. Sending a flier to a specific person instead of to a location required a more powerful, complex spell, which suggested the message was of some urgency. Tynthanal had been deep in conversation with one of his men, but when he saw the flier, he extended his hand. The device flew to him and released a scroll from its talons.

There was no particular reason Chanlix should find the appearance of that flier unnerving or have any notion that it had anything to do with the Abbey, and yet a chill of unease traveled down her spine. She watched Tynthanal read the message and wished he were not so far away. She would have liked to have seen the expression on his face.

Her fears that the flier brought bad tidings were confirmed when Tynthanal had a few words with his men and then entered the Abbey's gates.

"What now?" Chanlix asked out loud. She'd tried not to think about it too much, but the ominous flier reminded her of the three abigails who'd been arrested and taken by Prince Delnamal. She was certain that Mother Brynna had told no one about the spell she and her daughter and her granddaughter had cast. None of them had been foolish or stupid, and they knew full well that their actions would endanger all of the abigails. It would have been the height of folly—and cruelty—to share their secrets with anyone who could reveal them in the aftermath. But Chanlix knew all too well how the royal inquisitor could extract the information he wanted to hear out of a wretched prisoner who was desperate for the pain to stop. She had entered the Abbey at the age of fifteen when her unmarried mother had "confessed" to having poisoned her father. The charge had been leveled by her father's jealous wife, and it was absurd.

Neither Chanlix nor her mother had set eyes on the man since
Chanlix was five years old. But her mother had confessed anyway,
condemning herself to death and her daughter to the Abbey because the inquisitor had not believed her denial.

Chanlix took a seat in front of the bare fireplace. There was a
distinct chill in the air that would have made the fire's warmth more
than welcome, but the Abbey's stock of firewood had all been swept
away with the flood waters, and there was hardly enough money in
their coffers at the moment to keep everyone fed, especially when
there was little chance of the Women's Market bringing in any coin
in the near future.

It was not long before Tynthanal appeared in her doorway, and
it took no more than one quick glance to confirm that he was the
bearer of bad tidings. He had a naturally kind face—and a remarkably handsome one—and very expressive eyes. Currently, she read
sorrow, and pity, and a great dose of anger.

She had thought to receive whatever news he came bearing while
seated serenely by the fireplace, but the look in his eyes frightened
her so much she could not so easily sit still. She stood up and faced
him squarely, knowing her fear was plain in her face.

"What has happened?" she asked, certain that she had at least an
inkling what the answer would be.

"I have a . . . contact at the palace," he said.

"A spy, you mean."

He gave her a quelling look, though he didn't seem offended or
outraged by the charge. Nor did he deny it. "Your abigails have
confessed to conspiring with the late abbess."

She made a sound between a gasp and a sob, even though she'd
known her poor sisters would be vulnerable to the inquisitor's persuasions. One did not live to become an old woman in the Abbey
without learning to survive a great deal of both physical and emotional pain, so she did not want to imagine what her sisters had
suffered to make them confess to crimes they did not commit. Especially knowing that their admissions would most certainly condemn them to death.

Chanlix decided she needed that chair after all, her knees weakening and her eyes burning with unshed tears. She had loved Mother Brynna dearly, and still mourned her loss, but she cursed her, as well. The late abbess might not have known all the details of the damage her spell would create, but she had known the consequences would be significant and that the women of the Abbey would suffer for it.

Had she foreseen the earthquake and the flood? Had she foreseen three harmless old women being arrested and tortured simply for being old women of the Abbey? Mother Brynna had often told Chanlix she had the makings of an abbess, but those comments took on new shades of meaning now.

Chanlix had no handkerchief, so she used the sleeve of her robes to wipe some of the tears from her cheeks. "What will become of us?" she asked under her breath.

She did not expect an answer, but Tynthanal knelt at her feet and reached up to take one of her hands in both of his. She met his eyes, grateful for the small kindness. Until she saw from his expression that he had yet more bad news to impart.

"The king has ordered that the Abbey be razed."

She looked at him with incomprehension. "What?"

"The Abbey will be torn down."

"But . . . but . . . what will happen to all the women?" And where would the noble families send their unwanted daughters and wives, for there seemed to be a never-ending supply of those? Especially given the number of marriages that were crumbling in the aftermath of Mother Brynna's spell. The spell she knew others were beginning to refer to as the Curse.

"The Abbey is to be rebuilt." He drew out the scroll he had received from the flier, spreading it open so that she could see the map that had been drawn at the bottom of the page.

The map spanned all of Aaltah, from the coastal city of Aalwell all the way to the border of the Wasteland. And right on that border was marked a star to indicate the Abbey's new home.

Her mouth dropped open, and for a long moment she could not form a coherent thought.

The Wasteland was entirely uninhabitable, a vast barren desert devoid of life and devoid of elements. For miles before the true Wasteland began, elements and life were so sparse that there were no towns or villages or even solitary settlements.

Through all of history, it had always been clear that though the Abbey was peopled by unwanted women, the Abbey itself—and the services of those women, both magical and sexual—was indeed wanted. But if they were truly to be relocated in the desert so near the Wasteland, then the Crown had decided they were entirely unwanted, after all.

"How can we possibly survive out there?" she asked, shaking her head and wondering if what they had received was in fact a slow death sentence.

"I traveled to the edge of the Wasteland once before," Tynthanal said. "It is a truly desolate place, but there are a few small villages within a reasonable distance. You will be able to get the supplies you need."

"With what money?" she demanded. "From my understanding, there are so few elements in the area we will not be able to produce even ordinary potions and spells, and there are even fewer men than elements. How are we to fund our survival?"

"I do not know." He squeezed her hands between his, his touch warm and welcome, and yet powerless to truly soothe her. "I have here only an advance warning from my informant, not the whole of the plan. But though my father is a hard man, I don't believe he will send the entire Abbey to its death. He will make provisions for your survival, one way or another. And I feel certain your exile will be only temporary." He smiled faintly, though there was still sadness in his eyes. "I suspect he will find that the nobility of Aaltah will not be pleased to be denied access to the Abbey."

Chanlix suspected he was right, but that knowledge was little comfort when she imagined embarking on that exile and trying to survive its rigors until the king relented.

———

The magic lessons were progressing more slowly than Alys might have hoped, but progressing nonetheless. In their last lesson together, she and Jinnell had brought the number of elements identified up to thirty-five, but it was frustrating to go at Jinnell's pace, and Alys sometimes wondered if she should just skip ahead herself and let her daughter catch up.

The magic lessons were just one small part in Alys's strategy to protect her daughter. The more vital need was to find a husband who could protect Jinnell from Delnamal's schemes, but the more she'd thought about it, the more convinced she'd become that the only way to accomplish her goal was to involve her father—as delicate a prospect as that might be. Her preference was to marry Jinnell to someone outside of Aaltah and thereby keep her out of Delnamal's reach, but she did not have sufficient contacts of her own to make that happen.

So when she sent a flier to the palace requesting an audience with the king, she was not surprised to find it granted the very next day. Their last meeting had been undeniably tense, but she had no doubt that her father still loved her, and he was likely overjoyed to find her reaching out to him. It was only hours after she'd arranged for the audience that she heard the devastating news about the Abbey.

She wept tears of mingled anger and grief when she thought about the unfortunate women who would be punished so terribly for her mother's crime. She couldn't decide whose betrayal was the worst: her father's, for taking his anger out on these helpless women, or her mother's, for putting them in harm's way in the first place. It was apparent that Alys had never seen her mother as clearly as she'd thought, and no amount of suffering the woman had endured could excuse the heartlessness of her actions. She might not have foreseen all the consequences of her spell, but she'd had an inkling, and she had done it anyway. But at least she'd been acting on the noble ideal of improving the lives of women, whereas the king had no such benevolent motive. Razing the Abbey and banishing the women was an act of revenge, pure and simple.

Tempted though she was to invent a graceful excuse to back out of the audience she herself had requested, Alys knew that she could not afford to anger her father. His actions against the Abbey had almost certainly been prompted by Delnamal, and she dared not let her half-brother's influence grow any stronger than it already was. She had to follow through, and she had to contain her anger and hurt.

The only good news was that the risers were finally operational once more, so a trip to the palace was no longer a day-long commitment. Alys chose her wardrobe carefully, wearing as many of her father's gifts as she could coordinate. He had always favored rubies—the most feminine of stones in appearance, although they were a natural source of Del, a masculine element. She chose a large and stunning ruby brooch that ordinarily she found too ostentatious, a pair of dangling ruby earrings, and a luxurious fur-lined cloak that was perhaps her favorite gift her father had ever given her. Most of the jewels were simply too queenly for a woman of her rank, and the rest of the minor nobility would have thought her pretentious for wearing them. Even now, she kept the cloak tight around her to cover the brooch as her honor guard escorted her to the palace.

Alys experienced a pang when she set foot inside the Rose Room, for it had been her mother's personal favorite. She remembered helping Queen Brynna select the fabric for the soft yellow rose-embroidered curtains for the large west-facing windows that offered a spectacular view of the sunset in the evening. Back in the happy days of her childhood, before the divorce, she had often joined her mother in front of those windows to watch the sun sink in a flourish of red and orange and gold. And despite the change in circumstances and all the intervening years, neither the king nor Queen Xanvin had ever felt the need to redecorate.

Alys strolled around the room, indulging in memories of better days, while she waited for her father to arrive. She was running her fingers over a beautiful crystal vase that had been a gift from her father to her mother when she heard the sound of footsteps in the hall. She turned, and moments later her father stepped through the doorway. She bobbed a curtsy as she battled against all the emotions that swelled and roiled in her breast. She needed to keep her temper and her focus, for she would need the king's aid and blessing to find the most advantageous match for Jinnell.

Her father appeared rather more haggard than he had the last time she had seen him, and she was surprised that he was still wearing the spelled circlet that should have been unnecessary within the confines of his own palace. She wondered if Delnamal was whispering in his ear of imaginary threats, bending and manipulating the king to his will. Then she almost laughed at herself for imagining such cunning in her half-brother. He was not a man of subtlety, nor did he often bother to consider the consequences of his actions or form complex plans.

A maid entered the room carrying a tray with a shining silver tea service and a basket of currant-stuffed buns, a childhood favorite of Alys's. She glanced at her father as the maid carefully set the tray down and poured out two cups of fragrant tea stained vibrant red with rose petals.

"Rose tea in the Rose Room?" she asked her father, surprised to find herself smiling.

He returned her smile, though there was a wary look in his eye as he took a seat and gestured for her to join him. She did not need to put her feelings about the Abbey into words for him to know exactly how she felt about the order he had given.

"I was not trying to be clever," her father said as he picked up his cup and dismissed the maid. "The queen has taken it into her head that rose tea is calming for the digestion, and she insists I must drink one cup of tea for every glass of wine I consume over the course of the day. I am trying to stay ahead of the game."

Alys picked up her own cup and set a delicate currant bun on the saucer beside it. Rose tea was not greatly to her liking, though it was pretty to look at and smelled lovely. She took a sip to be polite, then popped the currant bun into her mouth and reveled in the explosion of flavor. Currants were a rare and expensive import from the queen's home kingdom of Khalpar, and though Alys's estate was sufficient to support her and the children with money to spare, she would not dream of buying currants for anything but a special occasion. A fact of which she suspected her father was well aware, just as he was aware how much she loved them.

She wanted very much to tell him he could not bribe her to silence with a few delicious currant buns, but all she had to do to stifle any such witticisms was remind herself of the danger to Jinnell.

The king sipped his tea and watched her eat, the tension in his shoulders proclaiming that he was ready to leap to his own defense the moment she launched an attack. One might almost imagine him the possessor of a guilty conscience.

"Is it truly necessary to banish all the abigails to the outer reaches of the kingdom?" she found herself asking despite all her best intentions to remain silent. At least she kept her voice level and reasonable. As attacks went, it was almost embarrassingly mild.

Fire flashed in the king's eyes, and he put his cup down with a soft click. A muscle twitched in his jaw, and Alys cursed herself for her lack of self-control.

"Your flier arrived before you could possibly have learned about the Abbey," he said. "I can only assume you had something else you wanted to discuss with me, as I am sure you did not reach out to me for the pleasure of my company."

Perhaps those words were meant as some kind of rebuke, but her father had never had much success in making Alys feel guilty, and this time was no different. However, there was no point in starting an argument, and if she could have gone back in time and stuffed the words down her own throat, she would have.

"Forgive me, Papa," she said, though it galled her to apologize. "You are right, and I have something important I want to speak with you about."

The anger faded to wariness once more, as if he were not convinced she would drop her grievance this quickly. "And what might that be?"

Here was where the situation immediately became delicate, for she knew better than to try to make her father see the poisonous hatred that lived within Delnamal. He would not call her a liar if she spoke of her half-brother's threats, but he would insist she had somehow mistaken her brother's meaning. At the very best, he would consider the threats empty.

"I was hoping to enlist your aid in finding a good match for Jinnell," she said.

The king looked vaguely puzzled. "I have already committed to increasing her dowry."

The dowry Alys could provide from her husband's estate would have been respectable on its own, but the additional contribution of the king's funds ensured Jinnell made a tempting match even to the highest ranks of the Aaltah nobility.

"Money is not an issue," Alys hastened to assure her father.

He nodded. "I'm glad to hear that. You aren't the type to have frittered away your husband's estate."

Very much to the contrary, Alys was conspicuously frugal without being miserly. "Her dowry is secure. But she is my only daughter, and I want to see her presented with the best options." She gave her father a wheedling smile. "I want her marriage to be as successful as my own."

Her father returned the smile, but still looked puzzled. He was trying to discern in advance where this conversation was leading, and so far he had failed to do so.

"I want that as well," he assured her. "She is, after all, my only granddaughter. We both wish her to have the best of everything."

Alys realized that his continued puzzlement meant Delnamal had not yet begun building the case for sending Jinnell to Nandel. "I would like to expand my search beyond the borders of Aaltah, but I have little familiarity with the noble houses outside our kingdom."

"Ah," said her father, finally understanding. The last bit of tension faded from his shoulders. Alys wondered just what he'd feared she would ask of him. She might have been hurt that he regarded her with such suspicion, but she couldn't deny that she had earned it through decades of mildly adversarial relations between them.

"I'm surprised you're willing to entertain the possibility of sending Jinnell away," he said with a curious tilt of his head.

"It is not my preference," she said, though of course that was exactly what she was trying to engineer. She would not compromise her daughter's safety because of her own selfish desire to have her near. "But when you were looking for a husband for me, you cast your net wide and presented me a quite dizzying array of options. I'm sure I would have loved Sylnin had he been the only choice I had, but I'm also sure I appreciated him more for having met so many other suitors."

It would not have been surprising at all if her father had chosen her husband without allowing her any input into the decision. Illegitimate as she was, she was still a king's daughter, and could very easily have been used to strengthen diplomatic ties or to induce favorable trade agreements. But despite their fiery relationship, he had clearly wanted her to be happy, and when she'd fallen for Sylnin—a man who could bring no additional benefits to the royal family—he'd given the union his blessing. She wanted the same kind of marriage for her own daughter while also moving her safely out of Delnamal's reach.

The king nodded. "You have my blessing to cast your net as wide as necessary to find a husband who will make my granddaughter happy. I know the late King of Rhozinolm had a grandson—illegitimate, but acknowledged—who is young and unmarried and well thought of. Prince Waldmir also has a young, unmarried nephew who was meant to marry Princess Ellinsoltah before she became queen. We certainly wouldn't want to send Jinnell to Nandel, but that doesn't mean we should not present the option. From what I hear, he is quite handsome and charming."

Alys suppressed a shudder. She had come to her father in search of options that did not include Nandel, but she supposed as long as he did not suggest the sovereign prince himself, she had no cause to object.

"You should schedule an audience with Shelvon and the queen. I'm sure they will have lists of the most eligible bachelors in all the kingdoms."

Of course they would, for helping arrange noble marriages was one of the queen's primary duties.

Alys had overcome the first hurdle and obtained the king's blessing for her search. Now all she had to do was find at least one suitable candidate who could take Jinnell away from here and keep her safe. Preferably while making her happy at the same time.

CHAPTER SIXTEEN

In her youth, Chanlix had often dreamed of leaving the Abbey, of escaping the oppression of its walls. But always in those dreams, leaving had been her own choice, and she'd been escaping to something much better. A life of freedom and self-respect. A life worth living.

Not a life as a desert nomad, eking out an existence while praying a vengeful prince would not order her and all the women under her protection killed.

At first light tomorrow, the Abbey would face its execution. Chanlix and the abigails were to travel on foot to the site of their new Abbey—a journey that would take the better part of two weeks if all went well. They would be "escorted" by a squadron of soldiers, led by Tynthanal, and those soldiers were tasked with "guarding" them in their new home. Chanlix could not help but dread the journey and doubted Tynthanal and his men were any happier about—or more deserving of—this banishment. At least the men had reason to

believe their mission would end and they could return home. Surely
the king did not envision Tynthanal's posting as a permanent one,
and there would be a regular changing of the guard.

There was no certainty all the abigails would survive to see their
new home. While Delnamal had arrested and executed the three
eldest, there were still several among them who were old and frail.
The thought that these women would be forced to travel on foot
for two weeks was more terrible than Chanlix could imagine. And
even once they reached their destination, there was nothing there
but open air. They would have to live with the minimal shelter of
tents while attempting to build a structure without any builders and
with only the most basic supplies.

Chanlix's musings were interrupted by a knock on her door.

"Enter," she called, hoping she was not about to be presented
with yet another problem she was unable to fix.

The abigail who entered her office was one of the most beautiful
women in the Abbey. Her lustrous auburn hair was entirely hidden
beneath her wimple, and the shapeless red robes hid her voluptuous
figure, but her face alone was enough to tempt men to sin. In the
five years that Rusha had been working the pavilion, she had
brought in double the amount of any other abigail. In the outside
world, her beauty would have been a great advantage. As an abigail,
it was a terrible curse, and she had been among those most brutally
abused by the prince's men.

Chanlix had no doubt the girl was enjoying this respite from
working the pavilion, but the simple pleasure of not having to service men throughout the day and night could not explain the light
of excitement that shone in her eyes as she entered the room.

Having found little cause for celebration since she'd been named
abbess, Chanlix felt a pleasant flutter of anticipation in her chest. She
would have loved to allow herself to hope that the king had relented
and they would not have to leave for the Wasteland tomorrow after
all, but good news of that sort would have come directly to her. She
tried to temper the surge of hope the young abigail's smile inspired.

"You look pleased about something," she said, and Rusha's
smile grew wider.

"I am indeed," Rusha said, practically jumping up and down with excitement.

"Well, what is it? I could do with some good news for a change."

Rusha pulled a slim volume out from the folds of her robes. The cover was worn so that Chanlix couldn't read the title. "I've been reading up on death curses."

Chanlix raised an eyebrow at that. Women of the Abbey were permitted a small amount of magical study, but their library had been completely destroyed in the flood, and they had never possessed a book on death curses—those most complex and most expensive spells that were triggered by Kai. What use did women have to learn of death curses when they were unable to see or produce Kai? Now that several women had the Kai to cast death curses, they were too busy scrambling to prepare for their exile to research the subject even if they dared. It seemed Rusha had both dared and found the time.

"Where did you get that book?" Chanlix asked.

"Perhaps best you not know."

As abbess, it was Chanlix's duty to reprimand the girl for her sauciness. If she was to be the true leader of the Abbey, it would behoove her to establish an air of authority, especially when she was so young for the position. However, she couldn't bring herself to quell Rusha's enthusiasm.

"We may have words later about how to treat your abbess with the proper respect," she said mildly, "but please do tell me what you've learned."

Chanlix was constantly aware of the mote of Kai that clung to her and to the other defiled abigails, and it was a nagging source of frustration that they could have possession of such a powerful element and not have any way to put it to their advantage. If it behaved like men's Kai, then it could be used all by itself to kill a single person—assuming that person was not using magic designed to repel Kai. Chanlix had refused to allow any of her abigails to test whether they could use their Kai in that way—the Abbey was in enough trouble as it was without any sudden, unexplained deaths, and Chanlix was fairly certain she'd made a convincing case with her abigails as to why they needed to keep their Kai secret.

"I think I've found a way to use our Kai without endangering the Abbey."

"Go on."

"According to this book, Kai can often be used as a negating element. For example, if you add Kai to a spell that would shield you from arrows, the spell would draw the arrows *to* you instead."

Chanlix gave a soft snort of laughter. "I wonder who was willing to waste a mote of Kai to discover that?"

Rusha laughed, too, though there was an edge to her laughter. "It's actually an improvisational battle spell for men who are not wealthy enough to afford a death curse. If their opponent has a protective spell active, they can force the Kai into the spell and reverse its effect. It also gets around Kai shield spells because those are meant to negate its ability to kill, not stop it from interacting with other active spells."

Chanlix imagined that using a spell to negate an enemy's shield would be prohibitively difficult in the heat of battle—especially when one was in the process of dying—but such a thing probably succeeded every once in a while.

"Regardless, that is merely an example," Rusha said. "But it started me thinking. Most death curses will be beyond our reach because they are worked with masculine elements—and because we dare not use them, of course. But it occurred to me that we might already produce a spell that could be used in reverse to a man's distinct disadvantage—without killing him." Her smile grew positively wicked, and her eyes sparkled with a malice Chanlix would not like to see turned on herself.

Chanlix was about to prompt the girl to continue when she realized herself just which spell Rusha was thinking of. "Oh!"

Some of the most commonly purchased potions of the Women's Market were those that contained spells for male potency. It was natural that men should be jealous of the ability of some women to climax repeatedly, and the best way they could simulate that ability was to keep their own . . . enthusiasm . . . from flagging after climax. It was a rare man who purchased the services of an abigail from the pavilion without assuring that he could pleasure himself multiple times with her body. There was also a milder form of the spell that would help a man who was unable to perform.

"You think adding Kai to a potency spell will render the user impotent?"

"Yes. And perhaps if we combine it also with Sur . . ."

Sur. The element of permanence. It was never used with potency spells, for as much as men adored their erections, they did not want to be in a permanent state of arousal.

Rusha giggled with what could only be described as pure glee. "Imagine it, Chanlix. Er, Mother Chanlix. Imagine if we could punish the men who attacked us with a spell that they might feel is even worse than death!"

"I must admit, there is a certain poetry to the idea," Chanlix said. "But of course we cannot be certain the spell will work as we think until we test it."

"Exactly," Rusha said, eyes shining once more. "One of my . . . admirers . . . has sent word he would like to reserve my services one more time before our exile begins. He has said he will arrive shortly after sundown and that I am to make myself available."

Chanlix snorted. That was not the way the pavilion worked. A woman of the pavilion went to the highest bidder the moment the auction was closed. A man could not reserve her services in advance.

"I thought maybe tonight we might make an exception to our normal rules," Rusha suggested. "Just for this one particular gentleman who has been such a devoted user of our services. A farewell gift, as it were."

"You are willing to use your Kai for this test? Even though it might fail?"

"I am more than willing, Mother. I am eager. And I don't think it will fail. Do I have your blessing to try?"

Chanlix tried to imagine exactly how Rusha would pull this off. She would need her customer to utilize a potency spell—that part should not be difficult.

"If our Kai is like men's Kai," she said, thinking out loud, "then it cannot be bound into a magic item or potion. It can only be used as a trigger."

Rusha nodded, rather reluctantly. "That does appear to be the case. I, er, tried to put it into a potion, and it did not take. I will simply have to wait until he drinks the potion and the spell takes effect before I use my Kai."

Meaning she would have to open her Mindseye—in front of a customer!—and then push her Kai into his body.

"I'll make sure he doesn't see anything," Rusha hurried to say, no doubt reading Chanlix's doubts.

But Chanlix wasn't sure Rusha's precautions would be sufficient. If her plan worked to perfection, the man would not know that she had manipulated the potency spell. But what he *would* know was that he'd used a potency spell and then been struck impotent. There was no question that he would blame the Abbey for his misfortune.

"I'm not sure this is such a good idea," Chanlix said. "It's too easy to imagine him linking his sudden ailment with drinking a potency spell."

"Then I'll make sure he doesn't know it's a potency spell. I will put one of the potions in wine, and we will both drink it. As long as he does not see me manipulating any elements, he will have no reason to guess he's been dosed. There are many ways a man can explain away his failure to perform without ever thinking of its being caused by magic." Another fierce grin. "And men are unlikely to want to discuss that inability with others anyway. I swear I will not put the Abbey at risk."

It was tempting. *So* tempting. Chanlix had never thought of herself as particularly vengeful or ruthless. Through all the abuses she—and her mother—had endured in her life, she had never struck back with anything but words. But she had to admit to herself that if she should ever be presented with an opportunity to hurt—or even *kill*—the men who'd defiled the Abbey, she would leap at it.

It was on the tip of her tongue to give Rusha the permission she requested, but she stopped herself before the words escaped. No matter what she claimed, Rusha could not guarantee her experiment would remain a secret. Chanlix had to consider the lives and safety of *all* her abigails. As satisfying as it would be to devise such a fitting revenge, she could not allow such a risk.

"I'm sorry," she said with genuine regret, "but it would be too dangerous. Perhaps after some time has passed and the Abbey is no longer the focus of so much attention we can revisit the issue."

Rusha's gaze dropped to the floor, her shoulders hunching in defeat. "Please, Mother—" she started in a voice that was holding back tears.

"I'm sorry," Chanlix repeated. She rose from her chair and crossed to Rusha, gathering the younger woman into a hug. It was the act of a fellow sister and friend, not one of an abbess, but it was an impulse she did not regret. "We will find a way to pay them back. I promise. Just not today."

Rusha waited in the barren playroom in breathless anticipation. In the days before the flood, the room had been draped in red silk, and the bed had been covered in plush red velvet to provide the comfort and luxury the customers demanded. All the bedding and drapes had been ruined by the flood, and with the Abbey's barren coffers, there had been no money to replace anything even before the Abbey had been condemned.

The room was now little more than a hovel, with a straw-tick mattress laid on the floor and covered with a thin linen sheet. Luckily, Yurvan had always been a great admirer of her mouth, and she would not need the comfort and padding of a luxurious bed to entertain him as he preferred.

Behind her excitement was no small amount of fear. If it had been Mother Brynna who had denied her request to test her Kai spell, Rusha would have had no choice but to obey. Brynna had ruled the Abbey with an iron hand and would have made sure Rusha regretted her disobedience for a good, long time. She was gambling that Mother Chanlix would be more lenient, but she was willing to take whatever punishment the new abbess doled out as long as her Kai spell worked as expected.

Carefully, she poured two generous doses of the potency potion into the decanter of wine, activating it with some Rho and adding three motes of Sur to ensure the effects of the potion would not fade with time. It was more potion than strictly necessary, but she couldn't be sure how much of the wine Yurvan would drink before he would be overcome with impatience. She had to make sure he had enough of the potion in him before she added her Kai to the mix. She took an exploratory sip to make sure he would not detect the potion mixed with the wine and was satisfied that he would not.

She didn't have long to wait. Yurvan had sent word that he intended to arrive a bit after sundown, but he had not had access to the Abbey's services since the earthquake, and he was no doubt half-starved for satisfaction. Unlike many of the patrons of the pavilion, who bought the services of abigails for convenience or for pleasures only a professional would be willing to provide, Yurvan was not the sort who could easily find a woman for his bed without having to pay. He would have spent these last two weeks with no lover save his own hand, so it was no surprise that he arrived a half an hour before he was expected. Not that Rusha minded. The sooner he arrived, the sooner she would find out if the spell worked.

Young Maidel escorted Yurvan to the appointed room. The two women locked eyes before Maidel closed the door. Rusha had told Maidel about her request of the abbess, and also about the abbess's refusal. She'd promised Maidel she would obey, but the look on Maidel's face said the girl hadn't believed the promise. Rusha put on her most innocent expression. Maidel shook her head and sighed, but made no attempt to talk her friend out of it. Smiling softly, Rusha closed the door and turned to her eager client.

Yurvan looked at Rusha as if she were a giant steak and he a starving man. He rushed to her and enveloped her in a smothering embrace. He gave a disgusting wet snuffle as she dutifully wrapped her arms as far around his soft, fleshy waist as possible.

"I'm going to miss you so much," he sobbed into her hair, and she rolled her eyes. The great oaf somehow imagined himself in love with her, and though he had never said so and she had certainly never encouraged it, she was certain he was under some delusion that she shared his feelings.

"There, there," she said as she rubbed his back and despised him with every fiber in her body. "I'm sure it will not be forever. The nobles of Aaltah will demand our return, and the king will see he has no choice but to comply unless he wants rioting in the streets."

It was something the abigails had been telling themselves repeatedly ever since they'd received the dreadful news of their exile, but Rusha was far from convinced of her own words. The men of Aaltah might find themselves hungry for the pleasures an abigail was required to give, but the more deeply the effects of the late abbess's spell were felt, the less kindly those men would look upon women in general and the abigails in particular. The Harbor District had always housed its share of cheap brothels, and with the Abbey gone, those brothels would quickly be rebuilt.

"But it's so unfair," Yurvan wailed like the great baby he was.

Rusha patted his back again, fighting her own revulsion. His doublet strained over his middle, and he was at just the right height that her face was on a level with his stinking armpits. He'd told her before that he bathed every day, but thanks to his gargantuan size, his skin was always damp with perspiration. She suspected that the stink returned within an hour of each bath.

When she could withstand his embrace no longer, she pulled away. He did not immediately release her, clinging and still blubbering, and she wondered just how much he'd had to drink before coming to see her. She hoped it was not so much that he would refuse the wine she was about to offer.

Eventually, she managed to squirm out of his embrace. "It seems to me that you are in need of a drink," she said, though it was in fact the last thing he needed. He was disgusting enough sober. He had only come to her drunk once before, but he had made quite the impression when he'd passed out the moment she'd started unlacing his breeches.

Rusha wished she'd known Yurvan was going to be drunk when he showed up. She could have mixed the potion with something stronger than wine. Then perhaps he would pass out once more, and she could add the Kai to the spell without ever having to lay hands or mouth on his cock.

"I don't need a drink," he insisted, making a clumsy grab for her arm and missing. "I need you."

Rusha ignored his words and poured them each a generous glass of dosed wine. "Well then perhaps it is I who needs the drink," she said, giving him her sexiest pout as she held out one of the glasses. "You don't want me thinking about my future life in the Wasteland while I'm sucking you, now do you?"

His frown made his bottom lip all but disappear into the folds of fat that formed a cascade of chins, and his eyes filmed with tears. If any of those tears had been for the cruel fate that was soon to face the woman he purported to love, she might have felt sorry for what she was about to do to him. However, he was weeping over his own sense of deprivation, not over the injustice and cruelty that the king was inflicting on every woman in this Abbey. He was far from the most distasteful of the men who'd degraded and humiliated her from the moment her father had disowned her and condemned her to the Abbey, but she hadn't an ounce of sympathy to spare for him.

"All right," he agreed reluctantly, then downed half his glass in one great swallow.

Rusha gave a soft sigh. Patience was far from one of Yurvan's great virtues. Not that she'd seen evidence he possessed any virtues at all, great or otherwise. She took a much more delicate sip of her own wine. The potency potion would have no effect on her, but she felt a superstitious reluctance to down too much of it.

Yurvan finished his own wine in two more quick swallows. The roll of his enormous belly and the skirting of his doublet hid his groin from view, but she could see by the almost immediate darkening of his eyes that the potion had already taken effect. No doubt he was at full mast, though sometimes she had to spend a tedious quarter hour bringing him to attention. She put down her nearly untouched glass of wine. Not surprisingly, he did not seem to notice that she'd barely drunk any, despite her claims to be so desperately in need of the alcohol.

"Come here," she said with a sultry smile that hid the hatred seething in her heart.

He eagerly obeyed, and she drew him toward her makeshift bed. Before the flood, each of the playrooms had been furnished with comfortable kneeling cushions, but now the thin mattress would have to do the trick. She made herself as comfortable as she could, then reached up under his doublet to find the prominent bulge in his breeches. He groaned when she stroked it, and it quivered with eagerness in her hands. She dared not stroke him again for fear he would finish too fast.

She raised the doublet, draping it over her head while she reached for the laces of his breeches. With a gleeful smile, she realized that her plan to wait until he was distracted by the pleasures of her mouth to open her Mindseye was unnecessary. With the skirt of the doublet hiding her head, he would not see her eyes go white. Even supposing he could see her at all over his swells of belly fat.

She moved very slowly to unlace his breeches as she opened her Mindseye. It was quite dark in the space under Yurvan's doublet, but she did not need light to see the mote of Kai that hovered inches from her breast. She freed one of her hands from the laces and took hold of the Kai mote, holding it cupped in her palm as she placed that palm against the engorged cock she had just freed.

The effect was so instantaneous she could feel Yurvan's member deflate the moment she touched him. He gave a tremendous groan of frustration, and it was all Rusha could do not to leap to her feet and dance like a madwoman. Her heart tripped over itself in her chest, and still in the shelter of the doublet skirt, she grinned broadly.

It had worked. She had created a devastating spell using Kai mixed with three elements that were abundant throughout Seven Wells and that almost any woman would be able to see and use. Never again would a man be able to rape a woman without fear of the consequences.

"This can't be happening!" Yurvan wailed, reminding Rusha that her mission was not yet complete. She had to make sure he didn't make the connection between the glass of wine she'd pressed on him and his sudden failure. At least not until she and her sisters had left Aalwell behind on their long journey to their new home.

"There, there, my lord," she said, patting a fleshy knee with one hand. "It happens to everyone every now and again."

She ducked out from under his doublet and looked up at him, but her feigned sympathy was lost on him. His face was bright red with embarrassment, his eyes squinched tightly in denial.

"This has never happened to me before," he said, and it was all she could do not to laugh at the predictability of men.

"You have, perhaps, had too much to drink," she suggested. "That can sometimes affect a man's . . . abilities."

He opened his eyes, and the misery in them was almost enough to make her regret her choice of victims. There were many more distasteful men she could have tested her spell on, but she had deemed pathetic Yurvan the least likely to tell tales even if he eventually came to realize what she had done.

"I am *so* sorry," he said. Apparently he believed her disappointed.

"I can give you a potency potion," she offered. "Free of charge. Consider it a farewell gift."

Hope lit his eyes, and she managed a smile for him as she pulled a vial of sleeping potion from the bedside table and poured him a fresh cup of wine. She'd used a formulation that tended to make memories fuzzy and indistinct—meant to be taken after a traumatic event. With any luck, he would wake in the morning thinking he must have performed adequately after taking the "potency potion," and that his memory was hazy thanks to the excess of drink. By the time he discovered the full effects of the Kai spell, she and her sisters would be long gone and out of his reach.

It was well past the hour when Chanlix would usually have retired for the night, and she knew she would regret the lack of sleep come morning, but the anxiety that filled her was too great to contain. The thought of lying still in bed held no appeal, so instead of sleeping, she was sitting before the fire in her sparse bedroom, staring into the flames instead of reading the book that lay in her lap. The tentative knock on her door interrupted her brooding thoughts, and for that she was glad—although a knock on her door at this time of night was rarely a good thing.

"Enter," she beckoned, and was surprised to see Rusha step into her room. She frowned at the abigail. "I thought you were with a client."

The Abbey had seen little enough business of any kind since the night of the earthquake, but the specter of their removal meant that, on this final night, a great many of the abigails who worked the pavilion were occupied.

Rusha bit her lip and smiled tentatively, and Chanlix groaned.

"Tell me you didn't test that spell when I expressly forbade you to do it!" she said, her heart kicking in her chest as her mind filled with all kinds of disastrous possibilities. Being banished to the outer reaches of the kingdom seemed a terrible punishment, but there were so many worse things that could happen if harm were to come to a client who visited the Abbey.

Rusha's shoulders hunched, but though her body language screamed remorse and apology, there was a flash of fire in her eyes that said she was not truly sorry. "I swear to you that Yurvan will never tell anyone what happened here tonight. He came to me so drunk he's unlikely to remember much of anything in the morning."

Chanlix looked at the younger woman and wanted to take her by the shoulders and shake her. "That is not the only issue," she growled, rising to her feet and glaring as fiercely as she was able. By all rights, the act of defiance deserved a blistering punishment. Mother Brynna would have ordered a thorough thrashing at the very least, and though it seemed harsh, everyone would have known it was for the good of them all. "You risked the lives of every woman in this abbey."

Rusha raised her chin. "You haven't even asked me if it worked."

"I don't *care* if it worked," Chanlix said, though that was a lie. She cared very much—and could already tell by Rusha's attitude that the test had been successful. "The point is that I forbade you to do it, and you did it anyway. I am your abbess, and I won't tolerate defiance."

It was all Chanlix could do to maintain a semblance of dignity, for she felt ridiculous making such statements. Some part of her *still* hadn't quite accepted that she was the abbess, and her reluctance to mete out a fitting punishment was proof of how unsuited she was for the position.

"I understand, Mother Chanlix," Rusha said, her voice calm and her eyes lowered demurely. "I knew what I was doing, and I am willing to accept the consequences." She glanced up at Chanlix through her lashes before lowering her gaze once more.

There was no doubt the abigail was expecting leniency, despite what she said. She was counting on Chanlix's youth and inexperience to make her soft and unwilling to punish someone who had only a short time ago been a sister. If she was going to be a proper abbess and earn the respect of her abigails—especially those who were more senior and might have expected to be named abbess themselves—Chanlix would have to get over her qualms.

But in only a few short hours, they would all be setting off on foot to their new home by the Wasteland, and it wouldn't do to have one of their young, able-bodied abigails hobbled by a beating when her older sisters might need her help. Chanlix could give her a healing potion after the punishment, but that would blunt the force of it.

Chanlix admitted to herself that her reasoning sounded suspiciously like an excuse. But she couldn't find it in herself to inflict an appropriate punishment on this of all nights. No matter how bad a precedent her leniency might set.

"We will table the issue for now," Chanlix said. "But don't believe this gives you license to disobey me. I will review your behavior once more when we reach the new Abbey, and you will be punished appropriately."

"Yes, Mother," Rusha said. "I understand. And I swear I will give you no further cause for complaint between now and then."

Chanlix very much doubted that would be the case.

Part Two

WOMEN'S WELL

CHAPTER SEVENTEEN

Ellin invited Semsulin to take a seat, trying not to make too much of the way her lord chancellor was looking at her. He'd cast more than one surprised—and speculative—glance in her direction during this morning's council meeting, and he was far from the only one. After a great deal of thought, she'd decided to appoint Lord Tamzin to the lord chamberlain seat, but she'd thought equally hard about how she wanted to present her decision. At the funeral, it had become abundantly clear that everyone expected her to meekly accept whatever decisions the council made, and she was determined to disabuse them of that notion as quickly as possible. And so instead of asking their advice on the appointment, she'd merely announced her choice. It had been almost amusing to see the discomfort her announcement had caused, but having chosen the candidate she already knew they wanted, she had neatly side-stepped any likelihood of debate.

Semsulin sat, watching her so closely she felt like squirming under his gaze. She had the uncomfortable feeling that he sensed the undercurrent of uncertainty that ran beneath what she hoped was a calm and cool exterior.

"I would like you to set up a meeting for me with each of my councilors," she said. "I wish to gain a better understanding of each of their roles and duties."

Semsulin looked pointedly at the stack of books on her desk—books she knew she would invariably end up taking back to the royal apartments at night to read, for she never seemed to find any time during the day. "Have you already finished all the texts I provided you?" he asked with a hint of amusement.

She gave him a frosty look. "While I'm sure every member of my council performs his duty to the letter of the law, I suspect there are variations in how each office is run, and it would behoove your sovereign queen to understand the day-to-day operations of her government."

Semsulin raised his eyebrows. "It is not necessary for you to understand every detail. The whole point of having advisers is so that you don't have to learn everything."

"And that's why royal boys are given no education on such petty details?"

Semsulin frowned, for of course boys of the royal family—no matter how far down the line of succession they might be—began learning the intricacies of running a kingdom almost as soon as they learned to read. "Naturally, a boy who might be king would be thoroughly educated, but—"

"Then why should I not be, when I currently sit on the throne?"

His frown deepened, his expression now almost laughably sour. "If you were planning to reign for the rest of your life, then I would agree that it was worth the effort to learn the minutiae. However, for a reign that will last no more than a year or two, it seems to me that there are better uses of your time."

She smiled sweetly at him, though she was sure the frost was clearly visible in her eyes. "I believe that as queen, *I* decide what is the best use of my own time. You may have expected me to sit quietly in the council meetings and sign whatever you and the council decide I should sign, but for however long I sit on the throne, I intend to rule. I will not simply act as the council's mouthpiece. Is that understood?"

She expected Semsulin to puff up with self-importance and tell her—in carefully couched terms—that a woman was incapable of grasping all the complexities of government, that he had urged her to sit on the throne as nothing more than a placeholder for the next king. Instead, he fixed her with another one of those piercing, too-knowing looks of his. His face looked as sour as ever, but there was a strange combination of speculation and maybe even respect in his eyes.

"I understand," he said slowly, "but I hope you'll forgive my need to make sure *you* understand, as well. You are right, and your council expected you to serve as nothing more than a figurehead. If they believe you are trying to pick up the reins and rule as a true sovereign, you will meet with a certain degree of . . . resistance."

She arched a single eyebrow. "Really? I never would have expected that when my own chancellor has already tried to put me in my place."

To her surprise, he smiled. "I did not intend to put you in your place, Your Majesty. I merely . . . misunderstood your intentions." The smile disappeared as if it had never existed. "You are a twenty-one-year-old girl with no experience in government, and with the exception of Lord Tamzin, every man on your council will be at least twice your age and have served under King Linolm almost as long as you've been alive. They are for the most part good men, but they can make your life difficult if they perceive you as a threat to their own authority. Your road as a figurehead would be considerably easier and less bumpy."

"And will you be one of the men making that road bumpy?"

"Not as long as you rule well and wisely."

"Which I am much more likely to do if I gain a full understanding of the duties of each member of the council. So set up those meetings for me."

Semsulin rose and bowed. "As you wish, Your Majesty."

Alys found herself unaccountably nervous as she waited in the ante-room for an invitation to enter the queen's parlor. As a young girl, she had—understandably, she thought—hated her stepmother, and she'd made no attempt to conceal her feelings. While Xanvin had absorbed her contempt with stoicism and calm, she had—equally understandably—never warmed to her stepdaughter. They had spo-ken only rarely since Alys's marriage, long ago, and yet now Alys had to trust her own daughter's future to a woman who would al-ways remember her as that spiteful, angry little girl who'd blamed her for her mother's disgrace.

As if that weren't bad enough, Princess Shelvon would also be taking part in the search for a husband for Jinnell, and it was pos-sible she bore Alys a great deal of ill will since her miscarriage. Not that Alys had any reason to think Shelvon blamed her for her moth-er's spell the way Delnamal did, but she imagined if their roles had been reversed, she herself would have harbored at least some re-sentment.

The parlor door opened, and a servant stepped out. "Her Maj-esty will see you now."

Alys smoothed her skirts and plucked at a stray fold of lace on her sleeve. It was all she could do not to reach out and pat her hair like a debutante about to make a grand entrance at her first ball. Mouth dry with nerves, Alys stepped into the parlor, dropping into a respectful curtsy.

Though the queen was no great beauty, she was certainly a hand-some woman, with a regal bearing and an aura of boundless calm. The roundness of her face had always given her a look of almost childlike innocence, although the gravity of her nature served to balance out that youthfulness with an air of wisdom.

Beside the queen, Princess Shelvon looked decidedly drab, her blond hair and pale skin making her seem colorless and almost sickly, though Alys knew full well her coloring was common for the folk of Nandel. Shelvon also had no eye for fashion, her dress decidedly matronly in cut and color, especially in comparison to the queen's stunning blue brocade ensemble.

Alys rose from her curtsy and had to fight a compulsion to smooth her skirts once more. The queen gave her a nod of greeting, but made no move to embrace her as a stepmother might.

"I hope you will forgive me, Alysoon," the queen said, "but I have another appointment I must keep." She turned slightly toward Shelvon and gave her daughter-in-law a surprisingly warm smile. "Shelvon and I have discussed the matter in advance, and I am certain I am leaving you in most capable hands."

Alys guarded her expression for all she was worth. She doubted the queen meant any great insult by this abandonment, but there was no question that it was at least a mild snub.

And how eager would you *be to discuss marriage arrangements with your husband's daughter from a previous marriage?* Alys asked herself. Perhaps she, too, would be looking for an excuse to step away had she been in the queen's position.

"Of that I have no doubt, Your Majesty," Alys said with as warm a smile as she could muster, although if truth be told, she had plenty of doubts. She knew very little about her sister-in-law, save that the woman was mousy and quiet and hailed from a backwoods principality in which women had little or no say in their own lives. It seemed to Alys that she lacked the qualifications to help arrange a court marriage, but perhaps she was being uncharitable.

The queen approached and took Alys's hands, belatedly bestowing a featherlight kiss on each cheek. "Then I shall wish you happy hunting and leave you to your work."

Alys dropped another curtsy as the queen swept out of the room, leaving her alone with her sister-in-law. Alys could not help but think that Shelvon would have absorbed some of her husband's unpleasant assessment of Alys's character, but she hoped that opinion would not also apply to Jinnell. For all that Alys had engaged in very little contact with her half-brother's wife, she did not think the woman cold or cruel. But then, what little contact she'd made had been before the abbess cast the spell that cost Shelvon her baby.

"Please come in and sit down," Shelvon said, waving toward a cluster of seats by the fireplace. Her smile was surprisingly warm and sweet.

They each sat on one end of a comfortable sofa. A long, awkward silence ensued, during which each woman waited for the other to begin. Alys was used to being more assertive than the average woman, but she shied away from being her usual assertive self with a woman who was so quiet and submissive by nature. Assertiveness might be taken for abrasiveness, and though she didn't need Shelvon to become her bosom companion, she didn't want to be disliked, for fear that would harm Jinnell's marriage prospects.

Shelvon clasped her hands nervously in her lap and let out a heavy sigh. "Perhaps we had best start by clearing the air," she said. "I know my husband has had words with you about . . . what happened."

Alys tilted her head to one side, surprised by the other woman's attempt at directness—while also wondering just what was covered under the title of "what happened."

"You know that he holds me responsible for my mother's actions," Alys said. "Is that what you're trying to tell me?"

Shelvon nodded and looked relieved. "Yes." She met Alys's eyes, but only for a moment. "I know what it is like to be tainted by the actions of one's mother."

Alys winced in sympathy, for she knew Shelvon's background. Her mother had been Sovereign Prince Waldmir's third wife, and had attempted to poison him. The attempt had been foiled, and Shelvon's mother had been executed as a traitor. Considering Waldmir's reputation and his treatment of his wives, it was something of a surprise that he had not repudiated his daughter, but just because he had not repudiated her did not mean theirs was a good relationship.

"So are you saying you do not share Delnamal's opinion of me?" Alys prompted, feeling a surprising surge of kinship with the younger woman. Some might think Shelvon the luckiest woman in the world to be the wife of the Crown Prince of Aaltah, but Alys doubted Shelvon would agree.

"I prefer to form my own opinions," Shelvon said, then wrinkled her nose. "I always have, though in Nandel such is considered an unpardonable offense for a woman." She managed a small, self-deprecating smile. "Only a year here in Aaltah, and I am beginning to adopt its decadent, unnatural ways."

Alys laughed, pleased to find Shelvon was not as pallid as she'd first thought. "I am glad to hear it. I do not envy the life of a woman in Nandel."

This time, when Shelvon met her eyes, she didn't look away. "And that is at the heart of your desire to find a husband for your daughter as soon as possible."

The laughter fled, to be replaced by a chill the fire had no ability to chase away. "You know what Delnamal has threatened," Alys whispered.

"No, but I can guess." Shelvon sighed and lowered her eyes. "He is not a hard man to read."

No, he was not, which made the king's refusal to read him all the more frustrating. "I mean no offense against your father," Alys said, "but he is not the husband I want for my daughter."

"No woman in her right mind would want my father for her daughter," Shelvon said with a hard glint in her eyes. "Don't think for a moment I will be offended on his behalf. I know what he is, and I will do what I can to prevent your daughter from being sacrificed to him."

Alys swallowed the lump that suddenly formed in her throat, absurdly grateful to this young woman she barely knew. She hadn't realized how desperately she longed for an ally until she found one unexpectedly.

"I still hope I may bear my husband a son," Shelvon continued, touching her belly self-consciously. "And as much as he might enjoy having a chance to hurt you, he, too, would prefer I give him a son and make a marriage to my father a moot point."

"But you agree that for safety's sake, it would be best for Jinnell if we arrange a speedy engagement."

There was a grim set to Shelvon's jaw. "Yes. I agree."

———

Ellin sagged into the chair at her dressing room table. It was well past midnight on a day that had stretched interminably as she continued to learn what a massive effort it was to lead a kingdom. If it was this exhausting in a time of relative peace and plenty, she couldn't imagine what it had been like for sovereigns before her, who were often faced with the grim spectacle of war.

What had it been like for Queen Shazinzal, a young woman very like her, who had unexpectedly found herself on the throne during a war that had nearly destroyed the kingdom?

Ellin took a deep breath and tried to relax as her lady's maid began unpinning her hair, releasing her long tresses and allowing her scalp to breathe. She met the maid's eyes in the mirror and smiled at her gratefully. Star had been her maid since she'd turned thirteen, and next to Graesan, she was the person Ellin held most dear in the world now that her family was gone. Warm and loving, if not all that much older than her lady, Star had comforted Ellin through many a bout of tears over the years and had been more understanding and sympathetic than her own mother.

The last of the pins holding her hair came free, and Ellin let out a little groan of pleasure as Star ran her fingers through the cascade of loose curls, then massaged her sore scalp. Star chuckled.

"Did I pull the coils too tight, Your Majesty?" Star asked.

"Not at all," Ellin assured her. "It's just that you have a magic touch."

Star began the nightly ritual of brushing Ellin's hair one lock at a time until it became perfectly smooth and glossy. Anxious as she was to crawl into bed and sleep, Ellin would not have missed this precious time for anything in the world. She let her lids grow heavy as she enjoyed the sensual pleasure of having her hair brushed, and she watched Star's almost hypnotic motions through half-closed eyes. She wondered for a moment if she was about to fall asleep sitting up.

"You are worth your weight in gold," she told her maid, forcing her eyes open once more. "I don't know how I'll cope if you ever get married." A lady's maid was meant to be unmarried so that the lady she served was her only responsibility, but Ellin knew Star had her eye on a young man of the palace guard, and while she would hate to relinquish her maid, she wanted Star to be happy.

Star laughed lightly and met her eyes in the mirror. "Is that your oh-so-subtle way of asking if there have been any . . . developments in my life?"

Ellin gave Star her most innocent expression. "Of course not. It was merely a casual observation of your place in my heart." She paused dramatically. "But now that you mention it . . ." She raised her brows.

"It is positively shocking that you would pursue this line of questioning. Shocking!" Star repeated as she held a hand to her breast to help emphasize her shock.

There were many people who would be scandalized by the thought of a queen asking after the personal life of one of her servants. Star was not one of them.

"Yes, I can see that smelling salts are in order. Now come on: out with it! What has happened?" She turned in her chair so she could look directly into Star's face.

Star put her hands on Ellin's shoulders and firmly turned her lady back toward the mirror so she could resume brushing. Ellin crossed her arms over her chest and gave her as stern a look as she could manage with her back turned. Star stroked the brush through her hair once more.

"The spell that Aaltah woman cast," Star said, not meeting Ellin's gaze, "the Curse, as some people are calling it. It's obvious she was telling the truth about what it did. There's no other explanation for all the miscarriages that occurred since it was cast." Another long stroke through Ellin's hair. "If we can't get pregnant unless we want to, then it is now possible for us to . . . have relations without fear that our bodies will reveal us."

Ellin thought about that statement and wondered how she had never come to that conclusion herself. It had always been the case that a man could take as many women as he wanted to his bed without ever having to fear that nature would betray his bad behavior. If the women became pregnant, he could claim he was not responsible, and no one could prove that he was lying.

Women had never been afforded that luxury. Unless they were wealthy enough to afford a contraceptive potion—and in a position that allowed them to hide it—any time they lay with a man, they ran the risk of all the world finding out about their "loose" morals. Women through the ages had taken that risk and paid the price, but women had also been forced to deny themselves the pleasures of the body when they were not willing to face the risk.

"So now you can take a man to your bed," Ellin murmured with something akin to wonder, "with as little risk as he takes joining you there."

Star nodded, and a small smile of satisfaction played over her face. "You may see evidence of many mysteriously cheerful women as others begin to draw the same conclusion."

Ellin watched the color bloom and deepen on Star's cheeks and neck. Clearly, she and her young man had taken full advantage of the spell's unexpected side effect. Star resumed brushing her hair. Ellin allowed the woman a couple of minutes of silence to fully regain her composure.

"So how was it?" she asked when the last signs of discomfiture had left Star's face.

Star shook her head and threw her hands up. "You are incorrigible!"

"You explained the mysteries of the marriage bed to me without ever having experienced them yourself." At least not as far as Ellin knew. Star had claimed her knowledge was all secondhand, and Ellin saw no reason not to believe her. "Surely you won't shy away from telling me how reality stacks up."

Star pursed her lips, the movements of the brush slowing as she thought about it. "It was both better and worse than I'd imagined," she admitted. "At least the first time was. The pain was sharp, but brief, so that was about what I'd expected. The sensation of having something inside was very strange and took some getting used to."

"And did you? Get used to it, I mean?"

Star's lips slowly turned up and the expression in her eyes turned warm and dreamy. "Oh yes, I got used to it all right." She gave a happy sigh. "And it continues to get better and easier with experience." Her cheeks were flushed again, but this time it wasn't with embarrassment.

Ellin thought of Graesan and felt her own cheeks flush. She had more than once daydreamed about what it might be like to kiss him, but she had never let her imaginings go further than that. The idea of having him in her bed had been so dangerous as to be completely out of the question. But if she did not have to fear an unwanted pregnancy . . .

She sighed quietly. There were far more obstacles between herself and Graesan than there were between Star and her lover. Enough that Ellin had no business entertaining fantasies.

Her impure thoughts had apparently been written across her face, for Star's eyes widened, and she stopped any pretense of brushing her hair.

"Princess Ellin," Star said in shocked tones, momentarily forgetting the change in her lady's station, "are you entertaining the possibility of—"

"Of course not," Ellin interrupted, rather too sharply. She dropped her gaze to her hands, which were demurely folded in her lap. For all her closeness with her maid, she had never admitted her feelings for Graesan, and whenever she'd complained of her marriage arrangement with Zarsha, she'd mentioned only her dislike of the man and of his homeland. She doubted Star would condemn her for her thoughts, but speaking them aloud was foolhardy. As powerful as she was now that she was queen, she was in many ways the property of her kingdom, charged with protecting its interests at all times. Giving the prize of her virginity to a man who was not her husband was clearly not in the best interests of Rhozinolm, and that she would even *think* of doing so was disgraceful.

"It's that Captain Graesan, isn't it?"

Ellin gasped and whirled around once more, her heart leaping into her throat. She had thought that both she and Graesan had been entirely discreet and hidden their attraction beneath a veneer of professional detachment. How many people had seen the longing they'd tried so hard to hide?

Star smiled at her reassuringly. "Don't worry, My Queen," she said. "I was only able to guess because I've known you so long and so well. I have never seen any overt hint of impropriety from either of you."

Ellin let out a long, slow sigh, trying to calm the racing of her heart. She reminded herself that despite Graesan's fears, she now had the power to protect him should anyone find fault in his behavior.

"I suppose I have ruined any chance of making you believe you are mistaken," she said as her shoulders lowered in defeat.

"You know I would take the secret to my grave if need be."

Impulsively, Ellin rose from her chair and gave her maid a hug. It might have felt awkward, for it was hardly common practice to embrace one's servants, but Star was so dear to her she didn't think twice, and beyond being momentarily startled, Star seemed not to disapprove.

"I'm so lucky to have you," Ellin told the maid, who blushed at the praise.

"The feeling is mutual. Now please do sit down so I can finish brushing your hair before dawn."

Ellin returned to her chair.

"Have you made your desires clear to Captain Graesan?" Star inquired as she resumed her work.

"I haven't thrown myself at him, if that's what you're asking." *Not that I haven't been tempted,* she added silently.

Star nodded. "And that is what you would need to do to break through his reserve. He is too conscious of his place to make any overtures himself."

That was the problem exactly, Ellin realized. Although Graesan never spoke of it, she knew his ignoble birth was a source of shame for him—one that his father could never erase by granting him his name and treating him like a legitimate son. She had once heard one of the palace guards with great distaste call him "Graesan Rai-Summer," proving that his fellow soldiers were very much aware of his lineage and scorned him for it. She knew they didn't appreciate his elevation to master of her guard one little bit, and that would likely have meant even more insults offered in private.

"Shouldn't you be telling me I must keep my distance from him at all costs?"

Star shrugged. "I don't see why I should. You are a grown woman, who has the right to make her own decisions. You are no longer engaged, you are not at risk of an unwanted pregnancy, and you have more power and freedom than most unmarried women of your age. You would have to be extremely careful, but that doesn't mean you shouldn't . . . explore the possibilities."

Star put the brush aside and began sweeping Ellin's hair into a braid for bed.

"You truly think so?" Ellin asked.

"Only if you think he's worth the risk."

Not so long ago, Ellin had faced the prospect of being shipped off to Nandel, never to see Graesan again. She was no longer facing that particular destiny, but she would never be free to marry the only man she had ever wanted. If it was now possible that she could, as Star termed it, *explore the possibilities*, how could she not take advantage of the opportunity?

"He's worth taking risks for," she affirmed.

"Even the risk of going to your marriage bed without your maidenhead?"

Ellin nodded solemnly. She couldn't imagine a man who would give up the crown to repudiate her for her lack of virginity. Her future husband might be unhappy to learn that he was not her first lover, but he would learn to live with it.

"Even that."

"Then perhaps it's time to be a little more . . . open with Captain Graesan about how you feel."

CHAPTER EIGHTEEN

When Alys and Jinnell had identified thirty-eight of the forty elements the magic lesson book required, they hit a wall. They tried for the better part of a week to find two more elements that Jinnell could see, but without success. Alys did not want to proceed with the lesson without Jinnell, but neither one of them had the necessary patience to keep looking.

"I'll learn what I can from you, Mama," Jinnell had said. "But it's clear Grandmother meant these lessons for you, not me."

Alys had been forced to concede the point, and had quickly filled in the last two elements. It had then taken her three tries to successfully pass the book's test of recognition, which she figured was not too bad when the book required perfection.

At long last, the page with the first lesson cleared and a new one appeared.

Lesson Two

Practice putting a spell together from a formula. Most potions (like the one below) require a relatively small number of motes and can be contained in most any liquid. More complex and powerful spells require alcohol, which is why wine is the most commonly used liquid for potions. For this potion, any liquid will do. To your liquid of choice, add:

1 mote of Zin (N, associated with binding. In this instance, being used to bind other elements into a spell vessel)

2 motes of Bryn (F, associated with beauty and sensuality)

4 motes of Lix (N, associated with matching and camouflage)

When you are ready to test your spell, add one mote of Rho and drink the potion. The vast majority of spells are triggered with Rho, as it is an element all but the Rho-blind can see.

If you have prepared it correctly, your gray hairs will change color to match the rest of your hair. On the following pages, you'll find pictures of a great many elements, in case you have not yet identified all of the elements in the spell.

Alys made a small sound of frustration. She had little interest in vanity spells in general, but she'd heard of this particular one and always found it especially silly. Why should she care about the gray in her hair when most of it was hidden under a headdress or a cap or a snood? The potions were absurdly expensive, and hardly worth it as far as she was concerned. Of course, she knew that people did buy them, so obviously someone thought they were worthwhile. She was surprised to find her mother was one of them.

"Well, if we needed any further proof that Grandmother meant this book specifically for you . . ." Jinnell mumbled, grinning impishly at her mother's glare.

Alys sniffed delicately and patted her hair, which was more visible in its nightly braid than it was in the daytime. "Are you suggesting my hair has gone gray?" She stroked the braid primly. There was no denying it was indeed shot with gray, as befitted her age.

Jinnell winked. "Let's just say it would not be a bad thing if you could craft this spell yourself."

They were as usual practicing in Jinnell's bedroom after the rest of the household had gone to sleep. There was no wine within easy reach, and it seemed imprudent to go looking for some, so they settled on a cup of water from the pitcher that sat by the bedside.

Alys skimmed through the book, looking for the element Lix, which she had not yet identified. She saw that it was a medium-light blue with circles of what looked almost like soap bubbles in it.

Opening her Mindseye, she searched the room for the elements she needed, finding them all and using Zin to bind them into the cup of water. Finally, she added Rho, to activate the spell, then closed her Mindseye. She saw Jinnell close hers as well, for she'd been following along with her mother as best she could.

"I can't see Lix," she said sadly.

"It's disappointing," Alys agreed. "But we may find there are other things you can do in later lessons." She wished her mother had produced a second book for Jinnell. In the back of Alys's mind was a clock that constantly ticked. Perhaps there was no magic that could protect Jinnell from becoming Delnamal's pawn, but a pawn needed every advantage she could get.

Jinnell nodded at the cup of water. "Go on. Let's see if it works."

Smiling at her daughter, Alys lifted the cup in a mock toast, then downed its contents. She and Jinnell both stared at her braid, waiting for it to change color.

"How long do you think this will take?" Jinnell asked.

Alys lifted her shoulders in a shrug. "I've never been one to take vanity potions, so I can't say." Though she was under the impression that most potions worked pretty quickly.

Suddenly, Alys's entire body flushed with heat. "Oh!" she cried, startled by the change that was so completely unexpected.

"Your cheeks have turned bright red!" Jinnell exclaimed.

Alys's pulse was hammering in her throat, and beneath the nightdress, her nipples tightened and hardened to pebbles. Moisture pooled between her legs, and she squeezed her thighs tightly together as a bolt of desire like nothing she'd ever felt before shot through her.

"What is it, Mama? What's the matter?"

"Nothing!" Alys said in a breathy squeak as she tried to swallow back the nearly uncontrollable hunger that had seized her. She desperately wanted to reach between her legs and ease the ache that had come out of nowhere, but she managed to keep her head and reached for the book instead. "I must have done something wrong," she choked out.

Jinnell touched her arm, understandably worried over Alys's puzzling condition. The touch—from her own daughter and nowhere near an erogenous zone—drew a gasp from her throat as she hastily opened the book to review the formula.

Lesson Three

Some elements look very similar to one another but have very different behaviors. Lix is an exceedingly rare element that looks similar to the much more common element, Sul. Unless you got very lucky, you have probably created the assigned potion with four motes of Sul instead of four motes of Lix. Study the two elements carefully and you'll see that Sul has a more green tinge to it, while Lix is purely blue.

The formula as written would temporarily change gray hair back to its original color, but the expensive potion you're no doubt familiar with also includes Sur for permanence. I was not cruel enough to include that element in this spell, knowing you were much more likely to create the aphrodisiac potion that is produced when you use Sul instead of Lix in the formula.

If you'd like to undo the effects, add one mote of Zin, one mote of Rho, and two motes of Grae to your liquid and drink that down. Grae is often used to reverse the effects of potions.

Alys glared at the book, then turned that glare to Jinnell when her daughter started laughing hysterically.

"Lord Kailindar has sent an announcement that he has taken a wife," Semsulin said to open the meeting of the royal council.

Ellin had been wondering how and when her uncle would make his displeasure at not being appointed lord chamberlain known. It had been three weeks since she had announced her decision, and though Kailindar had left the capital and returned to his own estate in a snit the day after the announcement, she had almost allowed herself to believe he would let the slight pass without further comment.

Kailindar had lost his wife a couple of years before, and it was no surprise that he wished to marry again. However, a man of his station required the sovereign's permission to marry. She had signed no such permission, and Semsulin would not be announcing the marriage with such a sour expression on his face if King Linolm had done so. No matter how improper it was to marry so soon after his father's death.

"I take it the king did not grant his permission?" she asked just to confirm her suspicion.

Semsulin shook his head. "He actively forbade the match. The woman Lord Kailindar has wed is a nobody, a woman he'd kept on the side for many years. Certainly not an appropriate bride for a king's son."

"That is an act of treason!" Lord Tamzin shouted, banging his fist on the table and making the nearly empty platter of refreshments near his seat clatter loudly. "He has actively defied the orders of our departed king!" His handsome face twisted in a snarl, and if Ellin did not know better, she would have sworn he was genuinely furious at this insult to his grandfather's memory.

Far from outraged, he was no doubt thrilled at this provocation that might lead to his uncle's punishment and humiliation. And with this forbidden marriage, Kailindar was about to put Ellin's rule to its first true test.

"The marriage is highly irregular, I admit," said Semsulin. His voice was even and calm, a marked contrast to Tamzin's feigned indignation. "And clearly it was not sanctioned, but the offense hardly rises to the level of treason."

"He directly disobeyed the king's command, and he disrespected our queen by not seeking her permission to wed. Just because we have a woman on the throne does not mean our lords can prey upon her weakness and inexperience to flout the rule of law."

Ellin clenched her fists in her lap, where no one could see the gesture, and hoped she did not visibly bristle at Tamzin's tone. Half her councilors were looking at Tamzin and nodding their agreement, and the other half were studying her with great intensity. There was not a man at the table who had not in one way or another suggested she was not up to the challenge of ruling, and though she felt certain Semsulin had developed at least a grudging respect, she still had much work to do if she wished to win over the rest. Rising to Tamzin's bait would not create the best impression.

"I assure you I don't need years of experience," *or a penis,* "to see when my rule is being tested," she said. "Besides, I have all of you fine gentlemen to advise me when I need it." She turned to Semsulin. "I presume there is some precedent for the Crown dealing with unsanctioned marriages?"

"Nearly as many precedents as there have been kings, I'm afraid. Punishments have ranged from toothless official rebukes, to exile, to writs of attainder. The law allows the council a great deal of leeway in how to treat the offense."

"The sovereign, you mean," she corrected immediately. She had not spent nearly every moment of her free time poring over books and discussing issues of law with both the lord chancellor and the marshal for nothing, and she was well aware of which decisions she could make on her own and which she needed the council to approve. How to punish an unsanctioned marriage would be her decision.

Semsulin bowed his head, while around the table she sensed a ripple of tension. "Of course, Your Majesty."

"Punishment of the offense is unquestionably for the sovereign to decide," the lord commander said, "but of course it is the duty of the royal council to advise Your Majesty before any decision is reached."

It was said with great tact and politeness, but Ellin did not think she was imagining the hint of challenge in his voice. She also didn't think she was imagining the spark of delight that lit the lord high treasurer's eyes. She had considered Lord Tamzin an antagonist—if not an active enemy—even before she'd put him on the council, but if she judged the atmosphere correctly, that label applied to the lord commander and the lord high treasurer also. Three of her highest-ranking council members seemed eager for her to fail. She glanced around at the most junior council members—the grand magus, the marshal, and the trade minister—and saw decidedly neutral expressions. They might not be actively against her, but they weren't *with* her, either.

"Of course I am happy to hear any advice you might have, Lord Commander," she said. "Please tell me what you feel is the appropriate punishment for this unsanctioned marriage."

"Kailindar is tweaking your rule because he believes you will offer no more resistance than a silly rebuke," Tamzin said as if the question were directed at him. "No doubt he thinks you will find his story of love denied tragically romantic."

Instead of being offended that Tamzin had spoken out of turn, the lord commander was nodding along. "Sometimes one must inflict a punishment that may objectively seem out of proportion to the offense in order to make a strong example."

"So you believe as does Lord Tamzin that the offense rises to the level of treason?" she asked incredulously.

"No, not that," he said, giving Tamzin an apologetic look. "Forgive me, Lord Chamberlain, but I don't believe we would like to start a reign of terror."

Tamzin crossed his arms and leaned back in his chair. Ellin doubted he'd actually believed he could talk her—or anyone else at the table—into leveling a treason charge for an offense so small. But he'd thrown out the outrageous charge in hopes of making a lesser punishment more palatable by comparison.

"Perhaps a treason charge is a bit excessive," Tamzin said. "But a strong message must still be sent. He must at least forfeit one of his many titles."

Ellin gritted her teeth to suppress a quick retort. She was certain Tamzin cared nothing about his uncle's insult to her reign. The only reason he was baying for the man's blood was his own personal enmity.

Or was it?

The vast majority of titles granted by the Crown came with generous grants of land and money. If Tamzin still entertained thoughts of sitting on the throne himself, then a logical first step would be to diminish Kailindar's resources and thereby eliminate the greatest potential source of resistance.

"Forfeiture of a title still seems like an excessive penalty for what amounts to a petty insult," Semsulin said. His voice and face were both a picture of calm, but Ellin doubted he had missed the threat that she had seen.

"He knowingly and directly disobeyed the command of his sovereign," Tamzin snapped. "That is more than a 'petty insult,' and it would be a bad precedent to let him get away with it."

"Do you have a list of Lord Kailindar's titles and assets somewhere in there?" Ellin asked, pointing at the stack of papers sitting in front of Semsulin. She was not intimately familiar with her uncle's holdings, but there was one particular title she wanted to check on.

"Of course, Your Majesty," he said, shuffling through the papers to find the one he wanted, then passing it to her.

She smiled when she skimmed down the list and saw that one of Lord Kailindar's first titles was Knight of the Realm. It was a military distinction with no associated land grant or income, but it did give Kailindar the right to wear a silver shield insignia. One which she had never seen him without, though he was years past his early military service. Losing that title would most definitely smart, but would not weaken him in any material way.

She pointed at the title as she slid the paper toward Semsulin. "Let the record show that the Crown has officially rescinded the title of Knight of the Realm from Lord Kailindar Rai-Chantah. He is to immediately cease wearing the insignia."

The array of facial expressions around her council table was almost amusing. Semsulin was giving her one of those speculative looks she was learning to hate, and the lower council members looked grudgingly satisfied. The lord high treasurer and the lord commander both frowned in thought as if searching for an objection, apparently with no success. And Tamzin stared at her with an almost frightening combination of malice and cunning. She might have proven herself not as easy to manipulate as he'd once thought, but perhaps she had been better off when he'd been underestimating her. He would bear close watching or he might undermine her rule before she truly got started.

The council meeting stretched to take up Ellin's entire morning. When it finally ended, Semsulin requested a private word with her. Her stomach protested, saying it was past time for lunch, and her brain protested, saying it needed a break. However, she was getting used to working past what seemed to be her limits, and weariness was becoming a familiar friend. She snatched a stale crust of bread from a refreshment platter that had long ago been stripped of anything appetizing and gnawed on it as her council filed out. When she and Semsulin had the room to themselves, she turned to him with raised eyebrows.

Semsulin's habitually dour expression always made his face look severe, but there was a shadow in his eyes that changed the severity into worry. It wasn't hard to guess the source of that worry. When he'd presented her with the prospect of taking the throne, he'd made it sound like her solid claim would snuff out Tamzin's ambitions. It was hard to see today's council meeting as anything but evidence of his continued hunger for power.

"I admire your elegant response to Lord Kailindar's challenge," Semsulin said, and he was obviously choosing his words with great care.

"But . . . ?"

"But it might have been better if you had let *me* make the suggestion and make a persuasive argument that might have swayed the council."

Ellin wasn't sure if she was more outraged or embarrassed. She'd been more than ready to pat herself on the back for her brilliant solution, but her lord chancellor was a far more experienced courtier, and he'd probably opened the council meeting with this solution already in mind. That did not mean she appreciated the rebuke, for there was no mistaking that was exactly what Semsulin was delivering.

"If you wanted a queen who would sit silent and passive while you made the decisions for her, you should not have pushed *me* to take the throne," she said in her iciest tone.

His eyes narrowed in a glare that once upon a time would have intimidated her. "I would not have thought you the kind of person who would refuse to hear criticism from someone who has been on the royal council for almost two decades and therefore has a great deal more experience than yourself."

"Are you my tutor now, Lord Semsulin? Do you think to punish me for speaking out of turn?"

His eyes flashed with anger, and his enunciation grew more precise and cutting. "Do you think yourself the only sovereign in history who has believed wearing the crown means not having to hear anyone's opinion but your own? I assure you, you are not—just as I assure you the history books are not kind to those sovereigns. You have no experience or training for your position, and only a childish fool would think herself able to tame a bucking stallion when she has never even sat on a pony's back. Are you a childish fool, Your Majesty?"

Ellin wasn't sure if the heat in her face was from anger or shame, for though he had no right to speak to her in such a paternalistic and condescending way, it was hard to deny that he had a point. A few weeks of intense study hardly made her an expert in running a kingdom, and while Semsulin had at first been taken aback by her decision to take an active part in the council meetings rather than to serve as a figurehead, he had been far more supportive than any of her other council members.

She couldn't manage anything that resembled acquiescence, so she settled for a chilly silence. Semsulin gave a small nod of satisfaction.

"Lord Tamzin will require careful handling," he said, then smiled at her narrow-eyed annoyance. "Yes, I know you know that. But sparring with him head-on is not in your best interests. He does not wish to kneel to anyone, much less a twenty-one-year-old woman whose reign is temporary. The less cause you give him for outrage—and damaged male pride—the better. Which is why you should let *me* present any news or decisions he might find disagreeable. I can weather his outrage in a way you cannot." Another smile. "As I'm sure you well know, I'm already roundly disliked. You are not—yet—and it is best for all concerned if you keep it that way."

She took a few moments to absorb everything Semsulin had said. It made a certain amount of sense to allow him to draw fire. However, she wasn't sure he was right about her not being disliked yet. Certainly Tamzin disliked her—and had even before this council meeting—merely for standing in his way. And if this meeting was anything to go by, the force of his personality had already won over two of her most senior councilors.

"Perhaps it would have been better if you had made the suggestion," she said. "But how could I have known you had already come up with a solution?"

Semsulin bowed his head. "That is my fault, Your Majesty, and I apologize. I made the foolish assumption that you would ask my advice instead of trying to solve the problem yourself. I promise I will not make the same mistake again." He met her eyes, and she thought she saw a hint of admiration in his gaze. "You are a formidable young woman. I doubt Lord Tamzin has fully absorbed that fact yet, but he will."

It remained to be seen whether that would be a good thing or not.

CHAPTER NINETEEN

Jinnell held the little vial of potion up to the light and shook it nervously, wondering if she was about to do something unutterably stupid. No doubt her mother would answer with a resounding *yes!*

For the third time, she opened her Mindseye and compared the contents of her cup with the contents of the vial she had pilfered from the household supply, and for the third time she assured herself that she had replicated it perfectly. At least as far as the elements were concerned. She wasn't sure what the liquid in the real potion was, except that it contained alcohol of some sort, so she had used wine for her own. She wished Mama weren't being so stubborn about slavishly following the abbess's lesson plan.

Jinnell was learning what she could from the lessons, but most spells she'd watched her mother work required at least one element she herself couldn't see. If Mama wanted her to learn magic, then it seemed only logical they should create their own lesson plan on the side. They did not need the abbess's formulas when the two of them together could look at existing potions in Mindsight and figure out what was in them.

"It's too dangerous," Mama had said the moment Jinnell had made the suggestion. "Without a formula, we can't be sure there aren't crucial elements in there we can't see."

Jinnell had sighed in frustration, not entirely surprised at the response. "You can see practically everything," she complained. "I seriously doubt that's a major danger."

Mama had raised an eyebrow at her. "Oh, so you've become an expert now, have you?"

Jinnell had made two more attempts to persuade Mama to be reasonable, to no avail. She supposed someday she would have children of her own and would understand Mama's protective instincts—that's what Mama insisted, anyway—but only if she didn't find herself shipped off to Nandel as a virgin sacrifice.

Putting down both the vial and the cup of homemade potion, Jinnell rolled up the sleeve of her nightdress. There was no reason to think there were any elements in the healing potion that she couldn't see. She could see the Zin, which bound the other elements into the potion. She could see Von, which she had learned during their very first magic lesson was often used in healing potions; and she could see Mai, a feminine element the book said was associated with mending and healing. Those, in combination with the obligatory Rho, should be everything she needed to create a spell of healing. And healing spells were so common that there was no reason to assume there was some higher-level element in there she couldn't see.

Still, Jinnell hesitated. Just because she couldn't think of some other property the potion might need didn't mean such a thing didn't exist, and she had seen a small glimpse of what could happen when one used an incorrectly formulated potion. Maybe now that she'd already put together her own version of the potion, Mama would be willing to examine the two side by side and confirm that she wasn't missing anything.

Then she sighed, for that was nothing but wishful thinking. Mama would never let her take the risk. If she wanted to test her ability to replicate a potion, she would have to do it in secret and tell Mama after the fact.

Impatient with her own dithering, she used a hairpin to draw a shallow scratch across her forearm, just barely enough to break the skin. She added a mote of Rho to the purchased potion, then drank it down, the sharp, mouth-puckering flavor making her grimace as it burned its way down her throat. As a child, she had always resisted taking the potion for her small hurts, preferring to suffer the pain than endure the taste, though her parents had occasionally overridden her wishes. Whatever the base liquid was, it clearly contained a high concentration of alcohol.

Moments after she downed the potion, the scratch on her arm knitted itself back together as she watched, until it faded to nothing but a thin red line that would be gone by morning. Nodding in satisfaction, she picked up the pin again and created an identical shallow scratch a little distance away from the first one. Then she activated her own potion and drank it down.

The first thing she noticed was that it tasted a lot better, though perhaps that was just because she was unused to whatever harder liquor had been used for the original. The wine of her potion had a slight, sour aftertaste as a result of the elements, but it was easy to ignore, and there was very little of that unpleasant burn in her throat.

Jinnell practically whooped in triumph when the little scratch sealed itself neatly, leaving a faint red line that was almost identical to the result of the first experiment. Mama would be furious with her for experimenting on her own, but surely this would be evidence that it was worth it!

Suddenly, and for no reason at all, her stomach gave an unhappy lurch. She closed her eyes and swallowed hard, thinking the nausea was a result of nerves and would soon pass. Her stomach twisted again, and she belched, tasting bile on the back of her tongue. She eyed her healing potion balefully. Surely it couldn't be to blame. It contained little more than a spoonful of wine. Maybe it was the strong alcohol in the first potion that was making her stomach unhappy.

Sweat broke out on her brow, and her stomach made a nasty rumbling noise. Jinnell breathed deeply through her nose, trying to keep her gorge down. She'd never reacted this way to a healing potion before. Which, unless she could convince herself otherwise, suggested that her mother had been right and there was something in it that she couldn't see.

For maybe fifteen minutes, she battled against the nausea, hoping it would fade away. Then she spent most of the rest of the night heaving into her chamber pot until near dawn when the nausea finally relented and she was able to snatch a couple of hours of sleep.

Semsulin gave Ellin one last disapproving look before stepping out of her private study and sending Graesan in. Ordinarily, her personal honor guard stayed at some remove when she was in the royal apartments, and Ellin could see that her summons had worried Graesan.

"You wished to see me, Your Majesty?" he inquired, bowing low and failing to hide his concern. He probably thought she was displeased with him or one of his men, the concern no doubt encouraged by Semsulin's dour expression when he'd left the room.

Ellin smiled at him brightly and saw his concern change to puzzlement. Her pulse was pleasantly speeding, and she was genuinely excited to share some good news, despite Semsulin's unsubtle opposition. She gestured toward a chair in front of her desk.

"Please have a seat," she said with a grin she could not suppress.

Graesan's eyebrows shot up in shock. "Excuse me? That would not—I mean . . ."

Her smile broadened as he continued to sputter. Members of her honor guard were *never* permitted to sit in her presence, and she had to admit she rather enjoyed seeing the usually stoic, unflappable Graesan put so off balance.

"I'm promoting you," she said, pointing more insistently at the chair. "There is no breach in protocol if you sit when I invite you to."

"Promoting me?" he said doubtfully, and still didn't take a seat. "But I'm your master of the guard. How can . . . ?"

"Graesan, sit down." Thanks to his ignoble birth—and despite his father's attempts to legitimize him—there was no question that master of the guard was an extraordinarily high rank for Graesan to achieve. She couldn't blame him for being unprepared for a promotion of any kind, though it saddened her that he couldn't just accept the honor as his due.

Eyes wide, a look of extreme discomfort on his face, Graesan sat on the very edge of one of the chairs, looking as if he was ready to leap to his feet at any moment. Ellin had imagined her announcement as a happy, joyful moment, and Graesan's reaction was more than a little disconcerting. Semsulin's resistance she had been expecting and was well prepared for, but Graesan's she had not.

"I'm removing you from my honor guard and making you my personal secretary," she told him. She was determined to take Star's advice and make a more concerted effort to let Graesan know exactly how she felt about him, but as her master of the guard, he was so rarely alone with her that she had found little opportunity. Her personal secretary, however, would have many an excuse to be alone with her during the day, and though that contact would not be extended—or uninterrupted—they would both be able to drop their public façades every once in a while.

Graesan shook his head as he scanned her face. "That would be most unwise, Your Majesty," he said. And, damn him, he rose from the chair once more.

Ellin sighed and leaned back in her own chair, hating the fact that Graesan had to pay such a price for his father's indiscretion. It wasn't *Graesan's* fault his father hadn't been able to keep his hands off a housemaid.

"I understand all the reasons why it would be an unconventional move," she assured him. "Believe me, Semsulin made certain of that."

"Then you should listen to your lord chancellor."

"No," she said decisively. "I need my personal secretary to be someone I can trust and with whom I feel comfortable. There is no one else I can think of who meets that description."

"I'm a bastard, and my mother was a housemaid!" he protested, his cheeks suffused with color. "I am not an appropriate choice for this position."

"Your father gave you his name for a reason," she explained calmly, "and—"

To her shock—and, by the look on his face, his own—Graesan interrupted her. "He cannot make me legitimate just by giving me his name, no matter how badly he would like to think so. There are a great many people who will be scandalized at the thought of a housemaid's son becoming personal secretary to the queen. You have enough challenges to your rule already."

"I've been through this with Semsulin." Who'd told her she was being stubborn and childish, although he had grudgingly been forced to admit she was within her rights. "While some people may disapprove, there is a limit to how scandalized people can be over the appointment of any member of my household staff. I'm not bestowing a title or a land grant upon you, so there's little anyone can do but mutter." She rose to her feet and moved around the desk so she could be closer to eye level with him.

"Accept this honor and the pay raise that comes with it," she urged him. Technically, he had no say in his promotion and was not free to refuse it, but it would hardly be an auspicious beginning to her planned seduction to force his hand. "You deserve it for your years of loyal service."

Graesan swallowed hard, and the expression in his eyes told her he was fighting an internal battle of some sort. Semsulin had warned her that the promotion would not be as easy on Graesan as she would have liked. There were those of his peers who already looked down their noses at him and whispered about him behind his back, and his elevation in rank would only make their jealousy grow stronger.

"Are you worried about how your fellow guardsmen will take

it?" she asked softly, moving just into the edge of his personal space. The sharpening of his gaze told her he was very much aware of her proximity, though he made no effort to move away.

"Those who already dislike me cannot dislike me any more than they already do," he said. "They call me Graesan Rai-Summer within my hearing to try to put me in my place. And that is my true name, no matter what my father says."

"But it is not your *legal* name," she insisted. "Appearances matter, and Graesan Rah-Brondar is of sufficient rank to be secretary to the queen even if Graesan Rai-Summer is not." She edged even closer, staring up into his face in what she hoped was an intimate way. "I will spend a great deal of time with my personal secretary," she said in a low murmur, and was rewarded with a distinct darkening of Graesan's eyes. "And some of that time will be in private."

"Perhaps that is another reason why the promotion would be unwise," he said, his voice suddenly hoarse.

"Or perhaps it's the best reason of all for you to accept it." She reached out tentatively to touch his chest. He was in uniform, of course, wearing mail under his tabard, so the touch was not as satisfying as it might have been, but she shivered and he gasped all the same.

Ellin thought perhaps she was finally breaking through, but Graesan took a hasty step back.

"Don't fool yourself into believing we are really in private," he said with a pointed look at the closed study door.

She felt his rejection like a slap in the face, despite his very practical explanation for it. "And if we were *truly* in private," she asked, "would you still have backed away from me?"

"We will never be *truly* in private," he said gently, and there was no missing the hint of regret in his voice. "Even if I am your personal secretary. If that's the only reason you wish to promote me—"

"It's not!" she protested, and it truly wasn't. Though admittedly, it ranked high on her list of priorities. She couldn't bear to put the distance of the desk between them once more, but she moved farther out of his personal space.

"I need a friend, Graesan," she said, and for the first time in what felt like forever, she stopped trying to put on a brave face. "I am surrounded by people who are constantly making demands of me while picking apart my every word, my every move, my every facial expression for signs of weakness." Tears stung her eyes, though she blinked quickly to clear them. "I need someone by my side with whom I don't have to pretend all the time. Someone who sees *me,* rather than Queen Ellinsoltah."

"You have friends . . ." he started, but he knew as well as she that the friends she grew up with were no longer enough. Many of them had married and moved away, and those who had not . . . What did Queen Ellinsoltah have in common with an unmarried miss whose life revolved around balls and parties and finding a husband?

"I need you," she said simply. "I won't insist you accept the promotion if you truly don't want it, but if there's any way you can see your way clear . . ."

Ellin was not strictly proud of herself or her behavior. She was quite aware that she was being manipulative, and though she would have liked to blame it on the influence of her courtiers, she knew it was all on her. But for this short time when she was a sovereign queen and unmarried, she had opportunities she would never again have in her life, and she was determined to take advantage of them. Graesan's rejection had stung, but the sting was eased by his obvious desire to accept her offers—both the one she'd voiced and the one she hadn't. And as long as he accepted the promotion, she would have other chances to change his mind.

"I still believe it is . . . imprudent," Graesan said. "For more reasons than one."

"But will you accept?"

His shoulders lowered in something very like defeat. "Of course I will accept."

CHAPTER TWENTY

Chanlix had never seen anything like the parched, barren land that the abigails were now traveling through. Instead of lush forest or fertile fields, everything around her was hard-packed dirt that gave off great clouds of dust with every footstep. The squadron of soldiers had kindly spread out to both sides of their straggling caravan, trying their best to keep the women from having to walk through the dust the horses and chevals and wagons kicked up, but the changeable winds made it impossible to escape entirely. Chanlix's skin felt gritty, even under the sweltering weight of her robes and wimple, as if the wind-borne dust and sand had passed right through the thickly woven fabric and adhered to every drop of sweat that coated her body.

Having never traveled outside of Aalwell before, Chanlix had never imagined such a land could exist, and the idea that the Wasteland itself was even more desolate was almost impossible to credit. For the last half day of travel, she had seen no hint of green. Even the small, scraggly bushes and grasses that grew in this inhospitable territory had a grayish tint that made them look half dead.

The journey to the Abbey's new location would have turned into a death march for the oldest and frailest of the abigails, had not Tynthanal been the one charged with their care. There were no horses or chevals for the women's use, and the wagons were too overloaded for passengers, but whenever someone seemed to be struggling, Tynthanal or one of his men would lift the woman onto his horse to give her a respite. He also refused to push them as hard as his orders specified, so the journey had already lasted several days longer than predicted.

Every day that Chanlix awoke, her body ached just a little more, her joints stiff and swollen and ever more reluctant to obey her orders. Maidel had many times urged her to take a healing potion, but as badly as her body hurt, Chanlix knew there were those with greater need.

She had entered into something of a daze, laboring to put one foot in front of the other, her eyes glazed and dull as the sun baked her skin and sucked the strength from her body. She was so dazed and distant that she did not even notice the approaching hoofbeats until a strong arm wrapped around her waist. She blinked and made a little bleat of alarm as her feet left the ground and she was hauled up until she was sitting on the horse's back. She gripped the arm around her waist and grabbed a handful of the horse's mane.

"Don't worry, Mother Chanlix," Tynthanal said with a laugh in his voice, "I will not let you fall."

Throughout this journey, she had repeatedly asked him not to call her Mother. She was only four years his senior, and she still felt like an impostor. It made her uncomfortable enough when the abigails addressed her by that title, but it somehow sounded even stranger coming from this handsome soldier who was practically the same age as she.

"What do you think you're doing?" she complained, although her body sagged in relief at not having to work so hard, at least for this short time. "Put me down."

"Why?"

She wriggled, though her efforts to free herself were half-hearted at best. The last thing her body needed was a fall off a horse. She felt brittle enough to break into a thousand pieces if she hit that unyielding earth from this height.

"Because I am fully capable of walking," she said tartly.

He snorted. "You realize you're the only woman here who has walked every step of this journey so far, don't you?"

"I am not!" she protested, though in truth she hadn't put any thought into it. It was true that most of the women, even the youngest ones, had occasionally spent at least a small stretch of time on horseback, but surely not *all* of them.

Tynthanal showed no inclination to set her back down, and if truth be told, she had no great inclination to fight him. It was her duty as the abbess to rule her women by example, and up till now, she'd considered trudging along on her own two feet the only proper example to set. But perhaps a more important example was to accept help when it was needed, and every inch of her body groaned that she needed it.

She was exhausted in both mind and body, by the long and arduous journey and by the weight of being named abbess with absolutely no preparation. Bad enough when they'd all been living within the familiar halls of the Abbey, with familiar, if often unpleasant, duties. What was she meant to do now, in this very different world?

Tynthanal's arm remained snugly around her waist, the reins held loosely in his other hand as his horse moved steadily forward with no visible guidance. They had been following a road up until this morning, when they'd passed through the tiniest, saddest village Chanlix had ever seen. The only reason Miller's Bridge was able to survive so far from any Well was that it was situated on the banks of the Endless River, which flowed from some unknown source deep in the Wasteland. The water made a few small, fertile fields possible and fueled a mill, but it was a place where life would always be difficult. The eponymous Miller's Bridge that crossed over the river was the end of the official road, though after crossing the river the earth was so hard-packed an actual road wasn't needed.

"How do you know we're going the right direction?" Chanlix asked. Every way she turned her head, she saw nothing but flat, dusty land, with no hint of a recognizable landmark.

"I have a compass," Tynthanal said, patting a small satchel that hung from the saddle. "But I'm not using it for guidance just now. We actually passed the spot where we were supposed to build the new Abbey about an hour ago."

She turned to look at him more fully. "What?" Surely he couldn't mean to lead them all out into the depths of the Wasteland! Not only were there no living things in the Wasteland, there were no elements at all. Explorers of yore had often journeyed into the Wasteland, hoping to find its end, but they'd all either turned back or never returned.

"Open your Mindseye," Tynthanal said, releasing her waist briefly to point, "and look over there."

Even as an abigail, Chanlix was unaccustomed to opening her Mindseye in the presence of men. She hesitated a moment, so Tynthanal opened his own, his warm, friendly eyes filming over with white. Whatever he saw put a smile on his lips, and she was curious enough that she had to take a look herself.

Opening her Mindseye, she looked out on the horizon and was astonished to see a thick cloud of swirling colors in the distance. All around them, the elements were as scarce as the plant life, with thin patches of Rho here and there around the growths, and scattered motes of Aal with the occasional mote of something else. Barely enough of anything to fuel even the most basic of spells.

But there was no mistaking that cloud in the distance for anything but a concentration of elements.

She closed her Mindseye and stared out into the distance. Now that she knew where to look, it seemed that one strip of land on the horizon was considerably darker than anything around it, right about where she'd seen that cloud of elements.

"What is it?" she whispered. "And did you know it was there?"

"It's a Well," he responded. "And I know for a fact that it was not there as recently as five years ago, when I led a training march in this area."

Chanlix shook her head in wonder. Wells didn't just pop up out of nowhere. "I've never heard of such a thing happening." She twisted so she could see his face better. "Have you?"

"No. And I've studied a lot of history."

She had never been this close to him before, had never noticed the lines that gathered around the corners of his eyes, made more prominent by his squint against the blinding sun. Because in this barren land water was too precious to waste on shaving, a short fuzz of black beard peppered his cheeks and chin, and his skin and shirt and jacket were streaked with dirt, but Chanlix was not so old that she couldn't appreciate the artistic perfection of his features.

"You want to know something else interesting?" he asked, showing no sign that he'd noticed her staring at his face like a smitten teenager.

"More interesting than finding a Well where no Well is meant to be?"

He lowered his voice, though their party was straggling so much there was no one close enough to hear—or with enough energy to notice much of what was happening around them.

"As far as I can tell, my men see nothing but a slight, unexpected concentration of elements. Barely enough to raise an eyebrow."

"How is that possible?" she asked, opening her Mindseye once more. As a magic user, she was above average—she'd probably have ranked as Prime had she been a man—but there was no mistaking that she was looking at a Well, not just an anomalous concentration of elements. Even if most of Tynthanal's men were of lesser magical ability, they should be able to recognize it for what it was.

"If I tell you something in strictest confidence, can I count on you to keep it to yourself?" he asked.

She closed her Mindseye once more and stared into his eyes. "Why would you put your confidence in me? You barely know me."

He shook his head and sighed. "Because I need to put my confidence in someone. And I believe I've already proved to you that you can put confidence in me." His eyes went filmy, and though she could not see his pupils through the film, she could tell by the angle of his head that he was looking directly at the mote of Kai that rode always by her left shoulder.

She shivered even in the blazing heat. She had hoped that because none of Tynthanal's men had seemed to notice the Kai that somehow it was not visible to them, that it was perhaps some kind of women's variation of Kai that men could not see. Apparently, that was not the case.

Tynthanal's eyes cleared, the warm hazel hue returning. "I am an Adept, and while I have never been in a true battle, I have seen Kai during skirmishes. What I see on you is recognizably Kai, but it does not look like the motes I have seen before. Yours and those of your abigails all look the same, whereas men's Kai motes share only their general crystalline form. It's Kai . . . but not Kai."

Something inside her shifted, as if her understanding of how the world worked took a step to the side. "It's women's Kai."

"So it would seem."

"And it's a feminine element. That's why no one but us seems to notice it."

He nodded.

"But *you* can see it."

He nodded once more. "I can see a fair number of feminine elements," he said. "Now that I know what my mother was capable of, I think my abilities are rooted in her blood."

Chanlix chewed over that thought for a few moments. Mother Brynna and Sister Nadeen had been the most powerful female magic users Chanlix had ever seen, able to see so many elements there was never any question that they would have been ranked as Adept had they been men. Perhaps poor, doomed Vondeen would have been the same. If they possessed that amount of power, it should be no great surprise that Brynna's son was also extraordinary.

She stared out at the horizon again. The dark patch she'd noticed in the distance was getting noticeably larger and seemed to have a faint green tinge to it. It looked for all the world like a patch of forest, rising from the dead lands around it.

"So you can see feminine elements," she mused, "and your men cannot see the Well we're approaching and that I can see quite clearly. You think the Well is giving off either primarily or even exclusively feminine elements."

"Yes. Which is why we may be able to get away with putting the new Abbey there. If it were a more usual Well . . ."

Chanlix grimaced and nodded. There was no war in the history of Seven Wells that couldn't be traced, directly or indirectly, to the desire to control a Well. Even the last great war between Aaltah and Rhozinolm—supposedly begun over a perceived miscarriage of justice—had been motivated by King Linolm's desire to lay claim to the Well in the Midlands, the principality that lay between the two kingdoms and that had at the time been a part of Aaltah. If this new Well on the edge of the Wasteland was deemed useful to men, there would be armies marching toward it the moment its existence was made public.

For the first time since the king had banished them from Aalwell, Chanlix felt a surge of hope. Instead of their new Abbey being a desolate, hopeless place where the abigails would have no access either to men or to magic, it was looking like they might have a burgeoning supply of the elements they used most commonly. And under Tynthanal's leadership, the men who'd been sent to trap and guard them had remained on their best behavior at all times.

"So what is it you wanted to show me?" Ellin inquired when she and Star were finally alone in her bedroom. There was a mischievous—even excited—twinkle in the maid's eyes, but Ellin was baffled by it and had been unable to wrest a single hint from her.

"Well," Star said, looking very pleased with herself, "you know your grandfather—and many a king before him, I might add—

considered his marriage vows as more of an ideal than an actual commitment."

Ellin rolled her eyes, for extramarital affairs were hardly the exclusive territory of kings. Although she had no proof of the matter, she felt fairly certain her own father had had women on the side, though he had been thankfully discreet, and as far as she knew, she had no half-siblings running around. "Kailindar did not come into being because of the king's dutiful devotion to his queen," she said with a heavy dose of irony. "What does that have to do with anything?"

Her impatience did nothing to quell Star's amusement. "Of course everyone knows about the king's dalliance with Chantah."

"If you can call a decades-long affair a dalliance." Kailindar was not the only fruit of the king's illicit union, although the first child, a daughter, had died long ago—at the hands of a duke of Aaltah, which had sparked the last war between their two kingdoms.

Star ignored the aside. "But just because everyone knew didn't mean the king felt comfortable flaunting his mistress in the queen's face." She moved to a large tapestry that adorned one wall of the bedroom, smoothing her hand over the intricately woven design. "So he took advantage of a convenience that has been part of this palace for as long as its walls have stood."

With a flourish—and not a little bit of effort, for the tapestry was heavy—Star swept the hanging aside to reveal a heavily bolted door set into the wall behind it. As Ellin gaped in surprise, Star lifted the bolts and pushed the door open to reveal a pitch-dark hallway.

Ellin shook her head. "How did you know this was here? And why didn't *I* know?" It was not a little disconcerting to discover there was a secret door into her bedroom, though she supposed that with the bolts keeping it securely shut, there had never been any threat of anyone sneaking in.

"I didn't know until earlier today," Star said. "Servants like to talk, and I overheard someone mention the passage. I took the liberty of bracing your steward for not having told you about it." She made a sour face. "He seemed to be of the opinion that because you are a woman, you would never have need for the passageway and that therefore there was no reason to mention it to you."

Ellin made a low growling sound of frustration. Her steward had served King Linolm before her, and was annoyingly stodgy and prudish. "I think I should have the right to know there's a secret passageway into my bedroom, whether I intend to use it or not!"

Star grinned at her. "But your steward was under the impression your innocent ears were not fit to hear the explanation for why the passage exists." Star pulled a folded piece of parchment from a pocket in her skirts. "There is apparently no official map of the secret passages in this palace, but I bullied the steward into marking the ones he knew about."

Ellin debated whether to have a word with her steward about his failure, but decided Star had probably upbraided the man enough on her behalf. While she did not much care for him, the offense seemed too minor to warrant dismissal, and she didn't relish watching him squirm.

"Do we know where it goes?" Ellin asked, peering into the darkness of the hallway.

"I investigated as soon as I found it," Star affirmed, pulling the door closed once more and securing the bolts. "It leads down to a hidden entrance in the servants' wing." She gave Ellin a wry smile. "Apparently, no one worries too much about servants knowing about the love affairs of kings."

Since the passageway was more about keeping up appearances than keeping actual secrets, Ellin supposed that wasn't entirely surprising.

Returning to her usual nighttime routine, Ellin took her seat at the dressing table, and Star began removing her headdress.

"How fares your new secretary?" Star asked as she gently extracted the headdress from Ellin's hair and set it aside.

Ellin gave a little huff of frustration. "Apparently, I have much to learn about the art of flirting and seduction," she said with some chagrin. "He watches me with the wary eye of a mouse in the presence of a hawk. I might think him completely uninterested, except every once in a while . . ." She shrugged. "You advised me to be more direct with him, but it is quite clearly not working."

Star made a noncommittal sound. "Just how direct have you been?"

"I've all but propositioned him outright!"

"And his response?"

Ellin crossed her arms protectively over her chest. "He says we aren't ever truly in private, even when we are behind a closed door." She caught a glimpse of herself in the mirror and saw that her expression was uncomfortably close to a pout, and she tried to smooth it out. Star, however, smiled.

"He might just be good enough for you," Star said approvingly.

Ellin frowned at her. "Which does me no good whatsoever when he's determined to reject me."

Star made a *tsk*ing sound. "He is being appropriately careful of your reputation. You do not want a man who thinks only of his own desires and ignores the dangers."

"Yes, I know, but—"

Star turned her head pointedly toward the tapestry behind which the secret door lay hidden. And for the first time, Ellin realized why her maid had been so excited to find it. Her jaw dropped open, and she hastily turned in her chair to stare up into Star's face.

Star looked astonishingly proud of herself. "I may not have just stumbled on that secret accidentally. I may have made some discreet inquiries as to how King Linolm had managed to maintain a mistress without undue scandal for all those years."

Ellin bit her lip and looked toward the tapestry once more. When she was alone with Graesan during the day, she was always "on duty" as it were, susceptible to interruptions and on a strict timetable. But once she retired to her room at night, the only person who would dare disturb her was Star.

"If you're sure what you want," Star said, "we can arrange for your young man to have truly private access to you. Without the fear of interruption and discovery, you might find him less apt to resist his own desires."

Ellin shivered suddenly in a combination of excitement and nerves. If she removed Graesan's practical objections and he rejected her advances anyway, she wasn't sure how her heart could survive the blow.

Shaking off her own fears, she stiffened her spine. If she made no advances, she would never know if he would have rejected them or not. While that might be far safer for her heart, she would question her own cowardice for the rest of her life.

"How would we go about getting him here?" she asked.

Star beamed at her. "You just leave that to me, Your Majesty."

CHAPTER TWENTY-ONE

When Tynthanal knocked on the doorframe of her quickly constructed cabin, Chanlix reluctantly closed her Mindseye. The elements that spilled from the Well they had built their encampment around were so abundant she couldn't even make out the faint shadow of his form when her Mindseye was open. When her vision cleared, he smiled at her, showing no sign that the sight of a woman with her Mindseye open bothered him in the slightest.

"Please come in," she beckoned.

The sun was low in the sky behind him, and as he stepped into the hut so that he was no longer backlighted, she could see from his sweat-dampened hair that rather than being a typical commanding officer, he'd been actively participating in the day's building effort. Not that she was surprised. He was hardly the kind of man to sit by idly while others worked.

It was only a couple of weeks into what was sure to be a lengthy building process—especially considering that the king had not seen fit to send any professional builders with their expedition—but the bones of the new Abbey were beginning to take shape already. Everyone in the encampment now had rudimentary shelter for the nights, and a space had been cleared where they could erect more permanent structures.

They had not yet progressed to such luxuries as furniture. Chanlix's seat consisted of a folded blanket against a log, but the blanket was big enough to allow Tynthanal to sit beside her without being uncomfortably close.

"Have you ever seen a place like this near the Wasteland before?" she asked.

He shook his head. "Never." He reached up and wiped away a drop of sweat that trickled down the side of his face. "I've checked and rechecked our coordinates and our map, and it seems our camp is just past where the Wasteland border used to be. There used to be *nothing* out here, not even Rho. I rode out deeper into the Wasteland this afternoon, and it's clear the Well's influence stretches for miles. I'm not sure where the Wasteland's borders are anymore."

Chanlix had been imagining a miserable existence in the scorching sun of the desert with no easy access to food or water or elements. But the elements that spilled from the Well had given the land back its life. Their encampment was near a crystal clear spring that seemed to be fed from somewhere deep beneath the earth, and while there were no full-grown trees yet, the spring was surrounded by grasses and shrubs and saplings. Birds and small mammals had found the oasis, and if they could avoid overhunting in these early days, it seemed possible that there would be sustainable populations come spring.

"Will the king let us stay?" Chanlix asked anxiously. While he hadn't said so explicitly, she knew Tynthanal had no choice but to report what they had found to the king. Tynthanal insisted the malice that had sent them all to live in desolate exile was Delnamal's, not the king's, but the king was clearly complicit. Would he order them to move their camp to somewhere less comfortable?

"I can't say for sure," Tynthanal said, "but my guess is that he will." He turned and gave her a crooked smile. "I might have forgotten to mention in my report that the Well produces a few rare masculine elements."

Chanlix laughed. The elements that came from this Well *were* overwhelmingly feminine. Every feminine element she was capable of seeing was available here, and having polled the rest of the abigails, she knew that was true of them, as well. The Well also produced a few of the most common neuter elements. Those were the only elements most of Tynthanal's men could see, and they were common enough that Chanlix couldn't imagine the king would feel any great need to exploit this Well.

Only Tynthanal could see any masculine elements coming from this Well, but then his magical abilities ranked at least two levels higher than those of any of his men. If the king were to learn some of these rare and precious masculine elements were abundant near this Well, there was no question that the abigails would be evicted and a new city would rise in the place of their settlement.

"I don't know how long the secret will last," Tynthanal said. "We are quite isolated here, and I can't think of a reason why any high-level magic user would come to see us, but it's bound to happen eventually."

"Eventually is better than *now*," she said with a fatalistic shrug. Maybe this was all too good to last, but after the hardships of the last months—after the great hardship that was part and parcel of the life of an abigail—she would happily take any respite the world cared to provide. Both she and Tynthanal had been sent to this place as a form of punishment, and there was a certain satisfying irony to having discovered the Well.

Impulsively, she reached over and put a hand on Tynthanal's leg. "I can't thank you enough for keeping control of your men as you have," she said.

She had hoped that with Tynthanal as their leader, the men would not be as vicious as Delnamal's had been, but she'd never dared believe that not once would any of the abigails be coerced into sexual relations. Tynthanal was an extraordinary leader—and he had handpicked the men who had accompanied them on their long journey. When he'd forbidden his men from taking any abigail to his bed without her consent, they'd obeyed. This new Abbey-in-the-making was about the closest thing to paradise Chanlix could imagine.

To her surprise, he covered her hand on his leg with his own, giving her fingers a squeeze and not letting go. She hadn't intended the touch to be flirtatious—at least, she didn't think she had—but her pulse sped up, and she found herself practically holding her breath.

He couldn't possibly be interested in *her*. That was ridiculous! There were any number of younger, more beautiful women who would jump at the chance to crawl into his bed. Chanlix had never been a great beauty, even before the strain of being a virtual prisoner of the Abbey had taken its toll. But Tynthanal still had not released her hand, and his thumb had begun stroking lightly over her skin. She swallowed hard, almost afraid to look at him. She was too old to play the shy miss, and yet she was too confused to know what to do. Maybe she was misinterpreting his touch. She *had* to be.

"Why have you never married?" she asked, then was shocked at her audacity. It was certainly none of her business. Blood heated her cheeks, and she wished she could take the words back.

She felt rather than saw his shrug. "It takes a certain kind of woman to be a military wife."

She risked a glance at him and found him looking at her with an expression of . . . tenderness? "You're a king's son," she said. *And ridiculously handsome, as well.* But she managed to keep that thought to herself. "I'd think you could find plenty of that 'certain kind of woman' if you wanted to."

He shrugged again. "Perhaps. But I have no lands or titles to pass on, so I have no urgent need for an heir. There seemed no point in rushing things."

"Because you certainly don't need marriage to lure women to your bed." She meant it as a compliment, but a hint of sharpness may have crept into her tone. Half the women of the Abbey were here because men had risked their ruin to enjoy their bodies outside of marriage. It was so easy for a man to have whatever he wanted without having to fear the consequences. She tried to move her hand away, but Tynthanal's fingers tightened on hers.

"Do you think so poorly of me, Chanlix?" he asked, looking into her eyes for all the world like her good opinion really mattered to him.

In all honesty, she didn't think poorly of him at all, but she wasn't ready to give up her anger just yet. "I think you are not a virgin."

Tynthanal laughed. "No, I am not a virgin."

"And you have not been a customer at the Abbey."

The laughter faded, and he moved a little closer to her on the blanket. The intensity of his eyes from close-up was too much, and she averted her gaze.

"I would never take a woman who didn't want me."

It was Chanlix's turn to laugh, though she still couldn't face him. "I think you could find many an abigail who wanted you."

"But if I paid for them, they'd have no choice. How would I ever know if they wanted me or not?"

She was startled enough that she looked at him again, then found herself trapped by his eyes and the earnestness of his expression. "You're sure you didn't avoid the Abbey just to avoid seeing your mother there?"

He closed his eyes, and this time it was he who turned away. In the fading light, she could see the hard outline of his jaw, and she knew that her words had wounded him. Possibly because there'd been a hint of truth in them.

"Forgive me," she said softly. "That was unkind of me."

He sighed heavily and opened his eyes, looking at her once more. He was not a coward, that was for sure.

"I believe I would have felt the same way even if my mother were not in the Abbey. But of course I can never be sure."

"*I'm* sure. You are a good man. I have been angry for a very long time, and I took it out on you." It was almost beyond comprehension that this man could share a parent with Prince Delnamal, who was as far from a good man as it was possible to be. How it must gall Tynthanal to be related to such a monster. She scooted closer until their sides were touching, trying to give him physical evidence that she was now stating her honest opinion.

He let go of her hand and put his arm around her shoulders. The intimacy of the gesture made her shiver pleasantly. "I'll try my best to live up to your good opinion."

She suspected he very rarely failed at anything he tried.

While she waited anxiously for Graesan's arrival, Ellin dotted on a couple drops of perfume, the sweet floral scent faint but noticeable. She then checked her reflection in the mirror, wondering how shocked Graesan would be at her dishabille. Her nightdress was of a featherlight white lawn, soft against her skin and translucent in the light, but she had covered it with a dressing gown of frothy white lace. Either garment by itself would be frighteningly revealing, but together they hid her from neck to ankles. Star had suggested that for the best hope of success, Ellin should do away with the dressing gown, but although having a man led through a secret passageway into her room at night was shockingly daring behavior already, somehow Ellin had felt revealing so much of her body would take things a step too far.

She heard the echo of footsteps from the passageway and whirled to face the tapestry, her heart leaping into her throat. This plan had felt like an exciting lark when she and Star had put it together, but now she felt something very akin to panic.

From behind the closed door, she heard the faint rumble of voices, one male, one female. She couldn't make out the words, but the woman's tone sounded coaxing and the man's suspicious. Ellin didn't know what Star had told Graesan to convince him to follow her through the secret passage, but he was certainly not expecting what was about to happen. Moments later, the door opened quietly on oiled hinges, and Star swept the tapestry aside to reveal Graesan standing in the passage at full alert, his entire body tense as if expecting attack.

He gasped audibly when he caught sight of Ellin with her uncovered hair and her nightclothes, and even in the dim light of the simple luminant Star carried, Ellin could see the flush of red that rose to his cheeks. She met Star's eyes, and the two women shared a conspiratorial smile.

"Well, go on in," Star said to Graesan. "I'm almost certain she won't bite. Unless you want her to."

Ellin suspected her cheeks turned a similar color to Graesan's as he stood there indecisively. If he wished to pretend even a hint of propriety in their relationship, he should have turned around and fled the moment he caught sight of her, but that did not seem to be his inclination.

Ellin licked her lips nervously, afraid to do anything that might frighten Graesan away or make him think better of entering her room. She felt the beat of her heart in her throat, and her breaths came short with a combination of nerves and yearning. Silently, she prayed that he would accept her invitation, that he would not turn out to be just one more man who believed she was incapable of making her own decisions.

Graesan visibly swallowed, the fingers of his right hand twitching as he closed and opened his fist in quick succession. Then he turned to fix his gaze on Star, and Ellin knew exactly what he was thinking.

"I would trust Star with my life," she said. "Whether you come in or whether you don't, she will tell no one."

"This is . . . a foolish risk," he said, but the rasp in his voice told her how very much he wanted to take that risk.

She walked closer, her loose nightclothes rustling and moving around her, giving him the occasional glimpse of barely covered leg. "All the good things in life are a risk," she countered, putting a little extra sway in her hips, hoping she looked alluring rather than awkward. "I happen to think this is a risk worth taking."

He stepped forward as if pulled by invisible hands. He hesitated for just a heartbeat more on the threshold, then stepped into the room. Behind him, Star beamed her approval.

"Have fun, you two," she said with an impish wink. "And be sure to bolt this door."

Then she closed the door, and Ellin and Graesan were alone in the bedroom.

He stood there drinking her in with his eyes, and she felt like she was about to go up in flames at the heat in his gaze. She drifted past him, heeding Star's last bit of advice and bolting the door to the secret passage. She couldn't imagine anyone trying to enter her bedchamber without permission, but there was no reason to take chances. Then she smoothed down the tapestry and turned to face Graesan.

The look on his face was equal parts desire and worry. Ellin's whole body tingled with nerves, not because she was afraid of the consequences of her actions, but because she feared some action of hers might cause him to change his mind.

"I want you," she said in a husky whisper. "More than anything else I've ever wanted. I hope you know that." And she hoped even more that he felt the same, though there seemed to be little doubt that he did. The only question was whether he would act on his desires.

He reached out and took her hands in his, drawing her close to him, but not all the way into his arms. She tilted her head up so she could look into those heated eyes, and the fire in them caused her skin to prickle with gooseflesh.

"I want you more than I want my next breath," he whispered, his hands squeezing hers tight. "But I'm terrified that you might be hurt because of me."

She offered him what she hoped was a reassuring smile. "I'm not afraid." Not of that, at least. "And I'm stronger than you think."

He let go of one of her hands so he could reach up and brush the back of his hand down the side of her face. "Only a blind man would fail to see the strength in you. And I am not a blind man."

She shivered at his touch, and his words flooded her with a kind

of warmth that had nothing to do with desire. He was not a courtier, not a man accustomed to dispensing empty flattery. If he said
he saw strength in her, then he meant it.

"Then why do you still hesitate?"

He cupped her cheek in his hand, and she closed her eyes and
reveled in the touch. "Because this cannot end well. You may not
have to marry Zarsha of Nandel anymore, but you will have to
marry *someone*, and that someone is not me. Any time we have together is but stolen moments, and every moment will make the inevitable parting hurt more."

Ellin swallowed hard, her throat suddenly filled with an aching
lump. How she wished she could tell him he was wrong, but such
was not possible. Various members of the royal council had already
started maneuvering themselves or their relatives into position to
contend for her hand. They would not push too hard just yet, when
her mourning was still fresh, but it had already become obvious to
her that they would expect her to choose a couple of prime candidates, if not name the future king himself, well before her year of
mourning was finished.

Even as he seemed determined to drive her away with his words,
Graesan pulled her in closer, until her body was pressed flush against
his and his arms slipped around her. Her skin under the thin layers
of lace and lawn felt exquisitely sensitive, and though his mail kept
her from feeling the contours of his body, she felt the strength and
warmth of him as she melted into his embrace.

"The greatest pain I can imagine," she murmured, "is to embark
on a marriage of state without ever having known love. When my
father contracted me to Zarsha, I thought all hope was lost, and I
had no ability to control my own destiny. Now I do."

Instead of waiting for him to overcome the last of his reservations, she lifted up on tiptoe and touched her lips to his. Graesan let
out a groan that sounded almost like pain, then crushed her body
against his and abandoned himself to the kiss.

Ellin's head swam as she tried to absorb all the glorious and unfamiliar sensations at once. The surprising softness and warmth of

his mouth on hers, the faint rasp of stubble on his cheek, the scent of his skin, the need that tightened her nipples and made her press her legs firmly together.

Still holding her against him, Graesan speared his fingers through the hair at the top of her loose braid, tilting her head back to get a better angle. His lips worked restlessly against hers, and she gasped when she felt the soft brush of his tongue. She and Star had discussed in detail the mechanics of joining their bodies, but they had mostly skipped over all talk of preliminaries. Ellin had thought she'd known what to expect, but she had apparently been mistaken.

Graesan's hands roamed restlessly up and down her back, the touch through the delicate fabric more intense than anything she had ever felt before. She tried to explore with her own hands just as Graesan did, but it was hard to feel much of anything beneath his mail. He tore himself away from her, and she was about to protest until she saw him pulling at the belt on his tabard. The length of leather came loose, and he took the belt and its attached scabbard and sword and laid it carefully on a chair. Then he pulled off the tabard to reveal the fine silver links of his mail.

The mail was attached by a series of buckles on both sides, and while Graesan began working the buckles loose on one side, Ellin began on the other. She found her hands were shaking, and she couldn't for the life of her have said whether the shaking was from nerves or excitement. Possibly a little of both.

Finally, the mail was unfastened, and she helped Graesan lift it off over his head. She was surprised by how heavy the mail shirt was, especially considering it was not full battle mail.

Underneath, Graesan wore a nearly translucent linen shirt to protect his skin. The shirt hung loose over a pair of tight-fitting tan trousers that tucked into his boots. Beneath the hem of his shirt, she could see how the lacings of those trousers bulged outward, and her heart skipped a beat. He watched her examine him, a smile playing over his lips as he let her look her fill. He even turned a full circle so she could take in the view from the back. She laughed breathlessly, and his lips turned down in a mock frown.

"Laughter was not the reaction I was looking for," he teased, and her smile grew wider.

"Well if you don't want me to laugh at you, you should probably stop preening."

He touched a hand to his chest with a gasp of outrage. "I am not preening. I am showing off. There's a difference."

She giggled at the silliness of his act, but the urge to laugh died in her throat when he reached out and grabbed the end of the sash that held her dressing gown closed. His eyes met hers with a renewed flare of lust.

"May I?"

Ellin couldn't find her voice, so she merely nodded as her pulse fluttered in her throat. Star had assured her a thousand times that Graesan would find her body pleasing to look at, but no amount of reassurance could entirely quell her anxiety as Graesan pulled on that sash and the dressing gown fell open.

Shyness caused her to lower her eyes, but her gaze never quite made it to the floor as her eyes locked on the fastenings of Graesan's trousers once more. Something inside her relaxed at this very visual evidence that he found her form pleasing indeed, so she reached up and gave the dressing gown the nudge it needed to slide off her shoulders and fall to the floor in a snowdrift of lace.

"You are so beautiful," Graesan whispered reverently as his gaze scanned up and down her body.

Her whole body flushed with pleasure at the compliment, but before she found the breath to offer one of her own, he was on her once more, mouth seizing hers in a kiss that drove all coherent thought from her mind.

This time, she could feel his body against hers. Her hands roamed over his back as Graesan kissed his way down her throat. She let her head fall backward to allow him access. She was disappointed that he needed to put some space between their bodies as his kisses traveled downward, but she loved the feel of his lips against her skin too much to complain. The hungry sound that rose from her throat hardly sounded like her at all.

Suddenly, Graesan pulled away. He was panting heavily, his eyes almost completely black with his desire as he took a double handful of her nightdress and tugged upward. Obediently, she raised her arms so he could pull the nightdress off over her head.

For the first time in her life, Ellin stood completely naked in front of a man, and she felt not even the tiniest sliver of embarrassment or self-consciousness. How could she see the way he was looking at her and not know he found her beautiful? Without taking her eyes from him, she backed up until she felt the edge of her bed against her legs, then climbed atop the mattress.

Graesan followed eagerly, and soon she was lying on her back with his body hovering over hers as his hands stroked every inch of her. Star's attempts to describe the experience, the pleasure clever hands could elicit, had been woefully inadequate. She had to bite her tongue to stifle her cry when the pleasure peaked. And this was just the prelude! What would it feel like when their bodies were finally joined? She was more than eager to find out.

Her lids felt heavy, and she panted as if she'd been running for miles with her stays laced too tight. Graesan smiled down at her, his expression filled with an intriguing mixture of tenderness and lust. She reached up and touched his cheek.

"You have every reason to be pleased with yourself," she told him, "but don't imagine you are finished yet."

Desire shone unabated in his eyes, but his brows pulled together in a small frown. "Are you sure? There are other ways—"

"I'm sure," she interrupted. Her hand slid down his back, slipping under the hem of his shirt until she found bare skin.

For one long, agonizing moment, he held still, staring into her eyes, his expression filled with doubt even as his body quivered with eagerness. She didn't know how she could bear it if he lost his nerve now. She reached up to cup his face in her hands, willing him to see her conviction.

"I'm sure," she said again, letting that certainty shine in her eyes. And finally, *finally,* he believed her.

CHAPTER TWENTY-TWO

Alys was working on the always tedious task of balancing the household books when Falcor knocked softly on the open door of her study. She had the various balance sheets spread out all over her desk and had been so absorbed in her work that she hadn't heard him approach. She didn't quite jump, but she must have shown some sign of being surprised.

"Forgive me, Lady Alysoon," he said. "I did not mean to startle you."

She waved off the apology, though her stomach muscles tensed in anticipation of bad news. Falcor rarely entered the house, taking pains to be as unobtrusive as possible. Sometimes, she felt guilty for keeping him and his men at such a distance, making it so clear to them that she would decline their protection if only her father would allow it—but not guilty enough to embrace their presence.

"You didn't startle me," she said. "Please come in." She hoped he didn't hear the reluctance in her voice. It showed something of her state of mind that she would have preferred balancing the books.

Falcor entered, and for the first time she saw that he held a familiar black-and-gold-painted flier in his hand. Even in her trepidation, a smile tugged at the corners of her mouth, for she would recognize one of Tynthanal's fliers anywhere. He had promised to write as soon as he could, once he reached the new location for the Abbey, and she'd been starting to worry as weeks passed with no word.

"This arrived in the message box this morning," Falcor said, laying the flier—still holding its scrolled parchment—on her desk.

"Thank you, Falcor," she said, though she knew he was here for some reason other than to deliver the flier. It was ordinarily her steward's job to check the message box.

She touched the flier, and it released the scrolled message from its metal talons—which meant it contained a privacy spell cued to her. With an ordinary flier, anyone could theoretically tug the message free and read it, if they didn't mind breaking the wax seal and revealing their intrusion.

"I gather there's something else?" she prompted, setting the message aside to open and read when she was alone. Those with suspicious minds—like Delnamal—might take the passing of privacy-locked messages between Alys and her brother as evidence that they were up to something treacherous, but she could not fault him for his caution. She would not put it past Delnamal to have a spy watching her house and trying to read any messages she received.

"I'm afraid so," Falcor said with a grimace. "I was hoping not to have to trouble you with this, but . . ." He trailed off and shook his head.

Alys sighed. "Go ahead and trouble me. What is it?"

"Someone has been leaving things other than fliers in the message box."

She frowned. "What sort of 'things' are we talking about?"

"Let's just call them messages of questionable origin."

"Let's not! Tell me what's been in the message box." Her hands had clenched into fists without her noticing, and she forced them to relax. It was already clear that Falcor was not speaking of a single occurrence—and it was also clear why it was *he* who had found Tynthanal's flier, when checking the box was ordinarily her steward's job. Clearly Mica had found something untoward in that box—and then reported the finding to Falcor instead of to her, at which point Falcor had taken over checking it.

Falcor shifted uncomfortably. "It started out with, er, excrement. Then there was a dead bird. And today there was a doll with its throat cut."

Alys ground her teeth, not sure if this news made her more angry or alarmed. She was not entirely surprised at how differently she and her children were viewed by their friends and neighbors since her mother's spell, but the censure had generally been of the subtle variety. Invitations that were turned down when they had once been eagerly accepted, friends who suddenly didn't have time to talk, smiles that had once been free and easy now tense and forced. But nothing in the behavior of those she knew had led her to expect threats to appear in her message box.

"I set one of my men to watch the box, of course," Falcor said, "but there appear to be at least two people behind it. One led my man on a fruitless chase, and the other placed the doll in the box while he was in pursuit."

"And he didn't catch either of them."

"No," Falcor said, bowing his head. "I must apologize for that failure, and if you would prefer to request a new crew—"

"Don't be absurd," she interrupted. "It's not your fault they were more organized than you expected."

"Thank you, my lady," he said with some relief. "I would like to bring on additional men, however. It is possible, maybe even likely, that this is all some juvenile prank, but just in case it represents a true threat . . ."

Alys shook her head. She already felt halfway smothered by her honor guard. The thought of having *more* of them around was far from appealing. "Let's not escalate just yet. I don't want to scare the children."

There was no doubt in her mind that Falcor saw straight through her and knew the children had nothing to do with her resistance. Just as she had no doubt he had seen her refusal coming before he'd even entered the room.

"I would strongly recommend you reconsider," he said, but he didn't sound like he expected his recommendation to sway her.

"I trust you can post more of your men to watch the box in the future—and that a decoy won't work on them a second time. If whoever it is keeps getting around you, or if the threats escalate in any way, *then* I'll reconsider."

Falcor was not happy with her answer, and she suspected he could find support for his own position if he were to take his concerns to the lord commander. But—for now, at least—he was willing to accede to her wishes.

Alys was glad she'd decided to wait until she was alone to read Tynthanal's letter. She didn't like to imagine what expressions her face must have worn when she read it the first time—or what others would have made of her reactions.

Alys rolled the letter up into a tight tube after she finished reading it for the third time, struggling to come to terms with the news of the new Well Tynthanal and the abigails had discovered in what was supposed to be the Wasteland. On the one hand, she was glad to know that the new Abbey would not be the miserable, barren encampment all of them had expected. Tynthanal seemed to think the women in his care would thrive in the presence of the impossible Well, and that the Abbey itself would prosper thanks to the wealth of feminine elements—some rare, and some that none of the abigails even recognized—available. But it was also abundantly clear that her brother was embarking on a dangerous game.

I have no choice but to report to my commander of the Well's existence, his letter had said.

> *However, I have done my best to downplay its significance. I do not want Delnamal to decide we are not suffering as he would wish us to and begin agitating for us to be moved*

elsewhere. We have already violated our exact mandate by setting up our camp at somewhat of a remove from our planned location, but I have made the case that it is to the Crown's advantage to allow the abigails unfettered access to elements that will help them produce enough potions to be self-sufficient.

Alys had no doubt that Delnamal would try to label Tynthanal's decision as an act of treason. She was still furious with the king for his cruelty in razing the Abbey and for his heartless decision to send Tynthanal into what amounted to exile, but surely he would not blame his eldest son for a decision that was clearly of benefit to the Crown's coffers.

Alys just wished Tynthanal had asked the king's permission before taking that dangerous step. She wished he had not given Delnamal more fuel to sow discord and attempt to poison their father's mind.

Alys threw Tynthanal's letter into the fire. While there was nothing overtly damning in it, the tone was somewhat less than respectful of the king and of Delnamal, and the open admission of his attempts at manipulation was best kept between the two of them.

Sighing, she watched the parchment curl and blacken as she told herself she absolutely did *not* envy her brother. He was in virtual exile, camping out in the open desert until he and his men could erect a ramshackle settlement. Even with the bounty of the Well, the conditions would be difficult for someone who'd lived all his life in the comfort of Aalwell. But in her heart of hearts, Alys had to admit she would love a chance to see that new Well with her own eyes. How much richer and more successful would her magic practice be if she had such a bounty of rare feminine elements at her fingertips?

But that was mere fantasy, she scolded herself. She still had so very much to learn here in Aalwell as she explored the secrets of her mother's book. It was foolish of her to dream of flying when she had not yet learned to walk.

The council meeting had begun on a contentious note, and it seemed to be continuing on that way no matter what subject came up for consideration. For all that Ellin felt she had served as a more-than-competent queen since she'd taken the throne, Lord Tamzin's opposition to her seemed to be growing daily, although his methods of expressing that opposition were increasingly subtle and understated. Rarely did he come out with an open challenge, instead letting his disagreement be known by facial expression and body language. And it was clear to anyone with eyes that both the lord high treasurer and the lord commander were actively taking their cues from him.

"If Sovereign Prince Waldmir has appointed Zarsha as his *special envoy*," Tamzin said, making no effort to hide his disdain for the newly minted position, "then it should be *his* obligation to fund the man's visit."

It was all Ellin could do to hold on to her patience. She always expected a certain amount of friction in the daily council meeting, but not over something so trivial as Zarsha of Nandel's continued status as a guest of the palace. While it was technically true that Zarsha was now in Rhozinolm as an official representative of the Principality of Nandel, it seemed petty to begrudge him the guest suite he had occupied in the royal palace since the day he had first arrived. He was, after all, still a member of the royal family of Nandel.

"Room and board for a Nandelite is hardly an extravagant expense," Semsulin pointed out. "The money saved by evicting him would hardly be worth the insult Prince Waldmir would take."

"The man doesn't belong in the palace," Tamzin persisted. "By all rights, he should have returned home after the king's funeral. Am I the only one who finds it odd that he is still here?"

"One does wonder what the purpose of this extended visit might be," the lord high treasurer agreed. "Nandel already has an envoy in Zinolm Well, so what exactly is Zarsha here to do?"

"I'm sure you haven't forgotten the trade agreements that are set to expire soon," Ellin said. She had taken Semsulin's advice to heart, and whenever possible, allowed him to be the voice of dissent against Tamzin's most outrageous provocations. However, she could not be an effective ruler while staying entirely silent, and the current discussion was patently ridiculous. "We can no longer secure those agreements through a marriage contract, but there is a great deal of negotiation to come, and I guarantee you those negotiations will be more effectively made through Prince Waldmir's nephew than through the regular envoy."

"If you ask me," Tamzin said, "we have already spent far too much time wringing our hands over the trade agreements with Nandel."

No one asked you, Ellin thought, then had to bite her tongue to keep the words from escaping her mouth.

"Waldmir thinks he can insist on better terms because he already has a profitable partner in Aaltah," Tamzin continued. "Let's see how profitable that arrangement becomes if we deny him access to our trade routes."

Ellin could clearly see from the startled faces around the table that she wasn't the only person surprised by Tamzin's proposal. It was true that by far the fastest routes between Nandel and Aaltah led straight through the heart of Rhozinolm. If Rhozinolm closed those routes, traders from Nandel would have to travel through the mountains all the way to the border of the Midlands before they would get to flat land and easy travel.

"You can't be serious," Ellin said, ignoring the look Semsulin shot her way. The look that urged her to be quiet and let him do the talking. "How do you imagine the Midlands and Aaltah would respond if we cut off their access to Nandel?"

"We wouldn't be cutting it off," Tamzin explained with exaggerated care. "We'd merely be delaying it a bit. Besides, Nandel would never allow it to come to that."

Semsulin spoke hurriedly. "I think, Lord Tamzin, that you misunderstand the nature of our agreements with Nandel."

Tamzin fixed him with a steely stare. "My estate is a good deal closer to the Nandel border than yours. I understand Nandel just fine."

"If that were true, you'd know that we need them far more than they need us," Semsulin countered with some heat. "You have never felt the effects of an iron embargo before, but I can tell you, it was devastating. You have no idea how much iron a kingdom uses until you have no supply."

Instead of watching Tamzin and Semsulin as they continued to bicker, Ellin looked back and forth between the other council members. She didn't like what she saw, didn't like the speculation on the faces of the lord high treasurer and the lord commander. Both were old enough to have felt the effects of the long-ago iron embargo, and yet they seemed admiring of Tamzin's militant stance.

"Perhaps we should table this discussion for a later date," she interrupted. "There seems to be little point in arguing over the trade agreements when we haven't even begun negotiations yet. I will allow Zarsha to remain in the palace as my personal guest so that he need not be a burden on the treasury." She gave the lord high treasurer a pointed look, and despite his obvious affinity for Tamzin, he did not argue.

To her relief, Tamzin allowed himself to be diverted. However, she had no doubt that if she didn't find a way to divert him more permanently, he would continue to agitate for Rhozinolm to take a hard line over the trade agreements. She wasn't sure if it was merely out of male ego and one-upmanship, or if he was actively trying to sabotage her reign, but either way, it was imperative that she find a way to stop him.

After the unexpectedly contentious council meeting, Ellin needed a little time to herself to regroup. She retired to her private study with a plate of fruit and cheese that would substitute for a luncheon, intending to catch up on some personal correspondence she'd been neglecting. She had no idea how King Linolm had had enough time in his day to fulfill his obligations without entirely neglecting his family, and though he'd always seemed busy, he rarely seemed as harried as she felt now.

On the top of her pile of correspondence was a letter from Alysoon Rai-Brynna, the illegitimate daughter of the King of Aaltah. Having assumed the letter was merely delayed condolences or an introduction, Ellin had put it aside when she'd received it more than a week ago, but now she finally broke the seal and read the contents.

While there was a brief introduction and greeting, the letter turned out not to be strictly personal, after all. Lady Alysoon was in search of a husband for her eighteen-year-old daughter, Jinnell. Although the girl was not in the line of succession, she had a substantial dowry that would make her hand more than appealing to many a man. Lady Alysoon was making an inquiry into the possibility of a match between her daughter and Lord Tamzin.

Ellin's first reaction was a deeply personal one. As much as most of the ladies of her court seemed enamored with her cousin, she would never recommend him as a husband for anyone she cared about. The past two months of seeing him every day in council meetings had strengthened her conviction that he was anything but a hero, no matter how shamelessly he played up that reputation. She might never know for sure what had happened when he and his men wiped out that enclave of bandits, but there was no doubt in her mind that he had at the very least embellished the story, if not out-and-out lied.

Ellin pulled back on the reins of her temper and tried not to let her dislike of Tamzin color her judgment. She had never met Lady Alysoon or her daughter, and it was her duty to think of the marriage in terms of its political impact. Tamzin was of an age to seek a wife, and a marriage between him and the King of Aaltah's granddaughter might be politically advantageous. Rhozinolm and Aaltah had spent much of their history at war with one another—mostly fighting over control of the Midlands and its Well. The Midlands was currently an independent principality per the agreement struck at the finish of the last war, but given some of Tamzin's more outra-

geous suggestions at today's council meeting, she wouldn't be entirely surprised if he might one day cast a greedy eye on that Well.
Perhaps if he were aligned with the royal family of Aaltah, his greed
might be tamed.

She considered the possibility for less than a minute before shaking her head. The last thing she needed, considering today's performance, was to give Tamzin even the slightest bit more power or
money. He was dangerous enough already. Any lady of rank would
bring power and money to the marriage, but Ellin would have to
make sure that money and power came from a sector over which he
already had great influence so that his sway wouldn't grow.

She was not entirely surprised when her private time was interrupted by the arrival of Lord Semsulin. A page showed him in, and
he bowed deeply before accepting her invitation to sit in a chair in
front of her desk. She still held the letter from Lady Alysoon, and
she saw Lord Semsulin looking at it curiously. She rolled it up and
set it aside.

"It seems King Aaltyn's granddaughter is in search of a husband," she said. Though she owed her chancellor no explanation,
she was curious to see if he viewed the match as poorly as she did.
"Her mother has written to me to inquire about Lord Tamzin."

Semsulin's head tilted to one side and his gaze became abstracted
as he considered the prospect. "The king's daughter is illegitimate,"
he mused. "And her mother was the late abbess of Aaltah."

Even when she'd been a princess with no thought of ruling,
Ellin had had a passing familiarity with all the royal houses. She
knew the story of King Aaltyn and his unfortunate first wife, and in
some abstract way, she'd known it was the former queen who was
responsible for the Curse. However, having not had sufficient time
to think about the proposal, she had not yet seen that very obvious
connection.

Lady Alysoon's daughter was a direct descendant of the most
reviled woman in the history of Seven Wells. That might make her
nearly unmarriageable. If she weren't also the granddaughter of a
king with a commensurate dowry.

"So you think Lord Tamzin will not be open to the possibility?"

Semsulin snorted in amusement. "I'd say it depends on her dowry. I suspect there are many flaws he would happily overlook for the right price."

She wrinkled her nose in distaste. She would never allow a daughter of hers to marry a man like Tamzin, and she had not failed to notice that Lady Alysoon had inquired not just about Tamzin's availability but also about his character. Ellin hoped that meant young Jinnell Rah-Sylnin was not for sale to the highest bidder.

Ellin allowed herself a small smile of amusement as she realized she'd just thought of a girl only three years her junior as "young." This past year—starting with her planned marriage to Zarsha of Nandel and ending with her taking the throne—had aged her what felt like a decade.

"And would such a match be to the benefit of Rhozinolm?" she asked. "Marriage to a king's granddaughter might blunt some of Tamzin's appetite for rebellion."

Lord Semsulin smiled at her, which was rather disconcerting considering how rarely he wore that particular expression. "I've been on your council long enough to have taken your measure by now. I feel certain you've already answered your own question."

She returned his smile. When she'd first taken the throne, he'd presumed complete naïveté on her part, and it had annoyed her. It seemed he was beginning to see her in a different light, which was heartening when her other most powerful councilors continued to regard her as a weak female with no experience and only borrowed authority.

"Maybe I should point Lady Alysoon toward Zarsha," she said. Not only was Zarsha the kind of good and charming man who would make most girls swoon, a tempting prospect such as Jinnell Rah-Sylnin might finally cause Zarsha to give up his vain pursuit of Ellin. She couldn't help thinking that his appointment as "special envoy" had more to do with his hopes of winning her hand—as impossible as such a prospect seemed—than truly serving as an envoy.

Two months into her reign, Ellin had finally come to accept that her initial dislike of Zarsha had been entirely unfounded. He'd been the wedge that separated her from Graesan, and she'd almost reflexively hated him for it. Now that she saw him with much clearer eyes, she believed that he was at heart a good man and would make a good husband for the right girl.

"If the lady is willing to consider sending her daughter to Nandel, then I'm sure she has already contacted him. But in truth we have a much more important marriage we must discuss."

Ellin heaved a sigh, knowing full well whose marriage Semsulin found so vital. "It's only been two months since nearly my entire family died. You can't seriously expect me to entertain marriage proposals so soon."

"Of course I can. You don't have to *accept* any marriage proposals, but you do have to entertain them."

"I'm in mourning!" she snapped, as if he hadn't heard her the first time.

He gave her a stern look that would have done her father proud. "Not so much in mourning that you haven't insisted on a coronation ceremony."

"It is traditional to crown the new king within his first six months on the throne," she said archly, but this was treading the same ground as all her previous "discussions" about the coronation with Semsulin. He had warned her that insisting on a coronation would anger her opponents, but she was adamant that she not be treated as a temporary ruler. If she were a king, she would be crowned despite the mourning, and she saw no reason that the same rule should not apply to her as queen.

"If you're willing to violate your mourning for a coronation, then you should be willing to do so for the vital business of determining the identity of our next king."

For all the respect she felt she had earned from Semsulin, even he habitually treated her as a temporary ruler. Which, of course, she was, but that didn't mean she had to act like it. "I will begin considering my prospects as soon as I'm crowned and not a day before."

The thought of reviewing her marriage prospects was enough to make her sick to her stomach. She had once entertained some hope that taking Graesan to her bed would help her get him out of her system, that once she'd experienced the mysteries propriety had so long denied them, she would be satisfied and ready to face reality.

Once again, she had proven herself embarrassingly naïve. With Star's help, she now spent as many nights as she could with Graesan, and far from becoming sated, she found her need for him seemed to grow stronger with each passing day. To look for a husband was to acknowledge that one day, she would have to give him up and break both their hearts.

Semsulin continued to give her that sternly paternal stare. "Since the decision about the coronation, I've heard the first stirrings of a disturbing rumor."

She watched him warily. "What rumor?"

"There are those who speculate that you have insisted on being crowned and have not yet begun considering potential marriages because you have no intention of ceding the throne."

"Don't be ridiculous." She forced herself to hold his gaze and not squirm. He would not find the *true* reason she was avoiding talk of marriage any more palatable.

"How is it ridiculous for me to point out a rumor that has started?"

"It's a ridiculous rumor. One that I'm surprised you've chosen to dignify by bringing it to me. I've made it very clear why I want to be crowned and why I won't discuss marriage yet. No one with any sense would interpret that to mean I'm planning to hold the throne."

Semsulin folded his arms and leaned back in his chair, the very picture of skepticism. "Even if the rumor were as ridiculous as you claim, you have to see how happily your enemies will pounce on it and spread it."

Unfortunately, he was right. Semsulin and the council had hoped that by putting Ellin on the throne, they could deprive both Tamzin and Kailindar of anything resembling a rallying cry for war. If one or both of them could convince the council that she planned to keep the throne for herself, that might be the very cause they needed to raise a rebellion. The rich and powerful men of Rhozinolm had always considered women the lesser sex, and that impression had not been improved by the unleashing of the Curse. The loss of life from the earthquake had been tragic—there had been casualties near every Well, though nowhere as devastating as in Aalwell—but the effects were continuing to be seen as marriage arrangements now had to take into account the bride's willingness to provide an heir. And there had been more divorces over the past two months than there had been over the previous two years.

Semsulin pressed his advantage. "If you want your throne to be secure, you must at least give the restive nobles a reason to believe you are working toward a marriage."

She furrowed her brow at his choice of words. "'A reason to believe'?"

"That's all you need to quiet the rumors right now. It stands to reason that Lord Tamzin is behind them and that your refusal to discuss marriage arrangements creates the fertile soil he needs in which to make those rumors grow. You need to salt the fields so that the rumors can't take root."

Was she imagining things, or was Semsulin suggesting she feign interest in a marriage for the sole purpose of quelling the rumor? "Out of curiosity, do you yourself lend any credence to the rumor?"

"I'm certainly not helping to spread it, if that's what you're asking."

"It's not, and you know it."

Semsulin thought for a long moment before speaking. "If I may be frank with you?" Ellin nodded and made an impatient gesture for him to continue. "I don't care who sits on the throne. My only concern is the well-being of our kingdom, and I will stand by anyone who can rule justly and keep us out of needless wars. So whether I believe the rumor or not is irrelevant."

Semsulin continued to reveal depths Ellin never would have

guessed. She'd have expected him to have an apoplexy at the very thought that she might not cede the throne, and here he was hinting he'd continue to support her for as long as she could successfully rule. Though perhaps the claim was meant merely to placate her, for he'd made it fairly obvious he did not believe she could successfully rule. At least not for long.

And if she didn't find a way to quiet Tamzin's opposition, he might be right. If Tamzin was going to oppose her in council meetings over something so trivial as whether Zarsha should remain a guest in the palace—and worse, continue to build support for such arguments from the lord high treasurer and the lord commander—then he might very well pull the throne out from under her. With the support of the royal treasury and the entire military, he could quell any rebellion from Kailindar before it got started.

So, what was the best way to stop Tamzin from laying the groundwork for an attempt to seize the throne?

A smile curved her lips as the solution presented itself. "I'm going to guess that you are at least as good at planting rumors as Lord Tamzin."

Semsulin cocked his head, and a line formed between his brows. It was gratifying to see his confusion, to see him try to figure out where she was heading and not succeed. Their minds often seemed to travel remarkably similar roads, but she suspected that this once, they had finally diverged.

"I may have some small skill, I must admit," Semsulin said.

"What would you think about planting the rumor that I'm investigating the precedent for marriage between first cousins?"

Semsulin's eyes went wide, and then he laughed. She'd have been insulted if the look of wonder and admiration on his face didn't tell her he was laughing *with* her, not *at* her.

"Do you think Tamzin might find himself with the proper incentive to be more cooperative?" she asked.

If Tamzin had any insight whatsoever, he would never fall for what was truly a ridiculous rumor. If there was a man in Seven Wells she was less likely to marry than him, she didn't know of him. But if Tamzin saw her as his easiest path to the throne, and if he thought she would allow him to become king without him ever having to suffer through the uncertainties of a war, then his ambition might well win out over his common sense.

Semsulin was still laughing. "And here I thought *I* was the one with a devious mind. I will begin rumormongering at once."

It was a temporary solution at best. Eventually, she would have to begin the search for a husband in earnest, and when that time came, it would shatter any illusions she'd managed to foster in Lord Tamzin's mind. But a temporary solution was better than no solution at all, and perhaps time would present her with better opportunities to quell the opposition.

CHAPTER TWENTY-THREE

Chanlix hiked up the skirts of her robe and stepped delicately into the crystal clear water that had no place in the middle of the desert. The cold sent an icy shock up her legs, but it was a lovely relief from the blistering heat of the noonday sun. The vegetation that had sprouted all around the water had not grown high enough to provide any shade, but Chanlix imagined that by this time the following year, the spring would be beautifully lush and provide ample shelter.

Under the soles of her feet, she felt the faintest vibration—the hum of the Well that lay at the depths of the spring. Like the one in Aalwell, this Well manifested as a deep fissure in the earth, seemingly bottomless, and the hum that emanated from its depths became more prominent the closer one came. But neither Aaltah's Well nor any of the other Wells around which the kingdoms and principalities were built also provided water. It seemed this Well provided the trappings of life itself, and though Chanlix knew the water had no magical properties—besides a high concentration of minerals that made it a more effective spell vessel than ordinary water—she found herself taking many a stolen moment to dip her feet in it. The cold and the hum of power were thrilling and calming in equal measure.

Chanlix turned at the sound of footsteps behind her and felt another little thrill when she caught sight of Tynthanal approaching. She hurried to get out of the water then lowered her robes, her cheeks heating in embarrassment at having been caught in so undignified a state.

Tynthanal grinned at her and shook his head as she stuck her feet haphazardly into her shoes. Then he plunked down on the damp earth and pulled off his own boots, revealing a pair of strong, work-calloused feet. Still grinning, he stood and strode into the water, his breath hissing in on a gasp as the cold bit into his flesh. Then he wiggled his toes and groaned in what sounded like ecstasy.

"Come join me," he beckoned. "That way I won't have to feel guilty for interrupting you."

She shook her head. "I should get back to work." As they continued to build and improve their little settlement, there was always more work to do, and after some initial reluctance, the men had allowed that the abigails need not confine themselves to only traditional women's work. More than one of Chanlix's women had shown an inclination to swing a hammer, though Chanlix herself was more apt to whack her own fingers than a nail.

"Join me," Tynthanal insisted. "I have something I need to talk to you about."

Chanlix hesitated. She had to admit that it was a little silly for a woman who'd spent nearly half her life as a whore to be so prudish about letting a man see her feet and ankles, but despite all her admonishments to herself, Tynthanal's good opinion meant a great deal more to her than it probably should.

She sighed and kicked her shoes back off. Tynthanal had been far from scandalized when several of her abigails eschewed their red robes for the convenience of borrowed men's breeches while they engaged in manual labor. He was no prissy nobleman, despite having once been the Crown Prince of Aaltah. Hiking up her skirts once more, she waded out to Tynthanal.

They stood together in silence for a few minutes, each quietly enjoying the fresh chill of the water and the peacefulness of the spring.

"What is it you want to talk about?" she finally asked. "Or was that just an excuse to goad me back into the water?"

He laughed. "Can't it be both?"

She tried to look stern, but the twinkle in his eye told her she had failed miserably. She had to fight the temptation to splash him, though she very much doubted such would quell his mischief. "Go on, then, and start talking." A bead of sweat trickled down her cheek, and with both hands holding her skirts, she couldn't brush it away.

"I'll start talking when you remove your wimple," he said, and she made a sound of outrage that had no effect on him whatsoever. "It's hot enough out here without wearing such a heavy head covering."

He wasn't wrong. The wimple seemed to trap the heat, and removing the sweat-soaked fabric at night was always a huge relief.

"Perhaps you can cut it down later to make a snood. That would keep your head properly covered without suffocating you. But for now, just take it off. It's only you and me, and I assure you I won't be scandalized at the sight of a woman's hair."

"Just because we're alone at this precise moment doesn't mean we will stay that way. *Anyone* could walk over here and see."

"Name me the person in this camp who you believe would faint away in shock and horror at seeing your head uncovered."

Chanlix bit her lip. Some of the older, more traditional abigails might grumble to themselves—they certainly grumbled about those who'd put aside their robes—but the discontent would not rise to the level of shock. She had never before considered taking the wimple off in public, but now that Tynthanal had mentioned the possibility, it was a powerful temptation.

The water rippled and splashed as Tynthanal closed the small distance between them and reached for her wimple. Chanlix started to jerk away, then forced herself to hold still as he carefully removed the pins that held the wimple in place. She should be telling him no in no uncertain terms—she knew him well enough by now to believe he would obey—but somehow that wasn't what she was doing.

Tynthanal pulled the wimple from her head and tossed the sodden length of fabric onto the shore beside their shoes.

"There," he said in a low murmur. "That's better, isn't it?"

Just then a faint breeze blew by, cooling the sweat that had pooled at the back of her neck. She had not felt the delicious kiss of the wind on her nape since she'd donned the red robes, a lifetime ago. "Yes, it is," she answered hoarsely, then cleared her throat and put a more respectable distance between them. It was becoming harder and harder to deny to herself that Tynthanal was flirting with her—as impossible as that was to comprehend—but she could not allow either of them to fall into temptation. No matter his near-exile, he was still a king's son, and she would not have been a fit companion for him even before she'd become an abigail.

"Now my wimple is off, and you may start talking," she said briskly. He cocked his head at her, and she knew he was debating whether to continue pressing. She was not sure if she was more relieved or disappointed when he chose to allow her to divert him.

"We had visitors this morning," he said.

"Yes. I noticed." A trio of riders had ridden into the encampment and met with Tynthanal and his second-in-command. The visit had struck her as curious, and perhaps just a little concerning. "What did they want?"

"They came from Miller's Bridge."

Chanlix remembered the little town that had been the last settlement they'd passed through on their journey to the new Abbey.

"Are they hoping to send some more women out to us?" she asked, though she frowned at her own question. The Abbey was meant only for noblewomen, though the occasional wealthy merchant's wife or daughter found herself banished there. Miller's

Bridge was on the edge of nowhere, hardly the sort of place where nobles or high-class merchants resided. "Or were they hoping the Abbey was open for business?"

Chanlix couldn't imagine the men of Miller's Bridge would be so desperate for paid sex that they would ride half a day out to a rough settlement in the desert to spend their hard-earned wages.

"Neither," Tynthanal said with a delighted grin. "As you know, I sent some of my men to the town to replenish our supplies, and they mentioned that we had found a Well that produces feminine elements. The mayor of Miller's Bridge is hoping we can come to an agreement to trade potions for additional supplies and man-power. With the help of experienced frontier builders, we can put up actual houses instead of one-room cabins and lean-tos, and we can eventually retire our little tent village altogether. And with our potions, Miller's Bridge can finally grow enough of their own food to not be so dependent on imported supplies."

Chanlix bit her lip, for it certainly sounded like an advantageous arrangement for both sides. The elements were so abundant at this Well—and the water so mineral rich—that a single abigail could produce dozens of vials of simple growth potions in a day. But it would be a most unorthodox arrangement, and the Abbey would not have the kind of taxable revenue the trade minister would ex-pect from them. Assuming he expected them to generate any reve-nue at all out here where there was supposed to be nothing.

"What did you tell him?" she asked.

"I told him I would discuss it with you and we would give him an answer within a week."

She gave him a startled look, though perhaps she should not have been surprised. He was as unlike his half-brother as it was pos-sible to be, and it would never have occurred to him to impose his own will on the women of the Abbey without consulting their ab-bess. Regardless of the harsh reality that she had no official power to make any such decision.

"I see no reason why any of us should live in shared tents and makeshift cabins when we can so easily make arrangements for bet-ter accommodations," he said. "Not when it will cost us so little."

Chanlix curled her toes into the sandy bottom of the spring. "I don't imagine the king sent us out here with the idea that we should live in comfort and ease."

Tynthanal snorted. "He can hardly expect us to ignore the resources available to us, no matter how unexpected they might be."

The king himself was not Chanlix's true concern, as Tynthanal clearly knew. Her most immediate concern was the trade minister, who would certainly object to anything he perceived as lost revenue. The Abbey's potions were meant to be sold, not bartered.

"Just how many growth potions can you be expected to sell?" Tynthanal asked. "Surely nothing close to the number you can produce with our resources. You could produce enough to fuel every farm and garden in Seven Wells and still have crates full of the stuff—to the point that it would have very little monetary value. If the trade minister should learn that you've bartered potions and objects, I will happily pay the taxes for you. It isn't as if I have much other use for my money out here."

"*If* the trade minister learns?"

Tynthanal shrugged. "I see no reason why my reports should contain information about the day-to-day running of the Abbey. And it seems unlikely the trade minister would be overly interested in the workings of a frontier town like Miller's Bridge. How would he know about a few bartered potions, unless you chose to report them yourself?"

Chanlix shifted uncomfortably, for while she could hardly argue Tynthanal's logic, she could not but think it was a dangerous game.

"If you would like me to pay your taxes on those potions, I will do it," Tynthanal said. "The labor and supplies will benefit me and my men as much as it will benefit you and your abigails. But it seems to me in all of our best interests to downplay the importance of this Well for as long as we can. We can build of our exile an advantage, and the more established we become, the harder we will be to dislodge if and when the Crown should want to do so. But I will leave the final decision to you."

Chanlix took in a deep breath and let it out slowly. The king had sent her and her abigails to this new Abbey with the express command that they undo Mother Brynna's spell, which she doubted anyone believed they could accomplish. Eventually, they would be punished for their failure—unless they had somehow made themselves vital to Aaltah's needs, which would take time.

"I'll make the potions myself," she said. "If this decision causes us trouble, it will be entirely on my head."

"No, it will not," Tynthanal said softly, then splashed his way loudly out of the spring so that he might pretend not to hear her response.

Alys was shocked at how wan and pale Shelvon looked. Her face was never exactly lively or full of color, but now her skin had an almost translucent hue, and there were dark circles like bruises under her eyes. Alys's heart ached for the young woman even as she struggled with her own fear of what it meant. Certainly it did not appear that Shelvon was suddenly flourishing in her marriage to Delnamal, with a happy announcement soon on the way.

Hiding her own distress as best she could, Alys smiled at her sister-in-law, clasping her hands and kissing her on both cheeks. Shelvon's hands were shockingly cold, although the Rose Room was comfortably warm.

As the two women sat by the fire, Alys decided not to pretend she couldn't see the decline in Shelvon's health. "Are you well?" she asked with a worried frown.

Shelvon smiled tremulously. "My husband has been combing the city to find fertility potions that were left behind when the Abbey was moved. There aren't very many to be found, but he's been quite resourceful. Unfortunately, they keep me up at night." Her eyelids drooped. "I can't remember the last time I had a full night's sleep."

Alys wasn't surprised to hear it. Every fertility spell she had learned from her mother's book included the element Shel, which was usually associated with energy and stamina. There being no official study of feminine elements and women's magic, no one had quite figured out why Shel was necessary, but from what Alys had read, the potions were useless without it. It was not at all uncommon for a woman taking fertility potions to have trouble sleeping. Which was usually not a problem, since the potions were fast-acting and effective under ordinary circumstances. Women rarely required more than two or three doses, and if they *did* require more, they either couldn't conceive at all or couldn't carry the infant to term.

"How many have you taken?" Alys asked gently, but she knew it was more than two or three.

"Enough that I *should* be pregnant by now." Shelvon touched her belly. "Of course without an abigail here to examine me, there's no way to know for sure whether I am or not."

Alys didn't think there was much uncertainty in the matter at all. Surely her mother's spell—a spell that shook the whole world, created a new Well, and changed the appearance of Rho itself—could not be circumvented by a potion any novice abigail could create.

Shelvon forced a smile and pointedly changed the subject. "How goes the search for a husband for Jinnell?"

Alys's shoulders drooped. "It seems I underestimated the effect my mother's spell would have on Jinnell's prospects."

Shelvon winced in sympathy. "I had hoped that would not be the case."

"I've received several very polite letters that simply said that marriage negotiations were already underway when I know for certain it's not true. And quite a number of people have failed to respond at all. Perhaps they're hoping I will think a flier got lost in transit and therefore not be insulted."

"What about Lord Tamzin?"

"I received a letter from Queen Ellinsoltah," Alys said. That had been a very different sort of letter, nowhere near as impersonal as the other responses she had received. Alys had immediately liked the other woman, even though her response had not been in the affirmative. "She said she did not believe my daughter and Lord Tamzin were compatible."

In fact, she had said a great deal more than that, but most of it was private. The queen was not rejecting Jinnell and seemed to bear no ill will toward her or Alys despite the devastating effect the spell had had on her family. What she had told Alys in strictest confidence was that Tamzin did not live up to his stellar reputation. The picture she had painted of the man as an ambitious, mean-spirited conniver had certainly not meshed with his public image. Alys had no good reason to trust the word of a woman she had never met, but she was inclined to do it anyway. Not that the explanation mattered near as much as the refusal itself.

"Perhaps I needn't worry about Delnamal sending her to Prince Waldmir," she said with a wry smile. "Perhaps he, too, will disdain her for her parentage."

It seemed an odd thing to hope, but then in Alys's opinion, there were worse fates in life than being unmarried, and being married to Prince Waldmir was one of them.

"I wouldn't count on it," Shelvon said. "Jinnell is young and lovely and has an attractive dowry. As you may have noticed, my father considers marriage a temporary inconvenience. Even if he thinks her the granddaughter of a witch, he would likely be happy to have her until he tires of her or she becomes inconvenient."

"But he needs an heir, doesn't he? And thanks to my mother's spell, he needs a willing wife to provide him with one. Surely despite his reputation, he could find a woman who would happily provide him an heir for the prestige of being his wife." Not that Alys could understand the type of woman who would sell herself in marriage like that. What good were social standing and money when your husband treated you like cattle and could destroy your life—even have you executed—on a whim? And yet she knew they were out there.

Shelvon shook her head. "You've never met my father. He has always believed himself a prize catch. My mother once told me she cried all the way to the altar and begged him to release her from the contract. And the whole time he smiled at her and assured her that she was the luckiest woman in all of Seven Wells." Shelvon's expression was usually so kind and mild that the fierceness that flashed in her eyes took Alys by surprise. "When she tried to poison him, he was genuinely shocked that she was that desperate to escape the marriage. He has no concept of what other people—especially women—think of him."

Alys wondered if Prince Waldmir had any idea how much his usually calm and placid daughter hated him. The look in Shelvon's eyes said just how sorry she was that her mother's assassination attempt had failed.

For all the troubles Alys had had with her own father after the divorce, it was nothing compared to what Shelvon must have gone through. How could a woman bear to even *look* at her father when he'd had her mother put to death? It was a strange irony that because her father had executed her mother rather than divorcing her, Shelvon was his only legitimate child. And it was because none of his wives had given him sons that he kept discarding them.

"So if my father offers him Jinnell," Alys said, "he will convince himself that she will provide him with children no matter how obvious it is to everyone else that she will do no such thing?"

Shelvon nodded. "I'm sure of it. Sometimes I think he believes he could tell the sun to stop shining and it would obey. You *have* to find another husband for Jinnell, just in case the potions fail." She rubbed her belly once more, as if force of will could make it swell with child. "What about Zarsha of Nandel? Have you had an answer from him?"

"I haven't contacted him yet," she admitted. "I left him as something of a last resort. Jinnell understands the gravity of the situation, but she does not want to go to Nandel."

Shelvon blinked at her as if she'd said something completely baffling. "You've discussed this with Jinnell?"

"Yes, of course. Why do you look so shocked?"

"Is that considered . . . normal here?"

Alys was fully aware that customs in Nandel were very different from those of Aaltah, and that women had even fewer choices there. She had not realized, however, that a girl expressing a preference for her marriage would somehow seem outside of normal.

"Well, the parents have the final say, of course," she said, "but it's certainly not out of the ordinary to at least ask our daughters what they want."

Shelvon looked awed by this information. "I've been here more than a year, and I still find myself occasionally surprised by things I didn't know. I was told that I was to marry Delnamal after the contract had been signed and arrangements for my travel had already been made. I don't even know if there were any other suitors."

Alys shuddered at the thought. Women had so little control of their own lives here in Aaltah, it was hard to credit that they had even less elsewhere in the world. "And there's a very good reason not to send Jinnell to Nandel."

"But marriage to Zarsha would be highly preferable to marriage to my father. You should at least contact him and see if he's interested. Maybe arrange to meet him to see for yourself if he's the kind of man you want for your daughter."

Alys had the sinking feeling she was running out of options.

CHAPTER TWENTY-FOUR

The temperature had plummeted overnight, and though Ellin longed for the calming solitude of a long walk through the gardens, she settled for a much more constrained—and comfortable—walk through the solarium instead. The sun beaming through the glass walls had warmed the room to a temperature both plants and people found pleasing, and there was a certain enjoyment in looking at the ice-frosted trees outside while being comfortably warm.

Solitude was a rare luxury for Ellin now that she was queen. She hadn't realized how much she'd missed it until she'd stolen that first walk in the garden; now she insisted on carving out at least thirty minutes each day to being both awake and alone. As her secretary, Graesan found her insistence on this quiet time inconvenient, but despite his grumbling, he always seemed to find time in her day for everything that needed doing.

By now, all the advisers and aides and servants of the palace were clear that she was not to be disturbed during her quiet time for anything less than a dire emergency. Unfortunately, Zarsha of Nandel was neither official adviser, aide, nor servant, and as she finished her first circuit around the solarium, she found him standing in the entryway, flanked by two members of her honor guard who had evidently refused to let him in.

Zarsha bowed elegantly. "Forgive my interruption, Your Majesty," he said as he rose, "but I was wondering if I could have a moment of your time."

Ellin suppressed a groan. She wanted to protect this little block of solitude she'd carved out for herself, but if Zarsha wished to speak to her, he no doubt had something important to discuss.

"It's nothing urgent," he assured her, "but your secretary seems to think you will not have time for me until at least next week, so I thought I'd ask."

Ellin sighed. The one person at court who seemed completely impervious to Zarsha's charm was Graesan, and she suspected he'd have trouble fitting her former intended into a day when she had no appointments whatsoever. While she had long ago stopped blaming Zarsha for the forced engagement, the same could not be said of Graesan.

"We can talk now," she said, "as long as you don't mind walking. I spend far too much of my day sitting still."

Zarsha smiled and gave her another half bow. "Of course. Shall we?"

He gallantly offered his elbow, for all the world like they were courting again. If you could call what they'd once had courtship. Ellin hesitated just a second—long enough for Zarsha to notice, but not long enough to be insulting—before slipping her hand into the crook of his elbow. Graesan would find the contact overfamiliar, though it was well within the bounds of court etiquette.

They strolled in silence, surprisingly companionable, until they were out of earshot of the guards who had resumed their posts outside the doorway.

"I've heard a very interesting rumor," Zarsha said with a hint of a smile on his face.

She gave him her most innocent look. "What rumor might that be?"

"That you've been looking for a precedent for royal marriages between first cousins."

She laughed and shook her head. Semsulin was a fast worker. She'd have thought it would take at least a week for him to plant the seeds of that rumor and at least two for the seeds to take root. "Where did you hear that?"

"Uncovering rumors and secrets is what I do best."

"You sound like a spy," she teased, and though Zarsha smiled at the joke, she could have sworn she felt a faint tensing of his muscles, which quickly relaxed. Had her joke perhaps hit a little close to home? Zarsha was Nandel royalty, but he seemed to spend very little time in his homeland. By all rights, he should have returned home after their engagement fell through, and yet here he still was.

"Is it true?" he asked. "Are you entertaining thoughts of marrying Lord Tamzin?"

"And now you sound jealous."

"That's not jealousy. That's fear for your safety—and your sanity."

"You being the avowed expert in court intrigue, why don't *you* tell *me* if the rumor is true or not?"

He stopped walking, and she took that opportunity to withdraw her hand and turn to face him. He peered into her face, blue eyes seeming to pierce through her skin and see everything that lay beneath. There was something so knowing in his gaze that she was tempted to look away, but she was not a coward.

After a long moment in which her pulse sped up with anxiety, Zarsha's face relaxed into his more customary expression of genial humor.

"We'll make a queen of you yet," he said with a rakish grin.

She glared at him, remembering why his humor had always rubbed her the wrong way. "I *am* a queen. I don't need you or anyone else to *make* me one."

He sobered and bowed his head. "Forgive me. That did not

come out how I intended." He met her gaze once more. "You are every inch a queen, and you have given everyone who expected you to fail a rude surprise. I suppose what I meant is that you are gaining skill as a courtier. When you first took the throne, you were honest and forthright to a fault. You've learned a great deal of subtlety since then."

Ellin would have liked to stay offended. Zarsha's praise was even more uncomfortable than his perceived insult. She would never have imagined that one day she would earn praise for being deceitful.

"Does that mean you don't believe the rumor?"

"It means I believe you're behind the rumor and therefore also behind Lord Tamzin's suddenly more positive opinion of you. I also believe you would sooner marry a venomous snake."

She couldn't help smiling at the image. "That sounds about right, though I hope Lord Tamzin and his followers won't see through me that easily."

"They won't," Zarsha assured her. "To be a good observer and to see through subterfuge requires an ability to understand other people, which requires one to actually *care* about other people enough to understand them. That is something Lord Tamzin is incapable of doing."

"And yet with few exceptions, you and I are the only ones who seem to see that about him."

"People see what they want to see. He is rich and handsome and powerful, and he is the grandson of a king. The perfect storybook hero. People need little encouragement to assign him that role."

She had to agree with this assessment. And it was clear Tamzin would be a problem for the entirety of her reign—and very likely the reign of her future husband, should she choose to marry after all.

Zarsha's voice dropped to little more than an unnecessary whisper. "There may come a time when to protect your throne, it will be necessary for Lord Tamzin to suffer an unfortunate accident."

She shivered and clutched her shawl tighter around her shoulders despite the warmth of the sun through the windows. She could not deny that the thought had occurred to her. It had probably occurred to Semsulin as well, though unlike Zarsha, he had the tact not to mention it out loud.

"But we are not there yet," Zarsha said, as if that could somehow erase the ugliness of his words. "For as long as you can keep him hoping he can take the throne without resistance or bloodshed, he will be at least marginally cooperative, although I don't believe he will stop altogether in his efforts to undermine you."

"No," she agreed. "The weaker my grip on the throne appears, the greater the need for me to name a husband and set a wedding date. Preferably on the day my mourning ends."

"There is a solution to all of your problems," Zarsha said, and something about the tone of his voice warned her she would not like this solution. "You could marry me."

She made a sound of exasperation and rolled her eyes. "We've been through this before."

"But let's examine it again," he pressed. "If you marry me, you would not only ensure the renewal of the trade agreements, but also gain a significant amount of military support. What do you think Prince Waldmir would give to have his brother's grandson on the throne of Rhozinolm?"

She glared at him. "If you think I'm handing over my throne to you—"

"I said *grand*son, Ellin. *Our* son. Your council will not be able to resist that kind of military alliance with Nandel as long as they don't have to put a Nandel-born man on the throne. And they would know that with the strength of Nandel behind you, neither Tamzin nor Kailindar could raise sufficient forces for an effective rebellion."

She shook her head. "How many times do we have to have this conversation? I'm not marrying you."

"Why?"

She opened her mouth to answer, but no sound came out. Because she had no good answer to that question. In the beginning, it had been because she thought she despised him, but now she knew better. She also had never taken seriously the possibility of staying on the throne. As long as her husband would be king, she had an easy excuse to turn Zarsha down as many times as he asked. But now keeping the throne no longer seemed as ridiculous an idea as it once had, especially with Semsulin's sly hints that he would support her if he thought she was good for the kingdom . . .

There was no good reason to reject him any longer, at least not without careful consideration.

"Is it because of that secretary of yours?"

The question took her so much by surprise that she couldn't even begin to formulate an answer. Nor could she stop the flush of color she felt rising up her neck and into her cheeks. Despite their clandestine meetings and the promotion she'd given him, she'd been sure she and Graesan had been entirely discreet in their relationship.

"Don't worry," Zarsha said. "As far as I can tell, no one else suspects. And believe me, if anyone suspected, I would know about it—as would every one of your courtiers."

Her stomach gave a sick lurch, and she cursed herself for not having prepared for such an accusation, no matter how unlikely she'd thought discovery to be. She could deny any impropriety with all the earnest sincerity in the world, but after her initial shocked reaction, Zarsha would never believe a denial.

"Is that a threat?" she asked in a voice raspy with incipient tears.

"No!" Zarsha said with enough vehemence that she believed him. "Why are you always so ready to think ill of me?"

Ellin might have felt more chastened if her mind weren't still reeling with the realization of how disastrous Zarsha's observation could be. "When I first met you, you were fully prepared to force me into a marriage you knew I did not want. Now you are once again in a position to force my hand, and you wonder at my suspicion?"

He sighed and ran a hand through his hair in evident frustration. "Do you imagine my uncle solicited my opinion when he decided a match with you would be beneficial to our principality? Because if so, you have no understanding of the mechanics of royal marriages at all."

It was ridiculous, but Ellin felt stung. "You didn't want to marry me?"

"Not once I knew you didn't want me. My uncle's last two brides openly wept at the altar, with good reason. That is not what I want for my bride, and not what I want for myself. I was given no more choice in the matter than you were, and I have no intention of blackmailing you into accepting my offer now."

He reached out and took both her freezing cold hands in his. She'd have pulled away from the overly familiar touch if she hadn't been seduced by his delicious warmth. He squeezed her hands and peered earnestly into her eyes.

"I did not bring up your secretary to blackmail you. I brought him up because I want you to know that I know about him and want to marry you anyway. I'm genuinely fond of you, I hope you know that, but our marriage would still be a business arrangement rather than a love match. I would not insist you give up your lover, as long as you continued to be entirely discreet—and as long as you are willing to bear my children instead of his."

For no reason she could name, tears sprang suddenly to her eyes, and her throat became so thick she could not speak.

Zarsha's offer was too good to be true. She knew that. Once they were married, he would never truly agree to share her with another man. She might be naïve, but she was not so naïve as to believe that. And could she honestly be sure she would bear children with Zarsha? She was well aware of the story of Princess Shelvon, who had many very logical reasons why she would wish to give her husband an heir, and yet had not become pregnant since the earthquake. Everyone kept saying it was a matter of time, that it had only been a couple of months, but Ellin had read the late abbess's letter. There was a subtlety to the woman's magic that Ellin suspected many others had so far failed to fully comprehend.

And even if all these other objections could be resolved, Graesan deserved better.

She was possibly the most selfish woman in all of Rhozinolm, holding on to a man she could never marry. The only truly decent thing to do was to set him free. If she weren't still stringing him along, surely Graesan could get on with his life, find a good woman who could make him happy and give him children. And who could love him openly and without shame.

"Just think about it," Zarsha urged. "Marrying me can solve a great many of your problems all at once." He flashed her a self-deprecating smile. "I may not be the man you want, but I do hope I've proven to have one or two redeeming qualities."

Ellin tried on a tremulous smile, though she still felt as if she could burst into tears at the slightest provocation. "I suppose I must concede that." She took a deep breath and let it out slowly, and the tears receded far enough into the background that she could steady her voice and her smile. "I promise I will think about it."

"That's all I ask."

CHAPTER TWENTY-FIVE

Alys carefully pulled the stable door open, wincing as the hinges creaked. She didn't think the sound would carry all the way to the servants' quarters that adjoined the back of the stables, but she herself was aware of even the smallest sound. The chirp of a cricket, the swaying of branches in the wind, the call of an owl . . . Each sound set her heart racing, her mind scrambling to call up the lie she had created to explain why she was creeping around the grounds of her own manor house at this hour of the night.

It was nearly pitch-dark in the stables, though a little moonlight filtered in from the high windows. Alys slipped inside and closed the door, then stood still and waited for her eyes to adjust. Her pulse hammered in her ears, but it was only in part because of her fear of getting caught. If she were being completely honest with herself, she had to admit there was a high level of excitement mixed in with those nerves.

For weeks after her disastrous attempt to work the first spell in her mother's book, she had followed the instructions to a tee, double- and even triple-checking each element to make sure she was using the correct ones. It hadn't taken long for her to realize she could see elements that were not included in her mother's book, and a quick, stolen glance at Corlin's primer had confirmed her suspicion that most of them were masculine elements.

Although her mother had anticipated that she might be able to see some masculine elements, there seemed to be no lessons in the book about how to work with them. Certainly there was nothing about combining masculine and feminine elements into the same spell, and Alys hadn't been able to resist seeing what would happen if she did. It was perhaps foolhardy to attempt to craft her own spells—especially in such an unconventional manner—when she had so much still to learn about magic, but it also seemed wasteful not to take advantage of her unique ability to see elements of all genders.

Every spell Alys had so far learned required the use of a potion as a means of delivery. Healing potions, vanity potions, love potions, even magical poisons. Potions were the cornerstone of women's magic. One of the masculine elements Alys could see was Tyn, which was used in a great deal of men's magic to create spells that could affect a human body without the need of ingesting a potion. It was Alys's theory that adding Tyn to some of the potion spells might make them take effect via touch rather than ingestion. And tonight she planned to put that theory to the test.

When her eyes had adjusted as much as they were going to, Alys crept forward across the stable floor. The dozing horses had all awoken at her entry, but aside from a little shuffling and shifting, they remained gratifyingly quiet as she crossed to Smoke's stall. The gray stallion looked at her with listless eyes, and she struggled against a surge of guilt that she would risk the poor creature's life to test her spell-crafting abilities. However, if he were to expire mysteriously during the night, she doubted anyone would be too surprised or think there was anything odd about it. Smoke had aged about ten years in the less than two years since Sylnin's death, and it was perhaps surprising he had survived as long as he had.

Alys stroked the horse's muzzle and took a deep breath. There was no reason to think her spell would kill the horse. It was a modified version of a women's sleeping potion, and while a sleeping potion made with too high a concentration of the feminine element Von could be deadly—a poison that would put its victim *permanently* to sleep—she would begin her experiment with only the three motes used for a mild potion and build up from there. If the spell worked at all, Smoke should fall asleep long before the concentration of Von became deadly.

Reaching into the small sack she had brought with her, she drew out the ring that contained what she hoped was a touch-triggered sleep spell as well as a pair of tongs she'd liberated from the kitchen. Holding the ring with the tongs so its spell wouldn't affect her when it was activated, she opened her Mindseye and added the Rho she needed to complete the spell. Then she touched the ring to Smoke's neck. She had to close her Mindseye to see what had happened and was disappointed to see the horse still blinking placidly.

So began an increasingly disappointing cycle. Open her Mindseye, add another mote of Von to intensify the spell, close her Mindseye, and see the horse still wide awake. She almost gave up when she reached a total of ten motes of Von, because that was the level at which sleep potions turned to poison. But she reasoned with herself that it would take more motes to affect a horse than a person, so with another apology to Smoke, she continued trying.

When she fed in the fifteenth mote of Von, she opened her Mindseye to see Smoke's eyelids drooping. With a sigh, he sagged downward until his belly hit the stable floor. His eyes closed. She opened the stall door to check on him, putting a hand to his ribs to feel the steady thump of his heart and the gentle movement of his breaths. His skin twitched under her hand, but he did not awaken. It was all she could do not to jump up and down and let out a victory whoop.

She could imagine any number of ways a touch-triggered

sleeping spell could be useful. Some of them were completely benevolent—she remembered a time when Corlin had been sick for a week with a stomach ailment that kept him vomiting at night and thought how useful it would have been if she could have helped him sleep without him having to drink a potion that would instantly come back up. Then there were a great many other, less benevolent ways it could be used. Ways that might help should Delnamal ever manage to turn their father completely against her and her children.

She caught a glimpse of movement out of the corner of her eye and whirled in that direction. She choked on a startled yelp when she saw the shadowed figure of a man standing by the stable door. The kitchen tongs fell from her hands, releasing the ring, which bounced and rolled across the floor.

Falcor stepped forward into a shaft of moonlight. It was enough illumination to show her his identity, but not enough to let her read his facial expression. The ring came to rest near his feet, and he looked back and forth between her and the ring.

How much had he seen? And, more important, was he likely to tell anyone what he'd seen?

Falcor bent down, and Alys realized he was about to reach for the ring. Which meant he hadn't seen her put Smoke to sleep with a touch. The horse seemed unharmed, but she had no way of knowing what a sleep spell built with fifteen motes of Von might do to a man.

She had a split second to make a decision. It would be safest for her and her family to let Falcor touch the ring. There would certainly be a lot of questions asked if he were to be found dead in the stables when the stable hands rose in the morning, but those questions were unlikely to lead anyone to her.

"Don't touch that!" she said when he reached for the ring. She took two hasty steps forward, holding out her hands in a warning gesture.

She wasn't entirely sure if she was more relieved or terrified when he rocked back on his heels and drew his hand away, staring up at her in silence. The shadows on his face still masked his expression, and she had no idea what he was thinking or feeling.

What she *did* know was that there was no innocent, logical explanation for her behavior. Except for the truth. She had already ruined her best chance to keep the truth hidden when she had stopped Falcor from touching the ring. She swallowed hard and prayed she wasn't making the wrong decision and condemning her entire family, but she believed Falcor was a good man. He might vehemently disapprove of what she'd been doing, but she didn't believe he would betray her.

Her knees felt wobbly as she squatted by the ring and opened her Mindseye. She heard Falcor's harsh intake of breath and tried to ignore it as she plucked the motes of Rho out of the ring, rendering its spell inactive once more. Then she closed her Mindseye and picked up the ring, slipping it onto her finger.

She and Falcor both rose at the same time and stood facing each other. Her heart was pounding so loudly she wondered if he could hear it.

"What would have happened if I'd touched it?" he asked softly.

She bit her lip. "I'm not entirely sure. It might have just put you to sleep." She gestured toward Smoke's stall, and saw Falcor's brows rise as he caught sight of the sleeping horse. They were moving and speaking quietly, but the noise was easily enough to awaken him under ordinary circumstances. "I'm just worried about what a spell strong enough to make a horse sleep might do to a man."

Falcor looked back and forth between her ring and the horse. "I've never seen or heard of a spell that does that before."

"No," she agreed.

He thought for a long time before he spoke again, and Alys bit her tongue and let him. She had no reason to volunteer any more information than absolutely necessary. Certainly she didn't want to face the questions he would ask if he knew the spell was of her own invention.

"You were testing it," he finally said. It wasn't quite a question, but she nodded anyway. "But a spell that puts a horse to sleep is merely an interesting parlor trick. Much more useful is one that puts a *man* to sleep. How were you planning to test that?"

She shrugged. "I haven't gotten that far yet." Which didn't

mean she hadn't thought about it. Agonized about it. Wondered whose life she could risk in the testing without herself expiring of guilt. The Academy utilized paid volunteers for its less dangerous tests and condemned criminals for the dangerous ones. She would have access to neither, since allowing a volunteer to know about her magic practice was far too risky.

"I can take care of that for you."

She stammered, momentarily at a loss for words. She hardly dared believe he would keep her secret, and yet he was offering to do far more. Well above and beyond the call of duty. "Why would you do that?" she asked, shaking her head in wonder. "Wouldn't it be far more prudent to report my transgressions to the lord commander?" She didn't need to know the details of a military contract to know Falcor was risking his entire career by keeping this knowledge to himself and would be risking far more if he actively helped her. It was not technically against the law for a woman to practice magic, and yet she doubted the law would protect her—or Falcor—if they were caught colluding in this way.

"Why did you help with the evacuation of the Harbor District rather than riding off to safety with your children?" he countered. "Surely it would have been more prudent to accompany them to the palace."

"That was different," she protested, then wondered what she was doing. It almost sounded as if she was arguing for him to turn her in.

"You did what you thought was right. Just as I did when I joined the effort instead of forcibly removing you, which was my duty."

"And you think *this* is right?" she asked with a sweeping gesture. "I doubt you'll find many men who agree."

"My duty is to protect you and your family. That cannot always be done with swords alone." He tilted his head so that the light hit it just right and she could read his grave and earnest expression. "There may come a time when you or Miss Jinnell or Master Corlin have need of a spell such as this." He looked pointedly at the still-sleeping horse. "I see no harm, and a great deal of potential benefit, in making sure you have access to such magic."

Alys let out a slow, shaky breath. She could hardly say she was comfortable with letting Falcor know her secret. For all that he'd been her master of the guard for well over a year now, she couldn't say she knew him well. But he *had* ridden out to the Harbor District with her on the night of the earthquake. If that wasn't an indicator of his basic decency—and his trustworthiness—she didn't know what was.

"Thank you," she said.

He bowed his head. "And thank *you*." She raised her eyebrows in inquiry. "For not allowing me to touch the ring while its spell was active. We both know that would have been a far more certain way to keep your secret."

She swallowed hard. "It probably wouldn't have killed you."

"Maybe not. But it would have made it very easy for you to kill me if you felt it necessary. Sleeping men make easy targets."

Alys did not want to think about what she might have done had he touched the ring and merely fallen asleep. She was very glad she didn't have to.

"Now, let's test that spell," he said.

She opened her mouth to protest, because she'd assumed he meant he would arrange for the testing of the spell, not that he would allow her to test it on himself.

"You must have a plan to lower the intensity of the spell for use on humans, right?"

"Well, yes. But it could still be dangerous even at its lowest intensity. I have no way of knowing."

"I'm a guardsman, my lady. I face some level of threat every hour of every day. I don't think a sleeping spell is that great a risk."

"All right," she finally said, resigned. In her heart, she didn't really believe the spell would harm him if she repeated the process she'd gone through with Smoke, starting with only one or two motes of Von and increasing them as necessary. "But let's wait until Smoke wakes up first. I'd like to see that there are no ill effects, and I'd like to know how long he'll sleep. It wouldn't do to test the spell and have you still sleeping when the sun rises."

He gave a soft snort of amusement. "No, it would not. And we

would be better served trying it somewhere a little more private."
He glanced at the door that led to the servants' quarters in the back
of the stables. They were probably lucky their quiet conversation
hadn't already roused someone.

"When Smoke wakes up, we'll go back to the house. We can test
the spell in my study. No one should disturb us at this time of
night."

Shelvon had lost weight since the last time Alys had met with her,
only two weeks ago. She looked so frail and ill that Alys's heart
ached for her.

"Are you still taking those fertility potions?" she asked her sister-
in-law as soon as they were alone together in the Rose Room for
what was becoming their biweekly strategy meeting. At this point
in the proceedings, Alys didn't really need any help from Shelvon in
searching for a potential match for Jinnell, but their previous discussions had given her a new appreciation for her sister-in-law, who
was clearly kind and good-hearted when she was comfortable
enough to let down her guard. Her shyness meant she had few
friends in the palace, and Alys had the distinct impression the poor
girl was painfully lonely.

Shelvon shrugged, though the effort of raising her shoulders
seemed to tire her. "I've poured out the last two Delnamal gave me.
They clearly aren't doing any good, but he keeps pushing them on
me." She managed one of her wan smiles. "I suppose I should be
flattered he's trying so hard to make it work. He could have given
up on me by now."

Alys wanted to gather the younger woman into a motherly embrace, to soothe away her fears and assure her everything would be
all right. If her detestable half-brother were actually trying to make
the marriage work, he would be showering Shelvon with love and
affection, not forcing her to drink potions that made her ill.

Shelvon shook off her melancholy—or at least its outer
trappings—and a small hint of life sparked in her eyes. For all the

unpleasant reasons behind finding a foreign match for Jinnell, Shelvon seemed to enjoy matchmaking.

"How goes the search?" Shelvon asked.

Alys frowned, hating that she had no positive news to help lift
the mood. "I've received a few more refusals, and a couple of vague
and tepid replies that indicate a willingness to entertain the possibility at some unspecified future time. I'm beginning to wonder if I
need to ask my father to increase Jinnell's dowry."

Not that she had any reason to think he would. Contributing to
the dowry at all had been an unnecessary kindness.

"Before you ask," she continued, "yes, I sent a flier to Zarsha of
Nandel, though I admit it was only last week, so it's not surprising
I have not yet received a response." Depending on wind and
weather, it could take up to two days for a flier to cross the distance
between Aalwell and Zinolm Well, where Zarsha was making his
extended visit.

Shelvon opened her mouth as if to say something, then shut it
with a snap. Looking over Alys's shoulder, she hastily scrambled to
her feet. Alys rose and whirled toward the door, knowing someone
must have come in while her back was turned.

With a shock, she saw that it was the king. She was so surprised
to see him that she was uncomfortably late giving him the necessary
curtsy. The king did not "pop in" unannounced. His schedule was
rigidly controlled, so that usually even his own children had to
make an appointment to speak with him.

"Please excuse my interruption," he said, then turned to Shelvon without awaiting a reply. Commanding them to accept his
apology, rather than asking. "I need a private word with my daughter, my dear."

Alys bit her tongue to keep herself from snapping at her father.
Rude enough that he was barging in on her conversation with Shelvon, but to then dismiss the future Queen of Aaltah as if she were
some serving girl . . .

"Of course, Your Majesty," Shelvon said, dropping into a deep
curtsy and averting her eyes. Alys had the uncharitable thought that

Shelvon was so submissive it never even occurred to her to be annoyed.

Alys crossed her arms and held her tongue as Shelvon scurried from the room and the king helped himself to her still-warm seat. Alys was sure her irritation showed plainly both in her facial expression and her body language. She hadn't expected a great deal of use to come from her meeting with Shelvon, but she would have liked more than five minutes of her sister-in-law's company.

"Please sit down, Alys," her father said when she remained on her feet, radiating displeasure. "I wouldn't have interrupted if it wasn't important."

Alys reclaimed her seat, sitting stiffly on its very edge as if perched for a quick escape. She could imagine no pleasant reason for this sudden need to speak with her. "You could have sent a summons."

"I saw no point in allowing your conversation with Shelvon to continue under the circumstances."

Alys's gut clenched in fear. Her father knew exactly why she'd been spending so much time with her sister-in-law lately. "What circumstances?" she asked, sure the blood had drained from her face.

"Don't panic," the king said, patting the air with his hand. "You should know I'm not prone to making rash decisions."

Alys could argue his assertion—if she weren't doing exactly what he'd told her not to do and panicking. "Then why don't you want me planning for my daughter's marriage?"

"She's only eighteen. There's no need to be in such a rush to find a husband for her."

Alys leaned forward in her chair and glared at her father. "She's *my* daughter. And that's *my* decision to make."

The king was unmoved by her anger. "But she's *my* granddaughter, so I'm afraid it's not. Not entirely, at least."

"You gave me permission . . ." Alys started weakly, but her voice died in her throat.

"I'm not rescinding it," he assured her in a tone that no doubt was meant to be soothing. "All I'm asking is that you slow down."

"Why?" As if she didn't know. As if the very reason he was asking her to slow down weren't the reason she had tried to rush this whole process in the first place.

"These are difficult times. I've given the Abbey very clear orders that they are to reverse your mother's spell on pain of death, but in all honesty, I'm not sure they can. Your mother was not a stupid woman, and she knew how the world would react to what she'd done. I'm sure she took every precaution to make the spell as difficult to circumvent as possible. Because of that spell, we may well need to . . . rethink certain alliances."

"In other words you intend to sell your granddaughter to the highest bidder for the sake of expediency!"

"Don't be such a child. You know how the world works, and you know what it takes to run a kingdom. I didn't educate you like a boy to have you act as if politics were some unfathomable mystery to you."

It was true that Alys both knew and understood Jinnell's potential value to the kingdom. Alys herself had escaped a marriage of purely political consideration because she'd come of age in a time of relative prosperity. Her father had solicited her opinion of her potential husbands only because he had no pressing need for a pawn. Now with the uncertainty about Shelvon's ability to produce an heir, Aaltah's most vital political alliance was in jeopardy.

Tears burned her eyes. "It's not childish to want what's best for my daughter. That's my duty as a mother."

The king sighed and rubbed his eyes. "I want what's best for her, too. Of course I do. But my duty as a king is to do what's best for the kingdom."

He leaned forward in his chair and took her hand, which was clenched into a white-knuckled fist. She jerked away and glared at him as a tear snaked down her cheek and she fought the need to burst into full-out sobs.

He grunted and leaned back, shaking his head. "If worse comes to worst and Shelvon fails to conceive, I will have no choice but to allow Delnamal to divorce her. He *must* have an heir. If he divorces her, I will need some way to compensate Prince Waldmir for the insult. But we are not there yet. Delnamal is impatient, but I reminded him that your mother didn't become pregnant until the second year of our marriage. It's only been three months since Shelvon lost the baby, and we have a long time still to wait before we give up hope. But until we know one way or another, Jinnell must remain available."

She stared at her father, the man who had destroyed her mother's life, who had disinherited his own children for cold political purposes, and who now commanded her to leave her daughter available to wed a monster. "You have no heart," she told him, her voice hoarse with suppressed tears.

She wouldn't exactly say he flinched at her bitter accusation, but there was a definite tightening around his eyes. She'd have rejoiced at having wounded him if she weren't so sick with fear for Jinnell.

"My kingdom will always come first," he said as he rose. "That doesn't mean I have no heart, and it doesn't mean this doesn't hurt."

"Good," she snarled, refusing to rise with him as protocol demanded. Her whole body shook with the effort of keeping her emotions contained. She wanted to throw herself at him and pound on his chest while she shrieked her rage. Never had she wished so desperately to wound someone.

The king closed his eyes and sighed, but his pain did nothing to ease her own. "It is still possible that Shelvon will conceive," he said, but he didn't sound as if he meant it. "And it's still possible the new abbess will find a way to break—or at least circumvent—your mother's spell. Let us both refrain from despair until such a time as all hope is lost."

Alys shook her head, for she saw little reason to hope. Tynthanal's letters had told her much about the abundant and unusual resources at the new Abbey, and yet he had reported no progress on the mission to reverse the Curse. The women were doing their best, experimenting with some of the rare elements the Well produced, and Tynthanal was helping them in whatever ways he could. He was by far the most magically talented person at the Abbey, but though he had admitted he could see some feminine elements, there were many he could not. It was even possible that the Well produced feminine elements that no one at the Abbey was magically gifted enough to see—but that maybe Alys could.

"I should visit the Abbey," Alys said, the thought tumbling from her mouth the moment it occurred to her. There was no denying that Tynthanal's reports about the new Well had intrigued her since she'd read his first letter, and she'd harbored some vague thought that she would be interested in seeing it. But she had certainly never thought such a thing would come to pass.

The king frowned at her. "Why would you want to do that?"

Alys was well aware that her brother was omitting a fair number of details in his reports, downplaying the importance of the Well that had been discovered. But news of the Well's existence was becoming common knowledge, even if no one outside the Abbey had yet realized its full significance.

"Because I am my mother's daughter," she said, rising and letting a fierce burst of determination chase off some of her anger and fear. While she was fairly certain her father understood that a woman born of two such powerful bloodlines—and whose brother was a gifted Adept—likely had advanced magical abilities herself, she thought it safer not to put that reality into words. "Mother said certain abilities had been bred into her bloodline. Perhaps—"

Her father waved off the argument. "If the abigails need blood from your mother's line, they have Tynthanal. I'm sure he would gladly donate for the cause."

"But he is not a woman," she persisted. "We don't under-stand—*at all*—how Mother's spell worked. Maybe I can't help in any way, but if there's even the smallest chance I can . . ."

Her father was still shaking his head. "I can't have my daughter going to the Abbey of the Unwanted even for a visit. That would not be proper."

"I visited Mother in the Abbey all the time!"

"But you weren't *staying* there. The Abbey's new location is remote, so it's not as if you could remove yourself to a respectable distance each night. You would be sleeping in a tent in the midst of an encampment of whores!"

Which showed just how much Tynthanal was leaving out of his official reports. Alys hardly thought she would be put up in a respectable inn, but she knew there were actual houses being built in the "encampment." Not that she could mention that without betraying her brother.

"Tynthanal is there," she reminded him soothingly. "He will serve as a more than adequate chaperone. And I will take my honor guard and my maid, and we can set up our own encampment at some remove. There will be no hint of impropriety."

Her father was still frowning fiercely.

"Please, Papa," she begged, giving him her most imploring look. "I will go mad if I must sit idly by while my daughter's future is in jeopardy. Let me at least *try* to help her."

"Even if you were to succeed, spending time at the Abbey would not help Jinnell's marriage prospects," he warned. "Tynthanal's presence will give you *some* cover, but those who think ill of you will feel their suspicions are being confirmed. You have no respectable reason to go there."

"Do you honestly believe my visit to the Abbey will cause someone to turn down Jinnell and her dowry if that someone has already decided to overlook the fact that she's my mother's granddaughter?" They both knew the "someone" they were discussing was Prince Waldmir. "It's not as if *Jinnell* would be at the Abbey. Would it be so shocking for me to go visit my brother, regardless of where he's posted?"

"When he's been gone less than three months?" her father countered.

Although she did not say so out loud, Alys had to concede that there was no socially acceptable excuse for her to go to the Abbey for a casual visit. "You could command me to go."

The king was so shocked by her words that he practically jumped. "What?"

"Tell everyone that you are doing everything you can to get the Curse reversed, and that you have commanded me to visit the Abbey in case my blood is the key to that reversal. Many will assume it's a sign that you're angry with me, and I will be disgraced. But I am disgraced already just by being my mother's daughter. If I can somehow help reverse the spell, then that will go a long way toward helping redeem my reputation. If I can't, I will not be any worse off, and neither will Jinnell."

That her father still wished to argue was clear in his facial expression and his body language, but he did not immediately respond. Her heart pattered in her chest, and it was all she could do not to fidget like a little girl as she awaited his judgment. If she went to the Abbey because the king commanded her to do so, then it was possible the blight on her reputation could eventually be smoothed over when he accepted her return. The same could not be said if she traveled to the Abbey of her own free will, regardless of the pretext of her visit.

"Do you honestly think there's a chance you can help them reverse the spell?" he asked, skewering her with a too-knowing gaze.

Alys was certain he understood that she meant to practice magic while she was at the Abbey, that her purpose in going there was not merely to donate blood for the abigails' experiments. While there was certainly magic that was worked using blood—such as the spell that analyzed bloodlines for signs that they could produce children—there were very few of them.

"Not a good one," she admitted, for he would know she was lying if her answer was an unqualified yes. "But any chance is better than no chance at all."

"Take some time to think about it." He held up his hand abruptly when Alys opened her mouth to argue. "If by this time next week you still feel traveling to the Abbey is the best choice, then I will command you to go. But this is not a decision to be made in haste."

"I understand," she said, though she knew no amount of thinking would cause her to change her mind.

The relief was so strong Alys threw her arms around her father's neck before she thought twice about it. She couldn't remember having hugged him since she was a little girl. Though he was clearly startled by the gesture, his arms quickly closed around her, and he held her as if he would never let go again.

CHAPTER TWENTY-SIX

Shelvon shivered in the cold air that blasted into her room as soon as she opened the window. Her nightdress flapped in the breeze, and her cheeks stung. The air smelled of snow, the lowering clouds thickly hiding the moon and stars. The first flakes were just starting to fall as Shelvon braced one hand on the casement and leaned over, making sure there was no one walking in the courtyard below. When she was certain the coast was clear and no one would see her, she tipped the vial that held her latest dose of fertility potion and let the magic-infused liquid splash onto the pavement, shaking out every last drop before retreating to the warmth of her bedroom and closing the window.

Setting the empty vial on the nightstand, she hurried to stand as close to the fire as she safely could, her skin prickling with gooseflesh as she absorbed the delicious warmth. Pouring out the potions had been the best decision she'd ever made, and she was now absurdly grateful for every sound night's sleep she had previously taken for granted. Her eyes and cheeks had lost that sunken look, and her skin had regained its color, and when Delnamal had ventured a guess her renewed vigor meant she was with child, she had encouraged him to believe it.

For seven glorious days, he'd been delighted with her and stopped trying to force the potions on her. He'd been solicitous and almost kind—at least as kind as he was capable of being. And then her monthly had begun, shattering the illusion.

When she'd poured out the first potion, she'd been frankly terrified. She was willfully defying her husband, which she had been raised to believe was an unpardonable crime. If lightning had shot down from the sky and struck her dead, she wouldn't have been entirely surprised. But nothing bad had happened. Delnamal showed no signs of suspecting, and instead of being punished for her audacity, her health was restored. Even as she shivered in the lingering chill, she smiled and reveled in that small act of defiance.

The door to her bedroom burst open, and Shelvon jumped and spun with a gasp to see Delnamal standing in the doorway, his face red with rage, his body practically vibrating with it. He slammed the door behind him so hard it sounded like a thunderclap, then advanced on her with unvarnished fury in his eyes.

"You stupid bitch!" he shouted.

Shelvon flinched from his vulgarity. He was often cruel and surly with her, but rarely vulgar, and never had she seen so much barely contained violence in his body language.

"How long have you been tossing out the potions?" he demanded as he crowded into her personal space.

Shelvon should have been afraid. She didn't know how Delnamal could have found out she wasn't taking the potions, but he clearly knew. Perhaps throwing them out the window hadn't been the best idea, after all. Just because she didn't see anyone didn't mean someone didn't see her. She had never witnessed her husband this angry before, and what he lacked in stature he more than made up for in weight and girth. He could break her in half, and he looked angry enough to do it, and yet though her pulse was definitely elevated, she did not cower or cringe. Instead, she looked him calmly in the eye.

"They weren't working, and they were making me sick."

"Well *you* make *me* sick!" he snarled, pulling back his hand as if to slap her.

A detached part of her mind thought that maybe she should take a step back or turn her head or at least put her hands up in an attempt to defend herself, but she did none of those things. She didn't even look at that raised hand, instead continuing to meet his eyes.

Instead of hitting her, he turned toward the mantel and sent a delicate crystal vase flying. It shattered against the far wall, barely missing her head on its way past. Then he grabbed her shoulders and shook her.

"Unless you want to spend the rest of your life spreading your legs for the highest bidder at the Abbey, you will do as you are told!"

His face was only inches from hers, and spittle splattered her cheek. She closed her eyes so she would no longer have to see the ugliness in his face, the hatred in his heart that shone so clearly in his eyes.

"If the potions were going to make me pregnant, they would have done so by now." She marveled at the continued calmness in her voice. But she'd been living in fear and misery for too long. They were still inside her, but they were now like old friends, quiet companions who made no demands of her.

She opened her eyes. "Divorce me if you must. But I will drink no more potions."

"Oh yes you fucking will!" He pulled back his hand again, and again she failed to flinch or in any way try to defend herself, even when she saw the back of that hand come toward her.

The impact with her cheek drew a short grunt of pain from her, but Delnamal was not a habitual abuser of women, and the blow had no teeth to it. In fact, he'd held back so much she doubted she'd even sport a bruise.

Something stirred from deep inside her gut. Something fierce and free and just as ugly as Delnamal's anger, and she found herself laughing.

"Is that the best you can do?" she mocked. "My tutor hit me harder when I was five and spilled a jar of ink." Delnamal pulled back his hand again, this time clenching it into a fist. "Do you have any idea how many beatings a child of Nandel takes in the course of growing up?" she asked. "Let's see if you can measure up to what I'm used to. Go on and give me a *proper* beating and see if it makes me submit."

Delnamal's whole body was shaking, and his breath was coming in great heaving gasps. His fist was poised and ready, and yet he didn't let fly.

How many times had she thought to herself that for all his many faults, her husband did not beat her? Here she had unquestionably given him good cause to break his own rules, and yet still he hesitated. Almost as if he were afraid of her, though she suspected it was more his own anger he feared. He did not like to lose control of himself, and he was perilously close to doing so now.

Self-preservation urged her to back down, to bow her head and apologize and promise to take the potions. If her husband truly did lose control, if he allowed all that rage to pour out of him unchecked, she might not survive the explosion that followed.

It came as somewhat of a shock when she realized how little that thought frightened her. Her future looked bleak no matter which way she turned, so in reality she had little to lose.

"Well?" she prompted, putting her hands on her hips. "What are you waiting for?"

He stood there for another excruciating few moments, panting and glaring and shaking. Then his hand dropped to his side, and he turned his head and spit on her carpet.

"You aren't even worth the effort," he growled, then turned and stalked out the door, slamming it behind him.

Shelvon stood staring at the door, waiting for him to change his mind and come back, but he didn't. A slow smile spread over her face.

Alys paced her room anxiously as she waited for Jinnell to arrive for their late-night magic lesson. She had put this conversation off for as long as she could, and she was lucky Jinnell hadn't noticed anything was amiss—and that Corlin had kept the news to himself after she had told him, as he had promised.

Jinnell slipped into the room without knocking, as was their habit. The less noise they made, the less chance someone would find out what they were doing at night after the household went to sleep. Not that the magic lessons were doing Jinnell much good any longer. The book spent very little time on the basics before moving on to advanced spells using elements Jinnell couldn't see. It was frustrating, because Jinnell could clearly see more elements than the average woman, and with the proper instruction, she could have learned many useful spells. Instead, she was quickly losing interest in the lessons, bored with watching the mixing of invisible elements to create spells she could not cast herself. And Alys spent a great deal of time practicing her magic in solitude.

Where once Jinnell would arrive for their lessons with a bounce in her step, she now trudged into the room yawning.

She stifled her yawn the moment her eyes lit on the three neatly packed trunks stacked near the door. "Are we going somewhere?" she asked with a furrow between her brows.

"Come sit down," Alys beckoned, patting the seat beside her on the sofa by the fire.

Jinnell's eyes narrowed with suspicion, but she did as she was told. "It wasn't my imagination, after all," she said as she sat. "I thought everyone was acting strange and told myself I was being silly." Her face seemed unnaturally pale in the firelight, but she raised her chin in an attempt to look bold and confident. "Are we going to Nandel so Prince Waldmir can appraise me?"

Alys gasped and shook her head. "No! I'm so sorry. It never occurred to me that you might think that."

Jinnell's shoulders sagged in relief. "Then what?"

"I'm doing everything I can to take Waldmir off the table."

"Okay. And . . ."

Alys squirmed on the inside, for though it had become obvious recently that she did not know her daughter as well as she'd thought, she felt certain she knew what Jinnell would think of what she had planned. "And I'm worried that the only way that can happen is if Shelvon gets pregnant."

Jinnell heaved an exasperated sigh. "Yes, I know that. We both know that. Just hurry up and tell me whatever it is you need to tell me."

"I think the best chance we have of Shelvon getting pregnant is if my mother's spell is reversed. The women of the Abbey are under orders to reverse it, but no one really believes they can do it. We know one of the things she did to create the spell was to manipulate bloodlines. You and I already know I can see some elements I have no business seeing."

"You think *you* can reverse the spell?" Jinnell cried.

Something inside Alys shriveled at the very thought of tackling something so impossible. Especially when her mother's letter had said explicitly that the spell could not be reversed. It felt like hubris even to *think* that she might be able to do it.

"Maybe with the help of the new abbess, and with the power of the new Well they've discovered . . ." Her voice trailed off, for the reality was she couldn't exactly claim to have high hopes. It was only sheer desperation that prompted her to make the attempt. Maybe it was nothing more than a purely selfish impulse, a desire to trick herself into believing she had control over something that was clearly beyond her.

"Even if you could do it," Jinnell said, "I wouldn't want you to."

"What?"

"I don't want the spell to be reversed," Jinnell repeated, speaking slowly and clearly and looking right into her mother's eyes. "Even if it means I have to marry Prince Waldmir."

Alys gaped at her. "But . . . why?"

Jinnell's eyes flashed. "Do you really think I'm that selfish,

Mama? I'm very sorry for Aunt Shelvon and the difficulties the spell is causing her, but think of all the women throughout Seven Wells whose lives have changed for the better." Her eyes welled with tears. "I have a lot of friends who will be married in the next few years, and for the first time, they have a bargaining chip. Few men want to marry a woman who won't give them children, and few women will give a man children when they are forced into the marriage. I can't take that away from every other woman in the world just to save myself from one of the few men who still thinks a forced marriage is a good idea."

It was . . . humbling, to say the least, to find that she had raised a daughter far more unselfish than herself. Alys hadn't thought twice about damning every other woman in the world in order to protect her daughter. "I'm sure Shelvon isn't the only woman who's suffering right now because of this spell," she argued weakly. "There have to be a lot of frustrated husbands everywhere, and many of them will take out their frustrations on their wives." It was clear that her mother's spell would not allow a woman to be bullied into "willingly" conceiving, but that wouldn't stop men from trying. And those women who did not provide heirs would soon find themselves divorced and sent to the Abbey to live in disgrace.

"Women will always suffer. Grandmother's spell did not change the basic nature of men. But as long as it keeps working, far fewer of us will be forced into marriages we don't want. Grandmother and your sister and your niece were all willing to die to make it happen. We don't even know for sure yet whether the king will offer me to Prince Waldmir, nor do we know if he'll want me. My blood is 'tainted,' remember? And if it comes to that, we will make it clear that I have no intention of giving him children. I could never live with myself if you reversed the spell just for me."

Alys closed her eyes and tried not to imagine Waldmir laying hands on her daughter. She could not adopt Jinnell's mature and unselfish position—though it would be counterproductive to say so.

Alys took a deep, shaky breath and let it out slowly. "It's highly unlikely I could have reversed the spell anyway."

Jinnell's eyes lit up. "Then you'll stay?"

Alys shook her head. "I had to ask the king for permission, of course, and now that I've made the offer . . ."

Jinnell's shoulders drooped. "He won't let you change your mind."

The king had insisted he would tell no one about his "command" until Alys had already left, on the off chance that she would think better of it. But Jinnell needn't know that. "I was very persuasive, and he decided I should go by royal decree. But it is perhaps not a bad thing for me to visit the abigails' Well anyway. There may be ways I can help that don't require reversing my mother's spell."

"Like what?"

"Tynthanal tells me there is an abundance of rare feminine elements at this Well. Maybe there are elements there I can't get here. Ones I can use to craft a spell to help Shelvon conceive despite my mother's spell."

"And thereby take away a woman's right to choose once more. The beauty of Grandmother's spell is that no one can force a woman to be 'willing.' Not even the woman herself. If the whole thing can be undermined by another spell, then everything Grandmother did was for nothing."

Jinnell was far too perceptive. Alys forced herself to think a little harder before speaking again. "Then perhaps I can invent a spell that will allow Shelvon to *fake* a pregnancy. If she seems to be pregnant, then that would reassure everyone that she will bear an heir. We might well be able to contract you to another before the false pregnancy fails."

Jinnell's face was the picture of skepticism, and Alys braced for yet another argument. But Jinnell was maturing at an almost dizzying speed and surprised her once more.

"I'm not going to talk you out of it no matter what I say, am I?" she asked.

Alys patted her daughter's hand. "No. I have to do this." No matter how unlikely it seemed that she could do anything to turn the tide—she was still a novice magic user at best, despite her natural aptitude—she had to at least try. To not try was to admit defeat, and that was something she refused to do.

Jinnell glanced over at the trunks. "And you're leaving tomorrow."

"This is not something that can wait."

"How long will you be gone?"

Alys bit back her initial urge to tell a soothing lie. "I can't say for sure. Probably at least a month, though if my efforts prove promising, it's possible I'll need to stay longer. You will run the household while I'm gone, but if you need anything, you can always go to your grandparents." Sylnin's parents might not be overly fond of Alys, but they adored their grandchildren, and Alys had seen no sign of that changing since the spell was cast.

Jinnell nodded, though she was worrying at that lower lip again. "I guess it will be good practice for when I'm married."

"That's a good way of looking at it. I'm also going to leave Falcor behind to watch over you and Corlin." Jinnell opened her mouth to argue, but Alys cut her off. "I will still have three honor guardsmen with me. Just not Falcor. I could not trust the life and safety of my children to anyone else."

Falcor had not been happy with her decision, and had he chosen to press the issue, he would have won. He still answered to his commander, not to Alys. But in the end he had understood her need to feel her children were safe in her absence, and he trusted his men. No doubt the fact that she would be under her brother's protection while she was at the Abbey had also factored into his decision.

Alys rose from the settee and opened the drawer of a nearby side table, pulling out two silk-wrapped packages. "I have a couple of gifts for you before I go."

Usually, Jinnell's face would light up like the sun at the prospect of receiving gifts, but she must have heard something ominous in her mother's tone, for she looked almost frightened. Alys handed her the larger of the two packages, watching as Jinnell unfolded the silk to reveal its contents.

"Stays?" Jinnell asked with a hint of distaste in her voice and a look on her face that said she suspected her mother had gone mad.

Alys smiled. It was indeed an odd gift, and the stays looked perfectly ordinary with their covering of plain white linen. "Open your Mindseye and look at them."

Jinnell did as she was told, her eyes going filmy as she regarded the stays once more, turning them this way and that. Alys's smile broadened as the frown on her daughter's face grew deeper.

"I don't understand," Jinnell said, closing her Mindseye.

"I learned how my mother hid the spell on her magic book. I don't have all the elements I need to re-create it fully, but I was able to adapt it. Someone who knows what they're looking for and is a skilled magic user could see through the camouflage, but under ordinary circumstances, no one will know the stays hold a spell." A necessary precaution, seeing as men frequently had to open their Mindseye to use minor everyday magics, and it wouldn't do for them to see the spell Alys had built into those stays.

"And what exactly is this spell hiding?"

"Feed a mote of Rho into the boning, and the spell will make you immune to most magic for about ten minutes. You can add up to four more motes to make it last longer, but I haven't been able to make it last for more than about an hour at a time no matter how much Rho I add." Alys handed her the next package, which was tiny enough to fit in the palm of her hand. "Now open this one."

Jinnell unwrapped the package carefully and found at its center a delicate gold ring with a blood-red ruby cabochon surrounded by diamond chips. "It's beautiful," she breathed, testing the ring on several fingers before deciding it fit best on her index finger. She held her hand up in front of her, admiring the way the diamonds sparkled in the light, then flicked a glance toward Alys.

"It's not just a ring, is it?" she asked.

"No. Once again I've hidden it, but I put my sleep spell into it. You can activate it by adding one mote of Rho. Be certain the spell in your stays is active if you ever need to use it, or the moment you put Rho into it, you will fall asleep where you stand."

Jinnell stopped admiring the beauty of the ring and lost a little color in her cheeks as she absorbed the implications of the spell. "So if I activate the ring, and I touch someone with it, they'll immediately fall asleep?"

"That's right."

Alys returned to her seat on the sofa and took both her daughter's hands in her own, looking into her eyes and willing her not to be afraid. "I'm sure you'll never need it," she said with as much conviction as she could muster. "It's only for use in the direst emergencies. But it will make me feel better to know you have it. Just in case."

Jinnell swallowed hard. "Just in case . . ." she whispered.

Neither one of them wanted to imagine any situation that would make it necessary for Jinnell to activate the ring's spell.

CHAPTER TWENTY-SEVEN

Every time Chanlix stepped over the threshold into her home—a *house*, if a small one—she experienced a little surge of wonder. She had spent most of her life sharing small, barren rooms with her fellow abigails, and even for the short time she'd been abbess in Aalwell, her dwelling had been nothing more than a single utilitarian room. Now here she was in her exile, and she lived in a two-room house with a proper parlor. There was a comfortable sitting area by the front windows, and a small but functional "dining room" by the wood-burning stove, and her bedroom was large enough that she could easily have partitioned off a dressing room, had she had any need of such a thing. Many of her younger abigails had stopped wearing the red robes, and though Chanlix had scolded at first, she found she didn't have it in her to insist. Just as she'd found she couldn't bear to part with her own.

Chanlix was stirring a pot of stew she had put together for the evening meal when there was a knock on her door. She had learned

some basic cooking skills at the Abbey, where there were no servants to take care of such things, but Mother Brynna had deemed
her to have no aptitude for it and banished her from the kitchens.
Here in Women's Well, she had asked Maidel to give her some re-
medial lessons, and she was now able to feed herself. However, she
was far from certain she was up to the task of feeding anyone else,
so she opened her door with a flutter of anxiety in her belly. Perhaps it had been an act of extreme overconfidence to extend an
invitation. Though in retrospect, Tynthanal had all but invited
himself.

The sight of him standing on her doorstep stole her voice. By
day, he labored side by side with his men and the growing population of visiting laborers from the closest towns, and she found him
quite lovely to look at with sweat-soaked, disheveled hair and dirty
clothes. But tonight, he was wearing his dress uniform as if attending some formal function at the palace, and his hair was tied back at
the nape of his neck in a tidy club. His face was clean shaven, and
he smelled faintly of the spicy soap brought to their little town by a
merchant who wished to set up a shop.

Tynthanal grinned at her. "I don't always look like a filthy barbarian," he teased.

She shook her head and tried to look stern, but she doubted she
succeeded. Her cheeks warmed in a way that said she was blushing,
and it wasn't exactly because of embarrassment. "I didn't realize
this was a formal occasion," she said, smoothing her robes, "or I
would have worn my own dress uniform." She stepped aside to let
him in, hoping her little quip hadn't come out sounding hostile. Of
course she *had* no dress uniform, for abigails did not have "occasions" of any sort.

"My apologies for my unintended rudeness," he said, sounding
not in the least apologetic. There was no question he had appreciated her admiring regard, as undignified as it might have been.
"Perhaps next time, you might consider shedding the robes and
wearing an actual dress. It seems to be a popular decision among
the younger abigails."

"And *not* so popular among we older ones," she retorted. "But you're getting ahead of yourself assuming there will be a next time."

"Have I offended you so much already?" His eyes twinkled with good humor, and his smile was contagious, no matter how hard she tried to fight it.

"You haven't tasted my cooking yet," she said with a rueful gesture at the pot on the stove. "I did mention I wasn't very good at it."

"If you were as bad at it as you like to claim, I doubt you would enjoy it as much as you do. You are still the abbess, and I've no doubt your abigails would happily cook your meals—as it is their duty. And yet you usually do for yourself."

She sighed, for his argument had some merit. She couldn't say she felt confident in her skills, but she *did* enjoy it. There was something that felt faintly decadent about making something meant entirely for her own consumption after years of making potions meant only for others.

"Besides," he continued, "you know full well I'm not here for the food."

She nodded briskly as she turned to the stove and pulled the pot off the heat. "Yes, we were going to discuss plans of building a town hall so that we might have an indoor gathering place." At least that was the excuse he had conjured up for why they needed to spend this time together. She tensed as she laid out a couple of bowls for the stew, waiting to see if Tynthanal would press the issue. She kept thinking he would tire of flirting with her. The town was full of pretty young women, many of whom would be more than happy to climb into his bed. Why he would pursue *her* was a mystery, but there was no mistaking his intent. Perhaps he was chasing her because she so assiduously insisted on running away?

But no. Tynthanal was not that kind of man—and that was the problem. He was the kind of man she could see herself losing her heart to. And despite his current disfavor, he was a king's son— a man who could never be hers. For all her adult life, her heart had been divorced from her body as countless men bedded her for no purpose but their own physical gratification. And yet her instincts told her that if she gave Tynthanal her body, her heart would go with it and ultimately be crushed.

Chanlix heard his quiet sigh of resignation and wondered if maybe she had finally managed to discourage him. She ladled stew into the bowls, giving the work more attention than it required as she attempted to hide her turmoil.

It took an embarrassing effort of will to meet his eyes and smile at him as she served the stew, but she desperately wanted to ease the tension that had arisen between them. Possibly the strained smile wasn't the best way to accomplish her goal, but Tynthanal came to her aid. He was much better at pretending to be at ease than she was.

"I *did* want to discuss plans for a town hall," he said, turning his attention to the stew so that she no longer had to squirm under his gaze. "But that will have to wait. I received a flier from Alysoon today. It seems she is on her way to Women's Well, though her explanation of *why* lacked a bit of clarity. We'll need to arrange lodging for her and her entourage, though it is thankfully small."

Chanlix's stomach did a flip-flop, and she could barely swallow the mouthful of stew she had taken. As much as the town had grown, they were hardly equipped to play host to a noblewoman of any sort, much less the king's daughter. What would the woman think of their town? Chanlix knew Tynthanal had been giving his sister much more truthful updates about their progress than he gave his own commander, but still . . .

What would Lady Alysoon think if she knew her little brother was spending so much time in the company of an abbess? Even if Chanlix somehow managed to put some distance between the two of them while Alysoon visited, she was sure to hear talk, for Chanlix wasn't the only person who'd recognized Tynthanal's courtship for what it was.

True, Alysoon had visited her mother in the Abbey and had treated the abigails with respect and kindness when she did. She was not the sort of woman to sneer at them or avoid them as if their disgrace were a contagious disease. But she could not possibly approve of her brother courting a whore. An *old* whore, at that.

Tynthanal reached across the table and laid a hand on top of hers, the warm contact startling her because she had become so lost in her whirling thoughts. She should have gently pulled away, but she couldn't bear to lose that touch, and her fingers curled around his as if they had a will of their own.

"All will be well," he said in a soothing croon. "Alys won't make unreasonable demands, nor will she tell tales of all that we've accomplished here. I would trust her with my life, and you may, as well." He squeezed her hand as if to emphasize his point.

Chanlix nodded her agreement. But if her life had taught her anything, it was that trust was a luxury a woman—especially an abigail—could not afford. "What we have here is so fragile," she whispered. "I wish we could just . . . seal the rest of the world out." Which was a terribly selfish thing to say to a man who still had family living in Aaltah. Everyone Chanlix cared about was within the borders of their little community, but the same could not be said of many others.

Tynthanal smiled at her, but there was a hint of sadness in that smile. "Let's not let fear of the future spoil what we have now. We are comfortable and thriving in a place where we were meant to be miserable. That proves how unpredictable the future can be."

He was still holding her hand, his thumb stroking idly over her knuckles. She met his eyes and felt an unmistakable stirring of desire in her core. No matter how unsuitable she found herself as a companion for a king's son, she feared that if he pressed the matter, she would not find the will to resist. She practically held her breath, her mouth going dry.

Tynthanal sighed and released her hand, turning his attention back to his stew. "Forgive me," he said. "I did not mean to make you uncomfortable."

Chanlix bit her tongue on the urge to correct him, to explain that her sudden stillness had nothing to do with discomfort. All it would take was a few well-chosen words, and she could have him in her bed this very night, she was sure of it.

She wasn't sure if it was cowardice or conscience that caused her to hold her tongue. But she did not correct his misinterpretation of her body language, instead steering their conversation into safer waters. And she spent that night alone in her bed, wishing for things an abigail had no business wishing for.

A lone rider on the back of an unencumbered cheval could have made the journey from Aalwell to the new Abbey in about three days of hard travel. The wealthiest of Aaltah's nobility, who could afford to put even their servants on chevals, could make it in about five if those chevals weren't weighed down with a lot of baggage and heavy carriages. Because Alys didn't own enough chevals for everyone to ride, she had to cut a few corners unless she wanted to spend two weeks on the road.

It was highly irregular for servants and honor guardsmen to ride inside a noblewoman's carriage, but she chose speed over protocol and bade Honor and one of her guardsmen to ride with her. That left two chevals to draw the carriage, two to carry the remaining honor guardsmen, and one to remain home with Jinnell and Corlin in case it was needed. She was sure the guardsmen were unhappy at being forced to ride chevals, but they could not have kept up with a cheval-drawn carriage on horseback.

Although everyone—especially the honor guardsmen, who were used to traveling rough—packed as lightly as possible, the carriage was still heavy with the coachman and three passengers and the baggage, and that made it impossible for the chevals to gallop. They still managed a respectable canter, which they could keep up indefinitely.

The journey stretched out over six days, with their party stopping at an inn each night. In Aalwell, Alys had been only dimly aware of the change in her image after her mother's spell. She'd certainly noticed the sudden lack of social engagements, but the nobility were as a whole too polite—and too worried about offending the king—to be openly rude to her. Whoever had been leaving threats in the message box had stopped after being chased by one

of Falcor's men, and there had been little in the way of overt hostility since then.

The farther from the capital she traveled, the less that was the
case. Few people in the countryside recognized her on sight, but
she was forced to identify herself at the inns, and there was no missing the animosity there. She dared not venture into the common
area for her meals, and for the first time in her life, she was grateful
for the honor guardsmen who surrounded her.

The influence of Aaltah's Well stretched for great distances into
the countryside, creating fertile farmland and majestic forests filled
with the famed Aalwood trees that grew nowhere else. Aalwood
was Aaltah's most prized export, as the wood was naturally infused
with Aal. The wood was hard and dark and lustrous enough to be
valued all by itself, but its abundance of Aal was its greatest selling
point to kingdoms and principalities that had little or no other access to that vital element. Practically every spell that required any
kind of movement required Aal.

The farther from the Well they traveled, the less lush the land
became. Forest gave way to plains, and those plains grew less and
less green with more patches of sand and bare dirt. Miller's Bridge,
the town in which Alys and her party spent the final night of travel,
was a sad little place where the tiny town center had a single market
and a single inn. Small houses were scattered about the dry plain,
the land so flat and bare that even the most distant residences were
easily spotted from the road. Tiny herds of goats clustered around
intermittent bursts of green where grasses were fed by underground
springs, and there was a strip of lushness on each side of the river by
which the town was built, but it seemed to Alys a hard life. The
thought that her half-brother had sent his best company of soldiers
and a bunch of innocent women to live out beyond even this meager bounty made her angry all over again.

Although Alys did not sense the same open hostility here that
she had in the previous towns, she chose to take her dinner in her
room anyway. The innkeeper's wife served a thick, gamy-tasting
stew made up almost entirely of root vegetables with the occasional

shreds of dark, tough meat that Alys presumed was goat, having not seen any larger animals around.

"Forgive the meager meal, my lady," the innkeeper's wife said, worrying at her apron and frowning fiercely. "We've had more travelers in the past month than we had in the past year, and it's all we can do to keep them fed."

Alys smiled at her reassuringly. "You have nothing to apologize for. It's a lovely meal." She scooped up a mouthful of stew and nodded as she chewed, trying to convey her appreciation. The stew was nothing she would serve at home, nor anything she would be eager to eat again, but the taste was not unpleasant, and it was nourishing. "Why have you had so many travelers?" she asked between bites. It seemed like this little town was on the edge of nowhere, and there was little reason for anyone to travel through it.

The innkeeper's wife looked surprised at the question. "Because of Women's Well, of course."

Alys blinked at her. "Women's Well?"

"Yes. Isn't that where you're heading to?"

"I'm bound for the new Abbey."

She nodded with satisfaction. "Yes. We call it Women's Well. Or had you not heard that there was a new Well there?"

Certainly news of the new Well had traveled. The unheard-of discovery of a new Well would likely have drawn a great deal more attention if not for its remote location and its failure to produce elements men considered useful. But though word of the Well had spread, this was the first time Alys had heard anyone refer to a place called Women's Well.

"Women's Well, eh?" she asked with a smile. It sounded like a bona fide town, rather than some half-hearted encampment. Perhaps Tynthanal's letters hadn't been as thorough as she'd thought, for though she knew to expect more than a gathering of tents, she certainly had not expected a town with a name. "And people are traveling there?"

"Oh, yes. I was out there myself last week. Never had much access to potions before, and never could have afforded them even if

I did, but I bought me some lovely ones for my garden." She indicated the bowl of stew with a jerk of her chin. "Was plumb out of carrots, but a little sprinkle on my garden and I have a fine new batch a week later."

Alys smiled again while inside she felt a prickle of unease. Delnamal—and the lord high treasurer—would not be pleased to know the women of the Abbey—of Women's Well—were producing potions inexpensive enough for an innkeeper's wife to afford. She imagined when the king had first sent the women out to the edge of the kingdom, no one had expected the Abbey to generate income anymore, not with elements so sparse and the nearest ragged town half a day's journey away.

In the first light of morning the next day, Alys climbed into her carriage once more for the final leg of her journey. The road had supposedly come to an end in the town, but the innkeeper's wife had clearly been telling the truth about the increase in travel. Where once the carriage would have bumped over unmarked desert, there was now a clear, hard-packed path leading out of town toward what should have been the Wasteland. The trail was thin and dusty at first, but a little bit more than an hour after they left the town, Alys noticed the color of the soil changing and darkening. Less sand and dust, and more earth. And the patchy grasses were bigger, more frequent, and more green.

With every mile they drove, the land changed. Her guardsman and Honor were both gazing out the carriage windows with rapt attention, but for safety's sake, Alys covered her eyes with her hand on the pretext of blocking the bright sunlight and opened her Mindseye. As she suspected, the air was alive with elements, many of which she'd never seen, and Alys knew she would have to spend some time with her nose in her mother's book to identify what she was seeing. Most of the elements she recognized were feminine, but there were also a reasonable number of neuter elements and she could even pick out a couple of masculine ones. She was delighted to see that the Women's Well produced a fair amount of Tyn, which had proved invaluable for creating her special sleep spell and with which she very much wanted to experiment some more.

Alys closed her Mindseye and sternly ordered herself to curb her enthusiasm. She itched to reach out and touch all the strange new elements she'd spotted, to crack open her mother's book right then and there and explore all the new possibilities. Her pulse was racing with excitement as she wondered what spells she could devise with the bounty of the Women's Well, but she was not here to play. She was in a race against a deadly clock, and no matter how tempting the abundance, she had to focus all her efforts on finding a way to save Jinnell from the fate Delnamal had in store for her.

Three hours after their day's journey had begun, their destination came into view. The trail the carriage followed was now lined with bushes and young trees, so it was no longer as easy to see over long distances as it had been in the plains and desert they'd been crossing the last couple of days.

A wooden archway had been erected over the trampled trail that might almost be large enough now to label a road. WELCOME TO WOMEN'S WELL was burned into the top of the wooden archway, and when the carriage passed through the archway, the town that had sprung up in the scant time since the women of the Abbey had been banished here stole Alys's power of speech.

This was no ramshackle collection of lean-tos and huts and tents, as she'd been expecting. Although the women had been sent here with only the most limited supplies and with only a company of soldiers to help set up their camp, they had clearly enlisted additional help and expertise. All along the main road were orderly, small wooden houses, and there were multiple smaller roads leading off in both directions. In the distance, Alys spotted the framework for a barn, outside of which was a large corral containing an impressive number of horses. On the far side of the corral, a young girl was tending a small herd of goats as the animals munched contentedly on the leaves of a lush, low bush with yellow-green leaves.

She had kept Tynthanal apprised of her progress via flier, so she was not at all surprised when he strode out of one of the houses and came to meet her carriage. She was out the door practically before the carriage came to a stop, not bothering to wait for the coachman to hand her down. She flung herself into her brother's arms and gave him a rib-crushing hug.

Tynthanal laughed as he returned the hug, lifting her briefly and easily off her feet before setting her back down.

"One would think you hadn't seen me for a year," he teased as she pulled back and looked up into his face.

She made a gesture encompassing the town. "One would think this place had been standing at least that long."

He grinned with apparent delight and looked around proudly. "You would, wouldn't you?"

The town was bustling with activity, and though many curious looks were tossed Alys's way, no one but Tynthanal seemed inclined to halt their labors to investigate. Though all the buildings within her immediate view were completed, the sound of hammers filled the air, a constant, low percussion.

She looked at her beaming brother and shook her head in wonder. "How?"

"Let's get you settled, and then we can have a long talk."

Ellin sighed contentedly and snuggled closer into Graesan's arms. Her breath still came short, and the hand that stroked over his skin came away damp with sweat. She patted his bare chest, feeling the hurried thumping of his heart behind his ribs.

"You've let yourself grow soft since you left the guard to become my secretary," she teased. "Where is your stamina?"

He grunted softly and rolled her over onto her back, his naked body a delicious weight pressing her into the bed. "I'll show you stamina," he panted, and took her mouth with a searing kiss.

She wrapped her arms around him and arched her back, but he had brought her to release three times already tonight, and they both needed a break before trying again—or falling asleep in exhaustion, as might be more likely.

Breaking the kiss, Graesan flopped over onto his back once more with a groan. "Okay, you win. I have no stamina."

She laughed and propped her head on her hand, enjoying the sight of him lying naked among the sheets in the flickering light of the fire. He was a beautiful specimen of manhood, lean and strong, with hard, corded muscles and sensuous lips that had kissed every inch of her body.

"Weren't we supposed to be discussing tomorrow's agenda?" she asked him.

His eyes twinkled in the firelight as he turned to look at her. "Council meeting. More meetings. Then lunch, and afterward . . . a bunch of people want to talk to you about stuff."

She laughed. "Yes, that about sums up my usual day-to-day schedule. Thank you for the detailed report."

"You'll be unsurprised to hear you have a full schedule." Some of the humor faded from his eyes and his lips tugged downward in the beginnings of a frown. "Zarsha of Nandel has an audience right after lunch. I've successfully put him off for two days, but he is getting most insistent. We can, of course, make something else pop up 'unexpectedly' if you don't wish to see him."

She had neatly avoided any private contact with Zarsha since his rather unusual proposal, although she saw him socially practically every day. So far, he had not pressed her for an answer and seemed perfectly content to wait as long as necessary. Whatever he wanted to see her about, she doubted it was to pressure her to marry him, or she would have sensed some impatience from him by now. Most likely, he wanted to give her his personal report on his observations of her courtiers.

"No, no," she said. "I'll happily see him. He is quite the fount of information."

Graesan's frown deepened. "You have an entire royal council to give you advice and information. Why do you need some foreign princeling? Shouldn't he have gone home by now?"

Ellin was taken aback by the sharpness of Graesan's tone. He had, of course, never been fond of Zarsha, just as he would have naturally disliked any man Ellin was slated to marry. She had expected that over time, some of those hard feelings would fall away now that the engagement was no more. But if anything, Graesan's dislike of Zarsha had grown stronger.

"He doesn't seem to be overfond of his homeland," she said, trying to keep her own tone casual. For all that her relationship with Graesan felt refreshingly open and honest when compared to all her other court relationships, she had chosen not to share Zarsha's proposal unless absolutely necessary. Why distress Graesan and raise the tension level when she still felt reasonably certain she would not marry Zarsha? "And as a foreigner, he has a unique perspective."

"As a spy, you mean. You know that's what he is, don't you?"

Ellin sat up, wrapping the sheet around herself and peering down at Graesan's face. "He's Prince Waldmir's nephew!" she protested. "Not a spy."

Graesan sat up, too, his square jaw taking on a mulish cast as something that looked suspiciously like jealousy flared in his eyes. "The two are not mutually exclusive."

"Members of royal families don't work as spies."

"Says who? There has to be a reason he's sticking around here now that the wedding is unequivocally off."

Ellin's heart skipped a beat, and she wondered if Graesan had somehow gotten wind of Zarsha's proposal, though she didn't know how that could be. Zarsha would certainly not have mentioned it to anyone. She rubbed a hand over her face, suddenly tired.

Graesan didn't have to know about the proposal to be jealous, though of course he would never admit to it. Only a blind man would fail to see how her relationship with Zarsha had thawed since she took the throne, and Graesan was hardly blind. Add to that Zarsha's famed good looks and charm, and it was hardly surprising Graesan would see him as a rival. She itched to tell Graesan he had no cause for his jealousy, but she sensed saying so would further fan the flames.

"You should send him home," Graesan concluded. "You've been more than generous in your hospitality, and he has no business being here. Not anymore."

The pulse of resistance that rose in Ellin's breast took her by surprise in its intensity. Regardless of whether she chose to accept Zarsha's offer or not, she didn't *want* to send him home. Dear as Graesan was to her, he had little understanding of—or interest in— the machinations of the court, and all her other advisers were either actively hostile, like Tamzin, or at least twice her age, like Semsulin. Zarsha might have ulterior motives for being a confidant, but at least he was honest about it, and his insights were keen. He had grown up a major player in a royal court, and he understood her position in a way that Graesan never could.

"I can't do that," she said, but she wasn't about to mention any personal reasons for her refusal. "I can't risk insulting Prince Waldmir by sending his nephew away."

Graesan shifted uncomfortably, perhaps because he understood the reasoning and didn't like it. "All right, then make yourself less available. I will shift your schedule so you don't have time for him tomorrow. It wouldn't be hard to do that continually. If he has no access to you, he'll eventually give up and go home."

She smiled faintly, and Graesan's expression darkened even further. "You underestimate the depth of his stubbornness. He will never just give up and go home."

"You don't know him well enough to be sure of that."

"Yes, I do."

Graesan's hands were clenched into angry fists, and the muscles of his jaw stood out in stark relief as he ground his teeth. Ellin cursed herself for speaking without thinking, for emphasizing her easy familiarity with Zarsha when Graesan was already struggling with jealousy. Zarsha had offered to let her keep Graesan as her lover if she accepted his marriage proposal, but based on Graesan's fiercely territorial behavior, it seemed unlikely he would accept such an arrangement.

"It isn't safe to cultivate a relationship with a spy, no matter how useful you might find his *insights*," Graesan persisted. "Especially when you have your own dangerous secret to hide. Imagine what a man like him would do if he ever found out about us . . ."

"He's known for quite some time," she told him, hoping to calm his fears with this evidence that Zarsha had not used the knowledge for nefarious purposes. The expression on Graesan's face said her words had had the opposite effect.

"What? How can he possibly . . . ?"

She shrugged. "I don't know. He claimed it was just an educated guess, but of course I gave everything away because I was so shocked."

Graesan swallowed hard. "Has he made any demands?"

So much for her hopeful assumption that Graesan would attribute Zarsha's failure to reveal what he knew as a sign of trustworthiness. His natural dislike of Zarsha made him jump to the immediate conclusion that she was being blackmailed, which made a tidy explanation for her failure to send Zarsha away.

"It's not like that," she said, but saw little hope Graesan would take her word for it.

"You cannot convince me that a man like him would not take advantage of knowing a secret so dangerous. Is that why you haven't sent him away? Because he's threatened you?"

Ellin groaned and rubbed her eyes. The only way to allay Graesan's suspicions would be to tell him the truth about Zarsha's proposal—and her refusal to dismiss it out of hand, just in case. She would rather have Graesan be angry than hurt.

"He's made no threats," she said, "and he promises he would never use the information against me. But . . ." She let the thought trail off, knowing Graesan would come to exactly the conclusion she intended. She was being a coward, running from an argument that was likely unavoidable, but she already had enough troubles in her life. When she tumbled into bed with Graesan, she wanted nothing but heat and comfort and support, and if she had to impugn Zarsha's character to bring this argument to a conclusion, then so be it.

"I can't send him away," she concluded, lying back down and pushing the sheet off her naked body. Even in his alarm and anger, Graesan's eyes roamed greedily over her, and though the sheet still covered him from the waist down, she had no doubt he was stirring to life again.

"Come here," Ellin commanded, reaching out to grab Graesan's shoulders and draw him to her. He could have resisted her easily had he wanted to, but he didn't. "Let's keep Zarsha out of our bed, shall we?"

Graesan made a low growling sound of mingled frustration and need. The need won out, and his mouth came down on hers, sending a spark straight to her center. She was under no illusion that the subject was closed. But for now, at least, they would enjoy each other's bodies without the interference of the outside world.

CHAPTER TWENTY-EIGHT

Tynthanal's home took Alys completely by surprise. He had lived in a barracks ever since he'd left home at age fourteen, and though his rank entitled him to a fair amount of luxury, a soldier's version of luxury was a far cry from a noblewoman's. Alys would have expected his home here in Women's Well to have nothing beyond the bare minimum—a bed, a table, and a chair, with a trunk to store his belongings.

Instead, she found a pleasantly comfortable two-room house with rugs on the floor and curtains on the windows. The first room was a living area, heated by an iron stove that clearly served more than one purpose, as evidenced by the rack of pots on the wall behind it and the kettle that sat on a table beside it. A table with four upholstered chairs was in one corner, and a small vase of cheerful yellow flowers sat on its center. There was even a cozy seating area by the window, with an armchair, a small sofa, and a delicate tea table.

Tynthanal laughed when he saw the way Alys was looking around. "You were expecting a barracks?"

She shook her head as she looked again at the flowers on the table. *Flowers.* "I wasn't expecting this," she admitted.

Tynthanal picked up the kettle, opening it and peering inside. "Would you like some tea?" Without awaiting an answer, he put the kettle on the stove to heat, then directed her to the sofa. "You probably have about a thousand questions for me while that water heats."

She sat and smoothed out the skirts of her traveling dress, not entirely sure what to do with this new, domesticated version of her little brother. "At least two thousand, I should think."

He flashed her a boyish grin as he dropped into the seat beside her. "The answer to your first is no, I did not decorate this place myself." He smoothed his hand over the back of the sofa, which was covered in a delicate floral print fabric. "Chanlix—the new abbess—and I have been spending considerable time together, and she couldn't abide my decorating tastes."

Alys's eyebrows rose to her hairline. While her brother was hardly celibate, his affairs with women had always been so brief and stormy that she rarely knew any of their names. Certainly none of them had the influence to cause him to change his living quarters. "The abbess, eh?"

To her surprise and delight, her brother blushed. "It isn't like that. We're the unofficial leaders of Women's Well, and so a great deal of the planning has fallen to us. It's a lot of work, building a town from scratch, especially when we were expecting to build nothing more than a few rough shelters in the desert."

She was sure her eyes were twinkling with humor and disbelief. "I see. It's all just business." Which was why he blushed at her teasing. "And how old is this abbess of yours?"

He glared at her, though there was no real heat in the expression. "Ancient. Older than *you.*"

She snorted. "How much older?"

He heaved a sigh and rolled his eyes. "Stop matchmaking."

"How much older?"

"One year."

She laughed. "Let me see if I have my math right. That would make her four whole years older than you. Right?"

Tynthanal waved that off, and the expression on his face quickly sobered. "She's a lovely woman, and we work well together. But Delnamal's men brutalized her."

Alys felt her own face stiffen. "And that makes her unfit for a man of your high character?" She was a fool to have made anything out of his silly blush and the décor in his house. He had never once visited their mother in the Abbey, had been so disdainful of the women there that he would not cross its threshold. How could she imagine he would take up with one of its denizens?

His expression turned to one of outright horror. "No! How could you think that of me? I meant only that she is . . . skittish. Understandably."

Alys reined in her outrage. It wasn't fair of her to hold his aloofness toward their mother against him. He'd been barely six years old when she'd been sent to the Abbey, and he had not been allowed to visit until he was ten, by which time he had practically forgotten her. Unlike Alys, he had only vague childhood memories to link him to her, and it had no doubt been easier for him to let her disgrace keep the distance between them.

"I'm sorry," Alys said, meaning it. "I know you're too good a man to blame her for what was done to her."

"I hope you do know that about me." That he was still angry and hurt by the accusation was clear in his eyes, and Alys wanted to kick herself.

"I do. And I look forward to meeting Chanlix."

"You will soon enough. She will join us after you and I have had a chance to catch up." He rose to check on the kettle, giving both of them enough time to regain their composure as he fixed two earthenware cups of tea and brought them to the table. The fragrance of mint wafted on the air, and once again Alys was surprised.

Mint did not love the soil of Aaltah, so it was either expensive because of its scarcity, or expensive because it was an import, depending on where it came from. While Tynthanal could easily afford it, she wouldn't have thought he'd have access to it out here in this remote outpost.

He smiled at her expression. "I brought some with me from home," he explained. "Then the abigails put together some growth potions, which we used on the last of my supply. Now, we have a mint garden. It actually seems to like the soil here."

Alys remembered the innkeeper's comment about her carrots, which must have flourished under the same potion, and felt her excitement growing. What sort of spells had they discovered here already, and what more were yet to be uncovered? Perhaps that growth spell could be a base on which to build a spell to simulate pregnancy.

Delnamal would be furious to see a flourishing town with plentiful supplies and naturally growing exotic herbs in a place he'd envisioned as a miserable prison encampment. "Are you selling it?"

"Not yet, but come spring when it's had more time to spread, I think we might."

"But you're selling potions already. At least the abigails are."

He nodded. "Mostly we're bartering them. The Well produces so many elements that the abigails can create growth potions by the gallon, and all the closest towns are thirsty for them. We give them potions, and they give us lumber and supplies in return. And also workmen."

"So that's how you've built such a sizable town in so little time and with so few supplies."

"Yes. The people of the outer provinces are used to living with deprivation, but they are more than happy not to have to anymore. You can see their gratitude all around."

He was glowing with pride over their accomplishments, but though Alys was suitably impressed, she could not ignore the danger Tynthanal and the abigails were courting. "And what happens when word reaches Aalwell that this town is bartering potions for its own enrichment? By law, the Abbey's profits are all payable to the Crown."

"It isn't *all* barter," he said. "Some potions we do sell, and those profits will make their way to the Crown's coffers."

"Which might appease Delnamal if he never finds out that you've built a town where he expected a prison, but you know he will. Word of a new town called Women's Well is surely spreading toward the capital even as we speak."

"No doubt much to his chagrin, Delnamal is not the king, nor is he the lord commander. I send weekly reports to my commander, and he reports what he feels is important to the king."

Tynthanal had told her long ago that he was withholding information in his reports, but he had downplayed just how many details he had failed to include. "So the reports Delnamal receives are filtered once through you, once through the lord commander, and once through the king."

Tynthanal nodded. "There may already be conflicting information trickling in, but since the lord commander and the king both trust me, they will take my word above silly rumors."

"For now. But distance will not protect you forever, and when Delnamal learns the truth . . ."

"I admit, it's risky." His lip curled in an ugly sneer. "Our brother will be most put out to hear we are not suffering as he had hoped." He smoothed out the sneer and replaced it with an expression of cool confidence. "But do you honestly think the king will let him punish us for flourishing? When the town is fully built and equipped, we will turn a tidy profit indeed, and the Crown's coffers will swell. Do you imagine our father will be anything but pleased?"

"It's not our father I'm worried about."

"I know. But Delnamal cannot act without the king's permission, and much as he hates to admit it, I am just as much the king's son as he is."

"And yet the king did not stop Delnamal from sending you out here."

"He might have if I'd asked him to. I came here willingly."

Alys's jaw dropped. It had never occurred to her that Tynthanal was not being forced to escort the abigails to their new home. It was clearly a punishment detail, after all.

He offered her a small smile. "I was not happy when Delnamal ordered me to guard the Abbey, but once my men and I took up that duty . . ." He shrugged. "I came because I knew my men could be trusted with the women's care, and anyone else . . . could not. Can you imagine an ordinary company of soldiers escorting a gaggle of whores on a long journey and guarding them in their new Abbey without taking egregious advantage of them?"

Alys shuddered. No, she could not. And in fact, although she respected her brother as a commander, it was hard to believe that his own men had been any more saintly than other soldiers might have been. "So your men are above such things?"

He shrugged. "Well, they're men. But I made quite the example of one who thought my orders did not apply to him, and everyone's been extremely cooperative since."

"As far as you know."

He leaned forward. "But that's just it, Alys. I *do* know." He rubbed his hands together. "There are some developments that I deemed too dangerous to put in writing, no matter how many secrecy spells I employed."

Alys could do little more than gape as her brother told her of the previously unknown element that was women's Kai.

"Once I saw it in Aalwell and recognized it for what it was," Tynthanal said, "I checked for it whenever I had a chance. It was . . . distressing how many women had it, though considering my admittedly rather cynical view on the self-control of men, there were fewer than I might have expected."

Alys thought of Shelvon and her loveless marriage with Delnamal. "Did you ever look at Shelvon?" she asked, then squirmed uncomfortably at her own question, as it seemed an invasion of her sister-in-law's privacy.

Tynthanal shook his head. "I didn't, but I suspect it would never have occurred to her to refuse her husband's advances, which, from what Chanlix and I have been able to piece together, is necessary for the generation of Kai. We have, of course, had to be very careful about which questions we ask and of whom."

"Do your men know about it?"

He shook his head. "Eventually, the knowledge will get out. Most women won't open their Mindseye to see the Kai, and many who do won't know what it is or what to do with it. But ours is not the only Abbey where women practice magic, and those who do will see and understand what is happening. Neither Chanlix nor I feel certain whether it will be an advantage to women or not, so we've chosen to keep it to ourselves for now."

"Is it like men's Kai? Can only the woman who produced it use it?" Belatedly, she realized that was not something a well-brought-up lady should know, but Tynthanal showed no sign of being shocked by her knowledge.

"Yes. No one else can touch it, and it can't be bound into a magic item."

That, at least, was good news. Alys didn't want to imagine a world where men could get hold of Kai by raping women and stealing it. "Have any of the women used it?"

"Only once," Tynthanal replied, telling her about an abigail who had created and tested a nasty Kai spell against a man who'd done nothing to deserve it. Although Tynthanal did not come right out and say it, Alys had the impression the test had not been sanctioned by the abbess.

"And after learning of this, none of the other women has used her Kai?" she asked disbelievingly.

"Chanlix promised that neither she nor any of her women will use Kai against an innocent victim again, and the guilty men are all back in Aalwell."

"Which is how you know they can't bind Kai into a magic object—because they've been trying to bind it into a spell they can send back to Aalwell."

"We, not they. I hope this won't shock your delicate sensibilities, but I've been working with Chanlix and a couple of her most skilled abigails to craft new spells. Spells using both masculine and feminine elements. I tried to help them bind the Kai—not without reservations—but we've had no success. It seems it can only be used to activate a spell and refuses to be bound. Just like men's Kai."

She nodded and gave her brother a long, assessing look. There was no law against men and women cooperating to craft magic together, but she could only imagine the horror polite society would react with if they knew what the king's favorite son was up to. "You're taking some big risks out here."

He took a sip of the tea, which he had so far ignored, and stared into the cup as he answered. "These are dangerous times for everyone in Seven Wells." He raised his gaze back to hers. "Father can threaten and bluster all he wants, but our mother's spell will not be reversed. When that fact becomes abundantly clear, everyone here in Women's Well will bear the brunt of the king's anger. I hope he still loves me enough not to order us all wiped out, but with Delnamal trying to poison him against us . . ." He rubbed his eyes as if suddenly tired. "We need to prepare ourselves for the worst-case scenario. So I'm helping Chanlix and her abigails as much as I can." A wry grin lifted the corners of his mouth. "And several of my more magically gifted men are, as well. One cannot have this many unattached men and women sharing one another's company for so long without attachments forming. There are already a couple of babies on the way. We have much to defend."

"Which brings me to why I'm here."

He lifted a brow. "You mean it's not to help reverse our mother's spell?" His tone said that he had never believed that lie, even though for a time Alys had believed it herself. But for her entire journey to Women's Well, she'd thought about Jinnell's selfless insistence that she didn't want the spell reversed, and by the time she'd arrived, she'd decided her time would be more wisely used if she tried to craft an illusion spell that would help fake a pregnancy. She was reasonably certain Shelvon would agree to use such a spell if it would spare Jinnell a forced marriage.

"I hope this won't shock *your* delicate sensibilities. But, you see, Mama left me this book . . ."

CHAPTER TWENTY-NINE

Ellin was just starting to drift off to sleep when something woke her—a soft, rhythmic tapping sound that barely penetrated the fog in her brain. She blinked in the darkened room, stifling a groan of annoyance. Ever since becoming queen, she'd found it difficult to surrender to sleep, her mind always whirling and worrying at problems the moment she lay down at night. It was easier when Graesan was there to take her mind off everything, but there was a risk whenever he came to her bed. They limited their trysts as much as they could both bear, and that meant she spent most nights alone.

The tapping went away for a second, and she entertained the brief illusion that she could now safely sink back into sleep, but the moment her eyes closed, it started up again.

She sat up and rubbed her eyes. Between the moonlight that shone through her windows and the amber glow of the banked coals in the fireplace, Ellin could see well enough without having to light a candle. As she came fully awake and her mind sharpened, she realized the tapping sound was coming from behind the tapestry on the far wall.

Alarmed, she swung her feet out of bed, grabbing for her dressing gown as she shivered in the chill air. The embers in the fireplace kept the worst of the cold at bay, but not until fuel was added and flames coaxed out in the morning would the room be comfortably warm. Sliding her feet into a pair of slippers, Ellin hastily tied the sash of her dressing gown and hurried toward the tapestry and the secret passageway it concealed. Not having expected Graesan tonight, she'd bolted the door, and her heart was in her throat with worry as she lifted the tapestry and started fumbling with the bolts in the dark. She couldn't imagine what would bring Graesan to her in the middle of the night unexpectedly, but she was certain it couldn't be for anything good.

Fear and cold made her clumsy, and it seemed to take forever to work the three bolts that held the door secure. Finally, the last one released and she pushed the door open. She gasped and covered her mouth when she found it wasn't Graesan standing outside that doorway.

"Please forgive the intrusion," Zarsha said. His hair was disheveled and loose around his face, and he was wearing a dressing gown open over a thin shirt of white linen and clumsily tied breeches. He held a small luminant in one hand, its dim light just enough to reveal his haggard expression as he sketched a quick and perfunctory bow.

"What are you doing here?" She instinctively kept her voice low, though she wondered if she should be screaming for help. Surely that was the sensible thing to do when a man unexpectedly appeared in her bedroom doorway in such a state—and when she was wearing nightclothes.

He shook his head. "It's a long story, best explained with visual aids. Please come with me."

He tried to turn away, presumably to lead her down into the passage, but she grabbed his arm and held her ground. He made a hissing sound of pain and grimaced. Ellin hastily let go, only to find a distinctive red stain on her hand.

"You're bleeding!" she cried, leaning forward to try to get a better look at his arm. His dressing gown was of midnight blue, and it was impossible to see it clearly in the dim light of the luminant. He twitched his arm out of reach when she tried to take a gentler hold.

"It's nothing serious," he assured her.

"What's going on? I'm not going anywhere until you tell me."

"You won't believe me until you see with your own eyes," he said. "Please trust me and come. I swear by the Mother you will be safe with me."

Having seen no sign that Zarsha held any strong religious beliefs, she wasn't sure how much weight to give his oath. However, despite all of Graesan's grumblings, she *did* trust Zarsha. Not to mention that if he meant her any harm, she had doomed herself the moment she'd opened the door to him. He didn't appear to be carrying a weapon, but he wouldn't need one to overpower her.

"How did you know this passage exists?" she asked as she stepped through the doorway and into the chill of the unheated passageway.

He flashed her a weak grin as he led the way down the long, dark hall. "I am extremely nosy. I've never yet set foot in a palace that doesn't have secret passages, and I always make it my business to find out where they are."

Ellin tied a couple more ribbons on her dressing gown, trying to make herself warmer even as she remembered Graesan's accusation that Zarsha was a spy of some sort. And wondering if it was because of his familiarity with the passageway that he'd known about her and Graesan. Had he lurked in hidden corners and seen Graesan coming to her room?

At the end of the hallway was a narrow staircase. Having explored the passageway, Ellin knew the stairs led down to the palace's ground floor, at which point another hallway would lead to an exit in the servants' wing. But instead of descending the staircase, Zarsha stopped about an arm's length short of it. His eyes went white as he opened his Mindseye.

Ellin gaped as Zarsha reached out to the empty air, grabbing something and pressing it against the wall. The wall turned into a door, and Zarsha's eyes cleared. She stared at him in openmouthed amazement. His grin had regained some of its customary mischief as he met her gaze.

"You didn't know this was here?"

She shook her head. "My steward will have some explaining to do," she said, wondering how the man could have failed to give her a thorough map of all the secret passages, for if there was one spell-hidden doorway she didn't know about, there were surely others. The steward had told Star there were no existing maps and his knowledge was incomplete, but she doubted he was truly ignorant of any passages that connected with the royal bedroom.

Zarsha shrugged. "He probably figured you didn't want to know about passages you couldn't use yourself."

She gave him a quelling look. "There's a difference between whether I *can* and whether I *should*. I know in Nandel a woman is supposed to prefer death over the dishonor of using magic, but we in Rhozinolm are more practical." There had been countless times in her life that Ellin had activated spells herself when it hadn't been worth the trouble of sending for a male servant to do it for her. As long as it was done where no one could see and people could just assume it had been done by a man, there was no reason a woman couldn't, for example, light her own luminant. "Besides, I'm less interested in whether *I* can use it than in whether *someone else* might use it."

Zarsha bowed his head respectfully. "Of course. I merely meant that there is likely no malice behind your steward's oversight."

"Maybe not, but I have the right to know about secret passages in my own palace."

"You'll get no argument from me." He opened the door and stepped through, holding it open for her as she followed. "I will give you a map of the passages I've discovered, in case your steward leaves anything else out when you ask for the full details."

Ellin followed in thoughtful—if somewhat resentful—silence as

Zarsha led the way through a series of halls and doors, none of which she'd known existed. It was downright humiliating that a foreign prince knew more about the layout of her palace than she did, and it made her wonder if she'd been harboring an unrealistic assumption about the power she held as queen. What other secrets were being kept from her?

After an almost dizzying series of twists and turns, Zarsha finally opened yet another secret door. Ellin blinked to find the doorway blocked with the back of a tapestry, which Zarsha swept aside. Tentatively, not sure what she was walking into, Ellin slipped under his arm and the tapestry and found herself in an aggressively masculine bedroom.

The first thing she noticed was the elegantly rustic décor, very unlike most of the palace. The colors were all muted and earthy, the furniture solid and heavy-looking, with only the most basic of adornments. Clearly, the room had been decorated with the express purpose of housing guests from Nandel, for whom simplicity was a way of life. A forest green silk counterpane lay crumpled on the floor by the massive dark wood bed, revealing densely woven white sheets marred by a splash of blood. Stepping closer, Ellin saw one of the pillows was rent and bloody, with a flurry of stained feathers spilling from the tear.

Beside the bed, a small night table lay on its side. Water from a fallen metal cup pooled on the floor around a broken luminant. On the floor, halfway under the bed, lay a dagger, its blade stained with blood.

Ellin took it all in in a series of quick glances. The scene, together with the blood that was drying on her hand, told a clear story. She turned to Zarsha. "You were attacked." It wasn't a question.

He nodded. "Luckily, I'm a light sleeper." He grimaced. "Not light enough to avoid this," he said, holding up his arm, "but it could have been a lot worse."

"Let me see," she said anxiously. There were more pressing issues than his injury—for instance, the identity and fate of his attacker—but she found herself reluctant to face them and all their implications. The diplomatic disaster of having Prince Waldmir's nephew attacked while her guest was unthinkable.

Zarsha put down the small luminant he'd been carrying—it was hardly needed in the bedroom, which was brightly lit—and slipped off his dressing gown to reveal a bloody tear in the arm of his shirt. "It's not bad," he assured her. "My sleeve and the pillow took the brunt of it." He pushed the sleeve up so she could see the short length of bandage he'd wrapped around his forearm right below his elbow. There were spots of blood on the bandage, but the edges were starting to dry, which suggested the wound was no longer bleeding. "It stings like a bastard, but it's shallow and barely more than an inconvenience."

Ellin was relieved he wasn't hurt more seriously, but it meant she could no longer put off the question she dreaded. "Who attacked you? And what happened to him?"

Zarsha hadn't made much effort to clean up the scene, hadn't even bothered to change his shirt, so that probably meant he hadn't had time to dispose of a body. But if he hadn't killed his attacker, then where was he?

Zarsha's face went grim, and his whole body visibly tensed. He opened and closed his mouth a couple of times, then huffed out a heavy sigh and shook his head. "There is no gentle way to do this."

He strode to a heavy wooden wardrobe across the room and threw the doors open.

"No!" Ellin cried, raising both hands to her mouth in shock and horror.

On the floor of the wardrobe, thoroughly trussed and gagged, his eye and his lip swelling from bruises, sat Graesan. The eye he could still open widened when he saw her, then he ducked his head, his shoulders and back drooping as he curled in on himself as if to escape her gaze.

Ellin's heart pounded in her throat, and no amount of willpower could stop the tears pooling in her eyes. Her immediate thought was that there was some kind of mistake, that Zarsha had to be lying. But there was no mistaking Graesan's body language as anything but guilt and shame.

She'd known Graesan was angry about her refusal to send Zarsha away. And she'd also known he was worried about what Zarsha would do with his dangerous knowledge of their affair. But she never could have imagined he would do *this*.

Tears flowed freely down her cheeks, and pain knifed through her whole body. Likely Graesan had been convinced he was doing this for her own good, that he was trying to protect her from their guilty secret, but no good intentions could overcome the crushing sense of betrayal that descended on her.

"I'm so sorry, Ellin," Zarsha said, his eyes full of sympathy.

Graesan's head shot up, and he glared at Zarsha's back, no doubt indignant over Zarsha's familiar use of her name. While it was patently inappropriate, this hardly seemed the time to be concerned about protocol. No protocol in the world would cover how a suitor should behave when revealing to the woman he's pursuing that her lover tried to kill him.

She took a deep, shuddering breath and scrubbed at the tears on her cheeks. She could not afford to lose herself in heartbreak. Not now. There was too much at stake.

For the span of a couple minutes, she stood there quietly, focusing on breathing, on fighting back the roiling emotions that tried to cripple her, on letting her reason be her one and only controlling force. And as she did so, she noticed two glaring incongruities in the situation.

Graesan had been acting as her secretary for the last month, but he was still a trained soldier, and he would never have risen in rank to master of the guard if he weren't a very good one. How had Zarsha, a spoiled prince's nephew lying unarmed and helpless in his bed, managed to fight Graesan off? Even after he'd missed with that first strike, Graesan should have been able to overpower him.

And since Zarsha apparently *had* fought Graesan off, why was Graesan still alive? And why had Zarsha brought *her* here instead of a squadron of palace guards?

The tears dried up, and the emotions subsided into the lockbox she'd built in her heart. She looked back and forth between Zarsha and Graesan.

"I'm impressed that you managed to fight off an armed, trained attacker while you were unarmed and supposedly asleep in your bed," she said as her gaze settled on Zarsha. "How did you manage it?"

"I'm good in a fight."

"So it would seem. Perhaps in Nandel it is customary for lords to receive more extensive training in the martial arts than it is here in Rhozinolm?" Any man of the nobility would have learned sword-play growing up, but only those with a military nature would keep up with it as adults. What use had a courtier for swordplay except perhaps for fun and a spirit of competition?

"We are a warlike people, so yes." His face was now a bland mask, giving away nothing.

He knew about secret passageways in the palace that even she as queen hadn't known of. And he was an experienced enough fighter to subdue a trained soldier even when unarmed and taken by surprise. Perhaps Graesan's assertions that he was a spy were not born of jealousy, after all.

"If you ask me a direct question, I will give you the truth," Zarsha said. "I will never lie to you. But some truths are best left unspoken."

It was as good as an admission, and it certainly explained why he had remained in Rhozinolm so long after their engagement fell through. It also explained why he had spent so little of his adult life in Nandel, why he had traveled from court to court to court.

He was right, however, and this particular truth was best kept silent. If ever he was caught, they would both be able to claim she knew nothing. She turned her attention to Graesan, who was unable to meet her eyes.

"Why didn't you kill him?" The emotions she'd been locking down tried to make an escape, and her voice cracked. A vision flashed through her mind of Graesan's body lying dead on the floor. She hastily thrust it away.

Zarsha crossed the distance between them and took her clenched hands in his, giving them a squeeze. Graesan made a muffled sound of protest from behind his gag, but they both ignored him.

"Because you love him," Zarsha said.

Strangely, she found herself flinching from the gentleness of his tone, and she was unable to meet his eyes.

"The sensible thing to do is kill him and dispose of his body," Zarsha continued. "Erase all signs of a struggle, and simply make him mysteriously disappear. You cannot afford the diplomatic ramifications of an attempt on my life, and the best way to hide it is to hide *him*." He jerked his chin toward the wardrobe, then let out a heavy sigh.

"If I were being completely practical, I would have done it already and you would never have known what happened to him. But I couldn't do that to you, not after everything you've already lost."

"So you brought me here to convince me to condemn him myself." She closed her eyes tightly, wishing this were nothing but a terrible nightmare.

"If you think it's best he should die, then I will take care of it for you," Zarsha confirmed. "As I said, it's the practical thing to do, the only sure way to keep a secret. And make sure he doesn't try something like this again."

She swayed on her feet and felt as if she might be sick. Zarsha was still holding her hands, and he gave them another squeeze.

"But I also want to present you with another alternative. It's very risky, and it would require your man's cooperation. It's probably irresponsible of me even to suggest it."

Ellin opened her eyes. She would happily grasp at any straw he offered, and he knew it. "What alternative?"

"Well, clearly he has to go. You cannot keep him close to you when he has shown himself dangerous and done something he surely knew you would not approve of. I know you love him, but you cannot trust him, not anymore."

"Don't you think I know that?" she snapped, hating him for rubbing her face in it.

"I can hire him away from you and send him to Nandel. I spend very little time there, as you know, but I do have an estate and a staff which operates it in my absence. That includes a security force, and though he would have to take a significant demotion, he can serve on that force."

"In Nandel," she murmured, her heart breaking all over again. She couldn't imagine taking Graesan back into her bed after tonight, but to send him to the land she herself had so dreaded . . .

"The only alternative is death. And if the murderous look he's giving me is any indication, he might prefer that alternative."

Zarsha finally let go of her hands, retrieving the knife from under the bed. He carelessly wiped the blade on the already-stained sheets, then crossed to the wardrobe and bent toward Graesan. Ellin almost cried out in alarm, but before a sound left her throat Zarsha had cut the gag and pulled it from Graesan's mouth. He then squatted so that their eyes were on the same level.

"Before you say something we all might regret," Zarsha said, "consider that if you refuse my offer, you will have a swift release from your suffering, but you will condemn Ellin to live with your death on her conscience for the rest of her life."

Graesan jerked backward as if he'd been slapped, as if he'd never even begun to consider anyone's feelings but his own. Ellin had always thought him sensitive and kind, had thought he'd seen her as a friend and equal as well as a lover. But tonight proved she'd been wrong about him in oh so many ways. He didn't respect her enough to trust her decisions. He didn't trust her love enough to tolerate a rival. And he didn't love her enough to take her feelings into account before trying to kill the man he saw as that rival.

"I made a huge gamble by not killing you," Zarsha continued. "I gambled that she would not want you dead and that I would not be putting that terrible decision on her conscience, and I gambled that your love for her is genuine and you would spare her that pain. Don't you dare destroy her just because you can't stomach the thought of working for me."

Graesan made a disgusted growling sound and spat at Zarsha's feet. "Someday, she will see you as the menace that you are, and she will wish I had succeeded."

"That may be," Zarsha said with a brief ironic grin. "The question is will you be around to see it, or will you be buried in some secret grave when it happens?"

Ellin held her breath as the two men stared at each other, both temporarily ignoring her. There was no missing their mutual desire to end the other's life. Zarsha had refrained for her sake, but could Graesan swallow his pride? And how could she bear it if he didn't?

Eventually, Graesan turned to look at her, and the anger and hatred on his face faded. There was longing and sorrow and pain in his expression, but there was love, also. He lowered his head and closed his eyes.

"I'll go."

With a rueful smile, Chanlix remembered the day when she'd blushed and stammered in embarrassment because Tynthanal had seen her ankles as she waded in the cooling waters of the spring. Now here she was, knee-deep in the water with the back of her robes pulled between her legs and tucked into a belt in the front to create impromptu breeches. Her toes curled into the sand, and she turned her face up into the warmth of the setting sun, enjoying the sense of peace she always felt in this place. The young trees had grown tall enough that there were pockets of privacy to be had along the spring's edges, so she could wade and relax unobserved.

She opened her eyes when she heard a rustle in the vegetation behind her. She was not surprised to see Tynthanal appear at the water's edge, smiling at her and giving her exposed calves an admiring glance. The familiar blush rose to her cheeks, but she made no move to drop her skirts and cover her legs. Meeting here and watching the sun set together had become something of a ritual for them. She was sure the people of Women's Well had noticed them disappearing together like this, just as she was sure most of them as-

sumed they were sleeping together. Which they weren't, although
Chanlix was finding it increasingly difficult to explain to herself why
that was so.

Tynthanal had been hard at work with training drills and sparring today, and was dressed in the standard military shirt and trousers, his jacket with its insignia marking his rank nowhere to be
seen. The shirt was plastered to his skin with sweat, and the great
swaths of dirt stains on his trousers said he had spent a fair amount
of those drills on his backside. She raised her eyebrows at him, for
both her own observation and the admiration of his men told her
he was a highly skilled swordsman. When he sparred, everyone else
stopped what they were doing to watch.

Tynthanal laughed to see her curious regard. "I added some
grappling work into the sword drills today," he said, pulling off his
sweat-soaked shirt with a sigh of relief. "It's hard on the clothing."

Chanlix had seen him without his shirt often enough that she
ought to be immune to the sight by now, but, damn it, her heart
skipped a beat every time. His body was lithe, but the muscles were
distinctly defined and in proportions that flirted with perfection.
She expected him to roll up his trousers and join her in the water,
and she tried not to fantasize about helping him splash the cool
water over all that beautiful skin he was revealing.

But instead of rolling up his trousers, he began unlacing them.

"What do you think you're doing?" she cried in what was meant
to sound like disapproval. Unfortunately, it came out sounding girl-
ishly breathless and excited.

"I'm taking off my trousers," he said matter-of-factly, seconds
before the laces came free and the trousers dropped to his feet, revealing drawers of white lawn so thin as to be almost transparent.
He grinned at her as he kicked the trousers aside, but the expression
in his eyes was more of assessment than humor.

Chanlix commanded herself to look away, to tell him in no uncertain terms that he must put those trousers back on immediately.
It was beyond indecent for a man to expose himself in such a way,
though perhaps he felt that as an abigail she had seen so many

naked men that she need not be afforded the same consideration as a respectable lady.

Chanlix swallowed hard, shoving that bitter thought to the back of her mind. She knew perfectly well he meant no such disrespect. His pursuit of her had never been anything but gentlemanly, and even when he pushed the boundaries, he did so with great care and gentleness. He was watching her carefully right now, gauging her reaction, poised to cover up if she asked him to.

Her heart seemed to flutter from somewhere in the vicinity of her throat. She had never in her life lain with a man who had not paid for her services, and though she had occasionally had clients who pleasured her—mostly for their own enjoyment—she had never before experienced true desire. When she had become too old to work the pavilion, she had happily laid that part of her life to rest and assumed no man would ever touch her in that way again. Then, after the attack on the Abbey, she had *hoped* that no man would ever touch her that way again.

And yet there was no denying the sudden racing of her pulse, nor the tug of desire she felt as her eyes drank in the beauty of Tynthanal's body—and the mingled desire and caution in his eyes.

When she couldn't find the voice to scold him, Tynthanal slowly waded into the water toward her. She smiled to see his skin pepper with gooseflesh at the chill. He came to stand within an arm's length of her, his eyes locked on her face as she struggled with her own warring emotions.

"Would it offend you if I rinsed off?" he asked, causing her to swallow hard again.

The drawers that were *almost* transparent now would be literally so if they became wet. And she wasn't sure how she could keep her hands off him if that happened.

"With all the beautiful young women in this town," she whispered, "I cannot for the life of me understand why you would want me."

One corner of his mouth turned up. "There are not a few handsome young men in town, as well. Surely you would find one of them more to your liking."

She scowled at him. "But you are a king's son, and I have lain with more men than you can imagine."

The look on his face hardened, and his voice took on a hint of a growl. "Do you really think so little of yourself for what was done to you?"

"I don't blame myself for what happened in that courtyard," she protested. She knew Tynthanal was concerned that she had been permanently traumatized by what had happened there. She doubted any man could truly understand the lifetime of traumas that came with being an abigail, of how little each individual indignity mattered in the grand scheme of things. If she was broken at all, it had happened long before that terrible day.

"That's not what I'm talking about," Tynthanal replied with some heat. "I know you are not so heartless as to blame the victims—even yourself—for my half-brother's barbarity."

She frowned in puzzlement. "Then what did you mean by 'what was done to' me?"

"I meant being sent to the Abbey in the first place! Would you have lain with all those men had you had a choice?"

Chanlix opened her mouth to protest, but no sound came out. Once she had entered the Abbey, she had resigned herself to her fate and been a dutiful abigail. She had loathed her time in the pavilion, but she had never cried and carried on as some of the abigails did when they first arrived. And she had never thought of selling her body to those men as something that was *done to* her. She had gone to their beds compliantly, if not exactly willingly.

"Even if you had lain with them willingly," Tynthanal said gently, "I would not condemn you for it." He moved closer to her, his hand rising to cup her cheek in a gesture that sent the most pleasant shiver imaginable through her. "You are kind, and courageous, and warm, and wise, and nothing in your past can change that."

He bent to kiss her lips, hesitating just a moment, giving her a chance to rebuff him. She tried to force a refusal out of her mouth, tried to do the only sensible thing. If she kissed him, she would be lost, her every defense broken down.

But was there truly any reason to keep denying herself what she wanted? She'd feared to give him her body because she was sure her heart would go with it, but if she were being entirely honest with herself, her heart had been his for some time now. Withholding her body would not protect her when eventually real life intruded and tore Tynthanal away from her.

With a needy moan, she stepped into his body and put her arms around his neck. His lips tasted of salt, and his skin smelled of sweat and desert dust, and yet it was the sweetest, most delicious kiss she had ever experienced. He untucked her robes from her belt and let the hem drop into the water, but before she thought to protest, he was hiking that hem upward, his hand sliding against the bare skin of her leg.

Chanlix broke the kiss and looked up into his dark, heated eyes. "Perhaps we should find somewhere more private," she suggested breathlessly, for now that they'd crossed that invisible boundary, she saw little chance that either of them could stop with just kisses and caresses, no matter how sweet those might be.

Tynthanal smiled and pressed himself against her. "I don't think I can wait that long. No one will disturb us here."

Having previously admitted to herself that people no doubt believed they were already sleeping together, she had to agree that they were unlikely to be interrupted, but that was not her only concern. "In the days when I worked the pavilion, I regularly took contraceptive potions, but I haven't since. I would feel . . . safer drinking one."

While Mother Brynna's spell meant that women could no longer conceive against their will, there was ample evidence a woman's conscious will and her unconscious desires were not necessarily one and the same—else Princess Shelvon would have conceived again by now. Chanlix had given up any hope of becoming a mother when she'd entered the Abbey, but she could not be entirely sure a kernel of that hope hadn't survived.

Tynthanal pressed a gentle kiss on her lips, though the fire still burned bright in his eyes. "That won't be necessary with me," he confided. "It seems I am not capable of fathering children."

Chanlix's eyes widened in surprise. "You aren't? How do you know?"

"I had my eye on a woman once," he said, "and I asked the abbess to examine our bloodlines—privately, because I did not want to propose without knowing in advance that our marriage would be sanctioned. Upon examining mine, she informed me that there would be no sanctioned marriage for me. Ever."

She looked at him in wonder and not a little sadness. She hadn't been aware that he'd had any contact with his mother once she'd been banished to the Abbey. Suddenly, his unmarried status made a lot more sense, and she knew it was a sign of his trust in her that he would tell her what many would consider the shameful truth.

"I'm so sorry," she said.

"I long ago came to terms with the fact that I am not meant to be a family man," he said, but she couldn't fail to hear the undertone of sorrow and regret in his voice. "Sometimes, I think it's for the better—especially when I see Delnamal's eagerness to strike out at Alys's daughter. I cannot imagine the horror that must be." He shook off the sadness, pressing close to her once more. "But let us set aside such weighty matters. At present, my inability to father children is decidedly convenient."

He waggled his brows at her suggestively, and she *giggled*. No such sound had escaped her lips since she was a little girl. He had an almost magical ability to make her cares disappear, to toss aside decades of hard living and degradation to make her feel hopeful and light of heart. And her body yearned for him in a way it had yearned for no other man.

She reached up to touch his face, and he turned his head to kiss her palm.

"I want you, Chanlix Rai-Chanwynne," he murmured, his breath coming short. "Will you have me?"

"Yes," she said, wrapping her arms around his neck and rising to her toes so she could kiss his lips. "Yes, I will."

CHAPTER THIRTY

Alys enjoyed the luxury of walking unguarded down the streets of Women's Well. During her first week here, her honor guard had insisted on doing their duty, surrounding her whenever she was in public. But what had felt natural and unremarkable in the capital city of Aalwell felt faintly ridiculous in this small frontier town, where there were no beggars or cutpurses or even painfully poor people. It was a remarkably cooperative community, and since at least a quarter of the residents of the town were soldiers, it was about as safe a place as Alys could imagine.

During her second week in Women's Well, her honor guard finally began to relax, and now during her fourth, they spent more time helping out with the seemingly never-ending work of building and expanding than they did guarding her. She was very glad she'd left Falcor with the children, for she doubted he'd have been as easy to shake.

The house she'd taken over since her arrival was about a ten-minute walk from Tynthanal's, which she ordinarily found convenient. She had spent countless hours in that house with her brother and Chanlix and various other abigails, combining their talents to create new spells. At first, the abigails had been clearly taken aback—and manifestly uncomfortable—with the thought of practicing magic side by side with a woman of her rank, and Tynthanal had worried about wagging tongues. But when Alys had made it clear she had no intention of carrying out her own experiments in secrecy, they had all gradually begun to accept her.

As Alys became more familiar with the elements available in Women's Well—and as she spent so many hours openly practicing magic, discussing it with others, and experimenting—she realized that she had found her true calling in life. Her heart sang with happiness and excitement, even as fear continued to simmer in the background. Within two weeks of arriving at Women's Well, she had concocted a potion that could create a convincing visual illusion of pregnancy, and she'd been sure it was only a matter of time before she would have just what she needed to fool Delnamal—assuming Shelvon was willing to cooperate and drink her potions. But since then, she'd run into roadblock after roadblock.

The visual illusion did not hold up to touch, nor could she make it last more than two hours at a stretch. And then there was the fact that a woman's body changes gradually during pregnancy, and Alys could only create a static illusion. And though the abigails and Tynthanal had tried to help, there was nothing in existing magic—neither men's nor women's—that seemed applicable. And so she had occasionally allowed herself to be drawn into other work as the magical practice at Women's Well had grown and expanded. They no longer met at Tynthanal's house, for there was now a dedicated building for experimentation, closer to the Well. Their very own Academy, they liked to joke. And their Academy was about to test a spell the likes of which the world had never seen.

The sun was setting as Alys walked to her brother's house for the third time that day, but instead of finding the short walk convenient, this time she wished she could stretch it out for longer, because once she entered that house, it would be time to make an irreversible decision that could doom Women's Well.

When she arrived at Tynthanal's house, Tynthanal, Chanlix, and Faltah were already waiting for her. Faltah had clearly been stunningly beautiful once. The right side of her face still was, but the left side was a different story. When Delnamal had attacked the women of the Abbey, beautiful Faltah had been one of the most popular targets. Despite the humiliation of being taken so publicly while she shivered with cold in the muddy courtyard, she had not resisted—until Delnamal's personal secretary, who was well-known to the women of the Abbey for his love of causing pain, came for her.

Even the women of the Abbey of the Unwanted had some protection under the law, and when Melcor purchased the use of an abigail, he was strictly forbidden from damaging her beyond healing. But the attack in the Abbey had not been an ordinary transaction, and Melcor had felt no fear that he would be punished for the damage he inflicted. He'd repeatedly struck Faltah's face as he raped her, crushing her cheekbone, her jaw, and her eye socket. The abigails were able to save her life in the aftermath, but there was no healing spell to realign all those badly broken bones into their original form, and they had not been able to save her eye.

Alys joined the other three at the table, sitting across from Faltah. It was hard to look at the poor girl's face, hard to see the devastating damage that had been done to her, but Alys did not allow herself to look away. Faltah's undamaged eye shone with a strange combination of excitement and cold, deadly fury, her breath coming short as Tynthanal laid a cloth-wrapped package in the middle of the table. He glanced from face to anxious face, then unwrapped the package to reveal a crudely carved, inert flier.

It looked more like a child's toy than an actual flier. Most fliers were made of deep black Aalwood, and they were distinctively decorated for their owners. Alys would recognize one of Tynthanal's fliers anywhere, but for the purpose of this spell, anonymity was key. Instead of using Aalwood, he'd whittled this flier out of a scrap piece of blond lumber, making no effort to sand down the rough knife marks. As the lumber didn't have the capacity for all the needed spell elements, a couple of iron nails had been hammered in, making the flier even uglier.

Beside the flier was a small scroll, with Melcor's full name printed on its outside. It was sealed with wax and marked confidential.

"If we do this," Tynthanal said into the silence as they all stared at the flier, "it is treason." Which was why they were meeting in the privacy of Tynthanal's house to test it, although the rest of the abigails of their fledgling Academy knew about it. Knowing it had been invented and knowing it was being used were two different things.

"No one will know we sent it," Chanlix said, fussing nervously at the red robes she still wore, though most of the abigails had abandoned them.

"It's treason whether we get caught or not," Tynthanal chided. "If we do this, we must do it with our eyes wide open."

Faltah, dressed in a drab brown kirtle and cloaked in anger that bordered on hatred, snarled at him. "Why would you help us craft this spell, then refuse to use it?"

Alys wanted to leap in and protect her little brother from Faltah's open bitterness, but Tynthanal didn't need her help.

"I'm not refusing," he said, seemingly unaffected by Faltah's hostility. "I'm merely pointing out that no matter how careful we've been, it's dangerous."

Faltah's rage burned on, but Chanlix silenced her with a hand on her arm. "That's enough, Faltah," Chanlix said, then nodded at Tynthanal. "We've heard your warning, and we know the danger. We're willing to risk it."

Tynthanal looked at Alys for yet another confirmation. They had all agreed that an open and obvious use of the women's Kai would be disastrous, although someone somewhere was bound to use it eventually. A respectable woman who was raped might never open her Mindseye to see that the Kai was there—and might not recognize it for what it was even if she did—but there were Abbeys throughout Seven Wells, and even outside of Abbeys, Alys was sure she wasn't the only woman who'd played with forbidden magic. Eventually, the existence of women's Kai would become common knowledge, and Alys had to agree with Chanlix's assessment that men like Delnamal would immediately think to use it to their own advantage.

But regardless of whether their complex, Kai-fueled flier spell worked as planned or didn't, it was unlikely its secret ingredient would be revealed. Tynthanal might not be the only male in the world who could see women's Kai, but there was as yet no sign of any other man seeing it. The flier would not reveal the existence of women's Kai, but it was still clearly a malicious spell, and if it was traced back to Women's Well . . .

"The women Melcor savaged deserve justice," Alys said. "It's worth the risk."

She knew she wasn't alone in wishing they could send the spell to Delnamal. He might not have raped any of the abigails himself, but it had been done on his orders, and he was arguably more deserving of punishment than anyone. But though odds were slim that Shelvon could provide him with an heir and thereby save Jinnell, Alys wasn't prepared to give up that last sliver of hope. Besides, there was no question that Faltah would rather target Melcor than the man who'd held Melcor's leash.

Tynthanal glanced quickly at Faltah, then away, his jaw working as he ground his teeth. "If a man of mine had done that, the whipping would not have stopped until he was dead." Even Faltah couldn't have missed the chilling truth in those words. "If this works, then one way or another, we will make sure all the men responsible are punished."

His eyes went white, and he fed some Rho into the flier, scooping it into his hand so it would not immediately fly away. His eyes cleared, and he held the flier out to Faltah, still keeping its wings trapped. In all their testing, they had been unable to find a way to bind Kai into a magic item; however, it could be used to trigger a spell in a magic item in the same way that men's Kai could. This flier contained a total of five spells, and all of them had to work correctly and in tandem.

Alys licked her lips and squirmed. She had tested the targeting spell she'd invented many times now—based on the spell that allowed fliers to be directed to specific people, it was one of her most heartening successes—and it had worked with everything she'd tried. When she attached the targeting spell to a sleep spell, the sleep spell would only work on its intended target, making the magic item that contained it entirely safe to handle even when the spell was active. But would the targeting spell work successfully with this untested Kai spell?

Faltah's eyes went white, and she reached above her. Alys knew she was plucking the mote of Kai that was the final element needed to complete the spell they had named Vengeance. She gripped the table with both hands, her body drenched with sweat as she wondered how she would live with herself if her spell failed.

For all the anger and hatred Faltah carried, she had not completely lost her better nature. Her hand halted just short of the flier, and her unfocused eyes rose to Tynthanal's face.

"Are you sure?"

Tynthanal looked distinctly nervous, with a thin sheen of sweat glowing on his upper lip, but he did not hesitate. "I'm sure."

I'm not! Alys wanted to shout, but she bit her tongue. Her brother was far too honorable to let any other man take this risk, and she loved him for it even as she feared for him.

Faltah pushed her Kai into the flier, speaking the full name of its intended target, and everyone held their breath. Alys opened her Mindseye to look, but the only elements she could see in the flier were components of the ordinary flier spell. The other spells they had put into the flier were well hidden.

Alys closed her Mindseye in time to see Tynthanal open his hand. The flier rose into the air and flew out the window he had left cracked open just for that purpose. Tynthanal closed his eyes, possibly saying a silent prayer that the Kai spell had not affected him. The fact that the self-destruct spell had not been triggered was a good sign, but because it was so difficult to test malicious spells—especially those using Kai—Alys didn't feel entirely comforted.

The corner of Tynthanal's mouth lifted in a smile, and he opened his eyes. "You can all relax, ladies. The spell didn't strike me."

Chanlix frowned at him in concern, putting her hand on his arm and biting her lip. "Are you sure?"

He covered her hand with his own and gave her a wolfish smile. "I've been imagining ways we can celebrate our success tonight, and I can tell you unequivocally that I am not affected."

Chanlix blushed like a virgin, for though everyone knew she and Tynthanal were sleeping together, she still seemed uncomfortable with acknowledging the relationship.

Alys grimaced, though she suspected her eyes were twinkling. "I did not want to know that about my little brother," she said. Tynthanal laughed, and even Faltah smiled.

Now there was nothing to do but wait. It would be a delicate matter to determine whether the spell was effective or not. They would not be present to see it strike, and Melcor was unlikely to want to talk about the effects if it worked. But Chanlix had some contacts among the madams who worked the brothels in the Harbor District, and when the flier had had enough time to reach its destination, she would discreetly contact them and inquire. If Melcor suddenly had trouble performing, the madams would tell her—and the experiment would be a success.

Chanlix laid the dress across her bed and shook her head in wonder. She had not worn an actual *dress* for twenty-five years, and the red robes she'd once hated had now become familiar and almost comforting. She donned those robes, and she knew exactly who she was, what her place in society was. But tonight when she'd returned to her house after sending the Kai flier on its way, she'd found this neatly packed little bundle on her doorstep.

For whenever you're ready, Tynthanal's note had read when she'd opened the package to reveal its contents. As if he knew something had permanently changed within her when she'd finally given herself to him, that she could no longer be Mother Chanlix. And yet even so, he was gentle and thoughtful about how to communicate his message. He did not hand her the package in person, which might have made her feel honor bound to accept and wear it immediately. There was no pressure, no demand. Merely an invitation.

She reached out to stroke the soft blue fabric. The dress was simple and modest, with few embellishments beyond a pleat here or there and a few accents of darker blue around the waist and neckline. Her eyes misted as she realized Tynthanal had known she would not want something exceedingly ornate and eye-catching, even if such might make a more extravagant gift. If she were to wear so simple a dress in the cosmopolitan center of Aalwell, people would assume her a commoner, for unlike the typical dress of a noblewoman, it was clearly designed to be donned without the help of a lady's maid. Which made it perfect for her at this moment.

Her belly fluttering with nerves, Chanlix reached up and unpinned her wimple, setting it aside. Then, she removed her red robes, smoothing the fabric in a gesture that was almost affectionate as she carefully folded them.

There was a single layer of petticoats attached to the skirt of the blue dress, and the fabric settled comfortably over Chanlix's hips. Laces along both sides of the bodice allowed her to snug the fabric around her waist and chest, though if she wanted the dress to show to its best advantage, she would have to invest in a more shapely set of stays.

Her only use for a mirror in the years since she'd been confined to the Abbey had been to help her pin her wimple in place. The single mirror in her possession was too small for her to examine the overall appearance of the dress, and she added a floor-length mirror to her list of needs. She moved this way and that, catching glimpses of herself in that small mirror, noticing how the dress accentuated curves the shapeless robes had long hidden. She did not flatter herself with delusions of beauty, but she would not be an embarrassment to her sex if she appeared in public in this dress. Provided she had a matching headdress and shoes, which of course she did not.

Did she dare imagine herself going *shopping*? For something she didn't actually *need*? That in itself would be a courageous act, even if she never mustered the courage to wear the dress for anyone's eyes but Tynthanal's.

Chanlix bit her lip as she examined herself in the mirror one last time. She had no personal finances whatsoever, for any money she earned belonged to the Abbey and the Crown. Perhaps she should settle for wearing the dress in the privacy of her own home. Certainly that was not what Tynthanal had had in mind when he'd bought it for her, but she suspected he would understand.

Nervous and excited in equal measure, Chanlix carefully removed the dress and changed back into her robes. Tomorrow, she would sell several potions with no intention of turning any of those profits over to the Crown. And with those profits, she would purchase everything she needed so that by dinnertime, she could dress like a free woman for the first time since she'd passed through the Abbey's gates as a heartbroken girl of fifteen.

A small smile tipped up the corners of her mouth as she imagined the surprised looks her abigails would give her. Everyone had been urging her to set the robes aside for weeks now, and yet she suspected they did not expect their persuasions to succeed. And the smile grew even broader when she imagined Tynthanal's reaction when he saw how she had embraced his gift.

She had a feeling she would not be wearing the dress for long after he set eyes on her.

Delnamal was shut up in his private study with Melcor, going over his schedule for the following day, when one of his guards knocked on the door. Delnamal grumbled at the interruption. It was past dinnertime, and his stomach was anxious to be done with the tedious schedule review so he could retire to the dining hall.

"Come in," he snarled with poor grace. His guards knew better than to disturb him when the door was closed, and they wouldn't do it if it wasn't important.

The guard opened the door and stepped in, bowing. "Forgive the interruption, Your Highness. A page has a flier for Lord Melcor.

It was trapped in a stairwell, and its message is marked urgent and confidential."

Melcor frowned, and Delnamal glared at the man for allowing his private business to interfere with his liege's schedule.

"I beg your pardon, Your Highness," Melcor said when he saw the glare. "I have no idea what this could be about. I can see to the flier after we're finished."

"No, no," Delnamal said, leaning back in his chair and making an impatient gesture toward the door. "Send the boy in. Clearly this message is of *vital* importance, and far be it from me to cause you any delays."

Melcor's face lost some of its healthy color, and the man's obvious fear and discomfort restored some of Delnamal's good humor. Melcor was an excellent secretary, but he had a somewhat inflated view of his own importance and dearly loved hearing himself talk. The only reason they were still shut up in this study going over the schedule was because of Melcor's insistence on discussing in great detail every silly rumor that reached his ears.

A young page, maybe about ten years old, with aggressively red hair and freckles, stepped into the room and bowed, holding the ugliest flier Delnamal had ever seen in his cupped hands.

"That thing could fly?" he found himself muttering in amazement. The child had plucked out the Rho that had powered the flier when he'd captured it, so that it lay inert in his hands.

"It was trying to go through a closed door in the stairwell, Your Highness," the page said in a piping voice. "It damaged itself."

Delnamal snorted. From halfway across the room he could see the clumsy knife marks that covered the entire flier and knew that damage had nothing to do with battering itself against a door. The page held the flier out to Melcor, whose frown had grown even more puzzled. Melcor shook his head and took the flier.

With a suddenness that made everyone in the room jump, the flier came to life, its crude little head with its crude little beak pecking downward with vicious speed. Melcor yelped and dropped the flier as blood beaded on his hand.

Delnamal leapt to his feet, pushing back his chair so fast it toppled over. The page cried out and backed away so fast he tripped over his own clumsy feet and landed on the carpet on his bottom. The flier, its beak red with Melcor's blood, dropped to the floor, inert once again. As Delnamal watched, the flier suddenly burst into white-hot flame, setting the carpet on fire.

The palace guard, who'd backed away from the flier when it first fell, acted quickly to stamp out the fire before the whole carpet was alight. The room filled with the stink of smoke, and all that was left of the flier was a crushed pile of ash.

The guard grabbed the page's arm in a brutal grip and shook him so hard the child's teeth chattered. "Who gave you that flier?" he roared.

The page immediately broke into terrified sobs, sputtering out nonsense that Delnamal was sure were denials of wrongdoing. He turned to Melcor.

"How badly are you hurt?" he asked.

"It's nothing serious," Melcor assured him, holding up his hand to show the small, bloody puncture. He put the finger in his mouth to suck off the blood.

The guard backhanded the page, sending the boy sprawling into the pile of ash. The boy curled into a protective ball, crying piteously as the guard advanced on him.

"Enough," Delnamal snapped, and the guard looked at him in surprise.

"But I can make him tell the truth!" he protested.

Delnamal frowned at the sobbing child. Was it possible someone had hired or coerced him to bring the flier to Melcor? If so, it would certainly be important to wrest the identity of the person behind this from the boy. The guard could probably get the boy talking without having to resort to the inquisitor.

But then he looked at Melcor, who was examining the cut again after having cleared away the blood. It was such a minor injury, and Melcor seemed more surprised by it than hurt. Surely it wasn't worth beating a child over.

Delnamal came around his desk and squatted by the fallen boy, wincing as his knees protested the position and his doublet strained.

"Look at me," he said in a voice of calm command. The tone—devoid of the guard's anger and accusation—was enough to penetrate the fog of the child's fear. Eyes still swimming with tears, nose running and quivering lip swelling from the guard's blow, the child met Delnamal's gaze.

"Did someone give you that flier to deliver to Melcor?" he asked gently. "I promise you won't be punished as long as you answer honestly."

It was a regrettably empty promise. If the boy admitted to being asked to bring the flier to Melcor, he would have to be punished harshly as an example to others. However, a child of his age was unlikely to understand such things well enough to see through the lie.

"I swear, sir," the child sniveled, "I found it in the stairwell. The door is all scratched up where it was trying to go through. I can show you."

"No need," Delnamal said, ruffling the child's hair then trying not to groan as he stood up once more. "I believe you."

The guard was still regarding the child with suspicion and distaste. Delnamal gave him a warning look.

"There's no reason to believe the boy was asked to deliver the flier," he said. "There would be no point in it self-destructing if we could learn who sent it by questioning the boy."

The guard bowed. "Yes, Your Highness."

Delnamal looked back at his secretary, no longer feeling so hungry. Someone had gone through a lot of trouble to send that flier, using some very expensive spells. Why would someone go to that expense and trouble to inflict so small a wound?

Melcor was looking at the little cut with some trepidation. One of the rumors he'd brought to Delnamal's attention was that the women of the Abbey were flourishing in their exile. Delnamal knew from hearing the lord commander's reports at the royal council meetings that the punitive exile had not turned out quite as planned.

But the reports said the women were producing potions at a pace that would be highly advantageous to the Crown's coffers, and everyone was pleased at the prospect of unexpected profits come tax time.

The rumors Melcor had mentioned suggested that the new Abbey was producing stronger, better potions than ever before. In fact, there had even been rumors that the Well that had sprung up in the Wasteland was producing feminine elements that were previously unknown.

But surely the crude flier was beyond the ability of any woman to craft, no matter how many feminine elements she had access to. The flier spell itself required Dar, which was a masculine element, as well as Aal, a neuter element, neither of which was produced by the new Well, or the reports would have mentioned it. So it *couldn't* have come from the Abbey in the Wasteland.

"Let me know if you suffer any ill effects from that cut," he ordered his secretary.

"Yes, Your Highness," Melcor said, his face pale, his eyes filled with worry.

"Let us send a tax collector out to the new Abbey. I would like to see some of these profits they claim to be making. And I would like him to make an assessment of the new facilities to compare to the reports sent to the lord commander."

Melcor's eyes widened in alarm, and he stared at the pile of ash on the carpet. The women of the Abbey probably weren't the only people in Aaltah who wished Melcor ill, but they certainly had one of the strongest motives to strike at him. Yes, Delnamal would be worried, too, if the Abbey turned out to be the source of the mysterious spell.

If he could find even a shred of evidence that the abigails were responsible—or if his tax collector should find evidence that the rumors Melcor had brought him were true—then he might finally have just the fuel he needed to destroy his half-siblings. And raze the Abbey yet again—this time for good.

CHAPTER THIRTY-ONE

The moment Delnamal stepped into the king's private study, he could see that his father was ailing, his nose red and swollen and a handkerchief clutched in his hand. Delnamal bowed, but his father was impatient with the formalities and quickly gestured for him to take a seat.

"You may want to keep your distance," the king said in a raspy voice that hinted at a sore throat. He sniffled and touched the handkerchief to his nose.

Delnamal made a face and took the chair farthest from his father. There were disadvantages to having the Abbey at such a remove, for though the abigails had never managed to create a *cure* for head colds, there were potions that could ease the symptoms appreciably.

"Have you no cold tonics in storage?" he inquired, for it was a rare household that didn't keep a supply of common healing potions.

The king coughed and winced. "I did. But several of my personal staff caught cold, and I hoped to avoid its spread by treating them. We have none left."

"I'm sure we can find some for you," Delnamal said. Surely someone in the city still had cold tonics available, though it was the season when they were always in high demand.

The king sighed. "There's no need to make a fuss. Common folk endure the symptoms of head colds all the time without the help of tonics."

Delnamal frowned, for his father was seventy-two, and illness tended to strike people of his advanced age harder. "Perhaps it is . . . unwise not to treat it?" he suggested, and the king smiled at him.

"Are you trying to mother me, my son?"

Delnamal squirmed and blushed. Surely the queen was already lecturing his father on the importance of maintaining his health. It was unbecoming of Delnamal to nag like a woman.

"I promised your mother I would send for a potion from the Abbey if my symptoms get worse or don't start getting better in the next few days. Now, what is it you wanted to see me about? I'm hoping to retire early this evening and get some extra rest."

Delnamal hesitated a moment, loath to add to his father's troubles and possibly disturb his rest. But if he saved his unpleasant report for later, his father would be furious with him when he found out. The king had little patience with coddling, which Delnamal should have remembered before he pushed him on the subject of the tonic.

"Melcor was attacked," he said, just as he could see his father was about to bark at him to get on with it. He told the king about the flier that had attacked his secretary, and of course he mentioned his own suspicions that that flier had come from the new Abbey.

"And why would the women of the Abbey want to attack Melcor in this fashion?" the king asked, and despite his cold, he was still capable of a fearsome glare.

It took an effort not to wither under that glare. Delnamal had never mentioned to the king exactly what he'd allowed his men to do when they'd visited the Abbey. The omission had been in part because he felt the king had no need to know, and in part because Delnamal knew full well he would not approve. The glare said he knew more than Delnamal would have liked.

"From what I understand," Delnamal said, hoping he looked entirely innocent and unconcerned, "Melcor has some exotic tastes when it comes to bedding women, and some of the women of the Abbey objected to his use of them." All of which was perfectly true. Delnamal swallowed hard and willed his father not to pursue the subject. He did not relish having to explain himself, and a lie would be unwise when it could be so easily disproved. There had been too many witnesses in that Abbey.

The king stared at him for a long, uncomfortable time, and if it weren't for the head cold, Delnamal was sure he would have pressed. As it was, a violent sneeze broke off the stare, and the king waved a hand in dismissal.

Delnamal rose from his seat and bowed, but before he exited the room, a sudden thought struck him, and he stopped a few steps from the door. He turned around and looked at his ailing father.

"Perhaps it would be best *not* to send for a tonic from the Abbey," he suggested. He would not put it past those bitches to hold his father responsible for their exile and strike out at him in retaliation.

The king's eyes widened. "Surely you don't think . . ." He allowed his voice to trail off.

Delnamal raised one shoulder in a half-hearted shrug. "Do I honestly think they would attempt to poison their king? Perhaps not. I only know that *I* would hesitate to drink one of their tonics at this time. They are not to be trusted. And as you said, common folk suffer through head colds without the aid of tonics all the time."

Delnamal left the room to the sound of his father loudly blowing his nose.

———

"What are you still doing here at this hour?" Chanlix asked.

Alys jumped and gasped, hastily closing her Mindseye and blinking in the darkened room. Chanlix stood in the doorway, clucking like a mother hen as she lit a luminant. Alys had been so absorbed in her work she hadn't even noticed the sun going down, and though she'd been vaguely aware of the room emptying out, of abigails saying good night, and of her own distracted responses, she'd had no idea she was the only one left.

"Sorry to startle you," Chanlix said, coming to join Alys at her worktable in their fledgling Academy.

Alys sighed and rolled her shoulders, trying to work out the stiffness. She'd been sitting there far too long, and her body ached and complained.

"You are pushing yourself too hard," Chanlix said gently. "Both your mind and your body need the occasional break."

Alys sighed. "I know. But I've had something of a breakthrough, and I couldn't bear to stop tinkering just yet."

Chanlix's face lit with delight. "You have?"

Alys pinched the bridge of her nose. "Not the breakthrough I was hoping for, unfortunately."

Chanlix gave her a look of sympathy that made her throat tighten, then gave her shoulder a gentle squeeze. Alys was pretty sure Chanlix thought she was on a fool's errand, but the other woman had been nothing but supportive and helpful and had not once put her doubts into words.

"I got frustrated with all my failures," Alys continued, "so I decided to try something different for a while. I was talking to one of Tynthanal's men the other day, and he mentioned a spell hunters use to hide snares. It's called a Trapper spell, and it uses Lix to make the snare blend into the background, effectively making it invisible. It can only work for something relatively small, and I was wondering if I could create something similar—and maybe larger—using Zal."

Zal was a feminine element associated with illusion, and in most of the world, it was exceedingly rare. It was rare enough that Alys had as yet discovered only one spell in her mother's book that utilized it—and yet in Women's Well, it was plentiful, and she was certain it had many, many other potential uses. When she'd first started working with it, she'd been hopeful it was the key to faking a pregnancy for Shelvon, but so far it had not panned out, and she'd thought perhaps trying a different application might break open some doors.

Alys smiled a little sheepishly. "It was just a whim, and there are probably more effective uses of my time, but . . ." She shrugged.

Chanlix nodded. "But it is enjoyable to tackle a challenge you're certain you can conquer."

Alys met the other woman's eyes and felt a surge of warmth. She had certainly not come to Women's Well in search of friendship, but she had found it nonetheless—and finally been forced to admit to herself how desperately she had needed a friend since her mother's Curse changed everything. She had always focused on the damage the social isolation was doing to her children, and had never allowed herself to acknowledge what it was doing to *her*, how lonely it made her feel. Back in Aalwell, Shelvon was the closest thing she had to a friend, and yet the woman was young enough to be her daughter.

"Show me what you've come up with," Chanlix urged, a glint of excitement in her eye. Her magical talent was considerably less than Alys's or Tynthanal's, but she made up for that lack of talent with a deep understanding of how elements would work together—even when speaking of elements she could not see herself. She also clearly loved to tinker with magic almost as much as Alys did.

Alys showed Chanlix the copious notes she had taken while testing different combinations of Zal with other elements and demonstrated the most promising of those, which caused her worktable to disappear from sight—along with the floor beneath it and the wall behind it, leaving a very strange empty space that was eye-catching, to say the least.

"I feel like I'm close," Alys said. "If only I could make it stay confined to the table itself . . ." She deactivated the spell so that the table came back into view.

Chanlix cocked her head at the table, a crease forming between her brows as she thought. "What you want is not so much for the table to *disappear,* as for it to be hidden from view."

Alys nodded. "Yes. But so far, I haven't figured out how to do that." Despite all her natural abilities, she was still a novice magic user at best. And as helpful as her mother's book was, it seemed clear the late abbess had not foreseen the elements available in Women's Well. The book's magic was centered on those elements produced by Aaltah's Well, with only passing mention of others.

"You want it to do what the usual Trapper spell does, only on a larger scale. Zal seems to be more potent than Lix, and shares some of the same attributes—camouflage is something like an illusion."

"Yes," Alys agreed.

"So why don't you try using them both together?"

Alys would have thought combining the two elements would be redundant, but she trusted Chanlix's greater experience. Opening her Mindseye, she found a couple motes of Lix and added them to the coin she was currently using to hold the spell. Then she added in Rho and held her breath.

When she opened her eyes, she saw that the entire tabletop had disappeared, though the legs were still visible. And there was no strange, gaping void to draw the eye. Reaching out, her fingers found the table's edge, then groped until she found her notes. When she lifted the notes off the table and away, they suddenly became visible in her hand.

She shared a delighted grin with Chanlix, though she wasn't sure how much use anyone had for a spell that made a tabletop disappear.

"And now it is time for you to take a rest," Chanlix said firmly. "End with this small victory. And tomorrow, we can work on making the illusion even larger."

Alys felt a surge of excitement. "If you have an idea, we can try it right now." She had sorely missed this almost giddy rush of success as she'd worked so long and hard on the illusion spell she wanted so desperately to create. The repeated failures had dampened her spirits more than she'd realized, and she felt like she could continue working all night now.

"I have an idea," Chanlix confirmed. "And I will tell you what it is—tomorrow."

Alys made a sound of frustration. "You are only one year my senior," she reminded Chanlix. "You don't get to mother me." She sounded sullen to her own ears, but Chanlix merely laughed.

"I'm the closest thing Women's Well has to a grand magus," she replied cheerfully as she hooked her elbow through Alys's and gave her a tug toward the door. "And I say the Academy is closed for the night."

She sighed when Alys didn't budge.

"Listen to the voice of experience," Chanlix insisted. "Experimenting with magic when your mind is weary is a recipe for disaster. If you weren't already weary, you would have thought of using Lix and Zal together without me."

Alys wasn't sure that was true—it would likely take her years to develop the kind of intuition Chanlix had demonstrated—but she *was* tired. And, come to think of it, her head was throbbing.

Still reluctant, she allowed Chanlix to steer her from the room and out into the desert twilight.

Watching out her window, Chanlix gritted her teeth as Rusha, dressed in the red robes she had previously tossed aside, led the tax collector to her house. The girl smiled and swished her hips, acting convincingly delighted at the prospect of selling her body once more.

"Come away," Tynthanal said, gently putting his hands on her shoulders and turning her away from the window and back toward the table where Alys sat, her hands cradling a cup of hot mint tea.

Chanlix saw that a second cup had appeared while she'd been anxiously watching out the window, and Alys pushed it toward her with a sad smile.

"I'm so sorry about this," Alys said, but Chanlix waved the apology off.

"It's hardly *your* fault Delnamal decided to send a tax collector to us." Chanlix knew *exactly* whom to blame for that, and she was powerless to do anything about it.

Alys turned her teacup around and around, staring at it as if in fascination. "If I hadn't come here, perhaps he wouldn't be paying so much attention . . ."

Tynthanal pulled back a chair with a deliberate scraping sound, startling both women. "Let's have done with the confessions of guilt," he said, then sat down with a thunk. "We knew he would not ignore us forever, and today's visit will buy us more time."

It was true that they had anticipated an eventual visit from a tax collector, and they'd had a plan in place to deal with such a thing. Thanks to Tynthanal's spies, they'd not only known a tax collector was coming, but they'd known which one, which had allowed them to tailor the bribe specifically to him.

"Do you think he'll keep his side of the bargain?" Alys asked.

"He'll keep it," Chanlix said, and she had no doubt of her own convictions. She had yet to meet a tax collector who wasn't a greedy bastard, and she was sure every one of them happily took payments on the side, but Julvin took that greed to an elevated level. Thanks in part to generous contributions from both Alys and Tynthanal, the bribe they had offered—paired with the promise of future payments of similar size—was a temptation Julvin could not resist.

It had been Rusha's idea to sweeten the pot by taking Julvin to her bed, playing once again the traditional role of the abigail that the women of Women's Well had thought was behind them.

"I was always his favorite," Rusha had said, and it was true, for Julvin had rarely come to the Abbey to collect taxes without visiting the pavilion—a visit he expected to be granted free of charge. "We don't want him to leave Women's Well unsatisfied."

Chanlix had curled her lip. "He'll have his money. How unsatisfied could he be?"

"Men are fickle beasts," Rusha replied. "He will expect to be serviced, and if he is not, he will wonder *why* not. We don't want him thinking about us in that way."

And still Chanlix had hesitated. All her abigails had grown used to being free to allow men into their beds by choice, rather than necessity, and it was a hard thing to take that away from any of them. But Rusha was insistent.

"You never did get around to punishing me for defying you back in the Abbey," she'd said with a wry smile. "Let this be my penance for endangering the Abbey. Now, I will ensure its safety instead."

In the end, Chanlix had been forced to agree, but that didn't mean she was untroubled by guilt. And beneath that guilt was the persistent worry that they would not be able to keep the secrets of Women's Well hidden forever.

"Julvin's report will buy us time," she said, tapping the table restlessly with her fingertips. "But one day, there will come a reckoning." She shivered and hugged herself.

Alys leaned over and put a hand on her arm, giving it a comforting squeeze. "But we have made such great strides in such a short time. By the time that reckoning occurs, we will be in a much stronger bargaining position."

"We?" Chanlix asked with an arch of her brow. "I was under the impression you'd be leaving us as soon as you perfected your spell for Princess Shelvon." Not that she showed any signs of even having *invented* such a spell, much less perfecting one. Chanlix knew she was still trying, but it was beginning to seem like a lost cause. Not that Chanlix would ever put that thought into words.

Alys colored. "That is still the plan, of course. I must secure my daughter's future above all else. But I desperately need those occasional successes to give me hope against all my failures. I don't know how much longer I can stay, but while I'm here, I will give you as much help as I'm able." She pushed back her chair. "And with that, I should get back to work."

"Perhaps you and Chanlix should spend some more time on that Trapper spell," Tynthanal suggested.

Chanlix cocked her head at him. "I thought we were ready to move on to something else. We've already re-created it for a much more affordable price, and it's capable of hiding much larger areas."

"But you haven't tested it to its limits yet. I'd like to see just how big you can make it." He gave Alys a hopeful look, and she shrugged.

"I'm sure we can expand it farther without too much effort if you think it's a valuable use of our time."

"I think it could be," Tynthanal said. "I can imagine any number of military uses for such a thing, if it could be made larger still, and that would make it a valuable commodity for us. Anything that increases our value to the Crown provides us another layer of safety."

Chanlix heard a hint of . . . something, she wasn't sure what, in Tynthanal's voice, and she glanced at him curiously as Alys agreed and hurried from the room, eager to return to the comfort and pleasure of her magical practice. He returned Chanlix's look with a studied blandness that only served to make her more anxious.

Tynthanal was not a common foot soldier: he'd been lieutenant commander of the Citadel, with the heavy expectation that he would one day be the lord commander. He'd received extensive training in tactics and strategy, and he was fully capable of planning for contingencies he saw coming down the road, no matter how distant they might seem.

"You don't want those Trapper spells larger because they make us useful," Chanlix said. "You think when our activities come to light we will be in danger no matter how valuable we've made ourselves."

"That is one possibility for our future," he admitted, though she could see he was tempted to offer comforting lies instead. One of the things she admired most about him was his ability to put aside the notion that women should at all times be protected from the unpleasant truth. "We crossed a dangerous line when we sent that flier to Melcor, and we cross another dangerous one when we bribe a royal tax collector. If I were the King of Aaltah, and I learned of what we have done out here in Women's Well, I might be inclined to brand us traitors to the Crown rather than celebrate our accomplishments. As much as I might want to protect my niece from Delnamal's marriage plans, I'd rather Alys focus her considerable talents on spells that might help defend us should the worst happen.

"My father isn't the kind of king who would condemn the townspeople for what we've done, but if we can create a Trapper spell large enough and strong enough to provide a securely hidden location for those at the greatest risk, I would sleep better at night."

That would require an exceedingly large spell—or a large number of smaller ones—for all of the abigails and all of Tynthanal's men would likely face the king's wrath if he condemned them, to say nothing of Alys.

"We're stepping closer and closer to outright rebellion, aren't we?" Chanlix asked softly as a lump of dread formed in her stomach.

"We're certainly flirting with it," he affirmed. "I think that if we can choose the time and the circumstances under which the king learns the truth about what we've been doing here, we can present it in such a way as to make it palatable. Everything we've done—except for that Kai spell—can be of benefit to the Crown, and he will see that and understand."

She gave him a wry smile. "And bribing the tax collector? Is that of benefit to the Crown?"

Tynthanal snorted. "Are you suggesting that Julvin and the rest are not already well accustomed to accepting bribes? Or that they are any more eager than we for those bribes to be made public?"

Chanlix tried to take comfort from that very reasonable argument. It was in Julvin's best interests in more ways than one to stick to their agreement. But they couldn't bribe every visitor to the town, and eventually the lord commander—and therefore the king—would start to wonder at the conflict between Tynthanal's reports and the rumors that were spreading throughout the kingdom.

Jinnell waited somewhat nervously in the anteroom to the king's chambers. She had been visiting him periodically ever since her mother had left, hoping that if she formed a closer relationship with him, he'd be less likely to send her away to Nandel. She had a feeling he knew exactly what she was up to—there was no missing the intelligence in his eyes—but he seemed to enjoy her visits nonetheless. Because of his strained relationship with her mother, she had seen very little of him growing up, and it was clear he felt the lack.

Today, he had sent word that she should not come, that he was feeling poorly—but she had come anyway. It was a rare king who would welcome defiance from any of his subjects—even his own family—but Jinnell had made the calculated guess that he would see her visit as a sign of her deep affection. It was worth the risk of catching his cold if she could endear herself to him further. She patted her reticule to feel the little vial of potion she had brought with her.

Since her first rather unfortunate attempt to create a healing potion on her own, Jinnell had learned that it did indeed contain an element that she could not see—a feminine element called Leel, which was associated with digestion. There were a fair number of potions—like most healing potions—that tended to irritate sensitive stomachs, and adding Leel to those potions eliminated that side effect. Leel occurred naturally in certain grain alcohols—which meant Jinnell could use it despite not being able to see it. All she had to do was use the right base fluid, and she could put together several minor healing spells—like cold tonics.

Knowing that cold tonics were in short supply since the removal of the Abbey, she had brought one of her own making—though naturally she would claim it had come from the household supply.

The door to the king's private parlor opened, and his manservant stepped out. Jinnell held her breath, for it was entirely possible she would be told to go home and come again when the king was feeling better, but the manservant told her to enter.

"Don't stay too long," the manservant whispered as she went by, an imploring look in his eyes. "He is more ill than he cares to admit."

It was a shocking break of protocol for the servant to speak to her so frankly, and the feeling of unease that had been with her since she'd chosen to ignore the king's advice to stay away strengthened. She looked up at the servant with wide eyes, but he had reverted to more formal behavior and was staring straight ahead, his face a bland mask.

"Well, come in already," the king's voice called, and it was so hoarse she could barely recognize it as his.

Jinnell stepped into the parlor, and it was all she could do not to gasp in dismay when she saw her grandfather, sitting wrapped up in a heavy blanket in front of the fire. His face had little color, save for the rosiness imparted by the glow of the fire, and his eyes looked dark and sunken. There was a sheen of perspiration on his brow, and yet he was shivering.

For all that, he still managed a wry smile, and there was genuine warmth in his eyes. "I look that bad, do I?"

Jinnell swallowed hard and dipped into a curtsy, her heart hammering. The king's message telling her not to come had said he had a head cold, but clearly this was something far worse.

"Of course not, Your Majesty," she murmured.

"Hmpf," the king snorted, but that brought on a fit of wet coughing that was painful to hear. When the fit passed, he spit discreetly into a handkerchief and sighed. "I have avoided my own reflection," he rasped, "for fear of what it would tell me."

Jinnell crossed the room, kneeling on the floor by his feet and gazing anxiously up into his face. Her purpose for visiting him had been entirely self-serving at the start, but just as their continued contact had made him more fond of her, she'd found herself more fond of him, as well. Always before, she had seen her grandfather through the lens of her mother's anger. Now she saw him for what he truly was: a kindhearted man who carried the weight of the kingdom on his shoulders and suffered under that burden.

"You should not have come," he scolded her gently. "And most especially you should not sit so close to me. I wouldn't want you to catch whatever this is I have."

Jinnell had no desire to catch it, either, but she stayed right where she was. "You should take better care of yourself, Grandpapa," she said, mimicking his scolding voice as best she could. "Surely there are potions that could make you better." Though she doubted the one she had brought with her was strong enough to do the job.

The king sighed and laid his head against the back of his chair. "It's just a head cold that has sunk into my chest," he said. "It will pass."

Jinnell shook her head at him. "I'm no healer, but anyone can see this is more than a simple cold."

"For reasons that need not concern you, my advisers would prefer I forgo healing potions if I can."

"By advisers, you mean Uncle Delnamal, don't you?" She could well imagine her uncle whispering into the king's ear about the dangers of women's healing potions. No doubt those whispers had only strengthened the moment Mama had arrived at the new Abbey, for Delnamal would see that as a way to further sow distrust between the king and his eldest children.

The king's eyes narrowed, and Jinnell cursed herself for speaking out of turn. Her mother had warned her that the king would hear no ill of his son, and Jinnell had found out for herself that such was the case.

"I mean advisers," he said in a repressive tone. His stern expression crumpled as another coughing spasm shook him.

Jinnell reached out helplessly to put what she hoped was a comforting hand on his arm. Even through the heavy blanket, she could feel the heat that radiated from his body.

"You're burning up," she said, touching his forehead with the back of her hand.

He pushed her hand away, though there was no impatience in the gesture. His breath wheezed in and out of his lungs, and the tight look around his eyes said it hurt. "I'll be fine," he assured her, when he could manage it, but his voice was weaker, and he looked exhausted.

Jinnell pulled her little vial of potion from her reticule. "I brought you this," she said, wishing she'd known how sick he was before she'd come. She didn't know how to make any stronger healing potion, but she could have at least looked in the cabinets at home to see if they had anything she could bring him. "I thought you had a cold, so it might not do any good, but . . ." She held the vial out to him.

The king hesitated for a moment, then sighed and took the vial. "We'd best keep this our little secret," he advised with a conspiratorial smile.

"You think your, uh, advisers would suspect me of trying to poison you?"

It showed how poorly he was feeling that he didn't respond to her pointed comment with more than a tiny shake of his head. She watched as he unstopped the vial and swallowed the potion in one great gulp, then grimaced at the taste. She winced in sympathy, imagining the burn of the alcohol must feel especially bad on his ravaged throat. He handed her back the empty vial.

"Thank you, my child," he said. "You are as thoughtful as you are disobedient."

She responded with a tremulous smile. "You need something stronger."

"It's just an ague," he argued. "Nothing to worry about."

"Maybe not if you were my age."

He groaned softly, but a smile played upon the edges of his lips. "You are so like your mother. She is never one to mince words." He reached out and cupped her cheek, and it was all she could do not to recoil at the feel of his hot, sweaty palm.

"Please, Grandpapa. Please take a stronger potion."

He closed his eyes and rested the back of his head against his chair. "All right, child," he finally said. "I'll ask the queen to track one down for me. I'm sure there are plenty of families who keep stockpiles. And if I can't find the appropriate potion, I'll send word to Tynthanal, and he'll send me one from the new Abbey. No one would suspect *him* of wishing me harm."

Jinnell wasn't sure that was true. Delnamal seemed able to think ill of just about anyone, and triply so for anyone related to her late grandmother. But she was so relieved at the king's agreement to take a stronger potion that she kept that opinion to herself.

CHAPTER THIRTY-TWO

Ellin used the secret passageways—to which she now had a full map—to intercept Zarsha and Graesan before they left the palace without having her honor guard hovering over her shoulder. Zarsha had kindly offered to "escort" Graesan on his way out of the city to begin his journey to Nandel, and he had urged Ellin to stay away. She agreed with him in theory—setting eyes on Graesan right now was rather like being punched in the stomach—but she couldn't let him walk out of her life without a goodbye.

Zarsha gave her an exasperated look when she stepped out of the shadows in front of them, and Graesan quickly looked down at his feet, unable to face her. It was strange to see him out of his uniform, dressed as an ordinary gentleman in riding breeches. She noticed immediately that the bruises on his face had been healed—no doubt to avoid any uncomfortable questions about how he'd gotten them—but there was a strange stiffness to the way he carried himself, and she instantly suspected there were unhealed bruises hiding beneath his clothing. Zarsha confirmed her suspicion when he slapped at Graesan's ribs, causing Graesan to gasp and wince.

"Bow when you see your queen," Zarsha reminded him nastily as he sketched his own courteous bow.

The look Graesan gave him would have melted steel, but he did as he was told, bowing low as his face tightened even more with pain. Ellin imagined a long ride on horseback would be terribly unpleasant, but it was hard to argue Graesan didn't deserve some suffering.

"Don't be petty," she said to Zarsha, who smiled unrepentantly.

"Not only did I spare his life, but I'm also giving him a graceful exit and decent wages after he tried to knife me in my sleep. I think I should be forgiven a little pettiness here and there, don't you?"

She supposed that was true, though she wasn't about to admit it. Ellin stared at the man she loved, her heart breaking all over again.

"Won't you even look at me?" she whispered, afraid she was going to start crying.

Zarsha gave Graesan's shoulder an overly hardy pat, making him wince again. "I'll just wait for you down the hall," he said, striding away. "Don't forget to tell her what you told me."

Graesan gave his retreating back another molten look, and Ellin hoped Zarsha wasn't going to inspire another murder attempt.

"What did you tell him?" she asked to distract his attention.

Graesan took a deep breath—the tightening of his eyes said that, too, hurt—then met her gaze. "I'm sorry." He swallowed hard, and she could see how badly he wanted to look away once more. "I let jealousy get the better of me and listened to rumors I should have known were suspect."

Her eyebrows rose. "What rumors?"

"I don't think he truly *knows* anything, but Lord Tamzin is aware that I . . . care about you more than a proper secretary should. It started out with him dropping hints here or there, not speaking directly to me but letting me overhear his innuendo. He suggested that Zarsha was still here because he had designs on you, and that you were too naïve to see the dangers."

Ellin suppressed a shiver and hoped her face didn't give anything away. She didn't want to know what Graesan would say or do if he knew that Zarsha had been quite open about his motives—and that she had let him stay anyway.

"You say that was how it *started*," she prompted.

Graesan nodded. "He began talking to me directly, asking me to advise you to send Zarsha home. I told him I didn't have that kind of influence on you, but he didn't believe me."

"But you did as he said. You advised me to send Zarsha away." Her voice came out sharp as she remembered their argument, remembered Graesan's vehemence.

"I thought Tamzin was right. I thought Zarsha was a clever spy who was working his way under your skin and getting too firm a foothold. Then when you told me he knew about us . . ." He shuddered.

Ellin closed her eyes and fantasized about slipping a knife between Tamzin's ribs. Apparently, starting the rumor suggesting she was considering him as a potential husband had not stopped him from scheming, after all. Tamzin might not have known about her trysts with Graesan, but he'd clearly known Graesan loved her, just as he clearly knew Zarsha was a potential threat to his influence.

"You thought Tamzin was right, and Zarsha was already blackmailing me."

"Yes. I thought I was protecting you."

Her eyes burned with tears for which she had no patience. She blinked them away. She wasn't sure if Graesan's motives made her feel better or worse. She was glad there was more than simple jealousy behind it, but it hurt to see such clear evidence of how little he'd trusted her judgment.

Graesan swallowed hard. "I know I hurt you, and I can't express how sorry I am for that. I let myself believe Zarsha was getting under your skin when the reality was it was Lord Tamzin getting under mine. I believed Tamzin's innuendo and ignored your assurances, and for that I have no excuse."

Her whole body twitched toward him, so desperate was she to put her arms around him and tuck herself into the comfort of his warmth. Her conscience twinged as she remembered her own lack of honesty. She had failed to tell him about Zarsha's proposal because she wanted to protect him, which was uncomfortably close to his own motivations. She was still furious with him, and she doubted she could ever truly forgive him for what he'd tried to do, but she still loved him so much it hurt.

"Be careful with Tamzin, Ellin," Graesan said. "He wants the throne more than anything in the world. Right now, he thinks you're the key that will help him take it, and he's focused on eliminating people who might be rivals or might talk you out of marrying him. But once he figures out you won't give him what he wants . . ."

She nodded. "I know, Graesan. I don't know what I'm going to do about him yet, but I know how much of a problem he is."

Graesan surprised her by reaching out and taking her hands, squeezing them. "Promise me you won't marry him."

For a moment, she thought he meant Zarsha, and she wondered if she could lie convincingly to his face and tell him there was no chance of that ever happening. Then she realized he meant Tamzin, and she made what she was sure was an ugly face. "If that man ever takes the throne of Rhozinolm, it will be over my dead body," she swore. Graesan paled, but she felt no inclination to take the words back. She would rather die than marry a man like Tamzin. Besides, it was her duty as queen to protect the kingdom, and that meant keeping manipulative, amoral, and cruel men like him off the throne.

"And be careful of Zarsha, too," Graesan finished. "He may not be the monster I allowed Tamzin to convince me he was, but his motives are not pure, either."

"I'll be careful. I promise." And she meant it. As fond as she had become of Zarsha, he was still something of an enigma. He had all but admitted to being a spy, but she wasn't sure why a spy would be trying to marry the queen of the kingdom he had infiltrated. And she had a feeling he understood her far better than she understood him. "I have a lot of questions to ask him when we next have some time."

"Good." He bowed his head. "I should go. Waiting isn't going to make this any easier."

He still had hold of her hands, and neither of them seemed inclined to let go. Ellin's throat was aching again, and she swallowed past the lump that was quickly forming there.

"Tell Zarsha I command him to heal whatever it is that's still wrong with you before setting out."

Graesan let go of her hands and rubbed his ribs gingerly as one corner of his mouth lifted in a wry smile. "It's just some bruises. When he stops finding it entertaining to poke them and make me wince, they'll hardly bother me at all."

She snorted. "He can afford a pot of salve."

"I'll pass on your request."

If Ellin truly wanted to be sure Graesan's ribs were healed before setting out, she would have to make the request herself. She doubted Graesan had any intention of asking Zarsha for anything— even if Zarsha were likely to grant that request. But if Graesan was too proud or stubborn to fix the bruises—he could afford a pot of salve on his own with what she'd been paying him as her secretary— then that was his problem.

Fighting yet again against tears, she watched as with one last yearning glance, he turned around and walked down the hallway after Zarsha.

Delnamal woke to feel a hand on his shoulder, shaking him gently. He blinked groggily, his body trying to drag him back into sleep, for he could feel in his bones that it was still the middle of the night. He reached up to rub his eyes, finding them gritty, then blinked to see his mother bending over his bed, a small luminant cupped in one hand.

Delnamal blinked again and sat up, stifling a yawn as his sluggish mind took in the sheen in his mother's eyes. He shook his head rather violently in an effort to wake up faster as his pulse suddenly kicked up and alarm prickled through him.

"What is it?" he cried. "What has happened?"

"The king has taken a turn for the worse," his mother said, then dashed away a tear that slid down her cheek. "The healer says—" She made a sound between a hiccup and a sob.

"What?" Delnamal yelled, dread making his voice come out sharper than he intended. "What does the healer say?" He threw back the covers and slid out of bed, grabbing for his dressing gown, for of course he already had a good idea what the healer said, based on his mother awakening him in the middle of the night.

"He's not expected to last the night," the queen said, then threw her arms around him and wept against his shoulder.

Delnamal had never known what to do with women's tears, and he was especially flummoxed by his mother's. Still, he put his arms around her and patted her back gently while inside, he tried to make sense of the wild swirl of emotions within him. To his shame, his own eyes burned with the hint of incipient tears.

"The potion," he said, blinking fiercely in an effort to keep his eyes dry. "Did he drink it?"

The healing potion had arrived from the Abbey—Delnamal refused to think of the place as Women's Well, no matter what delusions of grandeur had moved its inhabitants to so name it—earlier this evening, but the king had been asleep, and both Delnamal and the queen had thought it imprudent to wake him.

His mother shook her head, then pushed away from him, dabbing at her eyes. "I decided to wake him when I retired for the evening, but he would not rouse. That was when I summoned the healer."

Delnamal's gut clenched. They should have awakened the king the moment the healing potion arrived. Then his throat tightened as it occurred to him that what they *really* should have done was to send to the Abbey for a potion the moment they realized the illness was more than a head cold. And that the reason they hadn't was that he himself had put doubt into his father's mind about the safety of those potions.

If the king died this night, it might very well be Delnamal's fault. Something akin to panic swelled in his breast.

"We *must* get him to drink that potion."

The queen shook her head. "The healer says it is too late."

"Fuck the healer!" Delnamal bellowed, causing his mother to flinch away from him. He drew in a deep breath and tried to calm his temper. "He will drink the potion," he said in a steadier voice, "and he will get well again."

With his mother trailing along behind him, Delnamal marched to the king's bedchamber. "We should wake Shelvon," she said, clearly meaning that *Delnamal* should wake his wife.

"No need," he bit out. "We will not need a bedside vigil, for Father is not going to die tonight."

He continued through the halls, heedless of his mother's protestations. He burst into the king's bedroom unannounced, to find the healer, his apprentice, and a plethora of servants and honor guardsmen standing around the bed, looking grave and frightened.

"Everybody out!" he commanded.

There was no question that half the men in the room wanted to argue with him, but one look at his face was all it took to strike them silent. The healer tried to stay behind, but he hurried to follow the others when Delnamal glared at him.

The bed curtains had been tied back, giving Delnamal an unimpeded view of his father, who lay on his back in the center of the bed. The king's hair had been neatly brushed, though it was greasy and lank from lack of washing, and his beard had been trimmed for the first time since he had fallen ill only a little more than a week ago. The sheets had been pulled up to his chin, and Delnamal knew he had been groomed and positioned so as to retain what dignity he could during his final hours, when his household would stand vigil by his bedside. Delnamal snarled at the large bouquet of fragrant flowers that had been placed near the bed to help cover the stink of the sickroom.

"Get those out of here," he ordered his mother, and his mood was so fierce she leapt to obey.

The vial of potion that had arrived from the Abbey today sat forgotten on a bedside table. Delnamal snatched it up and sat on the bed beside his father. If it weren't for the painful, labored sound of his breathing, Delnamal might have thought him already dead. He put his hand on his father's bony shoulder and gave it a shake.

"Please, Father," he begged. "Wake up. You must take this potion."

There was no sign that the king was aware of him. Delnamal shook him a little harder, feeling his already fragile self-control fraying at an alarming rate.

"You *must*!" he demanded. "This *cannot* be my fault!"

This last came out on what sounded suspiciously like a sob to his own ears. He had thought only of his father's well-being when he had urged him not to send for a potion. How could he trust the king's health to those witches at the Abbey? Especially after they'd sent that flier to Melcor. If he'd had any idea his father was *this* ill . . .

Shaking had failed to awaken the king, so Delnamal tried slapping his face.

"Stop that!" his mother cried, reaching out to him, but he batted her hand away hard enough that she yelped.

He hadn't the energy to apologize, his focus entirely on his father's unearthly stillness. He had to admit to himself that the king was not going to wake up, no matter what he did. But he was not about to give up.

Delnamal pulled the stopper from the vial. "Hold his head up," he growled at his mother. She was too shaken by his ferocity to refuse, slipping one hand behind her husband's head and tilting it upward. Delnamal forced the king's mouth open and tipped the vial until a few drops of potion hit his tongue. The king's tongue made a sluggish attempt to move, but most of the potion trickled out the corner of his mouth, and there was no sign of swallowing.

Delnamal's hands were visibly shaking as he poured a little more potion, then attempted to hold the king's mouth closed so it couldn't escape. He then rubbed on the king's throat, as he might do for one of his dogs when inducing the beast to swallow a potion. The king's throat spasmed, but instead of swallowing, he coughed weakly, the potion bubbling out past his closed lips. Delnamal went to try again, only to find that the vial was now empty, most of the potion soaked up by the bedclothes. He let the queen gently take the vial from his fingers and set it aside.

"I'm not ready to be king yet," he whispered, hardly believing what was happening.

"Few kings are when they ascend the throne," his mother said, stroking the king's hair. She readjusted the bedclothes, heedless of the tears that stained her cheeks.

"I should have made him order the potion sooner," he said, expecting his mother to give him soothing reassurances that there was nothing he could have done. Instead, the look on her face hardened, and her eyes glinted with anger.

"Yes, you should have. And *he* should have. But it is the perpetual hubris of men to believe they are immortal. You are both to blame for this needless loss."

Delnamal recoiled from his mother's anger and pain. His immediate instinct was to defend himself, to reiterate his argument that the potions of the Abbey could not be trusted. But it was clear she was not open to hearing his point of view, and Delnamal couldn't help wondering . . .

Was there some part of him that had *wanted* this to happen? That had chafed at the king's insistence on protecting his bastard children and the traitorous women of the Abbey?

But no. Of *course* not.

Sunk in his own misery, Delnamal did not notice the moment when his father's labored breathing slowed, and then stopped.

Part Three

SOVEREIGN

CHAPTER THIRTY-THREE

Alys chewed her lip nervously as she placed the two paired fliers on the table in front of her.

"It will work this time," Chanlix assured her, her eyes alight with excitement.

"I hope you're right," Alys said as she opened her Mindseye and grabbed a mote of Rho. They'd been working on this spell for what felt like forever, Chanlix crafting the fliers with surprisingly skilled hands, and Alys and Tynthanal providing the needed combination of masculine and feminine elements. They were close, so close . . .

The visit from the tax collector heightened the pressure, driving home the reality that there was only so long Women's Well could go on as it was, operating in something very like autonomy. Alys no longer spent such a great proportion of her day trying to create a spell to fake a pregnancy and was instead spending most of her time helping invent new and powerful spells using the unique combination of elements available in Women's Well, as well as using masculine and feminine elements together. Tynthanal was her only blood family here, but in a way the whole town was beginning to feel like family as she spent so many hours working with them side by side. She desperately wanted to protect Jinnell, but she wanted to protect her brother and the townsfolk almost as much.

The fliers that she and Chanlix and Tynthanal had developed might very well be just the tool they needed to make the town of Women's Well indispensable to the Crown. Nowhere else was Zal plentiful enough to produce this particular spell—and even if the spell crafters of the Academy in Aaltah had access to Zal, they would be horrified and offended at the thought of combining their own magic with feminine elements. If this spell worked, then the town of Women's Well might no longer need to keep its successes secret.

Alys placed a mote of Rho into each of the fliers. One remained inert, while the other sprang to life. She trapped the active one with her hand, closing her Mindseye. "You belong to Tynthanal Rai-Brynna," she told the flier, speaking slowly and clearly to set its target. Then she released it.

Alys and Chanlix watched as the flier took wing and darted out the open window of Alys's house. Their hands met and clasped tensely together as they both stared at the remaining flier. And waited.

Alys imagined the flier she had sent speeding through the air, crossing the distance between her house and Tynthanal's in little more than a minute, then flying through the window he had left open for it. She silently counted the seconds. Tynthanal would be waiting as anxiously as she. Once the flier arrived, he would feed it the rest of the Rho it needed to activate the second spell, and then . . .

Alys hadn't realized she'd closed her eyes until she heard the soft chirp. She opened her eyes and saw that the flier on the table was now standing upright. Chanlix fed it some more Rho. And in front of the flier, transparent but clearly visible, a small image of Tynthanal appeared. He was sitting at his own kitchen table, his face split with a grin and his eyes alight.

"Can you hear me?" he asked.

Both Alys and Chanlix cried out in pleasure, impulsively hugging each other.

"I'll take that as a yes," Tynthanal said.

"Yes!" Chanlix agreed. "It's a yes!"

Alys's throat was too tight to answer. She was happy for the success of the spell and all the implications it had for the future of Women's Well, but she was even happier to know that soon she could see her children for the first time in almost three months. They exchanged letters by flier often, Jinnell supplying a constant stream of reassurances that all was well at home. But something in the last couple of letters had felt different, though Alys couldn't put her finger on it. She'd shown the most recent letter to Tynthanal, and he hadn't sensed anything off about it, so maybe she was imagining things. But she couldn't help feeling that Jinnell was beginning to worry about her extended absence. She'd told Alys she was visiting with her grandfather on a semi-regular basis, and Alys wondered if the king was beginning to drop more aggressive hints that a marriage with Prince Waldmir was in her future.

Alys should have headed home at least a month ago, when her hopes of finding a way to help Shelvon conceive or fake a pregnancy had all but died. There was little she could do at home to protect Jinnell if the king decided she should marry Prince Waldmir. But if nothing else, she could offer her daughter love and comfort—and they could formulate a plan to sneak her out of the kingdom under a false identity if it came to that. Alys would love to remain in Women's Well to continue her magical education, but this special flier was just the kind of breakthrough that would finally offer the town and its people protection. Which meant she could—and *should*—go home to her children.

Which, of course, she wanted to do quite desperately, for she had never been away from them this long before. She just wished she could return to them triumphantly with an arsenal of magic that would protect Jinnell from Delnamal's malice.

Chanlix and Tynthanal chattered away as Alys lost herself in thought, but her mind snapped back to attention when she heard both of them gasp with what sounded like dismay. She looked at the image of her brother and saw that a second flier was now sitting on the table before him. Her heart thudded against her breastbone as she took in the raven-black flier, which was holding a white parchment scroll sealed with black wax.

Only death announcements were sealed with black wax.

Alys met her brother's eyes and saw the same sick knowledge in his expression. He had no wife, no children, no mother. The only people in his life for whom he might receive a death announcement via flier were Alys, Delnamal, and the king.

Alys had never had much use for religion, but nonetheless she prayed silently to the Mother that the death being announced was Delnamal's. It wasn't that uncommon for young men in their prime to drop dead. Her husband, after all, had died well before his time, though he'd been far older than Delnamal was now.

Tynthanal removed the scroll from the flier's claws, breaking the seal and opening it. He read the message, and the look on his face said it all.

King Aaltyn was dead.

And that meant Delnamal was now the rightful King of Aaltah.

You are not *going to cry,* Jinnell told herself sternly as she wandered through the rooms of the manor house, ensuring that everything was in order. In each room, the furniture was draped to protect it from dust, and the curtains were drawn. Bedding had been packed away in storage trunks, and valuables moved to locked cabinets and cupboards. All but two of the household staff—some of whom had worked for her father's family since he was a little boy—had been told their services were no longer required. Jinnell couldn't imagine how the housekeeper and the steward alone could keep the place clean and in good repair, but there was nothing she could do about it. The king had spoken, and Jinnell had no choice but to obey.

Footsteps echoed loudly in the empty house, and Jinnell turned to see Falcor entering the once-cozy parlor where her inspection tour had petered out. He looked at her with undisguised sympathy, as if he knew exactly how she was feeling. Which perhaps he did. A master of the guard was meant to be distant and dispassionate, but she did not think Falcor's dedication to her family's safety was entirely a product of his sense of duty. He *cared*, and he had to know that her uncle's decree that she and Corlin should be his guests at the palace while her mother was away was not the act of kindness it might appear on the surface.

"Everything is ready, Miss Jinnell," he said gently.

A lump formed in her throat, and she swallowed hard. Surely she was being a superstitious ninny, but she couldn't shake the conviction that once she walked out of this house, she would never come back. But that truly was nonsense. Her mother would return to Aalwell for the funeral, and after that Delnamal would let them all return to the manor.

Then why did he dismiss all the servants and have the house packed up as if it were meant to stand empty indefinitely? she asked herself.

"I'll be along in a moment," she said.

Instead of accepting the dismissal, Falcor stepped farther into the room. "It will not get any easier," he said.

She blinked in an effort to hold back tears. "Do you blame me for not wishing to be my uncle's 'guest' any sooner than absolutely necessary?"

It was an imprudent question, revealing more of what she was feeling than was strictly wise. Her uncle was now the king, and where criticizing him before had been unwise, it was likely now *dangerous*. But she knew how much Falcor had helped her mother with her magic studies and was certain he could be trusted.

He gave her a wry smile. "I'm in no great hurry to place you under his care." The smile faded. "But you must be very careful of what you say once you reach the palace. Even to me. It is too easy to be overheard."

"I understand." She took a deep breath, hoping to find some

semblance of calm. She would never admit it out loud, but she wished desperately that her mother were here. Then she immediately felt guilty for the thought, because now that Delnamal was king, she feared her mother would be in great danger if she were within easy reach. He'd shown no great fondness for his niece and nephew, but he did not hate them like he did their mother. Jinnell did not like to think what might happen when her mother arrived for the funeral.

She looked up and met Falcor's kind eyes, dropping her voice to the lowest of whispers. "If I asked, would you spirit me and Corlin away to Women's Well instead of taking us to the palace?" She expected him to react with shock—and maybe to reiterate his warning.

Instead, he seemed to think it over. "I am sworn to protect you and Master Corlin, and I must do that at all costs. If I were to defy the king's orders and take you to Women's Well, then everyone involved would be subject to a treason charge. I'd be endangering you rather than protecting you."

"So that's a no."

He bowed his head. "That's a no. I'm sorry."

The "no" sounded unequivocal, and yet his manner of arriving at the answer suggested it might not be as irrevocable as it sounded. Perhaps once her mother returned, he would be open to the possibility of helping all three of them leave Aalwell to escape its new king's machinations.

"Can you imagine a situation in which that no might turn to yes?" she asked.

"I cannot," he answered quickly, then met her eyes steadily. "But then, I am not a man of great imagination."

Jinnell sighed, taking one last look around the room. "I have enough of that for the both of us," she said. But she felt encouraged by the careful wording of his answers. If all else failed, he seemed to be saying, he would do what he could to protect her and her family. Not that one guardsman could do much for them if the king found some excuse to condemn them. But at least they had one ally.

"I'm ready," she said, and allowed Falcor to escort her to the waiting carriage.

Alys murmured a half-hearted thank-you as Chanlix laid a fragrant cup of tea on the table in front of her. Tynthanal accepted his own cup more graciously, giving Chanlix's hand an affectionate squeeze.

Tynthanal had brought their half-brother's letter with him when he'd come to Alys's house to find her openly weeping on Chanlix's shoulder. The rim of red around his own eyes spoke to his own grief, though with typical male stoicism he tried to hide it.

Alys's eyes were dry now, so dry they burned. The devastating letter Delnamal had sent just one day after the death announcement—when she had been packed and ready to begin her journey back to Aalwell—had chased her grief into a dark corner and replaced it with a potent and poisonous concoction of fear and fury.

Apparently, Delnamal had not felt that news of their father's death was painful enough all on its own, and he'd felt compelled to dig the knife in deeper. His letter expressly forbade Alys and Tynthanal from returning to Aalwell for the king's funeral. Or for any other purpose. They were commanded to remain in Women's Well "until further notice." And then he'd shoved a second knife directly into Alys's heart.

You need not worry about the well-being of your children, dear sister, he'd written. *I have moved them into the palace, and I shall see to their care until such time as you are able to return.*

"If he were here in front of me," she rasped, "I swear I would rip his throat out with my bare hands."

Tynthanal made a snarling sound in the back of his throat. "Too quick a death. I'd slit his belly open till his guts spilled out and watch him slowly bleed to death."

Chanlix grimaced as she took a seat between them. "I have no love for your brother—"

"Half-brother," both Alys and Tynthanal chorused at once. Alys might almost have smiled at their simultaneous reaction, had she the strength for it.

"For Delnamal," Chanlix continued smoothly, "but fantasizing about his death isn't going to solve anything."

"He has my children," Alys said, "and there's nothing I can do about it."

Killing him wasn't enough to pay him back in full for his cruelty.

"Perhaps your husband's parents can contest the king's custody?" Chanlix suggested. "Surely grandparents should have a better claim to them than a half-uncle."

Alys would have loved to grab hold of that hope, but she knew better. "He's the king now. Even if my in-laws protest, who would support them? Most will probably think he's being kind and generous by installing them in the palace." They would not see that he was holding his own niece and nephew hostage to keep Alys and Tynthanal under control. Grief and terror threatened to swamp her again, helped along by a massive wave of guilt.

If she'd gone home a month ago, she would have been there to protect her children, to stop Delnamal from taking them. "I should have been there," she whispered.

Tynthanal rubbed her back. "Absolutely not," he said vehemently. "Delnamal would have found some excuse to have you arrested and take the children anyway. Then there really *would* be nothing you could do."

She shoved the tea away from her viciously, spilling hot liquid all over the table. Tea splashed on Delnamal's hateful letter, smearing the ink. "What is it you suggest I can do from here?" she snarled. She knew how unfair she was being, how little her brother deserved her ire, but the rage and fear inside her were too great to contain.

"Well," Tynthanal said calmly, unaffected by her burst of temper, "we did just invent a spell of immense value. Perhaps Delnamal would be tempted to release the children to you in exchange for the spell."

She laughed bitterly. The spell that had seemed the answer to securing the safety of Women's Well lost much of its value when it was Delnamal who sat on the throne rather than their father. "It's property of the Crown. He'll just seize it."

"He will want to. But he may not find that quite so easy to do.

At the risk of sounding boastful, my men are some of the best soldiers in all of Aaltah. There may not be very many of us, but we are formidable. And we have spells no one outside of Women's Well has ever seen before."

Alys swallowed back her anger and fear. Tynthanal was finally putting voice to something she knew they'd all been thinking. "You think we should revolt against the Crown." Which should have been a horrifying thought, should have filled her with fear. If their everyday lives, if their falsified reports to the lord commander, their very *existence*, weren't already the beginnings of a revolt. They could have negotiated with King Aaltyn to legitimize the work they were doing there, for he would have done anything in his power to avoid labeling his children as traitors. Such would not be the case with King Delnamal.

Tynthanal's eyes flashed. "I think we should do more than that. I think we should make Delnamal's life a living hell. *You* are our father's firstborn, not him."

Alys's mouth dropped open in shock. She tried to form meaningful words, but her thoughts were too badly scrambled. Chanlix was staring at Tynthanal as if he might have gone mad.

"You want to challenge Delnamal's claim to the throne?" she squeaked.

"Not me. Alysoon."

"But you are the firstborn son."

"And she is the firstborn. Period. Times are changing."

Alys managed a weak laugh. "They aren't changing *that* much."

"Rhozinolm has put a woman on the throne. There's no reason Aaltah can't do the same."

"But it would be much easier to put *you* on it," she protested. A part of her noticed how skillfully Tynthanal had managed to steer the conversation away from *whether* they should contest Delnamal's claim to *who* should contest it. "You have always been enormously popular. Much more so than Delnamal. The only reason you aren't already the heir to the throne is because our father signed a document retroactively delegitimizing you. You have clear grounds to contest the succession."

"I'm a career soldier who has kept himself as far removed from court intrigue as is humanly possible. I haven't the skill or the subtlety to rule, nor do I have the patience to play at politics."

There was an edge of hysteria in Alys's brief laugh. "And you think *I* do? I'm a career wife and mother, who—"

"Don't try to tell me you don't understand the intricacies of the court. I've seen how your mind works, and I know how well-versed you are in politics."

It was true that Alys had a good understanding of the inner workings of the court. While her marriage to Sylnin had removed her physically from the heart of the court, she had never lost touch or lost interest. It was probably true that she had the wherewithal to rule; it was also true that it would be infinitely easier to install Tynthanal on the throne.

"You have the respect of the lord commander," Alys insisted. "That means more than any court intrigue. If there's any possibility he might side with you—"

"He won't. The moment he finds out how badly I've lied to him, I will lose every drop of respect I've earned through years of serving under him."

"But—"

"I know the lord commander well. He is a good man, but his loyalty will always be to the Crown. Forwarding my claim would give us no advantage."

"This doesn't make any sense," she said, staring at her brother intently. "Why would you not want to claim the throne yourself? You and I both know that you would be the logical choice—if we decide to contest the succession at all, which we've somehow managed not to discuss yet."

Tynthanal stared at her in mulish silence. A silence that Chanlix broke to Tynthanal's evident horror.

"He can't have children," she said. Tynthanal turned to her, aghast, his face going red with either outrage or embarrassment or a combination of the two. She lifted her shoulders in a small shrug. "She's your sister, dearest. There's no reason to hide it from her."

Dearest? a curious voice in Alys's mind whispered. Chanlix no longer acted as if her love affair with Tynthanal were some deep, dark secret, but Alys had never heard her use a casual endearment like that before. It seemed that more and more of the former abbess's walls were coming down. Alys wished the current situation would allow her to feel happy for her brother.

"He looked to marry once," Chanlix continued, "and consulted his mother on his choice of bride."

Alys turned to her brother in open surprise. She'd been under the impression Tynthanal hadn't set eyes on their mother since the divorce, and she'd never guessed he'd ever been deeply enough enamored of a woman to seek to marry her.

"You went to see our mother," she said, shaking her head in wonder.

"It was just that once," Tynthanal said. "I needed to go to the Abbey for the bloodline test, but I didn't want anyone to know I was considering marriage until I could be sure it was approved. My visit might have been unusual, but no one would assume I was asking for a compatibility spell."

"So you visited for cover." Alys couldn't imagine how much that must have hurt their mother, that the one and only time her son had deigned to visit her was for the purpose of subterfuge.

Tynthanal squirmed, his eyes downcast. "It was not a comfortable encounter for either of us. Especially once she told me the test results. It was . . . a hard thing to learn at the age of twenty-two that I would never be a father."

Alys would have asked more questions, but Tynthanal shook off his melancholy and guilt and returned to the subject at hand.

"If we legitimize inheritance through the female by putting you on the throne, then you already have two direct heirs, while I will never have even one," Tynthanal said. "Which is why if we try for the throne, it should be in your name."

"And how long do you suppose my children will live if we challenge Delnamal's rule?" She shivered and hugged herself.

Tynthanal's face turned stony. "If we don't, then Jinnell is bound for Nandel, and Corlin will never survive until manhood. You know how Delnamal feels about us. Even if we show him our bellies, he will always see us as a threat to his rule. He will not rest until we are both dead, and when we are, he will turn on the only potential threat that is left."

Alys wanted to scream a denial, but she knew he was right.

Maybe in a couple days' time, they would all come to their senses and realize that their fears were unfounded, that trying to claim the throne was as unnecessary as it was dangerous. But an icy cold pit formed in her stomach as she came to the inevitable conclusion that this was not the case.

"We need an ally," she said. "Right now, Delnamal has no reason to negotiate with us or take us seriously as a threat, and as long as he has my children, he holds all the cards." She thought furiously. "Delnamal might think of the magic we produce here as belonging to Aaltah, but as long as we control the Well, it belongs to *us*. Perhaps we can forge an alliance with one of the other kingdoms. Offer them an exclusive supply of talking fliers if they will recognize our claim."

Tynthanal looked doubtful. "Khalpar has a strong interest in supporting Delnamal, and I'm not sure Rhozinolm will be willing to risk war with Aaltah now that King Linolm is no longer on the throne." He sighed. "But perhaps we can at least explore the possibility."

Alys suspected her brother was right about Khalpar. The whole reason King Aaltyn had divorced his wife to marry Xanvin had been to forge a nearly unbreakable bond with the royal family of Khalpar and end the last war with Rhozinolm. And the reason he'd not only divorced Brynna but declared her children illegitimate was so that Xanvin's son would be heir to the throne of Aaltah. Two royal families linked so closely by blood were unlikely to turn on one another without significant provocation.

Rhozinolm was another story. "Queen Ellinsoltah might not wish to spark a war with Aaltah," Alys mused out loud, "but she might also be leery of letting Delnamal control a second Well once she realizes its power. If we can offer her agreements she knows she will not be able to get from Delnamal, perhaps she will consider it worth the risk."

"Perhaps," Tynthanal said. "And I'll wager she will be more naturally inclined to align herself with you than with Delnamal."

She gave him a sharp look. For all of his dissembling, he had a canny mind. She suspected he was telling the truth when he said he did not want the throne for himself, but she wouldn't put it past him to have made that argument simply because he thought Queen Ellinsoltah might be more amenable to an agreement with the Sovereign Queen of Aaltah than with its sovereign king. She certainly hoped he was right.

"I suppose we should make a new pair of talking fliers," she said. "We can demonstrate one of our most unique spells and meet with Queen Ellinsoltah face-to-face at the same time."

And meanwhile, she would start devising a plan to get both Jinnell and Corlin out of Aalwell before it was too late.

CHAPTER THIRTY-FOUR

Delnamal suppressed a pleased smile when he paged through the marshal's crime report for the second week of his reign. He had no intention of continuing the practice of examining crime reports and was only doing so now on the pretext of getting a thorough understanding of each of his council members' jobs. What he'd really been looking for was on the first page of the report, which detailed the brutal murder of a well-heeled merchant who'd apparently been stabbed to death in a back alley with no witnesses.

Ordinarily, Delnamal wouldn't care about the murder of a merchant, no matter how wealthy. But this merchant had been the husband of Lady Oona Rah-Wylsem, and his death did not come as a surprise to Aaltah's new king. No, not at all.

He closed his eyes and tried to remember the taste of Lady Oona's lips, the feel of her satiny skin beneath his fingertips. He had never bedded her, despite their mutual desire, because he had loved

her too much to send her to the marriage bed spoiled and risk her
husband sending her to the Abbey. But now she was free, and after
a few months of respectful mourning for his father, he would divorce Shelvon and be free himself. Lady Oona would finally be his,
to bed to his heart's content. And with his disapproving father no
longer insisting the lady was beneath him, he would marry her,
making her his by law.

The smile kept wanting to break free, and thoughts of finally
having the woman he'd loved for so many years in his bed had him
hard and aching. He reminded himself sternly that he was in mourning, that his father had been dead less than two weeks and grief
should be his constant companion. It was unseemly to let the power
of the throne be such an effective balm against the grief. But while
he had lost a father, he had gained the right to have the woman he
loved, as well as the ability to banish his half-siblings from his sight
while fitting them both with a most effective leash. He felt more
inclined to celebrate than weep.

His celebratory mood faded when Draimel Rah-Draimir, the
grand magus, was shown into his private study. He had never much
liked the grand magus, whom he considered a pompous old fool,
and he suspected the feeling was mutual. However, Draimel was an
ambitious pompous old fool, and though he was already on the
royal council, Delnamal felt sure he had hopes of being elevated to
the lord chamberlain's or lord chancellor's position. His attempts
to curry favor were convenient, if overly transparent.

Draimel bowed and waited a beat for Delnamal to offer him a
chair. Hoping to keep the grand magus's report short, Delnamal
did not oblige.

Draimel cleared his throat and shifted awkwardly before he
spoke. "Your Majesty. I felt it my duty to tell you about some . . .
concerning developments that have come about in the Academy
over the course of this past day."

It had been six months now since the witch's Curse had changed
the appearance of Rho, and Delnamal had been under the impression the Academy had given up their search for a cure, or at the very

least given up hopes that their search would bring success. The grand magus had stopped taking up the council's precious time with reports of no progress, and Delnamal had been just as happy not to have to listen to the depressing news. The last thing he wanted to hear about was *concerning developments,* especially when he was fresh from the glow of reading the marshal's report.

"Perhaps you should bring those up at the council meeting tomorrow," he said peevishly.

"I thought perhaps you might prefer to hear my report yourself first in case you would prefer some aspects not be shared with the whole council."

Delnamal had to admit to a reluctant stir of curiosity. "Do go on," he said, debating whether he might want to offer the man a chair, after all. But no, he hadn't heard enough yet to feel inclined to invite a longer discussion.

Draimel cleared his throat again, and Delnamal's curiosity was tinged with just a hint of unease. The grand magus was a pompous fool, but he was generally stoic. These outward signs of discomfort warned the report would be worrisome indeed.

"Yesterday morning," Draimel said, "we received a group of prison volunteers from the dungeon."

Delnamal had visited the dungeons often enough to understand how prisoners might be desperate for any hope of escape. However, he could not imagine how anyone could be desperate enough to volunteer as a test subject for the Academy in exchange for a commuted sentence. And yet whenever the grand magus requested volunteers, he had no trouble filling his quota. They suffered greatly for their freedom, and for some of them freedom took the form of death, but they volunteered anyway.

"While we were sorting out who to use for what," Draimel continued, "a couple of apprentices decided to have some sport with one of the prisoners. She was a thief and a whore, and with the Abbey no longer available . . ." The grand magus's voice trailed off as Delnamal's eyes narrowed.

"I've heard of at least half a dozen brothels in the Harbor District that have reopened since the floods," he said in a warning tone. "Surely there are enough whores in half a dozen brothels to keep your men satisfied."

Draimel shifted. "Yes. Of course."

"But these men of yours, these apprentices, preferred not to have to pay for it, correct?"

Draimel's face had lost some of its color, and Delnamal wanted to laugh. If the old fool thought Delnamal would complain about a couple of young bucks enjoying the dubious charms of a whore who'd been locked in a dungeon for who knew how long, then he was an idiot on top of being tedious.

"Yes, Your Majesty," Draimel said, looking braced for a blow.

Delnamal lost patience with the game. "So they fucked her. So what? Surely you don't feel the need to report to the king every time one of your men feels the need to scratch an itch."

"No, no, of course not. It's not that. It's just that . . . Well, they planned to share her, you see. And when one of them tore her robe open, she opened her Mindseye and . . ."

"And what?" Delnamal demanded.

"I didn't witness this personally, you understand, but the other lad reported what he saw, and I have no reason not to believe him. The woman reached for something in the air while her Mindseye was open, and she touched it to the man who was to have her first. And he dropped dead."

A lump of dread formed in Delnamal's stomach as he absorbed the implications of Draimel's words. He was not a warrior, had never even seen a battle, much less been involved in one, but he was well-versed in magic as befitted a royal son. "That sounds like . . ."

Draimel nodded. "It sounds like she used Kai."

"Which, of course, is impossible." Delnamal finally relented and offered Draimel a seat. The man looked like he needed one.

"So I would have said," Draimel agreed, sitting with a sigh of relief.

"There has to be some other explanation."

"I took the liberty of visiting the women's section of the prison, examining the women with my Mindseye. I saw no sign of Kai anywhere—including on the whore in question."

And the grand magus was an Adept, so if there had been any Kai to be seen, he would have seen it. Delnamal tried to comfort himself with the thought, but Draimel was obviously not finished.

"I told myself the lad had been mistaken," Draimel said. "That perhaps his friend had a weak heart or some other defect that could explain his sudden demise. But I wanted to be absolutely sure. The whore had shared a cell with a woman who had been an abigail before her arrest. The abigail admitted under questioning that the whore had been taken against her will while imprisoned, and that something closely resembling a Kai mote appeared afterward. The men could not see it." His normally ruddy cheeks turned a sickly shade of gray. "I bade her examine all the female prisoners, and found five others with these perverted Kai motes. There was no indication that any of those women was aware of the Kai, but I instructed the warden to quarantine them anyway and to make sure their keepers activate a Kai shield spell before approaching them."

"How is any of that possible?" Delnamal asked in horrified awe.

"I made a few inquiries at the prison, naturally. Many of the prisoners have voluntarily traded sexual favors for special treatment, but the women who had Kai had each attempted to refuse such an agreement."

"In other words, they'd been raped," Delnamal snapped, impatient with all Draimel's careful wording. "Stop being so prissy about it. They're in the dungeon for a reason, and they deserve anything that happens to them there."

"Yes, Your Majesty. It appears the Curse has had yet another effect of which we were not aware until now."

Delnamal frowned in speculation. "That may not be the worst thing ever," he mused. "I imagine it wouldn't be overly difficult to induce a prisoner to use that Kai for the greater good." His heartbeat quickened at the possibilities. Spells triggered by Kai were the most powerful magics in the world, and yet they were so terribly limited in their usage, available only to powerful men on the verge of death. If there was a way to produce Kai in someone who was still alive and who could be coerced into triggering a Kai spell with it . . .

"I had that same thought," Draimel said, and his morose tone told Delnamal the news would not be good even before he spoke. "I tried to induce one of those women to use her Kai to trigger a death curse against another inmate. The thought of a renewable source of Kai was too tempting to resist, and I had to try right away. But it didn't work."

"What do you mean, it didn't work?"

"The Kai those women carry—it's very like men's Kai, but not exactly the same. The woman made a genuine effort to use her Kai to trigger the spell, but it did not activate. I then had her use the Kai directly on the prisoner, and nothing happened."

"How do you know she made a genuine effort? You said you couldn't see the Kai. Maybe she just *pretended* she tried to use it."

"Trust me when I tell you she would have done *anything* I told her to do by the time I was finished with her. She tried to use the Kai, and she failed. I purchased the remaining women for the Academy, and they are being tested as we speak. The only successful test we have seen thus far occurred when we offered a woman a target she was eager to kill."

Delnamal raised an eyebrow. "Not one of your own men, I presume?"

"No, no," Draimel hurried to assure him. "Merely another prisoner with whom the woman had a sordid history. More testing is needed, but my working theory is that the Kai can only be used with the woman's consent."

Delnamal cursed as all those tempting possibilities he'd glimpsed withered and died. What he was left with was the thought of women running around with deadly elements available for their use, if only they knew. He swallowed hard. "When you've finished testing the prisoners, make sure you use any survivors for . . . other testing."

Draimel inclined his head, understanding exactly what Delnamal meant. Those women could never be allowed to live once they knew about Kai.

But how many women knew? It was a comfort to know so few women ever opened their Mindseye—and to know that many who did would not recognize the Kai for what it was. But his mind went instantly to the Abbey of the Unwanted, to that muddy courtyard littered with torn red robes and sobbing females. *Those* women opened their Mindseye on a regular basis. And *those* women would know what they were seeing when the Kai appeared.

Suddenly, the flier that had attacked Melcor took on a whole new significance. Although his secretary had never reported any ill effects of the attack, Delnamal had heard rumors that Melcor had stopped visiting the brothels in the Harbor District. It was very unlike him, and when Delnamal had inquired—discreetly and through an intermediary, of course—of those brothels he knew were his secretary's favorites, he'd learned that ever since that flier's attack, Melcor had apparently been unable to perform. If those bitches at the new Abbey had figured out a way to harness that Kai and even use it over the long distance that separated them from their attackers in Aalwell . . .

They would have to be eliminated. Every last one of them.

"Do not tell *anyone* about what you have found," Delnamal instructed Draimel. "The fewer people who know about this, the safer we will all be."

For the first time, Draimel allowed himself a hint of his usual pompous smile. "There was a reason I did not want to discuss this in front of the entire council."

Some people would find out. There was no avoiding that. And those who had a sentimental attachment to the women in their lives would most likely let those women in on the secret. But it was to the advantage of men everywhere if women were to stay in a state of ignorance, and Delnamal would do all he could to make sure that was the case.

Ellin shut and locked the door to her private study, informing the guards that she was not to be interrupted save for a dire emergency. Then she put the little Aalwood flier on her desk and looked again at the cryptic letter that it carried.

"It would be safest if you'd leave the room and let me activate it by myself," Lord Semsulin advised as he took a seat across from her.

The letter had urged her to activate the flier's secondary spell only when she was in complete privacy, but doing so was out of the question. There was no reason to suspect Alysoon Rai-Brynna of meaning her any harm, but having never met the other woman, Ellin had no way of knowing. Their correspondence about Jinnell Rah-Sylnin's marriage prospects had been cordial and friendly, but hardly enough to give Ellin a feel for this stranger. And she couldn't imagine what Alysoon's purpose might be in sending this mysterious flier with its baffling instructions.

"You think the spell is malicious?" she asked.

Semsulin frowned. "I don't know. But it seems to me unwise for you to take a risk."

She met her chancellor's eyes across the breadth of the table. "My entire reign is a risk." She hadn't told anyone about Graesan's attack on Zarsha, nor had she told anyone about Tamzin's part in it. But she didn't need her council of advisers or even Zarsha's outsider's perspective to know that she was playing a dangerous game. She continued to refuse to talk with her council about a marriage arrangement, and it seemed clear Lord Tamzin no longer believed the rumor he had once so gladly embraced.

Lady Alysoon's letter promised she would find the secondary spell in the flier a valuable gift, and she was not in a position to refuse valuable gifts.

"Besides," she said, "Lady Alysoon was very clear in her instructions that I was to activate the spell myself."

Semsulin sniffed with distaste, his lip curling as if he smelled something rotten. "That in itself is reason enough for you to throw the cursed thing in the fire."

She gave the old man a droll look. Months of working closely with him had not exactly endeared him to her, but Ellin had to admit there were hidden depths to the man. He was also an excellent adviser, and far more open-minded than she ever would have guessed. "You are not that much of a prude, my lord."

"I am a proper gentleman!" he snapped, scowling at her fiercely.

"Then avert your eyes."

His scowl deepened. Ellin hoped she wasn't making a big mistake by activating the spell in his presence, but though her instincts told her the flier posed no danger, she'd had visions of following its instructions and activating it in private only to face some terrible spell that would destroy her with no witnesses to the crime. It was at least remotely possible that Tamzin's efforts to weaken her had spread to other kingdoms, that he'd reached out to Alysoon with promises to make her daughter the Queen of Rhozinolm.

Ducking her head slightly to hide her eyes from Semsulin, Ellin opened her Mindseye and fed a mote of Rho to the little flier on her desk. It made a chirping sound as her eyes cleared, but at first that seemed to be the only effect. Then the air in front of it shimmered, and a strange, translucent image appeared.

The image was of a middle-aged woman beautifully dressed in a black silk gown. A black velvet band held salt-and-pepper hair back from a narrow, almost ascetic-looking face, but what caught Ellin's eye most was the huge faceted sapphire pinned on the dress's high collar. A gem of that size was fit for royalty, and a non-royal woman would be considered pretentious in the extreme to wear such a thing, even if she could afford it.

Ellin gasped and nearly jumped out of her chair when the image blinked. Across the desk, Semsulin looked both puzzled and concerned.

The woman in the image smiled, and amusement danced in eyes that for all the world seemed to be focused on Ellin's face. And then the image spoke.

"I did tell you it was a valuable gift, did I not, Your Majesty?"

Ellin met Semsulin's wide, shocked eyes over the desk. She wasn't sure if he could see the image as clearly as she could, but he had certainly heard that voice.

"Forgive me for startling you," the voice continued. "I did not want to explain what the spell did in writing, in case the correspondence was intercepted. Until now, there were only three people in the entire world who knew this spell existed."

Ellin continued to gape stupidly at the image, her mind hardly able to encompass what she was seeing. Clearly, she was no expert in magic, but she'd never heard of any spell even remotely like whatever it was this little flier carried.

"Perhaps I should start over with a formal introduction. My name is Alysoon Rah-Aaltyn."

There had been no doubt in her mind that the image was Lady Alysoon. However . . . "Rah-Aaltyn?" Ellin murmured to herself. The letter the flier had delivered was signed only with a first name, but Lady Alysoon had signed her previous correspondence as Alysoon Rai-Brynna, which was to all appearances the correct appellation.

"Rah-Aaltyn," Lady Alysoon confirmed. "My father and my mother were lawfully married when I was born. He declared me and my brother illegitimate for the sake of a political alliance with Khalpar. Now that he is gone, I see no reason to continue the charade."

Ellin glanced again at Semsulin, whose face was pale and who was clearly speechless for the first time in his career. He held up his hands in a helpless gesture and shook his head. Word had reached Rhozinolm two weeks ago of King Aaltyn's death. Ellin's council had not seemed overly enamored of the new king, but there had been no talk of anything but a smooth and ordinary succession.

"My condolences on your loss," Ellin said, her own chest squeezing with sympathetic pain that six months of mourning had done little to alleviate.

There was a brief freezing of Alysoon's expression as she absorbed the grief then shunted it aside. Ellin felt almost as if she were looking into a mirror, sure she had made that exact same face time and time again since her parents had died.

"Thank you. It was quite the shock, as I'd never known him to be anything but healthy. But you, unfortunately, know all too well what it feels like to lose a father."

Ellin nodded. She wondered if Alysoon was aware of Semsulin, sitting out of her line of sight—presuming Ellin understood how the spell was working, which was perhaps not the safest assumption. She resolved to stop sending so many nervous glances Semsulin's way, not wanting Alysoon to know she was not alone as suggested.

"The flier I sent you is linked to one of mine," Alysoon explained. "Anytime you wish to speak with me, you have only to give the flier some Rho. Mine will chirp, and when I complete the spell with more Rho, we will have a connection as we do now. Naturally, the spell works both ways."

Ellin shook her head with amazement. "I've . . . never heard of such a thing. Never heard anyone *imagine* such a thing. How . . . ?"

"I'm not sure how far word has spread, but a new Well opened up in Aaltah when the earth shook six months ago."

Ellin nodded. "I'd heard tell of a new Well. One that produces primarily feminine elements, I've been told." Actually, what she'd been told was that the Well was all but worthless, useful only for producing frivolous potions and other minor magics, but it seemed hardly politic to say so. "I've also heard that you have been visiting that Well for the last months."

Alysoon raised an eyebrow. "It seems you are well informed indeed if you keep track of the current whereabouts of a foreign king's supposedly illegitimate children."

Ellin allowed herself a small smile. "It behooves a queen to keep track of all the most influential figures in foreign courts. Especially when such figures might decide to declare themselves legitimate."

Alysoon's eyes crinkled, forming a network of laugh lines that softened the angles of her face. They didn't make her look beautiful, but they did make her look more approachable—even as Ellin fully absorbed all the implications of the older woman declaring herself legitimate.

"Tell me," Ellin said slowly. "Has your brother Tynthanal decided to adopt a new name, as well?"

If Tynthanal was King Aaltyn's legitimate son, then he was the heir to the throne. Which was obviously problematic for the man who was even now coming to be known as King Delnamal. This unsolicited gift from Lady Alysoon had layers of meaning attached.

Alysoon looked down at something, then quickly looked up again to meet Ellin's eyes. "We don't know each other well enough for this, so forgive me if I'm being overly familiar, but would you mind terribly if we speak frankly?"

Ellin laughed. "I am not a diplomat, Lady Alysoon. When I want to exchange cryptic messages with layers of meaning that must be carefully deciphered after the fact, I send a courtier." She could almost feel Semsulin's disapproving frown, though she refrained from glancing at him.

Alysoon nodded in approval. "Very well then. I will give you the undiplomatic version of my message. My brother and I were both conceived and born within the bounds of marriage. By ordinary law, the crown should pass to the king's eldest son. But times have changed, and your succession may help set a new precedent. I am my father's eldest child, and Tynthanal would rather support my claim to the throne than make a claim of his own."

Ellin shook her head. "You cannot believe that either one of you has a legitimate chance to take the throne. If we're being blunt, we must admit that you would need a great deal of support to overthrow the reigning king. Thanks to your mother, neither one of you is likely to gain a great deal of support, even if you do convince people you are legitimate."

"You asked earlier about the flier, and I started to explain. Let me finish. This new Well we have found—you've probably heard that because it provides mostly feminine elements, it's mostly worthless. But that is very far from the truth. The town of Women's Well is peopled largely by the former abigails of Aaltah and a company of

my brother's men. With the bounty of the Well and with the cooperation between the men and women of this town, we are producing
new spells every day. Spells that combine masculine and feminine
elements, and which require elements that are exceedingly rare in
other places. Nowhere but in Women's Well is there enough Zal to
produce the spell in the flier I sent you. Feel free to ask the women
of your Abbey how hard it is to find Zal if you doubt my word."

"I don't doubt your word," Ellin said slowly, "but . . ."

"We've barely begun to scratch the surface of what we can do
here. Imagine what someone who chose to support us could do
with an exclusive supply of these fliers. And first access to any other
spells we might invent."

Ellin couldn't deny the usefulness of the spell Alysoon was dem-
onstrating. She could hardly begin to imagine the uses such a spell
could be put to. However, as valuable a commodity as it might be,
it was not worth fighting someone else's war for.

"It's a tempting offer," she said, though she wasn't truly
tempted, "but there's no question that my council would reject it
out of hand." Not only would they reject it, but Tamzin would
eviscerate her for even suggesting it. Her hold on her own throne
was tenuous enough as it was. "Unless you can find enough support within your own kingdom to make an attempt on the throne
viable, I can't see how it's in the best interests of Rhozinolm to
recognize your claim. I'm sorry."

"I would urge you not to make so hasty a decision," Alysoon
said. "Our kingdoms have a long and troubled history of war, and
if my half-brother gets control of Women's Well and all its resources,
it might tilt the balance of power in his favor."

"As it would do for you, if you took the throne," Ellin pointed
out, though Alysoon's words inspired a prickle of worry. Rhozinolm's ability to withstand an attack from a foreign power was
already at risk, thanks to the difficulties surrounding their trade
agreements with Nandel. If Delnamal should prove to be a warlike
and greedy king, then allowing a second Well to fall into his hands
could spell doom.

"But I will not be able to take the throne without your support," Alysoon countered. "We can come to an arrangement, you and I, that will ensure the safety and security of both our kingdoms." She flashed a small smile. "You would come into an alliance with me with a strong upper hand, for I need you and am motivated to be generous with my terms."

"I will think about it," Ellin promised. "And I will talk to my most trusted advisers before making a final decision."

"That's all I could ask."

Ellin removed the mote of Rho from the flier, deactivating the spell and looking across the desk to meet Semsulin's eyes. He didn't even wait for her to ask what he thought.

"The council would never agree," he said. "No matter how tempting the terms."

Unfortunately, Ellin knew he was right. She would have liked to have brought the proposal to the council for an extended rational discussion of the risks and benefits of supporting Alysoon's claim, but there was no point.

She nodded her agreement. "Certainly not with Tamzin as lord chamberlain, and probably not even without. There is no point in even mentioning that the offer was made."

Yet the glimpse of the future Lady Alysoon had offered was going to keep Ellin awake at night. If she could not find a way to secure the trade agreements with Nandel, arms production in Rhozinolm would be crippled, leaving them temptingly vulnerable to King Delnamal even without the addition of whatever mysterious spells could be produced in Women's Well.

History had been kind to Queen Shazinzal, had praised her brief reign and labeled her as an extraordinary woman who'd met the challenges of the throne with wisdom and courage and strength. If Ellin lost the trade agreements with Nandel and proved unable to protect her kingdom against Aaltah, history would paint her in a very different light.

CHAPTER THIRTY-FIVE

Shelvon found Jinnell curled up in a window seat in the parlor, reading a book. Between the strict protocols of mourning and the draconian restrictions Delnamal had put on her movements, the poor child had to be bored out of her wits. At least her brother had his studies to keep him occupied, but removed from the responsibilities of running a household, and with her social life almost nonexistent since her grandmother's Curse, Jinnell had nothing.

Jinnell looked up when Shelvon entered the room. She hastily dropped her book, struggling out of the seat to drop a deep curtsy.

"Your Majesty," she said, blushing and flustered.

Shelvon almost smiled, wondering what shocking subject matter she would find if she were to pick up the book Jinnell had dropped, but her purpose in seeking out her niece was too grim to allow for smiles.

"Forgive me for interrupting your reading," Shelvon said as Jinnell rose from her curtsy. The blush added some healthy color to her face while the black mourning dress attempted to leach it away. The girl was far prettier than her mother and managed to look fetching despite all that dull black. For a woman, beauty could be either a blessing or a curse. Jinnell would have been much better off were she ugly.

"Please sit down," Shelvon said, gesturing Jinnell into a chair. She tried to keep her voice neutral, but she could see at once that she had failed. Jinnell's blush faded, and there was a wary look in her eyes as she sat on the very edge of the indicated chair.

"Has something happened to my mother or Uncle Tynthanal?" Jinnell asked as she clenched her hands in her lap.

Shelvon wished she were possessed of more tact and sensitivity. The girl was rightfully fearful of what the new king might do to her mother and her other uncle, so it was only logical that she would leap to the worst possible conclusion on seeing Shelvon's distress.

"No, no, dear," Shelvon hastened to reassure her. "It's nothing like that."

"But there *is* something wrong." Jinnell held her head high as a mask of neutrality settled over her face.

Shelvon's own anger flared, and she hated her husband more than words could describe for making her be the bearer of bad tidings. *He* was the girl's blood kin, and *he* was the king. By all rights, he was the one who should be having this conversation. But the bastard was too cowardly to face his niece and acknowledge the suffering he was about to impart upon an innocent.

Shelvon knew of no gentle way to deliver the news, so she settled for blurting it out. "The king has decided to send you to Nandel to meet my father."

Jinnell blanched, but the expression on her face did not change. "Surely he knows I will not show to my best advantage while in mourning." Her voice was cold and leaden, but a spark of heat lit her eyes. She was by all accounts a very proper young woman, but that look in her eyes told Shelvon she was far from meek.

Shelvon's heart ached in sympathy. If Delnamal had had the

courage to deliver his orders in person, he no doubt would have explained all the logical reasons why it was to Aaltah's advantage to explore the possibility of another alliance by marriage. If he chose to explain anything at all, that is. He knew perfectly well that he was being cruel to a child who was in his care, and he could be counted on to lash out when he knew he was in the wrong. Perhaps he would merely have delivered a kingly order, then strode out of the room as fast as possible to avoid being faced with the distress his cruelty caused.

But he had sent Shelvon to deliver this message, and she would deliver it in her own way. "You do not have to show to your best advantage to interest Prince Waldmir. One look at your pretty face will win him over. I'm supposed to tell you that this is just a brief visit to explore possibilities and that no firm plans have been made."

The coldness in Jinnell's eyes was enough to make Shelvon shiver. "But we both know that if your father wants me, he will have me. Delnamal hates my mother too much to resist the lure of hurting her through me."

Shelvon leaned back into her chair as the energy drained from her body. She was the Queen of Aaltah, and yet she felt as powerless now as she had as a child growing up in Nandel. Delnamal could barely stand the sight of her, and he certainly had no interest in listening to anything she had to say. After their fight over the fertility potions, his visits to her bed had become more and more infrequent. They had stopped entirely after his father had died.

He was no longer making even a token effort to produce an heir, and that meant he had already decided to divorce her as soon as he could secure Aaltah's trade agreements with Nandel.

"I wish I could tell you otherwise," Shelvon said. She'd thought it was Jinnell who'd be in tears when this conversation was over, but it was she herself whose eyes burned and stung, whose chest ached. "But I can't give the king the heir he needs, and that is all the excuse he needs to divorce me."

"And I am the bribe to persuade your father not to be offended," Jinnell said bitterly.

"I'm so sorry, Jinnell. I've tried *everything* to give him an heir. When he first commanded me to speak with you, I lied to him and told him I was with child just to try to delay him. I don't think he believed me, but even if he did . . ."

Jinnell nodded. "Even if he did, what matters to him more than anything is hurting my mother by selling me to Nandel." Her jaw jutted out with stubborn resolve. "But the king underestimates how disagreeable I can make myself. Will your father still want me if I refuse to give him an heir?"

"I'm not even sure he believes in the power of your grandmother's spell. I've had no contact with him since my marriage, but I know how he thinks. It will take more than a few miscarriages and childless couples to convince him that women could possibly have had the power and intelligence to cast such a momentous spell."

Jinnell laughed, but it was a harsh, angry sound without any trace of genuine humor. "He need only open his Mindseye to see proof of my grandmother's power."

Shelvon wrinkled her nose. She had heard about the change in the magical element Rho, but she had never seen it herself. Even in the privacy of her own room, she couldn't convince herself it was acceptable to open her Mindseye. The horror of seeing her twelve-year-old half-sister beaten nearly to death because she'd been caught with her Mindseye open had left a scar on her soul that would never heal. Here in Aaltah, she was fairly sure every woman she met opened her Mindseye at least on occasion, but her own Nandel sensibilities did not allow her the same freedom.

"Maybe that's true. But Delnamal believed he could bully and berate me into carrying a child whether I wished to or no, and my father has fewer scruples. You can tell him you refuse to give him an heir, and he will be convinced he can bend you to his will."

Jinnell's face lost a little of the angry color it had gained. Perhaps it was cruel of Shelvon not to give the girl soothing lies, not to tell her everything was going to be all right. What purpose did telling her the truth serve, save to frighten her more? But despite her own logic, Shelvon couldn't bring herself to tell the pretty lies.

"Am I correct in believing you have no love for your father?" Jinnell asked.

Shelvon bit back the customary denial. No one who'd ever seen her interact with her father could believe she loved the man, and yet to have admitted her feelings would have been to condemn herself to the Abbey as a disrespectful daughter. "You are correct."

"And that you would like to save me from this marriage if you could?"

Shelvon became more wary. She did not want to see *any* woman, much less this girl who was at least nominally under her care, forcibly married to her father. But she was hardly in a position to "save" anyone—not even herself. She did not answer the question, but it seemed that Jinnell read some form of agreement from her facial expression.

"If I ask you an uncomfortable question," Jinnell said carefully, "would you promise me to answer truthfully—and to not tell anyone I asked it?"

Shelvon stared at the girl, trying to imagine what question she might be contemplating. "It's hard to make a promise when I don't know the question."

"I can't ask the question unless I'm certain you won't repeat it— or any conclusions you draw from my asking it."

If nothing else, Shelvon had to admit she was curious. Until Jinnell had been brought to live in the palace, Shelvon would have said the girl was a pretty—if flighty—teenager with little depth to her. A typical girl of the court, who giggled with her friends and considered choosing which gown to wear for dinner a challenging and desperately important puzzle. It hadn't taken long to see through that surface impression, though until now Shelvon had not seen the cunning intelligence that shone in Jinnell's eyes.

Shelvon had only to think of how her father would treat an intelligent wife to know that she would do what she could to help Jinnell—even if all she could do was listen and sympathize.

"All right. I promise."

Jinnell licked her lips. "Would your father still want to wed me if I were not chaste?"

Shelvon reared back in shock. In Nandel, a girl who was unchaste would be severely beaten by her family before her broken and bloody body was shipped off to the Abbey for the amusement of those men who could afford the indulgence—and did not mind the damaged husk that was left.

She took in a shaky breath and put her hand to her chest, where her heart was thudding painfully. She was not in Nandel. Delnamal would not break Jinnell's body as a man of Nandel would. But he would most definitely send her to the Abbey in disgrace, where she would spend the rest of her life as a whore and a virtual prisoner.

"I'm not afraid of the Abbey here in Aaltah," Jinnell said. "If I were sent there, I'd be with my mother and my uncle, and I know they would not allow any harm to come to me. But if the king marries me off to Prince Waldmir, then I will eventually end up in the Abbey in Nandel like his other wives—the ones he didn't kill, at least—and from all accounts, that is something very much to fear."

Shelvon crossed her arms over her chest, hugging herself. She of course had no personal experience with the Abbey—no respectable lady would ever cross its threshold or speak to an abigail—but she'd heard enough stories to know being incarcerated there was a fate worse than death. In many ways, Shelvon's mother was lucky she'd been put to death instead of divorced. Even in Nandel, most men would at least have some hesitation before divorcing their wives and condemning them to that hell, but Shelvon's father had shown no such scruples. If he married Jinnell, and the girl failed to give him an heir, then she would be sent to the Abbey as soon as he grew bored with her in his bed.

"Would he wed me if I were no longer a virgin?"

Shelvon's stomach gave a sick lurch. It went against everything she'd been taught as a woman of Nandel to in any way condone what Jinnell was suggesting, much less encourage it. A woman's virginity was her most prized possession, to be bestowed upon her husband on the first night of their marriage. Giving it away to some other man was a crime against the Crown and even against the Creator.

If Shelvon were a halfway proper woman, she would have Jinnell locked in her room for the duration of her time in the palace, and then send her to Nandel with guards specifically instructed to ensure her chastity.

Not that long ago, Shelvon might have done the proper thing. But something had changed in her on the night she'd first poured out a fertility potion her husband had bade her to drink, and there was no going back. Perhaps Delnamal had tasked her with giving Jinnell this news out of cowardice, but he had unknowingly given his wife a small chance to strike back at all the men who had made her life miserable.

"No, he would not."

"Corlin, please!" Jinnell said, grabbing her little brother's shoulder and trying to pull him away.

The boy twisted out of his sister's grip and continued to glare up at Delnamal with fury and defiance that sat oddly on the face of the usually cheerful thirteen-year-old. Clearly the boy had not been disciplined properly even while his father was alive, or he would not have had such cheek with any adult, much less the king.

"You can't do this!" Corlin growled, trying to sound fierce.

Delnamal sneered. "I'm the king, and the head of this family. So yes, I can."

"It's all right, Corlin," his sister tried, sounding desperate. "Nothing's been decided yet. I'm only going to *meet* him." She flicked a worried look at Delnamal, and he saw that despite her soothing words, she was fully aware what her journey to Nandel signified. He'd been half-expecting to meet with hysterics from her, and he'd been dreading it so much that not only had he had Shelvon deliver the news, but he'd tried his best to avoid seeing her despite her residence in the palace. What he had *not* expected was for her little brother to think himself man enough to defy the king.

Corlin's chin jutted out stubbornly, and his eyes flashed. The boy was small for his age and slight, but the ferocity of his stance hinted at the man he would become. Someday, he would be a man to be reckoned with. But not now.

"Your mother has obviously allowed you to run wild," Delnamal snapped. "Let me assure you I will not do the same. You will speak to me with the proper respect, or you will face the appropriate discipline."

Delnamal had interviewed the boy's regular tutor when he'd taken over the children's care and decided to discharge the man when he expressed reluctance to deliver beatings except in the most dire circumstances. A thirteen-year-old boy, who was naturally just starting to test out his manhood, needed a firm hand, and Delnamal had hired a new tutor who was less squeamish. Up until now, Corlin had been relatively well behaved, and his tutor reported having no cause to do more than rap his knuckles on occasion.

"I'm speaking to you with all the respect you deserve!" the boy spat. "You're not our father! We shouldn't even *be* here."

Jinnell gasped and covered her mouth with her hand, suitably appalled at her brother's gall. Tears sprang to her eyes, and she gave Delnamal a pleading look that made something squirm deep in his chest.

"Please, Uncle," she begged. "He didn't mean it. He's just upset."

This time when she grabbed her brother, she did so with more force. She was a slender young woman, but her protective instincts made her strong and she took him by surprise, pulling him backward, then giving him a shove toward the doorway. "Go to your room!" she ordered him. "Don't make this worse for me than it already is."

The squirming inside intensified, and Delnamal almost backed down. Jinnell was a surprisingly sweet girl considering her lineage, and she did not deserve the fate she faced in Nandel. Prince Waldmir would break her, and Delnamal would have to live with that knowledge on his conscience. In some ways, it was quite noble—if foolish—of her brother to attempt to defend her like this. Noble acts were often punished, but perhaps he should make allowances just this once . . .

"I *did* mean it!" Corlin spat. "And I'm not scared of you!"

Jinnell groaned, and though a part of him still regretted the necessity, Delnamal knew that he could not now back down. One way or another, Delnamal was going to destroy Alysoon and Tynthanal, and if the boy lacked the necessary respect for his authority, he could grow into a threat. A good beating now might make the boy think twice about future defiance. It might even prevent him from later involving himself with any treasonous activities that might lead to his unfortunate execution. So really it was for his own good.

"You should be," Delnamal growled at his nephew. "I will send your tutor to teach you just how scared you should be." Jinnell opened her mouth, no doubt to plead once again for mercy, but he'd had enough. "One more word from you, and you'll have a thrashing, as well. If you're going to act like a child, I will treat you like one."

She gaped at him, and he hoped she wouldn't test him. Having a thirteen-year-old boy thrashed was one thing, but he could hardly allow Corlin's tutor to see Jinnell's bare bottom, and he had no governess on staff who could take care of such duties.

The girl's eyes shimmered with tears, and her lower lip quivered as she put her arms around her still-defiant brother. Delnamal let out a silent sigh of relief, and it wasn't just because he didn't have to face the inconvenience of finding someone to thrash her.

It was a hard thing he was doing, sending her to Prince Waldmir. As much as he despised her mother, she was his niece, and she was an innocent. If only her thrice-damned grandmother hadn't cast that spell . . .

He would even now have an heir, with a likelihood of more on the way. His union with Shelvon would never have been a happy one, but it could at least have been fruitful. He wouldn't have to scramble to strengthen his ties with Nandel so he could have the divorce he needed without causing a diplomatic disaster. And Jinnell could have married whichever respectable young man of Aaltah would have made the best husband.

He was genuinely sorry for the pain he was causing Jinnell. He was even sorry that Corlin was so distressed about his sister's fate. But his decision to send her to Nandel had nothing to do with striking out at her mother and everything to do with political necessity. He could feel remorse for what he was being forced to do, but in the end, he had to remember that it was not his fault. The only person who should legitimately feel guilty over the girl's fate was her grandmother.

Too bad the bitch was dead.

CHAPTER THIRTY-SIX

I f Delnamal had not insisted on moving Jinnell and Corlin into the palace, where they were both always under someone's watchful eye, Jinnell had no doubt she could have easily rid herself of her virginity by now. She always displayed the proper maidenly modesty in front of others, but she was well aware that she was pretty. Everyone told her so, and she could not miss the occasional admiring glance from the men who crossed her path. But whereas at home, she was well versed in the art of escaping scrutiny, such was not the case in the palace, where she couldn't take a step without encountering a guard, a servant, or both.

Over the course of the past week, she had been carefully reviewing her options, and taking a close look at those men with whom she had the most regular contact. While she was not looking for a genuine romantic tryst, she did hope to find someone whose touch she would not find repellent, so she quickly dismissed many of the older men from consideration. Of those who were not old enough

to be her father, she felt Corlin's hateful tutor was the most interested, but she would no more let that creature touch her than she
would jump off the cliffs.

She had finally settled on Salnor, one of the most junior members of the palace guard. He had not developed the iron stoicism of
his elders, and was far more apt to make eye contact when she spoke
to him. He also had a free and easy smile that she could not deny
she found appealing. She was careful to speak to all the palace
guards from time to time so that no one would think she was paying undue attention to Salnor, but she was more generous with her
own smiles when he was around, and she noticed how the color
rose in his cheeks when she met his eyes. She had little doubt he was
interested, but she was not sure how to go about her own deflower-
ing.

She decided to start by stumbling and "turning her ankle" as she
passed him in the hall on her way back to her rooms after a walk in
the gardens. Since she was within the residential wing of the palace,
she did not have her honor guards trailing around behind her every
moment, which gave her at least a semblance of privacy.

She flashed Salnor a smile as she walked past him, then pretended to trip. She let herself fall to the carpet with a cry of pain
that was clearly convincing, for Salnor leapt from his post and hurriedly squatted before her.

"Are you hurt, Miss Jinnell?" he asked, his eyes wide with alarm.

Jinnell reached for her ankle, "inadvertently" pushing her skirt
up and giving him a teasing glimpse of leg. She moaned as she
squeezed the ankle, and though she could not quite manage to
make herself cry on demand, she blinked rapidly as if on the verge
of tears. "I really twisted it," she said with a wince.

Salnor reached out as if to test the ankle himself, then jerked his
hand back as he thought better of it. It was all Jinnell could do not
to smile when she saw that telltale flush of pink in his cheeks.

"Can you stand?" he asked, offering her a hand.

Jinnell took his hand and had to stifle a grimace of distaste at the
rough, calloused feel of his skin. As a junior guardsman, he still

spent a great deal of his time on drills and exercise, and his hands were much the worse for it. She did not imagine they would feel terribly pleasant against more sensitive skin—but surely they would feel more pleasant than Prince Waldmir's hands.

Leaning on the guardsman heavily, she climbed laboriously to her feet and tried to take a step, then clutched more tightly to Salnor's hand as she winced. "I don't think I can walk," she said.

The flush in Salnor's cheeks deepened, and he glanced up and down the hallway. For once, there was no one else in sight. Jinnell had chosen her ambush site wisely.

"I suppose I should carry you," he said doubtfully.

"I would be ever so grateful. If you can take me back to my rooms, I'm sure the ladies will know what to do with this dratted ankle. I broke it once when I was a little girl, and it's never been quite right since." That was at least half the truth, for though she had indeed once broken her ankle, a healer had been called for and it had been whole and healthy within a few hours.

Salnor swallowed hard as she slid her arm around his neck to make it easier for him to pick her up. He swept her off her feet with no difficulty—all that training had made him strong as an ox—and she settled comfortably against him as they began the long trek back to her rooms. She could feel the rapid patter of his pulse, and knew it had nothing to do with exertion. She wriggled a little, letting her breast rub against his chest. He swallowed again, proving he was fully aware of the contact despite the barrier of his mail. She smiled up at him brightly.

"I'm very sorry to have put you out like this," she said. "You won't get in trouble for leaving your station, will you?"

"Not under the circumstances," he assured her. "It's no trouble at all, miss."

She batted her eyelashes at him, though she failed to grasp why doing so was supposed to be a flirtatious gesture. "You needn't be so formal when I'm cradled in your arms."

His flush deepened, and he cleared his throat. "I would never treat you with anything less than the utmost respect, Miss Jinnell."

"You wouldn't?" she asked, widening her eyes in false innocence. "Why, I'm beginning to think that's a mighty shame."

His gaze darted all around, as if he were searching for rescue, and Jinnell feared she was moving far too fast for him. She knew how to flirt with an awkward young nobleman at a ball, but that was a very different skill than trying to seduce said awkward young nobleman into her bed. While he was on duty in her uncle's palace, no less. If he were to be suspected of inappropriate behavior with the king's niece, he would be subjected to a severe flogging at the very least. More likely, his punishment would be considerably more dire, and that possibility would be running rampant through his mind right now. It would behoove her to move as slowly as she dared, though she feared every day that passed led her closer and closer to an engagement that would spell the end of her life.

"I was just teasing," she said with a breathy little laugh. "That was terribly rude of me. I'm sorry."

"No apologies necessary," he said, but she was still very much aware of his stiffness and discomfort.

As she was trying to think of something else to say to both stimulate his interest and calm his discomfort, he turned a corner, and suddenly it seemed like every human being in the palace caught sight of them at once. They were immediately swarmed with servants and guardsmen alike, all asking after Jinnell's well-being. Despite her protests, one of the older guardsmen took her from Salnor's arms and insisted on summoning a healer right there and then. Salnor darted back toward his post with every evidence of being relieved, and Jinnell was left trying to assure everyone that her ankle was much better now and she could walk on her own.

As seductions went, clearly her first attempt had been a dismal failure, and though she had no doubt Salnor was interested, it would obviously take a concerted effort to overcome his sense of propriety. But she did not have the time to be slow and gentle in her pursuit, and that meant that however distasteful it might be, she needed to set her sights on someone less innocent and thoughtful. Someone who would be so eager to take what she was offering that neither his conscience nor his common sense would interfere with his desires.

Reminding herself that no alternative could be worse than a marriage to Prince Waldmir, she decided that she could stomach Corlin's tutor for long enough to do what needed to be done. And when her lack of chastity was discovered, she would happily confess the identity of her secret lover without any feelings of guilt whatsoever.

When next she had a moment alone with Master Wilbaad, she would bait the trap. Even if the very thought of letting that man touch her made her stomach turn.

There were very few things Ellin wanted to do less than have a private audience with Lord Tamzin. Bad enough that she had to sit in endless council meetings with him every day. Since he'd goaded Graesan into the ill-fated assassination attempt on Zarsha, the very sight of him made something clench in her belly, and it was all she could do to manage anything resembling civil discourse. However, the rumor that she and Semsulin had started so long ago, the one that was meant to plant hope in Tamzin's mind and tame his attempts to undermine her rule, was clearly no longer having the desired effect. Worse, it seemed to be spreading and gaining strength—no doubt thanks to Tamzin and his supporters.

When Tamzin had requested the audience, her first inclination had been to refuse. Indeed, everything in her had *begged* her to refuse. There could be no pleasant reason he wished to speak with her in private, and the temptation to hide from whatever trouble he was planning to cause now had been nearly overpowering. However, he *was* her lord chamberlain, and refusing to see him would be not only childish but irresponsible.

She did not immediately look up from the paper she was reading when Tamzin was shown into her private study. Not that she was actually *reading* the paper, mind you. It was nothing but a prop, meant to show Tamzin that she wasn't especially concerned about his request for an audience. It also gave her an extra few heartbeats to adjust to the tension his very presence caused—and to put the reins on her temper when she knew that, if not for him, Graesan would still be coming to her bed at night, warming her with his body and his love.

A few heartbeats was all she had, for instead of standing respectfully awaiting her attention, Tamzin dropped into one of the chairs before her desk without invitation. It was an unthinkable breach of etiquette even for a close family member, much less a member of her royal council. She put down her paper and glared at him, but there was no point in rebuking his behavior. His message of disrespect was best left unacknowledged.

"Lord Tamzin," she said in a flat voice that she hoped hid most of what she was feeling. "I only have a few minutes, so please be brief."

Tamzin grinned at her. "Yes, your new secretary informed me of your tight schedule. Whatever happened to the last one? I rather liked him, but I haven't seen him around in ages."

Ellin's heart leapt into her throat, and she felt as if she were choking on it. There was no question Tamzin knew why she had a new secretary, though she doubted he knew exactly what had happened to Graesan. It would not occur to someone like Tamzin that Zarsha was a decent enough man to allow his would-be assassin to live, much less give the man a home and a job. No, Tamzin thought he was poking at the open wound that was Graesan's death at Zarsha's hands, and he was enjoying himself.

"I sincerely doubt you asked for an audience to discuss the disposition of my staff," she gritted out. Try as she might, she could not hide her anger and her pain. She hated giving Tamzin even that much satisfaction.

Tamzin smiled. Somehow, when others saw that smile, they were charmed, but Ellin couldn't understand how so many missed the malice that she saw so clearly in his eyes. "No, I merely sought to satisfy my idle curiosity." His nostrils flared briefly, as if he could scent the pain he was causing. "What I truly wanted to discuss with you is a delicate matter, which is why I requested a private audience rather than bringing it up during a council meeting."

There was that flash of malice again, the flash that told her whatever "delicate matter" he wanted to discuss was something designed to hurt her in one way or another. She steeled herself, searching for a well of calm to mask her true feelings. "Well, what is it?" she asked, and was pleased that her tone betrayed nothing but impatience.

"There are some at this court who believe you have formed an . . . unhealthy attachment to Zarsha of Nandel. It is understandable, certainly, for a young woman to form an attachment to the man she is going to marry, but once that engagement is over . . ." He shrugged and made a regretful face. "Well, it's best for all that both parties move on."

Ellin was confident that the only member of her court who was concerned about this "unhealthy attachment" was sitting on the other side of her desk. If rumors had sprung up about any possible impropriety in her relationship with Zarsha, Semsulin would have heard of them and brought them to her attention. She was certain that neither she nor Zarsha had given the court any cause to suspect them of a romantic entanglement, and not even Semsulin knew that Zarsha was still pursuing a possible engagement.

"I won't even dignify that nonsense with a response," she said.

"But you should, Your Majesty. I'm sure you know rumors and rumblings don't have to be true to cause a great deal of trouble and inconvenience. It would be best for you—and for our kingdom—if you were to put those rumors to rest before they grow out of control."

"Is that why you tried to have Zarsha assassinated?" she blurted. Later, she might regret putting the accusation into words, but it was too late to swallow them now.

Tamzin widened his eyes in feigned shock. "I can't imagine what you're talking about, Your Majesty. Who would *dare* make such a baseless accusation?"

"If you had as much concern for the good of the kingdom as you claim, you would never have risked having the nephew of Sovereign Prince Waldmir murdered while he was a guest of the Crown."

"I must insist you present the evidence upon which you have leveled this outrageous charge!" The look in his eyes said he was far more amused—and entertained—by her accusation than worried by it.

Realizing she was only fueling Tamzin's hunger, Ellin forced herself to return to the subject at hand. "I will take your warning under advisement," she said coldly and with no sincerity. "And I would ask you to put the needs of the Kingdom of Rhozinolm above your own personal ambitions."

"And I would ask the same of you," he retorted. "If you wish to quell the unpleasant rumors before they take root, then send Zarsha of Nandel home so that we can all rest assured that he is not trying to woo his way onto the throne. And let us—discreetly, of course—make it known that you and I will marry when your mourning is over. Rhozinolm needs a king, and we both know I am the most suited for the position."

I would sooner take a poisonous snake to my bed than you, she thought, but thankfully she refrained from saying it. "As I have made abundantly clear, I have no intention of discussing my marriage arrangement until after my mourning is over."

Tamzin removed the mask of courtesy he'd hidden behind and fixed her with a look that chilled her to the marrow. "You may refrain from *publicly* discussing the arrangement until after your mourning has ended, but it is past time you let it be known to the members of your royal council. I'm sure you know they will happily support me, and I sincerely doubt you can find another candidate of whom you can say the same."

"I will take your warning under advisement," she said again, and with as little intention of doing so.

"You do that. But don't think about it too long, Your Majesty. I fear for the security of your throne if you don't act to quell the rumors about your relationship with Zarsha of Nandel. You cannot even begin to imagine the visceral outrage the thought of a Nandelite sitting on the throne of Rhozinolm would create in your people."

Ellin clenched her teeth to keep from voicing any of her thoughts. He hadn't *quite* gone so far as to openly threaten her, hadn't said enough to warrant a treason charge—even if she'd had a witness—but there was no question of his intent.

If she didn't send Zarsha home and agree to marry Tamzin, then he was going to start spreading whispers about her and Zarsha. He would rile up those who already opposed her and frighten those who were currently neutral. The rumor might even be ugly enough to turn some of her own supporters against her.

Once he'd sufficiently stirred the pot, Tamzin would take up arms against her. And as long as he had the support of the lord commander and the lord high treasurer, she would be helpless to stop him.

As a general rule, Delnamal seemed to take great pains to avoid seeing or speaking to Jinnell and Corlin, difficult as that was when they were all living in the same wing of the palace. Jinnell was perfectly satisfied with that arrangement, and would have been happier still if she never saw her uncle at all. It certainly would be safer for Corlin, who, far from being cowed by the vicious beating Delnamal had ordered, had discovered a taste for rebellion and a remarkable talent for getting under the skin of his elders. So she was far from pleased when Delnamal stepped into the sitting room where she was reading and instead of immediately finding an excuse to leave, strode toward her.

Reluctantly, Jinnell put the book down and stood so she could give him the curtsy protocol required. She bowed her head demurely and murmured a respectful greeting, which he failed to return. He picked up the book she'd been reading, and beneath her lowered lashes, she saw the look of surprise on his face.

"A Devotional?" he said in some astonishment. "I did not think you a pious sort."

"The dowager gave it to me and urged me to read it," she said, remembering the painful awkwardness of the moment. Jinnell had studied the Devotional growing up, as any well-brought-up lady should, but she could not say its teachings called to her. However, the dowager seemed to find great peace and serenity from reading it, and Jinnell had a desperate need for peace and serenity. Her safety depended on her ability to seduce Master Wilbaad, and yet she could not see him without thinking about his brutal treatment of her little brother.

"Your obedience is admirable," Delnamal said, and there was an unmistakable edge in his voice that made her pulse speed. He had no reason to be angry with her—unless he blamed her for not controlling her little brother's bad behavior—but she had little doubt that he was.

"Have I displeased you, Your Majesty?" she asked in a tremulous voice, racking her brain for something she might have done or said to draw his ire. Corlin might claim not to be afraid of their uncle, but Jinnell felt no shame in admitting that she was. There was so much anger in his heart, and he hardly seemed to see her and Corlin as people, much less as family. In his eyes, they were only their mother's children, and as such were weapons to be used to wound her.

Delnamal raised his eyebrows in feigned surprise. "Have you done something with which I should be displeased?" he asked.

Her eyebrows drew together in a frown of puzzlement, and she shook her head. "No, Your Majesty."

"So you have behaved with perfect propriety and decorum at all times since last we spoke." His narrowed eyes and growling tone made her long to take a step backward.

"Yes, Your Majesty," she said. She had certainly *intended* impropriety when she had "tripped" in the hallway, but since her intentions had not come to fruition . . .

"The captain of the palace guard reported to me that he was forced to reassign one of his men because you made improper advances."

Jinnell gasped in mingled fear and outrage. She had done nothing that might be considered improper!

Well, she *had* made an unwisely flirtatious comment to Salnor, but no one could know what she'd said. Unless Salnor himself had reported it to his superiors. She had known she'd made him uncomfortable, but she'd had no idea he was *that* much of a prig!

"I did no such thing!" she said indignantly, though she feared she sounded more frightened than angry.

"So the guardsman lied?" Delnamal sneered. "You did not suggest that he deviate from the proper, respectful behavior of a guardsman? Very well. I shall have him flogged. An offense of this magnitude requires a stern punishment. Perhaps fifty lashes."

The blood drained from Jinnell's face. Salnor had betrayed her, but that was hardly a crime worthy of fifty lashes. The pain would be immense, and he would bear the scars for the rest of his life. She could not allow that.

"I didn't say he lied," she murmured. "I said I did not make improper advances. I'll allow as how he might have misinterpreted my words, but I was merely teasing him to make him blush. I meant no offense."

"Hmm," Delnamal said, looking at her with glittering eyes. "It is a dangerous game for a pretty girl to 'tease' a young man like that. It is hardly surprising that he might have misinterpreted your intent, for that is often the way of young men. You are fortunate that he requested reassignment rather than acting upon what he saw as an invitation. Once a man hears such an invitation—whether it was intended as one or not—he often has a great deal of trouble discerning when that invitation has been revoked."

"I will be more circumspect in the future," she promised.

"See that you are. Your kingdom needs you fresh and unspoiled when you are presented to Sovereign Prince Waldmir, for those trade agreements are of vital importance. If through some naïve, childish error on your part, you were to find yourself unfit to be his bride, I might be forced to regard your behavior as something akin to treason, for it would not be only your own good name you dishonored—it would be Aaltah's."

Jinnell quailed, for she could see in Delnamal's eyes that he was deadly serious. Being branded unchaste would land her in the Abbey; being branded a traitor would land her at the block. Tears filmed her eyes, and her lower lip trembled.

"I have done nothing wrong, Uncle," she said, then cursed herself for the familiar form of address.

Delnamal's eyes continued to bore into her. "See that it stays that way. Do we understand each other?"

Jinnell bowed her head and closed her eyes, for she did indeed understand. Losing her virginity to avoid a marriage with Prince Waldmir was no longer among her options.

"Yes, Your Majesty."

CHAPTER THIRTY-SEVEN

"This is madness," Alys said, rising from her chair and stepping away from the table, unable to sit still. She was painfully aware of six pairs of eyes boring into her back as she crossed her arms over her chest and stared at the far wall to avoid all those expectant gazes.

"It's not madness," Tynthanal said, "it's necessity."

She shook her head, unwilling to answer in words. This had been a deliberate ambush. Every evening, there was a meeting in the east wing of the town hall during which the unofficial leaders of Women's Well would discuss the day's issues and successes. It had started out being just her, Tynthanal, and Chanlix, but then Tynthanal had included Jailom, his second-in-command, and Chanlix had begun bringing Maidel, a young abigail she'd taken under her wing, and then the chair of the building committee had invited himself and one of the merchants who'd taken up residence in Women's Well. Little by little, Tynthanal—who had at one time been the highest-ranking person in Women's Well and therefore considered by everyone as its leader—had started deferring to her, looking at her before taking a stand on any issue. She should have seen what he was doing, but perhaps she'd been willfully blind. Having not received any promises of aid from Queen Ellinsoltah, she had all but banished the thought of contesting Delnamal's claim to the throne, but now Tynthanal was angling toward a different goal.

"We are citizens of Aaltah," she said between gritted teeth. "We cannot—"

"Most of us are to all intents and purposes exiled," Tynthanal argued. "And technically, our town is located in the Wasteland, past Aaltah's border."

She whirled and glared at him. Neither she, nor her brother, nor Chanlix had mentioned to anyone that she might contest Delnamal's claim to the throne of Aaltah, and it was evident that Queen Ellinsoltah had not shared their conversation. Tynthanal had agreed that without the support of another kingdom, she didn't dare challenge Delnamal. And now here he was suggesting that Women's Well was not, in fact, a town within the Kingdom of Aaltah but was instead an independent principality. Worse, he was doing it not in private, but in front of all the most influential people of Women's Well, planting the idea in their minds because he knew full well it would take root.

"We both know that the king will not see it that way."

"Beg your pardon, Your Highness," Jailom said pointedly, "but every day we are here we break new laws. Even before you arrived, we were already flirting with charges of desertion and treason. We did not settle exactly where we were ordered to settle, we have not set up a functioning Abbey, the women no longer wear the robes or work the pavilion, and we have knowingly concealed a great deal of information."

Alys let out a grunt of frustration. She should immediately reprimand Jailom for calling her Your Highness, but she had so many other objections that seemed more pressing.

"If you think declaring our independence is going to improve our situation, you are as mad as my brother. As *both* my brothers."

Jailom leaned forward with his elbows on the table, radiating intensity. "How long do you think we have before he finds out how much we've already defied him?"

Chanlix took up the argument. "Word is spreading, and we are less isolated now than we were even a month ago. We have to plan for the moment when the king realizes he cannot simply forget about us just because we're so far away."

"We were always on borrowed time," Tynthanal continued, "but we had reason to hope Father would forgive our sins when we presented him with such useful magic. You and I both know that will not be the case with Delnamal."

Alys dropped into her chair, wishing she could just go back to her spell crafting. With her Mindseye open and the air alive with colorful motes, the world felt full of hope and possibility, and her mind tumbled over itself with new combinations she wanted to try. Even knowing that spell crafting was an inherently dangerous endeavor—especially when she was not possessed of years of training—she felt safe and in control when she was doing it.

The population of Women's Well was growing at an almost alarming pace. The people of the poor and struggling towns that edged up against the Wasteland were flocking to the bounty the new Well had produced, and the soldiers and abigails who had originally settled the place were now outnumbered. Tynthanal and his men had taken it upon themselves to uphold the law and keep the peace, but he had no official mandate that allowed him to discipline anyone but his own soldiers. Which didn't stop him from doing so.

In effect, they were already functioning as an independent principality, basing their laws and customs on those of Aaltah, but altering them to fit their own needs. And it was true that Delnamal was bound to find out sooner, rather than later.

She gave Tynthanal a pleading look. "He has my children. We don't dare provoke him."

"We provoke him merely by existing," he said gently.

"I won't do it," she said more firmly. "If you'd like to proclaim yourself the Prince of Women's Well, then go right ahead, but I will not support you while my children are in Delnamal's custody."

"That is not the plan."

While Alys and Chanlix knew the true reason that Tynthanal had no desire to make a try for the crown, he had told the rest of this little would-be royal council a different story: that it only made sense for the sovereign of Women's Well to be a woman. And somehow, because of the uniquely integrated society they seemed to be forming, he'd convinced the others to agree. They did not want Prince Tynthanal—they wanted Princess Alysoon.

"Then there *is* no plan," she said. "I will say this one more time: I refuse to provoke the king unless and until my children are safe." *Or until I have no other choice.* The anxiety that thought provoked was almost too great to bear, for she could not deny that some sort of conflict with Delnamal was inevitable.

There was some grumbling around the table, but Jailom cut it off. "Then we must simply find a way to make the children safe."

He said it as if it were a simple task, but of course it was impossible. The children would be well guarded in the palace, so there was little likelihood of spiriting them away to safety—even if safety could be found.

"When you have a way to ensure the children's safety," she said, addressing her statement to both Jailom in particular and the "council" in general, "then I will reconsider. But until such time, we are not discussing this any further."

"Then perhaps we should discuss how best to prepare for an attack," Tynthanal suggested grimly. "Because whether we declare independence or not, one is coming. I don't like our chances of surviving with potentially the entire army of Aaltah fighting to destroy us, but we can at least give them something to remember us by. And be prepared to evacuate as many civilians as possible before it comes."

Shelvon sat by Corlin's bedside and hummed tunelessly, stroking his sweat-dampened hair as exhaustion slowly overcame pain and his eyes became heavy. Her voice was unlovely to her own ears, but the boy seemed to find it soothing. Shelvon would never have a child of her own—and if she were being perfectly honest, she would admit she'd never felt any pressing drive to have one, save the drive that was imposed on her by custom—but her need to protect Alys's son made her whole body vibrate with helpless rage.

Far from being chastened by the first thrashing Delnamal had ordered, Corlin had taken it upon himself to rebel at every turn. Shelvon and Jinnell had both pleaded with him to be more circumspect, if not to protect himself, then to save them from the torture of seeing him suffer. For two whole days after the last beating, he'd been on his best behavior, but with Jinnell scheduled to leave for Nandel at first light tomorrow, today he'd been unable to contain his anger.

He had paid for it dearly. He'd been too modest to allow Shelvon to see the damage, but the spots of blood all up and down the back of his breeches had spoken volumes. Even in Nandel, a beating that left a child bloodied was considered excessive, but Shelvon was certain Delnamal would not balk at the brutality of the tutor he had hired for what seemed to be the express purpose of savaging his sister's son.

Corlin groaned softly and tried to find a more comfortable position in his bed. Shelvon winced in sympathy and wished she had a sleeping draught to give him. But even if sleeping draughts and healing potions had been readily available, she would not have been permitted to ease or shorten his pain.

There was a whisper-soft knock on the door, and then it opened and Jinnell slipped into the room. She had changed into a nightdress and dressing gown, her long braid coiled under a simple white cap. Shelvon doubted the poor girl would get much sleep tonight, and she cursed her husband and his damned tutor for making her last night at home more painful than it had to be. Jinnell's eyes were rimmed with red, though she held herself with admirable dignity as she approached her brother's bedside.

Corlin turned his head and looked at her, his eyes squinched in pain. "I'm sorry, Jinnell," he said softly, his voice revealing a depth of guilt that made Shelvon want to gather them both into a hug. "I shouldn't have . . . I shouldn't have . . ."

"Hush, little man," she said with a tender smile. "I wish I had half your courage and fight."

Shelvon moved to the side, ceding her place to Jinnell, who gave her a grateful smile.

Even in his pain, Corlin blushed at his sister's praise. "'Courage' is not the word Master Wilbaad uses."

"As if a grown man who beats children has any concept of courage!" Jinnell said with an unladylike snort.

Corlin stuck out his lower lip. "I'm not a child!" he said with all the dignity he could manage while lying on his stomach and making that pouty face.

Jinnell smiled indulgently. "No, of course not."

Shelvon thought to leave them in privacy, but as she was about to rise, she noticed for the first time that Jinnell held something clutched in her left hand, keeping whatever it was shielded by her body so that neither Shelvon nor Corlin could see it. Curious despite herself, Shelvon stayed where she was.

"Try to get some sleep," Jinnell said. A strange, sad expression passed over her face. "And I know we've fought a lot, but I hope you know I love you."

Corlin made a disgusted face. "Ewww. Can we save the mushy stuff for morning?"

Jinnell gave a shaky laugh. "Sure. We'll say the mushy stuff in the morning." She reached out to stroke the back of her brother's head, and Shelvon noticed that although she was dressed for bed and otherwise devoid of jewelry, there was a ring on her index finger—a stunning ruby cabochon, surrounded by diamonds that caught the light and flashed with fire.

The moment Jinnell's hand touched Corlin's head, the boy's eyes slid shut and his breathing evened out in sleep. Shelvon could do nothing but gape stupidly as Jinnell tucked whatever she was holding in her left hand under her arm and calmly opened her

Mindseye. She plucked something—doubtless a mote of Rho—out
of the ring, then closed her Mindseye and fixed Shelvon with a defi-
ant look.

"It was a gift from our mother," Jinnell said, untucking a set of
stays from beneath her arm and laying them on the bed between
them. "As long as you're in contact with the stays, the ring's spell
won't affect you. But as you can see, the ring induces immediate
sleep when it's active." She stroked her brother's hair fondly.

Perhaps Shelvon should have been shocked at the impropriety of
what Jinnell had just shown her, but the girl's grave expression told
her there was more to come.

"Why are you telling me this?" Shelvon asked.

Jinnell took off the ring and laid it on top of the stays. "Because
I want you to have these."

"What?" Shelvon frowned fiercely, her heart beating erratically
with some premonition of danger.

"Corlin is too fearless," Jinnell said, "and Uncle Delnamal is too
fearful." She stroked her brother's hair once more. "My mother
gave me the ring and stays to protect myself, but Corlin is in far
worse danger than I am. He is not willing to control his temper,
and you and I both know that Delnamal will eventually realize the
beatings aren't producing the results he would like. How much
more brutal do you suppose he will be if Corlin keeps defying him?"
Her eyes glittered with tears. "Eventually, he's going to start labeling it treason, and you know where that's going to end."

Shelvon jerked backward, shaking her head. "But he's just a
child," she protested.

Jinnell snarled and pulled down the covers, revealing Corlin's
bloodstained breeches. "He was happy enough to do *this* to a child!
And this is before my mother and Uncle Tynthanal have heard that
he's sending me away." She pulled the covers back over her brother,
her eyes pleading with Shelvon to understand. "How do you suppose they'll react when they find out I've been sent to Nandel while
they've been effectively exiled? That in all likelihood, they will never
see me again? My mother may not be able to do much to challenge

Delnamal's reign, but Uncle Tynthanal has a squadron of loyal men with him. What will Delnamal do with Corlin to keep Tynthanal under control? He's already threatened *me* with a treason charge, as you know."

Shelvon bit her lip in anxiety. Jinnell had told her about Delnamal's threat, and Shelvon had no reason not to believe he'd meant every word. He had brought the children to live in the palace so he could have total control over their lives—and threaten them at will. And there was a reason he'd endeavored to see so little of them once they were here. It was so much easier to hurt people—especially innocents—when you didn't have to face the results of your actions, when you didn't have to see the pain and absorb the guilt.

Jinnell rose and went to the door. Shelvon wondered where she was going—but she wasn't going anywhere.

Falcor, her mother's master of the guard, stepped into the room. He would not be traveling with her to Nandel—Delnamal had assigned her an entirely new set of guards for the journey and would likely dismiss Falcor entirely once she was gone. The man was too loyal to Alysoon and the children for Delnamal's taste. Shelvon should be scandalized that he was in the room when Jinnell was in dishabille, but there were far too many other dangerous undertones for the impropriety to matter.

Falcor bowed to her. "Your Majesty."

Jinnell licked her lips. "I've asked Falcor to take you and Corlin to Women's Well. The king will be occupied escorting me to the border all of tomorrow. If you leave as soon as we are gone, you will have at least a day's head start before he realizes you are gone. Maybe even more, considering how reluctant he is to risk running into Corlin and having to face his own brutality." She gestured toward the stays and the ring. "You can use them to help make sure you aren't seen. I know you don't want to use magic, but I hope you care enough about Corlin to make that sacrifice."

It was as if Shelvon had stepped into a waking dream. She looked between the sleeping boy, the earnest girl, and the grim-faced guard, and wondered how it was possible she found herself in this ridiculous position.

She was the Queen of Aaltah. She'd been raised since childhood to serve and obey the men in her life without question. Even with the more relaxed laws of Aaltah, her husband all but owned her, and would even if he weren't the king. And yet here was this teenage girl asking her to *kidnap* the king's nephew.

"You're asking me to commit an act of treason," she said in a small voice she barely recognized as her own.

There was no question as to what her duty was. Not only could she not do as Jinnell asked, she must also report the attempted treason to Delnamal. Because he needed her as his bargaining chip with Nandel, he was unlikely to execute Jinnell no matter how furious her plan made him, but Falcor was sure to die horribly. Shelvon had no particular attachment to the man—she barely knew him—but the thought of how the king would make him suffer before he died formed a knot of terror and revulsion in the pit of her stomach. He watched her with a calm and stoic resolve, but she could see from the look in his eyes that he knew exactly what he was risking.

Shelvon swallowed hard. Jinnell and Falcor might be suggesting treason, but it was only because they cared about Corlin so deeply. In her heart, Shelvon knew that Jinnell was right, that Corlin was in mortal danger. Delnamal would not tolerate the boy's defiance, and the older Corlin became, the more brutal the punishments would be. What even a man as cruel as Delnamal might hesitate to do to a thirteen-year-old, he would no doubt happily do in another couple of years.

"I'm asking you to save my little brother," Jinnell said. "You care about him, I can tell. And you see the danger. He can't stay here."

"You could have sent him with your man," Shelvon said, gesturing at the still-silent guard. "You didn't have to involve me."

"But the king will blame you if Corlin disappears while under your care. Now that he's given up hope that you'll give him an heir and has me to soothe your father's ruffled feathers, how do you suppose he'll react if he thinks you allowed Corlin to run away?"

The look on Jinnell's face was open and guileless, but if there was one thing Shelvon had learned from close association, it was that Jinnell was not half so guileless as she seemed.

Was she truly suggesting Shelvon flee Aalwell for her own good? Or was she trying to eliminate a potential witness?

Shelvon sighed softly. Jinnell's true motives didn't matter. What mattered was that by asking her to flee with Corlin, Jinnell had put her in an impossible situation.

Jinnell sat on the bed beside her. "I need your help, Aunt Shelvon. I need to get Corlin away from the king, and this is the only way I can think to do it. I'll soon be out of the king's reach, but you won't if you stay here. I know that you're a good, kind person, and I trust that you won't turn us all in. If you'd truly prefer to stay here and face the king's wrath, then so be it." She glanced over at Falcor. "My ring will look rather silly on him, and let's not even talk about the stays, but he cares enough about Corlin to risk his dignity as well as his life. We can do it without you, as long as you stay silent. But in my heart, I believe you will be safer if you go with them."

Shelvon chewed her lip as she thought. For all that her duty was to immediately report this talk of treason to the king, she knew that was the one thing she wouldn't do. That left her with the stark choice of fleeing with them or staying behind.

"When the king finds Corlin is missing, Women's Well will be the first place he thinks to look," she said.

Falcor nodded. "In all likelihood, we will have to leave as soon as we arrive. Once we reunite Corlin with Lady Alysoon, we should immediately head to Grunir. From there, we can book passage to anywhere in the world, and the king will have trouble tracking our movements."

"Unless the Sovereign Prince of Grunir hands you over." Grunir was an independent principality, but it was hardly in a position to defy the King of Aaltah.

"That's why speed is of the essence. I have secured chevals for all of us, and if we ride hard, we can reach Women's Well in a little more than two days' time. The pursuit will lag well behind, and by the time they reach Women's Well, we can be long gone and on a ship to Khalpar."

"The dowager queen is from Khalpar," she reminded him, as if there were any chance he'd forgotten. The marriage between the late King Aaltyn and Queen Xanvin had cemented an alliance with Khalpar for generations to come.

Falcor shrugged. "There will be risk wherever we go, and our lives will no doubt depend on hiding our identities. But our first priority is removing the boy from the king's reach."

While Falcor was talking, Jinnell had picked up the ring and the stays again, laying both in her lap. Shelvon glanced over at the girl and was faced with a suddenly neutral expression. She looked back at Falcor and noted that he was armed, as befitted an honor guardsman.

Her pulse picked up speed, and she wondered if Jinnell had activated the spell in that ring while she wasn't looking. If she refused to flee with Corlin and Falcor, would she soon find herself helplessly asleep under the ring's spell? And might Falcor be determined enough to take Corlin to his mother that he would prevent her from ever waking up?

Shelvon mentally rolled her eyes at herself. She was being ridiculous. Their flight to Women's Well would be over before it began if she were murdered in the night.

"If we left now," she found herself saying to Jinnell, "you could come, too."

But Jinnell shook her head sadly. "You will need every hour of distraction I can provide. I will slow down tomorrow's procession as much as humanly possible. Depending on how indulgent the king is feeling, I might even be able to delay us enough to force him to spend the night away from the palace. If we all left now, he would know we were missing by morning and probably have us back in custody by afternoon."

Shelvon could hardly believe she was considering doing this. Committing open treason. Defying the husband and king she had sworn to obey. If she did this and they were caught, beheading would be the least unpleasant of her likely fates.

But she was not willing to turn anyone in, and if she remained behind . . .

Her husband had never liked her, but ever since the night he'd struck her and she'd mocked him for it, she was fairly certain his dislike had edged over toward hatred. He would be all too glad to blame her for Corlin's escape, and she wouldn't be entirely surprised if that blame became an excuse to level a treason charge.

If she was going to face a possible arrest for treason no matter what she did, then she'd rather risk it in the name of saving a child's life.

"All right. I'll go."

Jinnell's shoulders slumped in relief. "Thank you." Her eyes went white, and she plucked at the ring she held in the palm of her hand.

The blood left Shelvon's face as she realized she hadn't been ridiculous, after all. Jinnell had truly been prepared to use that sleep spell against her.

"If it had been necessary," Jinnell said as her eyes cleared, "we would have kept you asleep until morning, then left you bound and gagged where you would not be found until long after we'd left. It would have made it easier to convince the king you did not willingly allow Corlin to be taken."

Shelvon shivered and said nothing. If that were all they'd planned, they would have told her from the start. After all, the stated reason why she should go with them was because the king would blame her, and they'd had a plan to divert that blame.

For a long moment, she battled a desire to press the issue, to try to force Jinnell to confess what she and Falcor had actually planned to do if Shelvon did not agree to go with Corlin. In the end, she decided she didn't truly want to know. The truth of the matter was that Jinnell was giving up her own chance at safety in order to save her brother's life. That she'd invited Shelvon to join in the attempt, that she'd given her an option other than being left alone to face Delnamal's wrath, was a luxury she had no right to expect.

CHAPTER THIRTY-EIGHT

Ellin grunted in exasperation when she heard the quiet knock coming from behind the tapestry. She was sitting at her dressing table, still fully clothed, while Star painstakingly removed the pins from the intricate headdress she'd worn for the evening's formal dinner.

Ellin met her maid's eyes in the glass. Star was fully aware of the disastrous end to Ellin's affair with Graesan, just as she was aware that there was only one person in the palace who would have the gall to come knocking on that secret door.

"Shall I let him in?" Star asked as she carefully lifted off the headdress and laid it on the table. Ellin's hair looked frightful in the aftermath.

Ellin wanted to say no. It was not only supremely impertinent for Zarsha to take such a liberty, but it was also dangerous. What if someone other than Star had been in the room with her?

And when is anyone but Star in the bedroom with me at night? she asked herself with a little stab of self-pity. She had received a brief letter from Graesan when he'd arrived in Nandel to let her know he was all right, but since then she had heard nothing. Zarsha insisted it was for the best that she cut her ties with her former lover entirely, but sometimes when she was alone at night in her bed, she battled tears of longing and loneliness.

"I suppose you had better," Ellin said, trying vainly to smooth down the tangled mess the headdress had made of her hair. "I'm sure he wouldn't be here if it wasn't important."

Twice before, he'd shown up at her bedroom door for the kind of private audience she could not grant him during the day without having to explain herself. The royal council—especially Semsulin—was extremely jealous of her time, and many of them were getting impatient with Zarsha's extended visit. Ellin had no doubt Tamzin was behind that growing impatience.

Giving up on her hair, she stood up and turned around as Star confirmed the identity of her nocturnal visitor, then opened the door and let him in. He was still dressed for evening in a simple gray brocade doublet and closely fitted black breeches. The ensemble was strikingly sober and highly unfashionable for Rhozinolm gentry with its lack of color and adornment, but Ellin found the simple clothing made his impressive physique and handsome face into an adornment all on their own. There was a reason the ladies of the court all swooned over his looks. Even Star was looking at him approvingly from under lowered lashes.

Zarsha bowed gracefully. "Forgive the intrusion, Your Majesty."

Ellin's mouth twitched with the beginnings of a smile at the way Star was looking at him. "Thank you, Star," she said. "I will call when I am ready for you again."

Star curtsied, but Ellin didn't fail to notice the tiny smirk and the twinkle in her maid's eyes. She had little doubt the woman was matchmaking again, for she had liked Zarsha from the very beginning and seemed baffled by Ellin's resistance to the match. Of course, considering she'd recognized the connection between Ellin and Graesan without having to be told, perhaps she'd never been as baffled as she'd pretended.

When the door closed behind Star, Zarsha invited himself to sit in one of the armchairs by the fireplace. She narrowed her eyes at him, and he grinned at her unrepentantly.

"I'm alone with you in your bedroom at night," he said. "I think the rules of propriety need no longer apply."

She snorted. "That's no excuse for being rude."

He heaved a long-suffering sigh and rose to his feet. A muscle in Ellin's jaw twitched. Ever since that night when Graesan had attacked him, Zarsha had been exceedingly relaxed and familiar with her, though admittedly his behavior in front of others was impeccable. It was true that since that night they had been co-conspirators of a sort and that perhaps that called for a little relaxation of the usual protocols, but he was taking it too far.

"Why are you here?" she asked, folding her arms and pointedly not inviting him to retake his seat.

"I suspect word will reach your own people by tomorrow or the next day at the latest," he said, "but I thought it best you have early warning."

"Warning of what?"

"Jinnell Rah-Sylnin is on her way to Nandel for a state visit."

Ellin suppressed a gasp as the implications immediately slapped her in the face. "Your uncle is in search of a new bride. And King Delnamal is trotting his niece out for his assessment."

Zarsha nodded. "There's no other reason the girl would be traveling to Nandel so soon after the late king's death. It's possible King Delnamal is seeking a divorce from Queen Shelvon and is trying to soften the blow in advance. It is also possible he is seeking to strengthen the bond between Aaltah and Nandel via a second state marriage, and that could be disastrous for Rhozinolm."

The only reason Ellin's council was not pressing her to expel Zarsha was because they were so concerned about the upcoming expiration of the trade agreements with Nandel—a problem that was brought to the table for discussion every once in a while without any sign of a resolution. Semsulin had even recently introduced the possibility of a renewed marriage agreement between herself and Zarsha—with the stipulation that Zarsha not be named king—

but had been quickly shouted down. He had floated the idea on Ellin's command to test the mood of the council, and the answer had been unequivocal.

After that meeting, Tamzin had once again demanded a private audience. She and Semsulin had hoped that during that "private" audience, Tamzin might forget himself and say something treasonous—which Semsulin would "just happen" to overhear—but either Tamzin had more self-control than they'd given him credit for, or he'd had some inkling that he and Ellin weren't as alone as it seemed.

A second state marriage between the royal houses of Aaltah and Nandel would all but destroy her chances to renew those trade agreements.

"We *have* to convince your council to let us marry," Zarsha said. "If you lose your trade agreements with Nandel while Nandel strikes exclusive agreements with Aaltah . . ."

She did not need him to complete the sentence. The last war between Aaltah and Rhozinolm had ended before she was born, but the bad blood that existed between the two kingdoms was still evident, especially in the older generations. During that war, both kingdoms had laid claim to the Midlands, the strip of land between the Twin Rivers that bordered both their kingdoms. The war had ended when both kingdoms had ceded their claims to the Midlands Well, and the Midlands had become—as it had been off and on throughout history—an independent principality. Ellin knew for a fact that many of the older members of her council—even Semsulin, with his generally steady temper—still considered the Midlands to be the rightful territory of Rhozinolm, and there was no reason to expect that the people of Aaltah did not feel the same way.

She shook her head. "The council will never agree." And even if they somehow could be persuaded, there was still Tamzin to be considered. He would happily sacrifice the good of the kingdom in service to his own ambitions. If he were somehow outvoted by the rest of the council, he would almost certainly begin preparations for war.

Zarsha said nothing, cocking his head and staring at her. It took her a moment to realize she had accepted his declaration without argument or demur. She waited for the surge of resistance that always rose in her when she considered the possibility of marrying Zarsha, but there was nothing but acceptance. She hadn't noticed it happening, but somehow within the past weeks and months she'd come to realize that marrying Zarsha was her only logical choice, and it wasn't just because of the trade agreements.

If she insisted on remaining unmarried, Tamzin would chip away at what remained of her support until she had a rebellion on her hands—which would swiftly be followed by a bloody fight between Tamzin and Kailindar for the throne. If she married anyone but Tamzin, she would face the same problem. And marrying Tamzin was out of the question.

"The council will *have* to agree to our marriage," Zarsha said. "They put you on the throne to avoid a war between Tamzin and Kailindar, and that is why they will want to keep you there."

She shook her head. He hadn't been in all those council meetings, hadn't seen the skillful way Tamzin had little by little captured more and more support. He'd whittled away at her authority—never openly challenging her, but finding countless sly ways to accomplish the same goal—and he'd even caused her to alienate Kailindar, who showed no sign of having forgiven her for stripping his ceremonial title.

"He has won them over, and they are all expecting me to marry him."

"Not Lord Semsulin," Zarsha said with authority. She probably didn't want to know why he felt so sure.

"No, not him," she agreed, for her chancellor clearly held Tamzin in the same contempt and distrust as she did. "But he's only one man."

A heavy silence descended on the room, and it was a long time before Zarsha finally broke it.

"If Tamzin weren't around to cause trouble," he said slowly, "do you suppose that would change the mood of the council?"

Ellin stiffened and glared at him. "If Tamzin were on the throne, he'd be just the sort to kill off all his rivals to make his life easier. I am not Tamzin."

Perhaps she'd overplayed her outrage, for Zarsha was giving her that assessing look again. She met his eyes coldly, hoping to mask the reality that, to her great shame, the same thought had more than once crossed her own mind. But she was neither a murderer nor a tyrant, and she refused to simply eliminate an inconvenient rival.

"As I see it, My Queen, you have three options," Zarsha said. "You can marry him, you can meet him on the battlefield, or you can kill him. Personally, I find the third option by far the most appealing. It can be handled in secret, with no blame falling to you. He has other enemies, after all, who would be more than happy to see him dead."

She shook her head. "There has to be some other way," she whispered.

Zarsha crossed the distance between them and put his hands on her shoulders. Another of his overly familiar gestures, but she was too shaken to protest.

"You are a good person," he said. "Your reluctance to condemn him is admirable and decent. But if you are to be a good queen, you cannot always be admirable and decent. Find some pretext to summon Kailindar to Zinolm Well, and leave the rest to me." He grinned. "Perhaps all we need do is have them both in the palace at the same time for an extended period to see our needs met without us having to make an effort."

"I will not have someone murdered in cold blood," she insisted.

"But summon Kailindar anyway. I promise I will not take any steps to eliminate Tamzin without your permission, but it might be best to have a scapegoat at the ready just in case."

"In case of what?" she snapped.

"In case Tamzin does something to make you change your mind. If he begins to feel threatened, if he begins to think he has not sufficiently cowed you into agreeing to a marriage, he could escalate in the blink of an eye."

Ellin hated the entire idea, hated that she would even contemplate the unlawful killing of a rival. She had no wish to become a tyrant. But loath as she was to admit it, Zarsha was right. Tamzin had made it clear he would stop at nothing to make the throne his, and if she could not find some middle ground, she would have to at least leave herself the option of eliminating him altogether.

"I'll summon Kailindar," she said. "But you'd better be certain nothing happens to Tamzin without my permission or I'll know you're behind it."

He put his hand over his heart and bowed. "You have my word I will not act without your permission. However, I must remind you that—"

"Kailindar and Tamzin hate each other. But if Kailindar takes this opportunity to kill Tamzin, I'll still know you're behind it. They haven't killed each other yet, and it would be too much of a coincidence if it were to happen just now."

Zarsha looked disgruntled. "I suppose I'll have to keep watch on Kailindar while he's here, then, lest I find myself unjustly accused."

"Just so we're clear—he dies without my command, and you will never be my husband. Understood?"

Zarsha bowed again. "Yes, Ellin, I understand. And I have every intention of becoming your husband."

Ellin couldn't tell whether that strange sensation in her belly was anticipation or dread.

When Tynthanal began standing whenever Alys entered a room, others quickly adopted the practice. Alys made the tactical error of making only a mild protest, when in fact she should have insisted unequivocally that everyone keep their seats. She could only blame the distraction of her fear for her children—and her concentration on the urgent research and development of defensive magic—for not seeing where her lack of protest would lead.

She was quicker to remonstrate—and more adamant—when Chanlix addressed her as "Your Highness" in a council meeting. Chanlix apologized and backed down, and Alys thought she had finally made her point. Even though the people of Women's Well still insisted on standing when she entered a room.

But it wasn't until Alys overheard a former abigail referring to her as "Princess Alysoon" that she truly recognized what was happening. Until then, she had thought only the members of their little town council knew about the discussion of declaring independence. Looking back, she realized that shortly after that meeting, even those closest to her had stopped calling her "Alys," as friends and family had always done. It seemed she was now "Alysoon" to her face, and "Princess Alysoon" when she was out of earshot. And she knew *exactly* who to blame for that.

The moment she overheard that fateful title, she marched straight for the area she referred to as the barracks—and which she knew others were calling the Citadel. As usual, Tynthanal was supervising his soldiers and trainees as they drilled and sparred, but she ignored all the activity around her—and all the curious stares—as she stamped toward him and pointed her finger.

"I want to talk to you! Right now!"

Tynthanal sighed and turned to the pair of teenagers he'd been training. "Carry on without me. And try not to kill each other while I'm gone." He turned away and gestured for Alys to follow.

She ground her teeth, for though his gesture was of a brother to his sister—rather than a subject to his sovereign—it was now easy to see in hindsight how much more formally he'd behaved toward her as of late. She was not fooled by the casual gesture, and she doubted any of his men were, either.

"You have to stop this," she growled at him the moment they were out of earshot.

He raised his eyebrows and attempted a look of innocence. "Stop what?"

"You *know* what," she snapped. "I just heard myself referred to as 'Princess Alysoon.' By someone who was not privy to our discussion of declaring independence, no less. That means someone—or multiple someones—from the council has been wagging his or her tongue in public."

"And you think that someone is me."

"You, and maybe Chanlix, too. I wouldn't put it past you two to gang up on me."

"We're not ganging up on you," he replied, putting his innocent act to pasture. "We're just—"

"Encouraging people to treat me like the sovereign princess over my clearly stated objections. If word gets back to Delnamal . . ." Her throat tightened in panic as she imagined what Delnamal might do to her children if he had any inkling she'd even *considered* declaring herself a sovereign princess.

Tynthanal gave a huff of impatience. "If word gets back to Delnamal about *anything* that's happening here in Women's Well, he will declare us traitors. And mark my words, Alysoon: it will get back to him. Sooner, rather than later. Your determination to deny what everyone else can see is the inevitable is absurd."

"That isn't your decision to make," she grated, wanting to shake him. His jaw jutted out stubbornly in a way that reminded her of their father when he was at his most implacable, her words bouncing off some invisible emotional shield.

"It isn't *yours,* either," he retorted. His temper had always been slow to rouse, but it was wide awake now. "The lives of every single man, woman, and child in this town are in danger because of decisions we've all made over the course of months. With Delnamal on the throne, we can no longer hope for leniency or tolerance. That makes *you* our only hope. The people of Women's Well have already declared you their sovereign princess, and it's not because of anything Chanlix or I have said. Every time you deny it, you are crushing our hopes."

Alys felt almost dizzy with panic. "Don't put this on me!" she wailed, closing her eyes, feeling like she might collapse under the impossible burden of expectation. "Don't ask me to choose between the people of this town and my children."

"I'm not *putting* anything on you, Alys," he said more gently. "I'm telling you that if you do nothing, we will eventually be condemned as traitors and we will die. If you imagine your children will live long and healthy lives after that happens, then you are lying to yourself."

Her stomach roiled, and for a moment she feared she might be sick. It was hard to argue Tynthanal's logic. Children of declared traitors rarely went on to live long and happy lives. Especially sons. And she had already given Delnamal more than enough excuse to declare her a traitor once he learned the truth of what was happening in Women's Well.

"None of us—not you, not me, not the people of this town, not your children—has a hope of survival unless we forge an alliance with Rhozinolm and revolt against the Crown," Tynthanal said. "Those are the bald facts, and denying them doesn't make them go away."

"I know," she whispered, her hands clenching into fists at her sides. She met his eyes. "I *know*. But just . . . give me some time."

"Alys—"

"Give me time to plan my approach to Queen Ellinsoltah. I would much prefer to secure an alliance *before* we make any public announcement."

Alys couldn't blame her brother for regarding her with such open skepticism. Even she had to admit to the possibility that she was stalling.

"Don't take *too* much time," he cautioned. "Every day you delay brings us one day closer to our doom."

Alys did not need that reminder.

Shelvon stood toe-to-toe with Master Wilbaad and refused to be cowed by his conviction in his own authority.

"If the king expected Corlin to have his usual lessons today, then he would have arranged for a healer to see to the boy's wounds," she said, crossing her arms over her chest. Beneath her dress, she wore the stays Jinnell had given her last night, and on her finger, she wore the ring. She and Jinnell and Falcor had agreed that Corlin couldn't simply fail to turn up for his lessons today. Master Wilbaad would scour the palace for him and sound the alarm when he couldn't be found.

"He will take his lessons on his feet," Wilbaad insisted. "A well-deserved thrashing does not excuse him from his responsibilities."

Wilbaad had the temerity to attempt to step around her, and Shelvon quickly put herself in his path. Her heart was pounding, and her palms were damp with sweat, for she was very aware that the man's life lay in her hands. If she could not persuade him to leave, then she would have to use Jinnell's ring to put him to sleep, and Falcor would kill him and hide the body. While she despised Master Wilbaad and believed he deserved to be on the receiving end of the many thrashings he had meted out, she had no wish to see him dead. Not to mention that the need to hide the body would delay their flight from the palace, which they could ill afford. They needed every hour and every minute they could get to distance themselves from the palace before they were discovered missing.

"I say it does," Shelvon said. "I am the queen, and I am the boy's guardian while the king is away. When the king returns, he may well overrule me, but he is not here now."

Master Wilbaad was not used to having his authority challenged, and Shelvon feared his masculine pride would not allow him to bend to a woman's will. But in the end, she *was* the Queen of Aaltah, and he had no authority to countermand her.

"You will spoil the child with your tender heart," he said stiffly, then sketched a perfunctory bow. "Your Majesty."

She sighed in relief as he left the room, all offended dignity and moral superiority. But it was *far* too soon for relief.

Scant moments after Wilbaad had left, the door to Corlin's room opened, and he and Falcor cautiously stepped out into the sitting room. Falcor had brought the boy a pain relief potion, but while it lessened the pain, it did not heal the bruises and welts and the damage they had caused. The boy walked stiffly and awkwardly, and Shelvon couldn't imagine what it would feel like to ride a cheval in his condition. Corlin needed the attentions of a healer, but they could not approach one when the king had expressly forbidden it.

"I'll be all right, Aunt Shelvon," Corlin assured her. "Don't worry about me."

Instinctively, she reached for him, wanting to hug him, but Falcor grabbed her wrist at the same moment she jerked her hand back and curled her fingers into her palm. It would be frighteningly easy to discharge the ring's sleep spell accidentally. Corlin paled a bit at the interplay, staring at the ring with a look that combined longing and fear and anger. He knew it was Jinnell's, knew his sister had given away their mother's gifts for his protection. He'd been so angry—and guilt-stricken—that Shelvon had feared she would have to use the ring's spell on *him,* though how they would escape while carrying an unconscious boy she didn't know.

"Let's go," Falcor urged. "The quicker, the better."

There were fewer servants and guards in the residential wing of the palace than usual, as many of them had accompanied the king and Jinnell. Shelvon walked as though there was nothing unusual going on, her left hand on Corlin's shoulder as if she were guiding him through the halls, Falcor trailing behind. Propriety insisted she not leave the residential wing of the palace without her honor guard, but she avoided that necessity by using the ring to put the master of the guard to sleep before he summoned his men—or even saw her coming.

"Now things get a little more difficult," Falcor muttered as they proceeded cautiously down a back staircase.

If they were to be seen outside the residential wing, Shelvon's lack of a full honor guard would be instantly regarded and questioned, so they crept down disused corridors and back staircases until they reached the level of the kitchens. Falcor hustled them into a small storeroom and pulled a large satchel out from behind a crate of bottled preserves so old the tops were coated with dust. He opened the satchel and withdrew a drab servant's kirtle and apron for Shelvon, and an equally drab doublet and breeches for Corlin.

"Change as quickly as you can," he urged. "From the looks of it, this storage room is rarely used, but I can't guarantee no one will come."

Shelvon felt the color rushing to her face and cursed her own naïveté. Falcor had said he had secured disguises for her and Corlin, but she had somehow imagined the disguise would consist of some outer wrapping—perhaps a hooded cloak. She had *not* expected to have to change her clothes, and the storage room was far too small to afford her any privacy.

"Corlin and I will look away," Falcor promised, turning his back and staring at the door.

Corlin looked almost as uncomfortable as Shelvon felt, but he also turned toward the door as he began unfastening his elegant doublet. Not wishing to catch even a glimpse of the wounds the brutal tutor had left on the boy's flesh, Shelvon also turned her back and started fumbling with the laces on her gown. Her hands were shaking, and her eyes burned with tears of humiliation, try though she might to scold herself out of her prudish horror of undressing in the presence of men. She reminded herself how important the disguise was, and that neither Falcor nor Corlin was looking at her. She reminded herself that she had found the courage to stand up to Delnamal and to Master Wilbaad. She reminded herself of Jinnell's bravery in turning over her magic items to help save her brother, and her own desire to be even half that brave. And still the tears insisted on dripping down her nose as she struggled with the laces and pins.

"May we turn yet?" Falcor asked softly, and all she had managed so far was to unlace the front of the bodice.

"No!" she cried, too loudly, then winced at the sound of her own voice. Her shoulders drooped, and she realized if she were to continue trying to get herself out of the dress, she would still be here an hour later. "I—I need help," she admitted, feeling like a small and helpless child. Not for the first time, she longed for the simple fashions of Nandel, though admittedly that was the only thing she missed about her homeland.

She heard a rustle of movement, then Falcor's hands were plucking at pins and untying laces along her back. His touch was impersonal and businesslike, and when he had loosened all the necessary fastenings, he turned his back once more. She took a deep, steadying breath, impatiently brushing away the remnants of her tears.

Today was the beginning of a new phase of her life. For as long as she could remember, fear had been the guiding force in her life, seconded by a crushing sense of inadequacy that both her father and Delnamal had taken pains to reinforce.

But as of today, she was neither Prince Waldmir's daughter nor King Delnamal's wife. Today, she was a fierce woman warrior, who would do whatever was necessary to save her friend's son from a fate he did not deserve. Last night, she had decided to risk her own life to save Corlin's, and that meant she was stronger than anyone—even she herself—had known. She was still frightened, and expected she would be for the foreseeable future, but she was done with crying.

She pulled on the rough servant's kirtle over the spelled stays, then shoved her silken court gown and petticoats into the empty satchel.

"I'm ready," she said as she fastened a simple kerchief over her hair. Her blond locks were the weakest point of the disguise, marking her Nandel origins, but she would not be the only servant in the huge palace who had some Nandel blood in her, so they hoped no one would take any notice of her as they hurried through the halls.

With Falcor taking the lead—and still trying to make sure they encountered as few others as possible—the three of them took to the back ways once more to find the chevals Falcor had secreted for them in a grove of trees just off the road outside the palace.

No one looked closely enough at the pair of servants and the guardsman to notice the queen and the king's nephew slipping away.

CHAPTER THIRTY-NINE

Jinnell smoothed her skirts nervously as the carriage slipped past the last few buildings of Aalwell proper. She had hoped to be alone in the carriage for the duration of the journey, but of course the king was too careful of her virtue to grant her such privacy, and she shared the carriage with a hawk-faced matron of the court who showed no interest in making conversation. Outside the carriage, the king and his honor guard rode their horses, thankfully slowing the pace of their procession, for the journey would have been over far too quickly if they'd all moved at the speed of chevals.

Jinnell's plan to further slow their progress required some degree of privacy—if the king should ever guess what she was doing, he would . . . Well, she didn't know just what he would do, but it was certain to be something dreadful. She wished her chaperone would fall asleep, but although the harridan never spoke except to scold, she remained ever vigilant, as if fearing Jinnell would debase herself with the nearest male if given the slightest opportunity. Jinnell momentarily wished she'd kept the ring her mother had given her, but she shook off that selfish thought. Corlin was in greater danger than she and would need it more. She hoped he and Shelvon and Falcor were already a long way from the palace, moving at a far greater pace than Jinnell's procession.

It wasn't until noon, when the procession stopped for a brief luncheon, that Jinnell finally had a chance to implement the plan she had devised in the early morning hours of her long and sleepless night. The royal party all but took over a small inn—which, based on the amount of food that was prepared, had been expecting them. Nerves stole Jinnell's appetite, but she forced herself to eat anyway.

It was a grim and quiet luncheon, and Jinnell experienced some small hint of satisfaction to see that while her uncle indulged his love of food and drank more than was strictly wise, he was in a surly and far from talkative mood. And he could barely stand to look at her, his eyes sliding quickly away from hers whenever their gazes accidentally met. He was well aware of the cruel fate to which he planned to subject her, and though he showed no signs of ceding to the dictates of his conscience, at least she had evidence that it troubled him.

When the uncomfortable meal was finished, Jinnell was allowed a visit to the privy, where she could for the first time all morning escape watchful eyes. With shaking hands, she lifted her skirts and removed a small pin she had concealed in one of the layers of underskirts. She slashed the pin over the skin of her calf, where no one could see the mark that was left. She reattached the pin to her skirts, just in case she might need it again, then removed the small vial of potion she had tucked into her pocket.

Never could she have guessed when she made her first attempt to replicate a healing potion that she would ever choose to make another just like it. With a grimace, she remembered the long night of misery that had followed the use of her Leel-free potion, but though she didn't look forward to repeating the experience, she was determined to do what she could to aid her brother's escape from Delnamal's clutches.

Steeling herself as best she could, Jinnell activated the potion and downed it, then tucked the empty vial back into her pocket. Lifting her skirts once more, she watched anxiously for the little scratch to heal. She suspected it was not strictly necessary for her to wound herself before taking the potion, but she wanted to replicate the previous circumstances as closely as possible to make certain her plan worked. The scratch sealed itself up nicely.

Delnamal was seething with impatience by the time she emerged from the privy, the procession all mounted and ready to go. She was fully prepared to embarrass him with a description of women's troubles if he dared to question what had taken so long, but he merely snapped at her to make haste. She climbed into the carriage as the first lick of nausea roiled her stomach.

They had barely made it past the outskirts of the small town when Jinnell shouted for the driver to stop the carriage. Her chaperone squawked at her manners, and the driver showed no inclination to follow her orders. The best Jinnell could manage was to stick her head out the carriage window and vomit out her lunch onto the road while Delnamal and his men watched in horror and revulsion.

At first, Delnamal insisted the procession carry on, dismissing Jinnell's sickness as a sign of girlish nerves. The next hour was one of the most miserable in Jinnell's memory. Someone brought her a slop pot so she didn't have to stick her head out the window, but the stink that soon filled the carriage did not improve her nausea. Her traveling companion was beginning to look fairly green herself and was pressing her body against the far side of the carriage when Delnamal finally conceded that it was best they come to a halt.

Once again, their party found an inn to take over, although this one was not expecting them and was likely put out by their invasion. Delnamal muttered darkly over the inn where they'd eaten lunch, and Jinnell hoped he would not take out his wrath on that innkeeper.

"No one else seems to have taken ill," she pointed out to him. "Perhaps you are right, and this is a result of nerves." She moaned softly and closed her eyes as her stomach made an unbecoming burbling sound. "I'm sure I'll be better in a few hours. Or by tomorrow morning at the latest."

He still grumbled about it, but as far as she could tell he didn't order the innkeeper's arrest. "We will continue on our journey tomorrow morning, whether you feel up to it or not," he told her.

Jinnell's knees were too shaky to manage a curtsy, but she lowered her head demurely. "Yes, Your Majesty."

Her stomach had long ago expelled all its contents, but that did not keep it from heaving regularly for the next several hours as she lay miserably on the bed in the inn. But because of her illness, her chaperone occasionally left her alone. In one of those brief windows of opportunity, Jinnell refilled her potion vial from the dregs of a goblet of wine and added the necessary elements to create another dose.

Her attempt to make herself unappealing to Prince Waldmir by losing her virginity had been foiled, but the disgusted and horrified way Delnamal and his men had regarded her while she was green with nausea had sparked a new idea. One that would be even more unpleasant to carry out. However, she could tolerate a couple of weeks of sickness if it would save her from a lifetime of marriage to a monster.

No one called the private meeting room at the town hall a "council chamber" in Alys's hearing, but she had the distinct impression the term was being used behind her back. Just as she suspected that the people with whom she met every day were being called her "royal council." It was Tynthanal's doing, no doubt, as he continued to lay the groundwork for Women's Well to declare its independence from Aaltah despite her insistence that she wasn't yet ready.

She'd had an exciting—if disturbing—day at the Women's Well Academy, where the former abigails worked side by side with her and several of Tynthanal's most skilled magic practitioners developing new spells that could be produced nowhere but in this one strange border town that had once been a wasteland. Two spells that had previously failed in testing had finally been perfected, and she was glowing with the satisfaction of success when she entered the meeting room to find the people who were not her royal council waiting for her.

Alys noticed the somber mood of the room the moment she entered. Everyone rose—a habit she had finally given up grumbling about—but no one made eye contact, and there were no smiles of greeting. Standing directly to the right of her usual seat was Tynthanal, and she saw a parchment scroll clutched in his hand. His jaw was clenched, his eyes full of worry, and foreboding chased the last hints of triumph from her mind.

Alys made her way around the table toward her seat, not sure if she'd rather hurry to reach her destination and end the suspense or run from the room and remain in blissful ignorance. She was not, after all, a sovereign of any kind—no matter if she was treated like one—and there was no requirement that she face bad news immediately.

The room was eerily silent, and Alys tried to prepare herself for the worst as she took her seat, thereby giving everyone else silent permission to sit. Holding herself stiffly upright, she turned to Tynthanal and braced herself.

"What is it?"

"The king has sent Jinnell to Nandel."

Alys's lungs seized, and for a long moment it seemed as if even her heart had ceased to beat. She had, of course, been fully aware that this was what Delnamal was planning, but she'd been sure she had plenty of time to figure out how to . . . Well, she didn't really know what exactly she'd been planning, except that it was to get both her children away from Delnamal.

"She's only eighteen," she said weakly when she could find her voice. "And she's still in mourning for her grandfather."

"She is apparently being sent merely to meet Prince Waldmir. There are no plans for a wedding as of yet, and that's how the king has justified sending her while she's still in mourning."

It was a cold comfort at best, and with a shiver she realized that Tynthanal had not relaxed after delivering the news. "There's more, isn't there?"

He nodded, the muscles in his jaw flexing as he glanced down at the parchment, which was tightly scrolled, as if it had been delivered by flier. "My informant in the palace tells me Corlin and Queen Shelvon have gone missing."

A tiny sound of distress escaped Alys's throat, and she clamped her hand over her mouth.

"It doesn't seem they've been hurt," Tynthanal hurried to assure her. "The king and his entourage escorted Jinnell to the Midlands border to formally place her in the care of a delegation from Nandel. There were some delays, and he was away from the palace for a day and a half. He returned to find Corlin and Shelvon hadn't been seen since the morning he and Jinnell left, and one of Jinnell's honor guardsmen is also missing. There was no sign of foul play."

Alys let out a shaky breath and pulled together the shreds of her composure as her mind began processing what Tynthanal had just told her—and what it meant that he had told her in front of these leaders of Women's Well whom she refused to call her council. "You think they've fled Aalwell together."

Tynthanal nodded. "It's what the king thinks, too. According to my source"—he raised the scroll—"treason charges are even now being leveled against all three of them, and he sees no reason to believe the council will not ratify those charges."

That Delnamal would charge his wife and thirteen-year-old nephew with capital crimes was unsurprising. He had never made any pretense of caring for Shelvon, and he hated both Jinnell and Corlin simply because they were Alys's children. Why should she hope he would show any family loyalty to them?

"They're coming here," she said, because there was nowhere else she could imagine them fleeing to.

"Almost certainly," Tynthanal agreed. "If I were orchestrating an escape from Aalwell, I would travel on cheval to put as much distance between myself and pursuit as possible as fast as possible. If they are on chevals and left Aalwell the moment the king's procession departed, they should be nearly here by now."

Alys nodded absently. The flier—which traveled faster than a cheval, had no need for rest, and could travel in a straight line—could cross the distance between Aalwell and Women's Well in about one day's time, and this flier had been sent after Corlin and Shelvon had been discovered missing.

And now Alys fully understood why Tynthanal had chosen to break this news to her in front of all these other people, rather than in private.

"The moment they arrive in Women's Well," Tynthanal continued, "we cease to be beneath the king's notice, and no matter what we do, a treason charge will follow swift on their heels." His eyes bored into her, and she had no trouble reading the message he was trying to convey: she was out of time.

"Even if we handed your son and the queen over to the king's forces—which of course we won't," Chanlix said gently, "we will have drawn his attention, and he will crush us."

Alys shook her head. It was too soon! "Your men are good, but the king can send ten times as many against us if he wishes." And though she had designed a number of spells specifically meant to tempt Queen Ellinsoltah into an alliance, reaching out to Rhozinolm while Delnamal's forces were marching on Women's Well reeked of desperation. How could she expect Ellinsoltah to take her seriously under those circumstances?

"We can make it difficult for them," Jailom said. "He will not immediately send an army. Why should he think he'd need to? We have magic he has never seen before and that his commanders will have no defenses against."

Alys frowned at him. "Very little of our magic has the power to scare anyone." With the exception of one of the spells that had finally succeeded today, the magic of Women's Well was best suited for health and growth and defense.

"But we do have Kai," Chanlix said with a gleam in her eyes.

"Lower your voice!" Alys snapped, glaring at the former abbess.

Everyone in the room knew about the women's Kai, but it was—as far as Alys knew—still Women's Well's best-kept secret.

Chanlix lowered her voice as asked, but did not subside. "It cannot stay secret forever. And perhaps it *should* not. The only reason we sent that first flier to Melcor was because we still hoped Delnamal would father an heir. That is no longer a possibility, and it's past time he paid the price for what he did."

Alys started to object, but Chanlix kept talking.

"If it becomes known that we have this power, that we have harnessed it in such a way that we can strike with it from a distance, it would be a powerful deterrent against any who wish to attack us."

"It won't deter Delnamal if he's already been struck," she retorted. "I can't argue that he doesn't deserve it, but I can't see how it would further our cause to so enrage him."

"He's enraged anyway," Tynthanal said. "If we were to make him incapable of fathering an heir, then perhaps we could persuade his royal council he is no longer fit to be king." He leaned forward, as eager to strike as Chanlix. "And if the council doesn't see it that way, perhaps we can remind certain key members that we have more Kai available, as well as having the only known method of delivering it over a distance. We are not as defenseless as you seem to think."

Alys stared at this new, bloodthirsty version of her brother, and wondered whether he was thinking more about the well-being of Women's Well or getting revenge for the attack on the woman who now shared his bed. "You would do that to the lord commander?" she asked, for Tynthanal had always seemed to respect his commander and had more than once called him a good man. And there was no way they could turn the royal council without the lord commander's support.

"I will do whatever it takes to protect the lives of the people of this principality."

"We are not a principality!" she objected. "Not yet, at least."

"You are the only one who has so far failed to acknowledge that you are our sovereign princess," Jailom said. "Tynthanal is your lord chancellor; I am your lord commander; Chanlix is your grand magus." He looked at the other three members of the would-be royal council. "Trade minister," he said, pointing at the merchant, before frowning at the last two members. "I'm not sure who is the lord chamberlain, the marshal, and the lord high treasurer, but we can work that out."

Alys fought the panic that was building in her chest. When she'd contacted Queen Ellinsoltah and declared herself the rightful Queen of Aaltah, it had felt . . . unreal. So ridiculous and unlikely to work that her nerves had barely troubled her. But with Delnamal already provoked and with Shelvon and Corlin coming their way, it all felt very, very real.

There was a reason she'd been trying so desperately to buy time, and it wasn't entirely because of fear or indecision. The defenses Tynthanal had laid out were only temporary measures.

"Even if we choose not to unleash the Kai spell, we can withstand the initial attack," Tynthanal insisted. "I know the lord commander, and he trained me well. He will send what he thinks is an overwhelming force, but they will be completely unprepared for the magic of Women's Well. His overwhelming force will not be enough."

"These will be men you trained with and fought with since you first entered the Citadel," she reminded him. "Are you really so eager to kill them?"

He and Jailom shared a look. "We are not eager," Tynthanal said, "but we won't have a choice." He glanced at Chanlix. "How many Trapper spells do you suppose we can produce in the time it takes the king to muster the forces to attack us?"

By the time Chanlix and Alys had finished modifying the Trapper spell, it was capable of creating an illusion large enough to hide an entire house from view.

Chanlix smiled. "Quite a few, now that we know how to do it. We have plenty of Zal. And since the spell can be contained in stone, we have plenty of available spell vessels."

Tynthanal nodded in satisfaction, his eyes gleaming with excitement once more. As if he was actually looking forward to the battle, though Alys supposed that was not particularly unusual for a life-long soldier. "We can create an ambush the likes of which the world has never seen. And by the time Delnamal regroups and sends a force large enough to overwhelm us, we may well have developed new and unexpected spells. And found new allies."

That was the key, Alys knew. Tynthanal was probably right. Women's Well could likely withstand the first wave Delnamal sent against them simply because he would not know what he was up against. And once they survived that first wave and had demon-strated the usefulness of the unique magic they produced, Queen Ellinsoltah would be less likely to see an overture as an act of des-peration.

"We will lose a lot of good men," she said. "Even a victory against that first attack will be costly."

"Not as costly as doing nothing," Tynthanal countered.

Everything within her recoiled at the thought of staging such an open rebellion with no allies to support them. But no matter how she looked at it, Tynthanal was right. If they did nothing, then Women's Well was doomed, and many of its inhabitants would be put to death, including herself and her brother—and very likely Shelvon and Corlin, when they arrived. She could not let that hap-pen!

There was a long silence as everyone at the table stared at her with hopeful eyes. They were all frightened—even those who hid their fear most successfully—but there was not a person at the table who didn't wish for her to take this fateful step.

"Very well," she said, hoping her voice didn't shake. "I will be the Sovereign Princess of Women's Well." She turned to Chanlix. "And we will punish Delnamal for the atrocity that was committed on his orders. Let's send him a gift he will not forget."

If Delnamal lost his ability to sire an heir and also suffered a hu-miliating defeat at the hands of their fledgling principality, then it was possible that not only would Women's Well win its indepen-dence, but that his royal council might decide he wasn't the rightful King of Aaltah, after all.

CHAPTER FORTY

Shelvon had never ached so terribly in her entire life, nor had she ever been half so exhausted. She hadn't admitted it to anyone, but she'd never ridden a cheval before, and so was completely unprepared for how physically demanding it could be. Especially when Falcor set so punishing a pace in hopes of outrunning any possible pursuit. He pushed the chevals to their top speed and kept them there, galloping headlong down the road at a pace that made staying seated a life-or-death proposition, with few stops for rest.

People noticed them when they tore through towns along the way, but they were through all the major ones by the time fliers started arriving and demanding their arrest, and the smallest towns did not have militias capable of stopping them. And still Falcor pressed, urging them to greater speed despite the toll it was taking on them.

For all her pain and misery, Shelvon did not complain, for poor

Corlin's ride was pure agony, and the pain potions Falcor gave him barely took the edge off. The bruises deepened, and the welts opened up, leaving his breeches stained and stuck to his legs and backside. By the second day, he was weak and woozy enough that Falcor insisted on strapping him to the saddle lest he lose consciousness and fall off.

"He needs a healer," Shelvon had insisted tearfully as she watched the boy slump in the saddle while Falcor strapped him in with belts and ropes.

"If we stop for a healer," Falcor insisted, "we will be caught." He patted Corlin's thigh. "I'm sorry, Master Corlin, but we need you to hold on just a little longer."

Corlin nodded, his eyes dull and glazed with pain. "I know," he rasped, then tried to put on a brave face as he looked at Shelvon. "I'll be all right, Aunt Shelvon," he assured her, but it was hard to believe him when he looked so haggard.

And yet, they had no choice but to keep riding, as fast as the chevals could go and as long as they could endure.

By the time they reached Women's Well, their pace had slowed considerably, as Corlin could no longer keep himself in the saddle and had to ride double with Falcor, his head lolling as the guardsman guided the cheval with one hand and held him about the waist with the other. Shelvon herself could barely stay upright, and when Falcor brought the chevals to a stop and the townspeople came flooding toward them, she felt herself tipping sideways. She made a weak grab for the saddle, but her movements were too sluggish. She saw ground coming up to meet her.

Corlin would be mortally embarrassed to know his mother was there when Chanlix cut away his bloodstained breeches and revealed the ravages of a beating no child should ever have been forced to endure. Alys had been so filled with helpless rage that she'd screamed and almost punched the wall, as she'd seen a couple of boneheaded men do over the course of her lifetime. She held back before she needed a healer herself, but she was shaking with the need to strike back at whoever had done that to her son.

Chanlix assessed the damage with a degree of detachment that both angered and impressed Alys, touching the ugliest of the open wounds and nodding. She met Alys's eyes and nodded again.

"He's going to be fine," she said, and there was no hint of doubt in her voice. "There is some infection setting in, but our potions can fix that."

"And are they strong enough to close those gashes?" Alys asked anxiously. They looked long enough and bloody enough to require battlefield healing spells, which were in scant supply in Women's Well. Alys wished she'd put more time into experimenting with ways to augment women's healing magic. She had a feeling they were going to need it.

Chanlix nodded. "They are not deep, even if they are ugly. Go and talk to your master of the guard. By the time you return, I'll have him cleaned up and well on the way to mending."

Alys hesitated, reluctant to let her son out of her sight. But she had ordered Falcor to wait for her downstairs when Corlin and Shelvon had been carried into the house of healing, and though he appeared to be whole and healthy, he certainly needed rest.

Sighing, she glanced around the partition to the neighboring bed, where Shelvon lay deeply asleep, aided by a potion that had been pressed on her when she was barely conscious. Her body had been pushed beyond endurance, and though Alys would have liked to talk to her, she understood that rest had to come first.

Emotions heaving and lurching within her, Alys descended the stairs to the first floor of the house of healing, where Falcor stood waiting, practically swaying on his feet in weariness. She didn't know whether she wanted to hug him for bringing Corlin to her or scratch his eyes out for not bringing Jinnell.

"Tell me everything," she demanded, and he obeyed.

Rarely did Alys allow herself to cry in public, but she could not hold back the tears when she heard of Delnamal's brutality toward Corlin, and she moaned in agony when he told her how Jinnell had given up her magic items to aid their escape. Her little girl was on her way to meet Waldmir with no way to protect herself, and there was nothing Alys could do for her.

"Miss Jinnell is an extraordinary young woman, with an extraordinary mind," Falcor told her. "By the time she came to me with her proposal, she had worked out every detail."

Alys's throat tightened. "And you believe she was right, and you could not have brought her with you."

Falcor bowed his head. "If she had come with us—or if she hadn't delayed the procession so that we had such a significant head start—we would all be in a dungeon right now. Even Corlin, for it is clear that the king has no familial loyalty even to the children."

Alys shuddered and hugged herself, proud of her daughter and terrified for her.

"I would have given my life if that could have gotten her to safety," Falcor said softly. "I hope you know that."

Alys blinked and looked at the man before her, the man who'd been protecting her and her family ever since Sylnin's death—and whom she'd resented and treated unfairly for a good deal of that time. He had shown his loyalty when he'd helped her with her early magical experiments, but never would she have expected his loyalty to stretch this far. He had committed *treason* for her, and because of him her son was now safe. Or at least as safe as anyone in Women's Well could be.

"I don't know how to thank you for all that you have done," she said, shaking her head. "Thank you for bringing Corlin to me."

He bowed. "There is no need for thanks, Your Highness," he said. "King Delnamal would savage a child in service to his own anger. *You* would ride into danger to save people you don't even know from the ravages of a flood. I would rather pledge my service to you a thousand times, no matter what the danger, than carry out his bidding in safety and comfort."

There were no doubt those who would consider the gesture inappropriate, but Alys reached out and squeezed his shoulder in thanks. "You are a good man. One of the best I know. I don't have much to offer just yet, but rest assured your service will be rewarded."

"Reward is even less necessary than thanks."

She was too emotionally exhausted to manage more than a small smile. "It is necessary to me." And she still had seats to fill on her royal council. She would talk it over with them before making an autocratic decision, but she had a feeling she had just found her lord chamberlain.

Nandel was like no place Jinnell had ever imagined, much less seen. She'd heard stories about the mountainous principality, about its soaring peaks and its bleak, inhospitable land, but nothing could have prepared her for its raw and savage beauty. Snowcapped mountains disappeared into lowering gray skies, and valleys filled with thick fog that made it feel as if the procession was traveling through a dreamscape. Jinnell was assured that the rough road upon which her carriage bounced and jolted was not the only one in all of Nandel, but it certainly felt that way. The settlements they passed through were small and sparse, and unlike her royal escort in Aaltah, the delegation of Nandelites who had taken over escort duty saw no cause to stop and rest when Jinnell was ill.

Jinnell found she had even less privacy when she and her chaperone and her honor guard were handed over to the Nandel delegation, who had brought a chaperone of their own to instruct her on the ways of Nandel. Most of the "instruction" came down to two simple rules: be quiet and do as you're told.

Practically the only time she wasn't under someone's watchful eyes was when she was in the privy, but she reasoned that someone might become suspicious if she became ill *every* time she visited the privy, so she took care to dose herself with her special healing poison whenever she had the slightest window of opportunity. She learned to conceal the vial in the palm of her hand, and had once brazenly poured it into a cup of wine during dinner in front of everyone, with none the wiser. No one had any cause to guess her bouts of violent nausea were of her own doing.

Although the delegation refused to stop for her illness, she was certain she slowed the procession down. The men of Nandel did not have the same discomfort as those of Aaltah about riding chevals, for the culture of Nandel valued practicality above all else, and even with the rough roads and the difficulties caused by harsh weather, the journey through the mountains should have lasted only a few days, but it was almost a week before they finally arrived in The Keep, Nandel's imposing capital city. By then, Jinnell had lost enough weight that her clothes hung on her awkwardly, and there were deep, blue-black hollows beneath her eyes. And yet still she dosed herself whenever she had a chance—and whenever she could bear it.

The Keep was the most unlovely, unwelcoming city Jinnell had ever set eyes upon. Set into the side of a mountain, it was built entirely of bleak gray stone, with roofs of near-black slate. Even the poorest quarters of the city were stone, for wood was by far harder to come by in these barren mountain passes. In her carriage, Jinnell shivered and huddled deeper into the furs that had become necessary the moment they'd passed into Nandel. While her retinue from Aaltah had come prepared with warming spells, her Nandel escorts had forbidden their use, for warming spells were women's magic, and therefore considered unclean.

Curious despite herself—and perhaps hoping to distract herself from her misery—Jinnell peered out the window as the carriage clattered through the snow-covered streets toward the palace, which looked more like a fortress than a place of residence. If she didn't occasionally cast her gaze back to the interior of the carriage for reassurance, she might have thought she had lost the ability to see colors, for The Keep showed her nothing but black and white and shades of gray. Even the huddled figures of its people blended into the background like ghosts, no touch of color on any of their garments. Every once in a while, someone would glance up, and she would see a flash of blue or green eyes, but mostly those who walked the streets kept their heads down, tucked into scarves or hoods to protect against the frosty bite of the wind.

Even without the prospect of Prince Waldmir as a husband, Jinnell would have despaired at the thought of having to spend the rest of her life with this bleak city as her home.

The palace itself was little better, cold and drafty and dark. Jinnell's room held a narrow, hard bed, a blocky, unadorned wardrobe, and a straight-backed chair before a distressingly small fireplace. By the bedside was a rectangular wooden table on which sat a metal pitcher of water in a basin, which she assumed was meant for washing up. There was no dressing table and no mirror, and Jinnell was briefly thankful to the king for sending a lady's maid with her, for she knew none would be granted to her by the palace staff. The maid was not a particularly warm or friendly person, and she'd often expressed impatience with Jinnell's illness, but her attitude softened somewhat when she saw her lady's accommodations.

"Fine hospitality these barbarians show to the niece of Aaltah's king," the woman muttered as she helped Jinnell out of her traveling clothes. Jinnell did not like to think what the servants' quarters would be like in a place like this.

Jinnell had a few hours to rest before she was to be presented to Sovereign Prince Waldmir, and she spent them huddled under her bedclothes, shivering despite the merrily crackling fire, which was too small to heat the whole room comfortably. She had refrained from drinking any potions for the last few hours of the journey, for just the thought of downing one had brought on a spell of dry heaves. Her stomach was currently at peace, except for a gnawing hunger that was her constant companion when the nausea eased.

The mourning gown Jinnell donned for her meeting with her future husband was the most drab item of clothing she had ever worn. The silk was fine enough, save that it was completely unadorned and draped in unfashionably straight lines. The black fur at the cuffs and collar was soft and glossy, and a cape of the same fur kept some of the chill at bay, but when the maid found a mirror tucked into the baggage and allowed Jinnell to view her reflection, she almost recoiled. The unadorned, uninterrupted black stole every inkling of color from her already pale face, and her complexion reminded her uneasily of her grandfather's the last time she had seen him. The hollows beneath her eyes had deepened, and the dress hung loosely on her shoulders.

"It's a good thing Nandel men like their women pale and waif-like," her maid said callously as she tucked Jinnell's hair into a black net snood.

The words sent a bolt of alarm through Jinnell's system, for she wondered if the pallor that looked so terrible and sickly to her eyes would indeed be considered attractive here in this place where color was so noticeably absent. Her stomach took that opportunity to grumble loudly, and her maid gave a grunt of exasperation.

"Do you think perhaps you could keep some bread and broth down?" she inquired. "It won't do to have your stomach making such unseemly noises when you meet the prince."

Jinnell's stomach fairly howled at the thought of food of any sort. "I think I might," she said. "Perhaps I am finally over the worst of it." She tried a tentative smile, but it was wasted on the maid who was already halfway out the door.

While the maid arranged for the bread and broth, Jinnell rooted through her traveling dress and once again palmed the vial of potion she had created during their last overnight stay at a dismal Nandel inn. Tears stung her eyes as everything within her rebelled at the thought of suffering through even more hours of misery, and she was sorely tempted to forgo the potion and gamble that she already looked unappealing enough to discourage her would-be suitor. Then she looked around her room and shivered once more in the cold, and it reminded her how very much was at stake.

Fortuitously, her maid was unable to obtain the bread and broth until scant minutes before Jinnell had to make her way to her formal presentation to the prince. The rush made it easier for Jinnell to pour in the potion unobserved, and it meant that the nausea had not yet begun when she was led into the austere receiving room where Prince Waldmir awaited her.

Jinnell studied her nightmare of a would-be husband as she was ceremoniously announced. She had come to associate all things unpleasant with her uncle, and therefore had somehow imagined

Prince Waldmir would resemble him in some way. But whereas Del-namal was short and fat, with a round, pudgy face, Waldmir was tall and thin and severe-looking. He wore a simple charcoal-gray dou-blet adorned with polished metal fastenings over black breeches that tucked into plain black leather boots. A sword was belted at his side, and if not for the thin iron circlet around his head, Jinnell might almost have mistaken him for a palace guard.

She curtsied deeply and lowered her head as the prince ap-proached her and her entourage backed away to create a semblance of privacy.

"I hear that your journey to The Keep has not been an easy one," he said in a surprisingly warm, deep voice. His Mountain Tongue accent was less pronounced than Queen Shelvon's.

Jinnell rose from her curtsy and looked at him more closely. He was more than old enough to be her father, and yet she still would describe him as moderately handsome. His hair was an almost me-tallic shade of silver, and his eyes were the deep gray of storm clouds. A neatly clipped snowy white beard surrounded full lips that curved into the hint of a smile at her regard.

"You were expecting an ogre?" he asked with a twinkle in his eye.

Jinnell blushed and lowered her gaze. "Of course not, Your Royal Highness," she hurried to say.

"Come sit by the fire," he beckoned, and she saw that there was a cluster of chairs before the hearth, and a tea service sitting on a low table at their center. "Your lips are practically blue."

Almost as if on command, she shivered, for once again the fire was far too small to heat a room of this size. Prince Waldmir guided her into a chair and poured a cup of tea for her without asking. She knew from talking to Shelvon that the nobility of Nandel was far more self-sufficient than what she was used to in Aaltah, but she never would have imagined the sovereign prince pouring her tea for her! She accepted the cup with a murmured thank-you, although the first uneasy stirring in her gut made her unwilling to take more than the tiniest sip.

"Are you still unwell?" Prince Waldmir asked solicitously.

Jinnell set the tea aside. "I had been feeling better for a while, but now I'm not so sure." She gave him what she hoped was an apologetic smile.

"I'm sorry to hear your journey was so very unpleasant."

To Jinnell's surprise, he sounded like he meant it. "Yes, me too," she said dryly, and once again he smiled.

"As you know, we of Nandel do not avail ourselves of women's magic." His nose wrinkled slightly in distaste. "However, we have some herbal remedies for maladies of the digestion. I will send some to your rooms, and perhaps you will find one to ease your symptoms."

"That's very kind of you, Your Royal Highness."

"We are not so very formal here in Nandel," he said. "You may address me as 'my lord,' at least until we are acquainted enough to permit the use of first names."

Jinnell's eyebrows rose at that. "That will . . . take some getting used to."

He grinned. "I imagine much about Nandel will, especially for someone used to a king's court. Here, we value simplicity and honesty and practicality. I won't pretend there isn't a great deal of intrigue, just as there is in any other court, but even so we are a great deal more plain-spoken than you are no doubt accustomed to."

If Jinnell didn't know this man's history—and if she weren't destined to a forced marriage with him—she might almost lower her guard enough to like him. Her stomach turned over, and she closed her eyes briefly, dreading what was to come.

"I will send for a digestive tonic straightaway," the prince said, beckoning one of his servants over without awaiting a reply.

"I doubt I could drink anything at all just now," she said mournfully, but he sent the servant off for a tonic anyway.

"It won't do any harm to have it ready, should you change your mind," Prince Waldmir said.

She swallowed down her gorge. In Aaltah, she would have been expected to retire from public view the moment any hint of sickness was revealed, but nothing about this encounter was meeting with her expectations.

"I think perhaps I should return to my rooms," she said, sure her face was turning that particularly unattractive shade of green that was becoming all too familiar.

"Will you feel any less sick there?"

She blinked at him. "Um, no. I suppose not."

"Then perhaps best to stay here, where the fire is warmer."

The servant returned, bearing both a cup of the promised herbal tonic, and a covered basin. She gave the prince another astonished, helpless look, and he shrugged.

"Honesty and practicality, remember? We are not offended by sickness, and there is no need to pretend it doesn't exist by hiding it away."

Tears stung Jinnell's eyes, caused both by her misery and a sudden shift of understanding. She had expected Prince Waldmir to be disgusted by her illness and the damage it had done to her appearance. Her gorge rose, and she spilled the meager contents of her stomach into the basin. When the heaving stopped, Prince Waldmir handed her the cup of tonic and bade her to rinse out her mouth even if she didn't feel up to swallowing. Then he ordered a fresh basin brought in. She sniffled and dabbed at her eyes.

"An auspicious first meeting," she mumbled, and he smiled. All the hours of misery she had suffered, all her careful planning had been for naught. One by one, her hopes of escaping this dreaded marriage were slipping away.

Delnamal had not been able to hold still since the moment he'd learned that Alysoon had had the gall to declare herself the sovereign princess of a nonexistent principality named Women's Well. Every time he thought of it, his hands started shaking with rage, and his jaw ached from the constant clenching and grinding of his teeth. He wasn't sure how he could bear to sit behind his desk long enough to sign each one of the arrest warrants Melcor had just stacked there, the pile intimidating in its height.

"Has the lord commander dispatched his men?" he asked, delaying the inevitable as he paced the confines of the room.

Melcor, wary of his mood, bowed low before answering. "Yes, Your Majesty."

Delnamal nodded in satisfaction. The lord commander had asked for a few days to plan the journey to Women's Well, for he wanted as much advance reconnaissance as possible, but Delnamal had scoffed at that foolishness. From all indications, there at most one hundred able-bodied men in the whole place, most of whom would have no armor nor any but makeshift weapons. A company of three hundred and fifty men, well-armed and well-trained, would break them with no effort whatsoever. The faster the petty rebellion was quelled—and the more of its leaders could be marched back to Aaltah in chains to face a very public trial and execution—the easier Delnamal would rest.

He expected Melcor to take a hint and scurry from the room, leaving him to sign all those warrants at whatever pace he could tolerate, but the secretary remained where he stood. Delnamal stifled a groan of irritation.

"Well, what is it?" he demanded.

Melcor waved at the pile of warrants that declared every known inhabitant of Women's Well a traitor to the Crown. Most of those warrants would be made unnecessary when his soldiers took the "town," for Delnamal's orders had been to kill everyone but the leaders. He would have looked forward to signing them anyway, were it not necessary for him to sit down and hold still to do it.

"The one on the top there," Melcor said. "It's one that was . . . unexpected."

Delnamal snatched the top warrant and scanned it quickly, but the name of the traitor did not look familiar, and he hadn't the patience to read through the document to find out why this particular warrant was different from the others.

"Who is this?" he demanded. "And why should I care?"

Melcor shifted uncomfortably. "He is a man who squired for Lieutenant—" He cleared his throat as he realized he was about to grant a traitor a title he did not deserve. "Who squired for Tynthanal when he was young. He's now a member of the palace guard, and it seems he's been in regular contact with the rebels. We can't be certain the full extent of his treachery until he's been thoroughly examined, but there's little doubt he has shared a great deal of sensitive information. He was caught this morning trying to send a message warning Tynthanal of the arrest warrants and the departure of our troops."

Delnamal did not appreciate the reminder that some of his own soldiers felt a bone-deep loyalty to his traitorous half-brother, but it made it even more important that Tynthanal be brought to justice and publicly humiliated as quickly as possible. His petty rebellion and its ignominious defeat would go a long way toward quelling his shiny public image.

Delnamal's face twisted into a sneer of distaste, and he leaned over his desk so he could scrawl a quick signature on the warrant before thrusting it back at Melcor.

"Make sure the inquisitor examines him *thoroughly*. I want him longing for his execution day well before his trial begins."

Melcor bowed. "Yes, Your Majesty."

CHAPTER FORTY-ONE

Alys looked back at the town of Women's Well in awe as, at Tynthanal's signal, the Trapper spells were activated one by one. Even having known what to expect, the sudden vanishing of all those buildings and men took her breath away. What was left was a cluster of tents, brought out of storage to create the illusion of just the sort of settlement Delnamal's men would likely expect to see, and a scattering of small wooden buildings that were in truth the farthest outskirts of the town proper. All the civilians would be huddled in the town hall, far from where the fighting was expected to take place and hidden beneath several layers of Trapper spells.

Beside her, Tynthanal's horse shuffled and tossed its head, and Alys turned to see a grim and troubled look on her brother's face. Jailom, too, looked pale in the bright sunlight.

"It will be a slaughter," Jailom mumbled, and his hands clenched on the reins.

What had seemed a stunning tactical advantage during the plan-

ning stages now took on a grimmer mien as the reality set in. She
knew both her lord chancellor and her lord commander were imagining what it would be like for their former comrades-at-arms to
march into this deadly trap.

Alys bit her lip. She believed Tynthanal and Jailom when they
proclaimed their victory was almost assured, and yet there was no
tactical advantage overwhelming enough to make her feel secure
with Tynthanal insisting on joining the fighting himself. No member of the royal council save the lord commander was expected to
be present on the battlefield. Certainly not the lord chancellor. But
Tynthanal had lived all his life as a soldier, and he would not leave
his men to face the enemy without him, no matter what the risk—
and no matter what his sovereign princess demanded. "But the
numbers . . ." she said, and let her voice trail off.

Friendly neighbors in the closest towns—towns that had come
to depend on the magic of Women's Well—had given them warning of Delnamal's forces closing in. By tomorrow morning, there
would be three hundred and fifty well-trained, well-armored soldiers with plenty of magical support bearing down on Women's
Well, where they would face fewer than a hundred fighters, most of
whom were mere civilian militia.

"Delnamal could have sent twice as many and we still would
have had a good chance of winning," Tynthanal said. "You have
never experienced a battle. You have no idea how devastating an
ambush can be."

She opened her mouth to retort that *he* had never been in a true
battle before, either, for Aaltah had been at peace since they were
children.

"They will not even have activated their battle magic yet," Jailom said before she had a chance to speak. "We are trained not to
trigger the spells in our armor or weapons until the last possible
moment to reduce the risk of having them fail in the heat of battle.
Having your spells run out during the fighting is a death sentence,
for you cannot afford to cloud your vision by opening your Mindseye. Twenty-five men with spelled weapons can cut through an

army of one hundred in ordinary armor in the blink of an eye. They will die in droves before the true fighting even begins."

"It is a foul tactic we use," Tynthanal agreed. "But it is our only chance for survival." The muscles of his cheek worked as he ground his teeth. "A fair and courteous warrior is a *dead* warrior."

Alys swallowed her worries and tried not to imagine the hell that would reign on this battlefield tomorrow as Tynthanal and his men slaughtered men who had once been their friends. Men who were doing their duty by following the commands of their king. Even a victory would take a heavy toll, and the consequences of a loss were unthinkable.

"I'm not arguing that it's not necessary," Jailom hurried to assure him. "But I am not required to feel good about it."

Tynthanal sighed heavily. "No." He shook his head, then turned to Alys. "Make sure you keep all the civilians indoors and away from windows. Some will be tempted to watch, but a stray arrow or bolt—especially a spelled one—can travel a long, long way and can easily break through a window."

She suspected that particular warning was aimed straight at her. She raised an eyebrow. "I thought they wouldn't have time to activate their spells."

He shrugged. "The stray arrows don't have to come from the enemy to be deadly."

"Besides," Jailom added, "we are sure to meet *some* resistance once the shock wears off. They are more likely to retreat than attack, but they would certainly want to cover that retreat with a hail of arrows."

As they rode back toward the town, Alys pulled up beside Jailom's horse, hoping the sound of the hooves would keep Tynthanal from hearing her.

"Whatever happens," she said, giving him a steady stare, "you make sure my brother is safe tomorrow. I cannot lose him."

Jailom returned the stare. "You will not lose him, Your Highness."

And he said it with such conviction that she couldn't help believing him. There was now nothing she could do but wait. She glanced over her shoulder in the general direction from which the attack would come.

Even if the battle was not the success Tynthanal and Jailom assured her it would be—even if they all fell to Delnamal's men—she would have her revenge. Just before riding out here to inspect the workings of the Trapper spells, she and Chanlix and Tynthanal had presided over the sending of a Kai flier to Delnamal. There was some comfort in knowing that whether the battle was won or lost, Delnamal himself would lose something he held dear.

With the town of Women's Well itself in its infancy, there were very few children packed into the town hall with all the women and other noncombatants, but it seemed to Alys that every single one of them was crying. If Delnamal's forces somehow made it past the town's defenders, they would have little trouble finding the hidden heart of Women's Well, despite the Trapper spells that concealed the building from view.

Not that Alys could blame those children. Even those too young to know what was happening could sense the tension and fear in the room as the first shouts of battle sounded from the distance. Alys clasped hands with Chanlix, and the two women shared an anxious look as they imagined Tynthanal out there in the middle of the fray. As sovereign princess, Alys was naturally concerned for *all* the men who were out there risking their lives, but it was fear for her brother that had her squeezing Chanlix's hand painfully tight. On the table before them was the mate to Tynthanal's talking flier, and they both stared at it as they waited breathlessly for it to chirp.

At least Corlin wasn't out there, despite his impassioned arguments that he should be. He was only a few weeks short of his fourteenth birthday, at which time he would be considered from a soldier's perspective man enough to fight, and he'd been adamant that they had too few warriors to spare him. Alys thanked the Mother that Tynthanal had sided with her and turned a deaf ear to Corlin's pleas.

Corlin sat with Shelvon in resentful silence, his arms crossed over his chest as his jaw worked in frustration. He was still capable of a world-class sulk. Alys couldn't understand what made men so eager for battle, for pain and terror and death. Corlin acted as if it were all some great game that his mother was stubbornly refusing to let him join, but she would happily face his disdain to have him safe and whole here with her.

The town hall was far enough from the ambush site that only faint cries reached Alys's ears, but the sounds made her wince none-theless. Men were dying on her doorstep because of the choices she'd made, and guilt gnawed at her insides.

"You did not start this fight," Chanlix said, shaking Alys out of her downward spiral—and proving herself a very perceptive woman.

"If I had not declared myself sovereign princess—"

"*You* didn't. *We* did. And it was necessary. You know it was."

She let out a shuddering breath. Yes, she *did* know. "That doesn't make this any easier to bear."

To that, Chanlix had no reply.

Less than a quarter of an hour after they'd heard the first shout, the communicating flier—or talker, as the folk of Women's Well were now calling them—chirped. She and Chanlix shared a look of shock, for though the faint sounds of battle had faded already, they could hardly credit that it was all over in such a short time. Alys activated the talker, and both she and Chanlix let out loud sighs of relief when Tynthanal's image appeared before them. He was sweaty and dirty, and there were spots of blood on his mail coat, but he was whole.

"All went as expected," he reported, and there was a haunted look in his eyes that told her just how much he had hated their un-gallant plan of attack. "The enemy has fled. Those who survived, that is."

"How many dead?" Alys tried to keep her voice steady and dis-passionate, but she doubted she'd fooled anyone.

"I don't have a count yet. We've lost perhaps five men, with about twenty more wounded. The enemy's casualties were . . . a lot more significant. Keep everyone in the town hall until I contact you again. The women and children do not need to see this."

"But you have wounded who need tending," Chanlix said.

"Send some of your abigails," Tynthanal conceded. "But only those with the strongest stomachs." His head turned in a slow circle as he looked around him. "This is not a pretty sight."

Chanlix snorted. "As if any battlefield is."

Tynthanal deactivated his flier, and Chanlix chose a handful of her former abigails to go with her to the battlefield to heal the wounded. Although Alys had no desire to see the devastation, she felt it her duty as the sovereign princess to tour the battlefield, and so she went with Chanlix despite the other woman's attempts to dissuade her. And when Corlin begged to come along—to prove what a man he was, she supposed—Alys allowed it, though it felt like cruelty. The boy had lived a more sheltered life than he realized, and it was time he come to grips with the reality that war was not a game to be eagerly plunged into.

When Alys caught her first glimpse of the battlefield, her whole body went cold, and it was all she could do to keep her feet moving forward. Chanlix and her abigails rushed forward, preparing healing spells as they ran with blind eyes, leaving Alys and Corlin to cover the remaining distance alone.

Alys knew in her head that it had been a very small battle, nothing like the battles that occurred in most wars, and yet the enormity of it made her eyes sting with tears. So many dead, so much blood, so much gore. And the stench was enough to make her stomach turn. Worse were the bodies that moved still, the men who cried and groaned and whimpered in pain and misery.

To her surprise, Corlin slipped his hand into hers, his earlier anger forgotten. His face was pale and his eyes too wide.

"You've seen enough, Mama," he said. "Go back to the town hall. I will find Uncle Tynthanal and see how I can help. The danger is past now, so you needn't worry about me."

Her heart swelled with love for her son, and she very much wanted to gather him into a hug. Of course, he would have been mortified by such a gesture, so she refrained.

"I'm all right, Corlin," she assured him, though it was beyond her to make the lie convincing. "I'm not the sort to order men to their deaths and refuse to acknowledge the consequences."

Still holding her son's hand, she started forward once more, fighting the nausea that swam in her stomach. Tynthanal's men were sorting through the fallen, separating the dead from the wounded—and relieving both of their weapons and armor, for Women's Well did not have the necessary masculine elements to produce spelled weapons or armor.

She spotted Tynthanal—carefully laying out the body of one of his men—at the same time he spotted her. Corlin let go of her hand and veered off, and she let him go as Tynthanal shook his head and grimaced. The look he gave her combined exasperation and sadness as he picked his way across to her. One of the wounded—a boy who looked no more than sixteen and had a gaping wound in his belly and one on his thigh—grabbed weakly at Tynthanal's leg.

Tynthanal glanced down, and Alys saw him quickly assess the boy's wounds. Then he squatted by the boy's head, saying something she couldn't quite make out in a soothing tone. He laid a gentle hand on the boy's forehead, and Alys saw the boy's eyes slide closed as if in relief.

With a suddenness that made Alys gasp, Tynthanal whipped a knife out of his boot and jammed it upward through the boy's throat. The boy's body jerked once, then was still. Tynthanal wiped the blood from his knife and stuck it back in his boot.

Alys covered her mouth and feared she might collapse in horror.

"He would not have survived that injury," Tynthanal said as he approached. "Better to end it swiftly."

"But we have healers . . ." Her voice died, for that wasn't strictly true. They had abigails with healing potions, but they did not have Academy-trained battlefield healers, who were capable of healing more grievous wounds. To tend the damage men did to one another in battle required men's magic.

"Even the best healers would not have saved that boy," Tynthanal said. "There are limits to what magic can do."

Alys surveyed the battlefield once more and saw that the abigails were delivering potions to Tynthanal's wounded men, while the wounded attackers were left to lie in the dirt. A small band of Tynthanal's men were making their way through those wounded, occasionally striking killing blows, but leaving many others alive and suffering. In all their previous planning for this battle, Alys had never stopped to think about what to do with wounded enemies.

"In an ordinary battle," Tynthanal said, "we would take the enemy soldiers prisoner and perhaps ransom them. But we don't have the men or the facilities to keep prisoners."

"What do you recommend we do with them, then?"

"From a military standpoint, the most practical thing to do is kill them. Such a solution is hardly unheard of, though it is considered barbarous. Then again, our ambush has already shredded any pretensions of honor we might have."

Alys shook her head. "It's not their fault they were fighting for the other side. They were just following their orders."

"The same can be said of almost all enemy combatants. It does not change the stark reality that we cannot hold them."

Alys chewed on her lip as she thought. The "barbarous" ambush had been an unavoidable evil in the face of overwhelming numbers, but *surely* there was an alternative to killing the wounded.

"We can heal them and then let them go," she said. "Without their armor and weapons, of course. We can never hope to compete with Delnamal in sheer numbers, and returning a couple dozen fighters to him will do us no harm."

Tynthanal frowned as he thought about it. "I'm not sure that would be doing them any favors. Delnamal doesn't understand the depth of the magic we have here. He will think of those healing potions as expensive resources, and he will question the loyalty of any man on whom we would 'waste' a potion."

"Then perhaps you can explain that to them and then give them the option to stay and join us if they prefer. We could use more fighters. These are your former friends and comrades-at-arms, and they respect you."

Tynthanal snorted. "I very much doubt that after today. But

you're right—I'd much rather give them that option than kill them."

Alys let out a sigh of relief. There was more than enough death on this battlefield already. She just had to hope that all those deaths might help Women's Well entice an ally and prevent an all-out war.

A blast of frigid wind stole Jinnell's breath as she and Prince Wald-mir stepped out onto the observation platform. At the very top of the highest tower in the palace, the platform offered a breathtaking view of the city below and of the soaring cliffs on all sides. For the first time since Jinnell's procession had crossed the border into Nandel, the sun was shining bright in a nearly cloudless sky, the snowcapped peaks nearly blinding in the light. She pulled the heavy fur mantle more closely around her as her breath steamed.

"If the cold is too much for you, we can go back inside," the prince offered solicitously, but she shook her head.

"It's worth a little cold to see this," she told him, taking in a deep breath of bracing mountain air. There was so much about Nandel that was bleak and forbidding and inhospitable, but there was an undeniable beauty and grandeur to the land, as well.

The prince smiled, his eyes crinkling with crow's-feet that she suspected came more from squinting in the sun and snow than from smiling. She could hardly claim to know him well after a mere two days' acquaintance, but she had already formed the impression that he was a deeply unhappy man. While he smiled at her a great deal, she rarely saw him smile at anyone else. And she doubted that smile would make very many appearances once she was bound to him.

Prince Waldmir put a hand on her back and gently guided her toward the battlements at the edge of the platform. Although he had brought her here to show her the beauty of the view, there was no missing the true purpose of this place, where there was always a lookout on duty. Despite all the twists and turns the road took to thread its way through the mountains toward The Keep, Jinnell could see most of its curves for miles into the distance. A hostile force foolish enough to launch an attack would be remarked long before they arrived at the city's walls.

The wind whistled through the battlements and whipped Jinnell's skirts around her legs, the chill sinking deep into her bones till she could hardly remember what it felt like to be warm—and this was supposed to be spring. She shuddered to think what the temperature would feel like in the height of winter.

"I would not make a good wife for you," she said baldly. She glanced up at Prince Waldmir's face, internally wincing at her brazen, impolitic remark. She hadn't meant to say it, but the words had tumbled out with no forethought, and they were hardly the kind she could take back.

The prince leaned his forearms on the battlements, looking relaxed and unaffected by the cold—or by her rude words.

"I don't need a good wife," he said, not looking at her. "I need a son."

Jinnell swallowed hard, her stomach threatening to turn over. She had stopped taking her poison potions, but they seemed to have had a lingering effect, and she could eat very little without paying for it. She had no idea how to respond to his uncomfortably frank response to her uncomfortably frank statement.

"My first wife was a good wife," the prince continued. There was a hint of wistfulness in both his voice and his expression. "She bore me three daughters, and she was everything I could have wished for." His expression hardened. "None of those births was easy. But then she bore me a stillborn son, and the birth almost killed her. The midwives warned that she could not survive another pregnancy." His lips pressed together into a thin, hard line. "I am the Sovereign Prince of Nandel. I *must* have an heir."

"So you divorced her. Sent her to the Abbey to rot." Her voice was all sharp edges and accusation, and she quailed to think that that would be her own fate if she was forced to marry him and did not give him the heir he desired.

The prince closed his eyes in what looked like pain. "I deemed a life at the Abbey favorable to a death in childbirth."

Jinnell wondered if his wife would agree. "And what about your second wife? Did you divorce her for her own good, as well?" Perhaps if she were sharp-tongued and disagreeable enough, he would decide to seek a better wife elsewhere.

He stood up straight and turned to face her. The expression in his flinty gray eyes was chilling and repressive, and yet he answered calmly enough.

"I understand that my marital history does not make me a young woman's dream husband, so I will share with you details I might not share with others, with the understanding that these details are not to be repeated. Do I have your agreement?"

By now, Jinnell was far too curious to do anything but nod.

"My second wife was barren and did not quicken even once over the five years we were married. That marriage was not as successful as my first even before her barrenness came to light, but it was at least . . . adequate. We were not happy together, but we were content. Had I not needed a son, I never would have divorced her."

If the Nandelites weren't so squeamish about women's magic, they could have known in advance that the marriage could not bear fruit, but Jinnell kept that thought to herself. She didn't imagine that the fate of a barren woman here would be any better if she never married in the first place.

"After that, I married Shelvon's mother," Prince Waldmir said with a curl of his lip. "I had no illusions that she would ever be a good wife, but then how many good wives can one man hope to have? I had no sons—and far too many scheming nephews—and securing the throne was of paramount importance. I know you are aware of how that marriage ended, and I doubt even my daughter could argue the execution wasn't warranted."

Jinnell remembered well the anger and dislike Shelvon had expressed toward her father, and she suspected Shelvon would indeed have argued. Though perhaps her argument would be that Waldmir never should have married a woman who didn't want him, rather than that he should not execute one who tried to kill him.

"And your most recent?" she inquired with a raised brow. "I presume she was also found lacking in some significant way?"

Waldmir glowered at her. "While I hope I can make a case that I am not the ogre you've been led to expect, I cannot pretend to endless patience. When you are my wife, I will expect you to hold that pretty tongue of yours, and if you do not, you will pay a price."

Jinnell jerked back, unaccountably surprised by this sudden change in his demeanor. He had been surprisingly personable so far, and she had let her guard down.

He sighed and shook his head. "Forgive my harsh words. I did tell you we are more plainly spoken here than you are accustomed to, but there are limits. I will not pretend that marriage to me would be easy on a girl used to the ways of Aaltah."

She swallowed hard, fighting a surge of fear. "What you mean is that *men* may speak more plainly here, but that the same is not true for women."

"Something like that," he agreed. "But to answer your question, my last wife was lacking in one very significant way." His cold eyes glinted with anger, and it was all Jinnell could do not to back away from him. He was not as openly unpleasant as Delnamal, but the look in those eyes told her he was just as dangerous.

"She was a whore," Waldmir said. "She bore me yet another daughter, and perhaps if given time she would have borne the son I need. But I could never have been certain any future children were mine."

How stupid would a woman have to be to cheat on Prince Waldmir after he'd just had his previous wife beheaded? Jinnell wondered if Waldmir had simply tired of her and chosen to interpret her behavior with other men as a sign of infidelity when she was in fact innocent.

Apparently, he read her doubt on her face. "I found her with her lover when she thought I was away. She gave me just cause to execute her for treason, but I chose to divorce her instead. No matter what people think, I am *not* a monster."

How many monsters know they are monsters? Jinnell wondered. She was tempted to ask what had happened to his wife's lover, but decided she didn't want to know.

"You don't think it's monstrous to marry a woman against her will?" she asked, allowing a slight quaver to enter her voice in hopes of deflecting any anger the accusation might cause.

He looked at her askance. "Even in Aaltah, it is a girl's family who arranges her marriage, not the girl herself."

"Yes, but if her family is good and kind, it takes her will into account."

"And if her family is royal, her will is of no consequence at all."

"And that seems fair and right to you?"

He shrugged. "I am a sovereign prince. Do you really think my will is of any more consequence than yours? *My* will was to grow old with my first wife by my side, even if I dared not lie with her again until such time as she could no longer quicken. But my duty is to provide an heir to the throne, and I chose my duty over my desires."

"But you *chose*."

He leaned on the battlements once more, looking over the city with thoughtful eyes. "And what would *you* choose, Jinnell Rah-Sylnin? Would you choose to return to Aaltah having been rejected by a sovereign prince, for that is how anyone would interpret the lack of an engagement. Do you imagine your uncle would find you a husband who would please you? You are the granddaughter of the most reviled woman in the history of Seven Wells. Do you imagine suitors would flock to your door?"

Jinnell ducked her head to hide the color that rose to her cheeks. Suddenly, she was glad for the dry air and cold wind, for it sucked the moisture from her eyes before tears could form. She had never put any thought into what would happen if Prince Waldmir decided he didn't want her. Even if her chastity was not the issue, Delnamal might blame her for the failure. As cruel as he was, she doubted he would charge her with treason for having been sick—as long as he didn't know she'd done it to herself—but he would certainly not be inclined to generosity. Part of the appeal of sending her to Nandel had been the pain it would cause her mother, and he would no doubt look for another husband who would be just as repellent, if one could be found.

"I don't mean to be cruel," Prince Waldmir said. "I only mean to point out that marriage to me is perhaps not the worst possible outcome for you, no matter my faults. We can approach it as a business arrangement, if you'd like. I meant what I said: I have no need for a 'good' wife. All I would ask is that you not whore yourself out to others and that you give me a son." He stood up straight once more and looked into her eyes. "Once my heir is born, you need never again come to my bed nor spend any more time in my company than required for ceremony."

Jinnell opened and closed her mouth a few times, searching for words, but they proved elusive. There was so much truth to what he said, so many other unpleasant possibilities for the course of her life. Prince Waldmir was not an especially *nice* man, but he was far less inclined to cruelty than Shelvon's descriptions had led her to believe. Perhaps she had not taken into account how Shelvon's opinion of her father was skewed by what happened to her mother.

"What will happen to me if I say no to you?" she asked. "Will you marry me anyway?"

He shook his head. "It is hard for me to credit that your grandmother's Curse could so profoundly change the laws of nature, but I've seen enough evidence to suggest it is so. If you do not wish to bear me a son, then you will not do so, and therefore it is not to my advantage to marry you. I am too old to waste time with another fruitless marriage, and the older I get, the more ambitiously my nephews eye the throne. One way or another, I must find a wife who will bear me a son, the sooner the better. So no, I will not offer for you if you do not wish it."

Those words should have made her sag with relief, but they instead caused a flutter of panic in her breast. Waldmir had painted an all-too-realistic picture of what her future held if she returned home to Aaltah ostensibly rejected. It was a sign of how terribly her life had changed that marriage to Prince Waldmir might actually be the lesser of any number of evils.

"You don't have to decide now," Waldmir said. "We will have many more occasions to talk over the course of your visit, and I will show you more of the great beauties of Nandel when you are fully well again. Perhaps I can persuade you that marriage to me would not be quite so dire a fate as you might have feared."

He managed a self-deprecating smile that Jinnell might almost have found charming, were she not so chilled by today's realizations. Perhaps marriage with him might not be as horrible as Shelvon had led her to believe, but it would hardly be pleasing. There was a hardness about him, a coldness that made him dangerous—she'd already seen a flash of his temper, and was sure it would be more in evidence over longer acquaintance. And though she might come to think of him as a lesser evil, she had no way of knowing if she'd be able to bear him any children at all, much less a son. She had only to look at Shelvon to know that one could not *will* oneself to want something, and it was hard to imagine herself wanting to bear this man's children.

"I will endeavor to keep an open mind," she said, for that was the best she could promise him.

"That is all I would ask."

CHAPTER FORTY-TWO

Ellin remembered fondly the days when a full night's sleep had been a regular feature of her everyday life. Even when she'd first become queen and her days had been scheduled and choreographed down to the minute, she'd had sufficient time in her night to eke out a satisfying sleep.

Those days were now long past as her reign stretched into its eighth month and her year of mourning marched inevitably toward its conclusion. It seemed as if every day, the council grew more and more enamored of Tamzin, more and more entrenched in the idea that she would marry him and make him their king in a few months' time. Tamzin himself was so secure in his position that he no longer bothered to make threats, leaning back comfortably in his chair and smirking when she reminded the council for the thousandth time that she had not made any decision about her marriage yet. And while he occasionally made snide comments about Zarsha's continued presence in Rhozinolm, he had not followed through on his veiled threat to start spreading unsavory rumors. A fact she was sure would change if Tamzin stopped feeling that he had the upper hand.

"You've but to say the word," Zarsha told her as the two of them sat alone together in her bedroom sipping tea when she should by all rights have been fast asleep. With tensions rising, she found Zarsha knocking on her secret door at night more and more frequently. He was not an uncomplicated friend, but he was a true one. His mind was at least as sharp and subtle as Semsulin's, and yet he was possessed of a level of kindness Semsulin could never match, and he seemed to genuinely care about her as a person as well as a queen. Time spent in his presence was a balm against all the scheming and plotting—even when he held a pivotal role in much of that scheming and plotting.

She shook her head and sipped her tea. Her body ached with fatigue, but even if she'd been comfortably in bed instead of entertaining a forbidden visitor, she doubted she'd be asleep right now. The harder she tried to extract herself from the trap Tamzin had built, the tighter the jaws clamped down on her. And yet still she hesitated to murder a man in cold blood.

Zarsha grunted in exasperation. "I respect your sense of honor. I really do. But you are beginning to lose even Semsulin."

"I said no!" she snapped, angry because he was right. Not that he should know of Semsulin's new inclination to support a marriage to Tamzin. Her conversations with her chancellor were private—at least the open and honest ones were—and that was the only time he expressed any weakening of his opposition to Tamzin, which he insisted was based on necessity rather than inclination. "And I'll thank you to stop acting so much like a spy."

Zarsha laughed and settled into his chair more comfortably. "I cannot be other than I am, Your Majesty."

She blinked in surprise. "You're actually admitting it?" The closest he'd come to admitting he was a spy was not denying it.

"I'm admitting that I have what might be considered an unhealthy interest in others' business. And a singular skill at learning secrets. There's more than one reason a man with my skills and inclinations might spend the majority of his adult life away from his home and the court to which he is beholden."

She looked at him with new eyes, casting aside Graesan's accusations, which she realized had colored her judgment even when she'd denied believing them. Prince Waldmir was Zarsha's uncle, but she'd never seen any sign that Zarsha had any great affection or respect for his uncle. And a man who would so callously marry and then discard respectable young women without regard to the offense to their families was doubtlessly engaged in all sorts of unappealing behavior that he preferred to keep private. Such a man would not want to have an overly curious nephew living if not within the royal palace, then within The Keep.

She was still sorting through her thoughts and feelings when she heard soft chirping coming from a drawer in her bedside table. Zarsha heard it, too, his head swiveling toward the window, which was the only logical source for the sound. When the chirp sounded again, obviously inside the room and not from the window, he frowned in puzzlement. Ellin was pleased that for all his skill at digging up secrets, this one had apparently escaped him. She was less pleased that she would now have to admit she'd been keeping one from him.

She rose from her chair, heading toward the table. She had stored the flier from Lady Alysoon there because it was about as secret a hiding place as she had available. The last thing she wanted was to carry the little bird around on her person and have it start chirping at an inopportune moment.

"What is that?" Zarsha asked, his face alight with curiosity.

"I'll explain later," she said as she unlocked the drawer and pulled out the chirping flier. "Please stay where you are and don't make a sound."

She resumed her seat, holding the flier in her cupped hand with its head facing toward her. Wondering if Zarsha would be scandalized, she opened her Mindseye so she could feed some Rho into the flier and activate its communication spell. When her vision cleared, she could see him gaping at her, but the image that shimmered into being in front of her soon distracted all his attention.

Lady Alysoon was seated in a fire-lit room in a high-backed chair ornamented with intricately carved flowers and vines painted in gold. She was still dressed all in black as befitted her mourning, but unlike the last time the two had spoken, she wore no headdress but a delicate gold circlet studded with diamonds.

Ellin was aware of the revolt Lady Alysoon had instigated in Aaltah, just as she was aware that King Delnamal had sent his forces to crush it. She had, in fact, expected to receive a desperate plea for help much sooner than this. Based on the information her spies had gathered, King Delnamal's forces had to be on Alysoon's doorstep by now, which meant no aid Ellin could send would reach her in time.

Not that Ellin could have helped the woman even with a more timely appeal. She was in no better position to offer alliance now than she had been the last time the two had talked, though she would dearly love access to the talking flier spell.

Ellin nodded her head in greeting, taking in the crown Alysoon wore and the throne on which she sat. If nothing else, she was making a good show at being a true sovereign princess.

"It is a pleasure to hear from you again," Ellin lied. She was not looking forward to dashing the other woman's last hope, but she had no intention of dragging things out any longer than absolutely necessary. "I regret to inform you that nothing has changed since the last time we spoke."

To her surprise, Alysoon smiled. "Perhaps not in Rhozinolm. The same cannot be said of Women's Well."

"So I have heard," Ellin said. "You have declared your independence from Aaltah, is that right?"

Alysoon inclined her head. "Yes. I am now the Sovereign Princess of Women's Well and stand in direct conflict with my half-brother."

Ellin winced. With the exception of Nandel, which had a distinct advantage because of its mountainous terrain and nearly limitless supply of metal and gems, none of the independent principalities could long withstand an attack from one of the three kingdoms. And Women's Well, in its infancy, was far smaller than any of the established principalities.

"I am familiar with your situation," Ellin said, "and it seems clear your wisest option would be flight. If you can get to Rhozinolm, I might be able to grant you shelter. That is something I can probably arrange without the approval of my council, though I would of course be acting as a private citizen and not as queen."

Through Alysoon's translucent image, she could see Zarsha making frantic slashing gestures, warning her off that particular course. He was probably right—offering shelter to Alysoon was of no possible benefit to Ellin or to Rhozinolm and carried tremendous risks. If King Delnamal found out about it, she would be forced to either hand Alysoon over or face a war.

Logic told her the offer was unwise at best, actively stupid at worst. The only reasonable thing to do was rescind it immediately, but that turned out not to be necessary.

"I thank you for the generous offer," Alysoon said, "but we will not flee. We have made a great deal of progress with our magical development here."

"I'm sure your magic is impressive," Ellin said, realizing as the words left her mouth how condescending she sounded, "but even the best, most innovative magic will not stop an army."

Alysoon's smile broadened. "Not an army, I'll grant you. But come tomorrow when the news reaches him, Delnamal will find he needs more than a single company of soldiers to defeat us."

Ellin gaped in surprise. Apparently, her initial assumption that Alysoon was contacting her with a desperate plea for help as the soldiers bore down on her was incorrect. She supposed it was possible that Alysoon was attempting to deceive her, but there seemed little point to such a deception.

"Unless my information is mistaken," Ellin said, "you have fewer than a hundred men in Women's Well."

Alysoon nodded. "We do. And most of those are not trained

soldiers. But I am not exaggerating the unprecedented nature of the magic we are producing here. It was enough to allow us to withstand my half-brother's first assault, though he is sure to send more men against us the next time. We were outnumbered three to one, and yet we didn't just defeat Delnamal's men, we *routed* them. If Delnamal takes Women's Well, he will have access to that magic, and you can be certain he will not share it with Rhozinolm—or any other kingdom.

"I understand that your council may be reluctant to support my claim, but perhaps in light of recent events you may want to reconsider your decision. Our continued existence should be convincing evidence that you would prefer to work in cooperation with us rather than face a historically hostile kingdom that has acquired our magic. But in case that isn't convincing enough, I have sent you a selection of some of our most innovative new spells. The fliers should arrive with them sometime tomorrow. Contact me when you've had a chance to look them over. And think about whether you want Aaltah to have exclusive access to that magic—and whether you might rather secure that exclusive access for Rhozinolm."

"I don't—"

"Rhozinolm and Aaltah have been at peace for all of your lifetime and most of mine, but I'm sure you know our history. If Delnamal gets his hands on the magic of Women's Well, I guarantee he will see an opportunity to expand his power and that he will use it. Ask your council whether they're willing to let him have it."

It sounded like a giant bluff to Ellin, but she had to admit she was intrigued. The magic of the communicating flier was so great that it was hard to remain completely skeptical of Alysoon's claims.

"I must warn you that under current conditions, I might have trouble convincing my council to approve a declaration that the sky is blue," Ellin said, and she thought Zarsha might reach through the ghostly image and strangle her. She had to fight off a smile at his predictable reaction to her honesty. "But I am curious to see these spells of yours and will reserve judgment until I do."

"That is all I ask," Alysoon responded. "I look forward to speaking with you again."

Ellin removed the mote of Rho from the flier and took a moment to enjoy Zarsha's outrage as he glared at her. "Before you berate me for being too open and honest," she said, "consider that for all the time we've spent together recently, you did not know about this flier or about my previous conversation with Alysoon."

Now he looked almost comically annoyed, though he had no counter. He showed her far more respect than most men of her acquaintance, and he had never once hinted that he thought her unsuited for the throne. But just like Semsulin, he seemed to think he had some right to be consulted before she made any decisions, as if she could not act without the male stamp of approval.

"I hope you're not thinking that I will be some kind of figurehead for your rule if we marry," she said. "Because that is not at all how I see our relationship going forward."

She thought he might be offended, but he smiled and held up his hands. "I am very clear as to what our roles will be. You are the queen, and I will never be anything more than an adviser." For the briefest moment, something very like longing flashed in his eyes.

Ellin dropped her gaze and squirmed, telling herself she'd imagined it. Or if she *hadn't* imagined it, that he'd let her see it on purpose in an attempt to take advantage of her soft heart. It was vain and ridiculous to think he actually wanted her as a woman. He had offered to turn a blind eye to her lover! Not something she could imagine a man in love doing.

"I'm glad we're in agreement," she said.

"Oh, I wouldn't go that far. You seem proud of yourself for keeping vital information from me, but I can hardly be expected to give the best advice if I am kept in the dark."

"You are not yet my husband. And until you are, you remain a man of Nandel with no sworn allegiance to me. I share far more with you than I have any right to do, but you cannot expect me to share everything." She gave him a wry smile to take some of the sting out of her words. "Just as I cannot expect you to share everything with me."

He nodded his agreement, though his facial expression remained sour. "Unless you're willing to take action against Tamzin, I don't see how I can ever become your husband. He will never be persuaded to allow a marriage to anyone but himself. And he will not support another woman's claim to a new throne in Women's Well, no matter how impressive her magic might be."

"Maybe not. In which case we're going to have to work to turn the other council members against him."

It seemed like a nearly impossible task. But something was going to have to change and soon, or Tamzin would rip the throne out from under her either by marriage or by force. She could not allow that to happen, and she was not willing to resort to assassination.

She would have to hope one of the spells Alysoon had sent her would be the key to winning over her royal council, even against Tamzin's resistance.

Unfortunately, she could not imagine a spell that could have such an effect.

Delnamal was standing at the window, sipping from a goblet of wine and staring out at the distant harbor when he heard the sound of footsteps in the hall outside his private study. He entertained a brief, pleasant fantasy that they would pass right by and leave him in peace. His temper had been eating away at his self-control ever since he'd learned of Alysoon and Tynthanal's pathetic attempt at rebellion, and it was easier for all involved if he interacted with others as little as possible.

He glared down at his wine when he heard the inevitable knock on his door. The stuff might as well have been water for all the soothing effect it had on his frayed nerves. Nevertheless, he gulped down the last swallows before inviting his unwelcome visitor to enter.

Melcor looked the same as always, impeccably dressed and groomed and with a back so straight Delnamal often wondered if his secretary wore stays beneath his doublet. And yet Delnamal had trouble holding the man's gaze for more than a few seconds at a time these days, his whole body tensing as he tried not to let what he knew show on his face.

Of course Melcor had never mentioned to Delnamal that he had suffered what appeared to be permanent ill effects from the strange flier's mysterious attack. He sometimes stroked the scar on his hand as if it were a badge of honor earned on the battlefield, and he was as pompous as always. But Delnamal had heard enough rumors to be convinced that Melcor had been unable to perform ever since the attack. Which meant that the flier had somehow delivered a heretofore unknown spell. Thanks to the grand magus's disturbing discoveries about women's Kai, Delnamal had an uncomfortable suspicion he knew how the spell had been achieved. He'd taken to wearing an enormous belt buckle that contained a Kai shield spell, keeping it activated at all times except when he was asleep. He'd also ordered all windows to be kept firmly shut and refused to receive fliers from anyone except his most trusted friends and advisers.

"Are the traitors in custody?" he asked Melcor, for his men should have reached Women's Well the day before, and he expected a flier announcing their victory to arrive sometime today. He planned a simple beheading for Shelvon and young Corlin—though the council might wish to defer the punishment until the boy reached maturity—but for Alysoon and Tynthanal, he had other plans. They would die just as surely, but a great deal more slowly.

"No, Your Majesty," Melcor said, and for the first time Delnamal noticed how pale the man was. Beads of sweat stood out on his brow, and there was downright fear in his eyes. He was definitely not a man who had come to report a victory to his king.

"Why not?" Delnamal asked. He thought he'd kept his voice calm, but Melcor looked even more alarmed. Delnamal was aware his temper had been easy to rouse lately, that the irritant that was Women's Well had caused him to act with unaccustomed harshness. His own mother was barely speaking to him, and though Lady Oona had come to his bed within a week of her husband's funeral, she was not the free and easy companion she'd been in their youth, always looking at him with a hint of what might be distrust. As if she had some inkling that her husband's death might be attributable to something other than a random act of violence.

"The company was defeated, Your Majesty," Melcor said. "The witches of Women's Well have apparently developed a more robust version of the Trapper spell. The captain reports that nearly the entire town was hidden behind the spell, and when his men marched in to take the small collection of buildings they could see, they were ambushed and never had a chance."

Delnamal clenched his fists, barely able to contain the fury that flooded his veins. Women's Well was barely a *town,* much less a principality. It was inconceivable that the place could still be standing!

"Send a summons to the lord commander at once!" he shouted. "I will have that captain flogged and demoted for gross incompetence."

Melcor cringed. "Yes, Your Majesty."

Delnamal closed his eyes and tried to regain control of himself. This was a setback—and an embarrassing one at that—but in the grand scheme of things, it was only a temporary inconvenience. The next time the army marched on Women's Well, it would not be a single company, and Delnamal would be at its head to make sure there were no more blunders.

When he opened his eyes again, he wasn't exactly calm, but he was no longer in a blinding rage, either. His reign was getting off to a shaky start, but once Alysoon and Tynthanal were no more, everything would return to normal. He would order his men to take the leaders alive so that their disgrace could be made public, but all other inhabitants of Women's Well would be slaughtered. Knowledge of their insidious Kai spell would be destroyed with them, and Delnamal would guard that Well so closely that the spell would never be reproduced.

A loud crash—the sound of shattering glass—caused both Delnamal and Melcor to start. They whirled toward the sound, which had come from one of the closed windows, to see something small

and fast winging its way across the room. Heading straight for Delnamal.

Delnamal held his arms out in front of himself as if to ward off
the flier, though he knew the gesture was useless. In battle, a Kai
shield would defend against any spell fueled by Kai, but he could
not be entirely certain it would work against women's Kai. He
backpedaled frantically, not wanting to test the shield.

Melcor stepped between him and the flier, shoving his king to
the floor and blocking the attack with his own body. The flier tried
to duck around him, but Melcor had surprisingly quick reflexes and
blocked it once more, grabbing for it with both hands. It took three
tries, but he eventually managed to trap the flier, which struggled in
his grip. Pinning the wings with one hand, he opened his Mindseye
and reached out to pluck a couple of elements out of the flier until
it went still.

Breathing hard, feeling sick to his stomach, Delnamal lay on the
floor and looked up at his secretary. The man had saved him from a
fate worse than death—for there was no question in his mind that
the flier held a Kai spell, and there was no guarantee the shield
would have stopped it. Sweat drenched his body, and in the aftermath of that fear and dread came a wave of fury greater than any he
had ever felt before.

Delnamal pushed himself into a sitting position. Melcor kept a
firm hold on the inert flier with one hand and held out his other
hand to help Delnamal up. Delnamal wasn't ready to stand yet—
and though he was loath to admit it, he feared that his continually
increasing bulk was more likely to pull Melcor down on top of him
than to help him to his feet—so he waved it off.

The cursed flier had been a "gift" from Alysoon, a way to kick
him when he was already down, to humiliate him on a personal
level on top of the public humiliation of his troops' defeat. Well two
could play at that game. And no matter what delusions of grandeur
the bitch operated under, he had the upper hand. He was going to
win this game, and she was going to regret having dared to challenge him.

"I want you to send word to Miss Jinnell's entourage that they are to return with her to Aalwell at once," he ordered Melcor. Word had reached him of Jinnell's inelegant meeting with Prince Wald-mir, and though the prince claimed to still be interested, Delnamal couldn't help suspecting his enthusiasm had dimmed. He had been promised a beautiful and tempting young woman—ripe and fertile soil in which to plant seeds for a son. Instead, he'd received a sickly, sallow shell who could not keep a meal in her stomach even when she *wasn't* with child. Delnamal had been tempted to recall her to Aalwell the moment he'd returned to find Shelvon and Corlin miss-ing, but he'd refrained. Having no choice but to condemn Prince Waldmir's daughter as a traitor, he couldn't very well have justified also depriving the man the consolation of a marriage to the King of Aaltah's niece.

"What shall we tell Prince Waldmir?" Melcor asked, shifting un-comfortably from foot to foot.

"Tell him that we are recalling her for the sake of her health and will send her once again when she is well. Once she is formally ar-rested and charged with treason, he will thank us for not saddling him with a woman who is not worthy of him."

Melcor looked doubtful, and not without reason. "But what will we—"

Delnamal made a slashing gesture. "Bring her back. Immedi-ately, and in chains. Prince Waldmir will not want her once he real-izes what a blight her whole family is on the world." And really Delnamal's marital and diplomatic difficulties were not the secre-tary's concern.

Not long ago, Delnamal had harbored at least a trace of familial loyalty toward the girl, whom he'd allowed himself to think of as sweet and innocent. But there was no innocence to be found any-where in the issue of Brynna Rah-Malrye, and it was best for all concerned if her line was wiped out entirely. He should have con-demned them all the moment King Aaltyn died. Now he would rectify that error and drive a dagger into Alysoon's heart. One that would cause her so much pain she would come to beg for the death he had no intention of granting her until she had fully atoned for her crimes.

"See that we are not disturbed," Ellin told her guard as he opened the door to her private study and allowed Semsulin and Zarsha to enter.

"Yes, Your Majesty," he said.

Eying her curiously, her lord chancellor and Nandel's "special envoy" each took a seat before her desk. She had insisted on privacy when opening the bundle of magic items sent to her by Princess Alysoon earlier this afternoon, and she was certain both men were highly curious what she had found in that bundle.

It was clear from the wonders of the talking flier—and from the ability of Women's Well to fight off an attacking force three times its size—that the magic of the new Well was deeper and more significant than anyone had guessed, and yet Ellin *still* hadn't been prepared for what Alysoon's gift contained. To think that those powerful, unheard-of spells had been developed in the scant months that Women's Well had existed was . . . unsettling. And the thought of what they might be able to develop with *years* of study and experimentation was downright terrifying.

The door to her study closed with a comfortingly firm thunk, and she laid out three of the four magic items she had received on the desk for Semsulin and Zarsha's inspection. A bronze coin; a smooth, rounded pebble; and an unlovely metal hairpin clearly meant for utilitarian rather than decorative purposes. The bundle had contained yet another magic item, but Alysoon's letter had suggested Ellin might wish to keep that item's existence to herself. When Ellin read what the thin gold ring could do, she had shuddered and agreed.

"I gather from the look on your face that you have found Princess Alysoon's gift to be of great interest," Zarsha said, provoking a disapproving scowl from Semsulin for his insolence in speaking first.

"Indeed," she said, taking a deep breath to quell the sense of unease in her chest. "And they have shown me once and for all that it is not in our best interests to allow King Delnamal to have access to the magic of Women's Well."

Opening her Mindseye, she added the necessary mote of Rho to activate the spell in the hairpin, then stuck it haphazardly into her hair. Then she activated the spell in the pebble and heard both Semsulin and Zarsha gasp, their chairs scraping back. She closed her Mindseye and smiled as she watched both men scan the room with rather frantic gazes.

"I'm still here," she said before either man could panic, and once again she had the satisfaction of seeing them startle. "The hairpin makes me immune to magic, so I cannot see the effect of the pebble's spell, but I gather from your reactions that it is functional."

Zarsha was staring in her direction, but his eyes did not lock on her. Semsulin was blinking rapidly, as if unable to believe what his eyes were telling him—which was that Ellin and her desk had vanished from sight.

"Alysoon tells me it is a modified version of a spell used by trappers to hide their snares," she explained. "It is powerful enough that with larger spell vessels, it can be used to hide entire buildings. That is how Women's Well defeated King Delnamal's soldiers."

Zarsha nodded his understanding. "One cannot fight what one cannot see."

"Exactly." Once more, she opened her Mindseye, plucking the mote of Rho out of the Trapper spell and making herself visible once more. Bending close so she could see through the haze of elements, she picked up the bronze coin and activated both the spells it contained. She had tested both the immunity and the Trapper spells already in the privacy of her study, but the coin's spells required test subjects.

"Semsulin Rah-Lomlys," she said, then reached out her hand and closed her Mindseye once more. "Zarsha, I would like you to touch this coin."

She almost laughed at the wary look in his eyes as he reached out and touched the tip of his finger to the coin that lay in her palm, then frowned.

"Has something happened that I can't see?" he asked.

"No," she replied, then held out her hand to Semsulin. "Your turn."

Semsulin's expression was rarely pleasant, but at that moment, his scowl was as deep as she'd ever seen it. "I've never heard of magic of this sort, but you did not just say my full name for no reason. Whatever the spell in that coin is, it will affect only me, correct?"

"Yes."

He ground his teeth and stared at her, no doubt willing her to tell him what the spell would do to him. It was perhaps cruel of her not to volunteer the information, and if he asked, she would answer. But Semsulin was not a man apt to trust, and she wanted to know how much he trusted her.

Enough to trigger the spell without knowing what it would do, she soon learned when he touched the coin with the tip of his finger, wincing in anticipation.

The moment he made contact, Semsulin's knees gave way, his eyes sliding closed. He would have collapsed to the floor, except Zarsha reached for him and held him up, guiding him into the chair he had vacated. Semsulin's head bowed to his chest, his limbs flopping bonelessly so that Zarsha had to work to keep him supported by the chair.

"Alysoon's letter says he will only sleep for a minute or two," she said as the old man began to snore. "She says she has more robust versions that require gemstones to hold all the necessary elements."

Zarsha shook his head in wonder. "How is this possible?" he asked, but not as if he expected an answer. "I'm not a skilled practitioner myself, but I've studied magic, and I've never heard tell of anything even remotely like these spells."

"You've studied *men's* magic. There is no official study of *women's* magic, nor has there ever before been a concerted effort to combine the two." Which seemed to Ellin like a foolish oversight, fueled by prejudices that made little sense. "There are also elements at Women's Well that have never been seen before. Dismissing its importance because it doesn't produce a great number of masculine or neuter elements is clearly a mistake."

Semsulin came instantly, fully awake when the spell wore off. He bristled with offended dignity when Zarsha and Ellin explained what had happened, but she could see he was suitably impressed—if somewhat disturbed—by the demonstration.

"Do you now both agree that it would be dangerous to allow Aaltah to control this Well?"

Zarsha and Semsulin shared a look with many hidden meanings.

"The council will argue that we are not at war with Aaltah, and that we therefore need not treat them as an enemy," Semsulin said.

She huffed in frustration, for she was sure that was indeed what Tamzin would argue—and his cronies would immediately fall into step with him. "And I would argue that throughout history, a kingdom has never held control of two Wells without becoming a danger to the rest of the world. Can we really expect that Aaltah will gain control of Women's Well and *not* decide it is time to 'take back' the Midlands?"

"I said the *council* will make that argument, not that *I* would," Semsulin reminded her.

"What you really mean is that *Tamzin* will make the argument, and the council will be inclined to side with him over me."

"It amounts to the same thing."

Ellin took a deep breath and let it out slowly, for she had, of course, come to the same conclusion. No matter what was best for the kingdom, Tamzin would always look out for what he perceived to be his own interests first. Right now, his interest was in securing the throne, which he could best do by continuing to weaken her authority and bend the council to his own will.

"That is why we must remove him from the council once and for all," she said. "And I believe I have a plan to bring about that removal."

CHAPTER FORTY-THREE

Alys knew she looked distinctly unregal as she leaned against the fence and watched the ragtag army of Women's Well sparring and drilling under the lord commander's watchful eyes. Her heart lurched when she saw Corlin lose his footing and land in the dirt, and she stifled a protest when his instructor increased the indignity by whacking him on the rump with the flat of his sword. She saw Corlin's glance dart in her direction as he climbed back to his feet.

"Let the boy have some pride," Tynthanal's voice said from behind her, and she jumped, for she had not heard him approaching. "Hitting the dirt is embarrassing enough without having your mother—and sovereign princess—watching."

"I don't like him drilling with the men," she said, not for the first time. "No matter what happens, he is *not* fighting."

"That is no reason for him not to learn to defend himself. I've half a mind to set up some training for our women, as well."

She turned toward him, forcing herself to look away as Corlin raised his training sword once more. She thought perhaps Tynthanal was teasing, but the expression on his face dispelled that notion. "You're serious."

He nodded. "We can discuss it in council, but I see no reason why those women who'd want it shouldn't receive some training. They won't turn into seasoned warriors overnight, but at least they wouldn't be completely helpless."

For the first time, Alys noticed the curled parchment he held in his hand. She jerked her chin at it. "You've finally heard from your informant?"

Ever since Women's Well had declared its independence, there had been an ominous silence from Tynthanal's informant in the palace. At a time when they most desperately needed information, there was suddenly none forthcoming.

Tynthanal shook his head. "Still no word. But I have other friends in the army—men I trained with and fought with—who still feel some loyalty to me." He held up the parchment. "I've been informed that the army is on the march, and that Delnamal is leading them.

"He's taking no chances this time," Tynthanal continued grimly. "He's mustering troops as he goes, and my friend estimates there will be nearly ten thousand men by the time they reach us."

Alys blanched. She looked back over her shoulder at the drilling soldiers. An army of ten thousand could march over them without breaking stride, no matter how good their magical defenses. Especially now that those defenses would no longer be a total surprise.

"We need Rhozinolm to declare its allegiance," Tynthanal said. "That is our only hope."

Alys chewed her lip and nodded. "I will contact Ellinsoltah again tonight. She will have received my gift by now."

"It may not be enough," Tynthanal warned. "Even if she is suitably impressed, she will have to win over her council, and that might take time. The closer the army is by the time Delnamal hears we have an ally, the less likely he will be willing to turn back. Can you imagine what a blow it would be to his ego to choreograph this preemptive victory march and then have to turn around with his tail tucked between his legs?"

She shook her head helplessly. "Then what else can we do?"

The muscles in his jaw worked. "There is nothing."

Ellin took a deep, shaky breath, sure her face was ghastly pale. Zarsha gave her an encouraging smile, while Lord Kailindar was too busy staring at the door to the council room with an unnerving glitter in his eyes to notice her hesitation. Semsulin frowned fiercely.

"Are you sure about this?" he whispered, and she saw an unmistakable flash of fear in his eyes. That her ordinarily unflappable chancellor was frightened both reinforced her own fears and made it easier for her to tuck them into a hidden corner of her soul.

She couldn't manage a smile, but her legs felt steadier as her tripping pulse slowed. "I'm sure," she said, despite the lingering quiver of nerves in her belly. "We cannot go on as we have." And although Zarsha's plan to quietly eliminate Tamzin would be personally easier to face, it would not erase the damage he'd already done to her royal council. She had to not only eliminate Tamzin but to win support from some of the council members he'd subverted, and a back-alley assassination would not accomplish that.

"You are gambling with all our lives," Semsulin said.

"We've all already agreed to the gamble," Lord Kailindar growled. "Let's not mince about like frightened little girls."

Semsulin gave Ellin a pointed look, which she had no trouble understanding. Lord Kailindar was playing the role of ally merely because of his hatred for his nephew, not because of any loyalty to his queen. If this meeting went as planned, she might well be replacing one enemy with another—it had become patently obvious in speaking with Kailindar that he still had not forgiven her for stripping his title—but at least Kailindar did not have Tamzin's popularity. He would have a much harder time gathering support than Tamzin did.

Ellin nodded at Zarsha, who bowed his head and opened the door to the council chamber. Holding her own head high while the weight of the crown tried to push it back down, she strode into the room, silencing the chatter and replacing it with the scraping sound of chairs being pushed back. She saw that the platter of seed cakes she'd ordered sent to the council chamber had been appropriately decimated while they awaited her. Her ribs seemed to tighten around her lungs, and she prayed she would never be forced to reveal just why she had selected that particular treat—one of Tamzin's favorites—to serve at this meeting.

Semsulin followed on her heels, as usual, but she could sense the astonishment of the rest of the council when they saw Zarsha and Kailindar. Tamzin especially went stiff, his eyes blazing.

"Please be seated," she said as Semsulin pulled back her chair. She was not entirely surprised when Tamzin remained on his feet while everyone else sat.

"Your Majesty," he grated through clenched teeth, "I must ask that your . . . guests be excused before we bring this meeting to order."

"You are relatively new to the royal council, Lord Tamzin," Semsulin answered for her, "so you may be forgiven for your unfamiliarity with protocol. It is within the right of any member of this council to bring in guests who might have a vested interest in the proceedings."

Ellin had to fight the urge to smile at how gracefully Semsulin had cut Tamzin's legs out from under him—while both offering an excuse for Tamzin's unacceptable outburst and condescending to him at the same time. Semsulin might not be fully convinced that Ellin was doing the right thing, but one never would have guessed his doubts looking at him right now.

The look on Tamzin's face was so murderous that for a moment Ellin thought he might press the issue. Kailindar's smug, delighted grin as he dropped into a chair by the wall behind Semsulin did not help matters. She glanced around the table, taking in the expressions of the rest of her council. Most looked vaguely uncomfortable with the unsubtle undercurrents, but the lord high treasurer, who was proving to be one of Tamzin's most ardent supporters, was scowling deeply.

Eventually, Tamzin resumed his seat, though he moved slowly enough to be sure that no one missed the disrespect. The whole point of today's exercise was to provoke Tamzin into showing his true colors, and it seemed Ellin would not have to work terribly hard to succeed.

"My ascension to the throne has left the Kingdom of Rhozinolm with an unresolved issue of which we are all aware," Ellin said without preamble. "Namely, the trade agreements with Nandel that are set to expire and that Prince Waldmir has seemed reluctant to renew. When I was free to marry Zarsha, it seemed we had secured Waldmir's cooperation, and we have as yet failed to find another way of encouraging his support."

She could almost see some of the councilors rapidly losing interest, thinking the council meeting was sure to devolve into yet another long, pointless discussion of options that had long been picked clean and discarded. Nandel's territory was small, and its population even smaller. However, thanks to the mountainous nature of that territory, the land was riddled with mines, producing metals and gems that were sought after the world over. At least seventy percent of the iron available anywhere in Seven Wells originated in Nandel, and for some gems that percentage neared a hundred. Rhozinolm needed those trade agreements, and under the current circumstances, Nandel had no reason not to change the terms and make their prices extortionate.

"I submit to this council that a marriage between myself and Zarsha is still the most certain way to secure those trade agreements."

Her words provoked a moment of shocked silence. Then everyone began speaking at once. She sat and listened, taking in the mood of the room. Several of her advisers seemed to think she meant to make Zarsha king and voiced vociferous objections. Tamzin was the loudest of all of them; his chair had scraped back as he leapt to his feet, and he was now glaring at her in a way that was completely inappropriate. The lord high treasurer, seated beside him, put a hand on Tamzin's arm, looking up at him and saying something she couldn't hear. Whatever it was, it convinced Tamzin to sit down once more, though he was practically shaking with anger—and perhaps just a touch of eager anticipation.

The clamor began to die down as others decided to sit back and enjoy the show. When the noise level was reduced to a low murmur, Tamzin leaned a forearm on the table and fixed her with a penetrating stare.

"Do you mean to abdicate the throne?" he asked, his eyes gleaming with excitement at the thought, though he followed up the question with a suspicious look in Kailindar's direction. No matter what his own ambitions—or how much support he had among the members of the royal council—Kailindar's claim to the throne would be stronger than his own if Ellin were to abdicate.

Ellin ignored his question and asked one of her own. "Does anyone disagree with my assessment?"

Everyone looked back and forth, but no one immediately answered. Semsulin stepped into the ensuing silence. "I cannot see that we have any other inducements to offer Prince Waldmir. Though I would be delighted if someone were to propose a solution we have not yet considered."

The tension in the room was so thick it was almost visible as minds whirred and calculated. Those trade agreements had weighed on everyone's mind ever since Ellin had attended her first council meeting—and judging by her original would-be engagement to Zarsha against her strenuous objections, had no doubt done so long before.

Ellin gave them all time to think, time to recognize just how vital those trade agreements were, and just how important her hand in marriage might be in securing them. She did not have to be an expert statesman to see that her words had had exactly the desired effect. On everyone but Tamzin, who was still staring at her with naked suspicion in his eyes.

"Do you mean to abdicate the throne?" he asked again. His eyes rose briefly to the heavy ornamental crown on her head. One that she generally wore only for state occasions, as it was hardly a comfortable accessory.

He already knew the answer to his own question, which was why he was not already sitting there contemplating how he could convince the council to name him as the next king over Kailindar.

"I am the lawful Queen of Rhozinolm," she said. "If I had a son to whom I could pass the crown, perhaps I would consider abdicating for the good of the kingdom. However, as I have no clear, unchallenged heir, abdication is not an option."

"You are *not* giving the crown of Rhozinolm to some filthy barbarian warlord," Tamzin snarled, pounding the table and causing everyone in the room to jump. Some looked nervously at the "filthy barbarian warlord" who was seated quietly next to Kailindar.

Zarsha showed no sign of being offended, despite the outrageous insult. "I assure you, I have no designs on the throne of Rhozinolm," he said with a self-deprecating smile.

Semsulin did not take the insult with such aplomb. "Lord Tamzin, as the senior member of this council, I must ask you to sit down and refrain from speaking out of turn, or you will be removed from these proceedings."

More nervous murmurings as everyone in the room waited to see whether Tamzin would accept the rebuke. Ellin prayed he would sit down. Disrespect of Zarsha and Semsulin might result in a toothless censure from the rest of the council, but she needed to push him into flagrantly disrespecting *her*, which was a far more serious offense.

Stiffly, Tamzin resumed his seat, his face still red with anger.

"I have no intention of giving my crown to anyone," she said, turning her gaze to the Marshal of Rhozinolm, who was the highest-ranking officer of the law. "I understand that while there is legal precedent for a queen ceding her crown to her husband, the law doesn't specifically stipulate that she must do so. Am I correct?"

All eyes turned to the marshal, one of the more taciturn members of the royal council, who immediately looked uncomfortable with all the attention. "There has only once before been a sovereign queen in Rhozinolm," he said, "so there is very little legal language to cover such a situation."

"Is there a law that says my husband must be named king, or isn't there?" Out of the corner of her eye, Ellin could see the fire blazing in Tamzin's eyes as he saw the throne receding from his grasp.

"You are a woman!" Tamzin spat before the marshal had a chance to respond. "You are not fit to sit on the throne in anything but a temporary capacity."

"And yet right now I *do* sit on the throne, and I asked the marshal a question: am I legally required to cede the throne to my husband?"

The marshal squirmed even more, but everyone already knew the answer, so he finally admitted that no, there was no such law.

"Then I propose I marry Zarsha—after my mourning is complete, of course—and thereby secure renewed trade agreements with Nandel in the only way any of us can imagine it happening. I will remain as queen, and Zarsha will become the prince consort, and we shall proceed from there."

Tamzin was not the only person at the council table who did not like her proposal, and she had not missed the few subtle nods of agreement that had met his outburst about a woman's fitness to rule. But she had baited the hook generously, making it obvious that if they rejected her proposal, those trade agreements would never be renewed. Some of them might not mind if Tamzin led a revolt and seized the crown for himself, but she had just shown them a major shortcoming in such a coup. They *needed* her, and even those who harbored the most obvious loyalty to Tamzin—the lord high treasurer and the lord commander—looked doubtful.

Tamzin stood once more, and this time when he spoke, his voice was deadly calm. "The council obviously made a terrible mistake in putting you on the throne," he said, his eyes staring daggers as his lips curled into a sneer. "Rhozinolm's queen need not spread her legs for Nandel to gain access to the supplies we need."

Even having come into this meeting fully prepared to provoke

Tamzin, she could not help but be chilled by the way he was looking at her.

"You go too far, Lord Tamzin," Semsulin warned, also rising to
his feet. "You tread dangerously close to treason."

In his seat against the wall Kailindar sat up straighter, his own
eyes alight with expectation. In seconds, Tamzin would say something even his admirers would admit was treasonous, and Semsulin
would move that the council vote to arrest him. His followers
would be loath to do it, but faced with the alternative . . .

Kailindar could fill the lord chamberlain's seat "temporarily,"
until Tamzin could have a full trial and be found guilty, and Ellin's
throne would finally be secure. As long as the council realized the
only way to secure the trade agreements was through her marriage
to Zarsha, they could not allow Tamzin to shove her aside.

Tamzin ignored the chancellor's warning, not so much as flick-
ing a glance Semsulin's way. Instead, he fixed his gaze on the lord
commander. "We have ten times as many men as Prince Waldmir.
Why should we have to bow and scrape and beg and," he sneered
at Ellin, "whore ourselves to gain the bastard's favor when we can
simply take what we want?"

In all her plans for today's confrontation, Ellin had never once
seen that absurd suggestion coming.

"Are you mad?" Kailindar shouted. "The Keep is the only city in
all of Seven Wells that has never been conquered!"

"Sit down, *Uncle*," Tamzin snarled. "You have no voice in this
council and no place in this room."

"I move Lord Tamzin be removed from this council effective
immediately," Semsulin said. His face might have turned to stone
for all the expression in it, and his voice was steady and sure, as if he
actually believed his motion would be heard and fairly considered.

But everyone was staring at Tamzin, considering. He was a self-
declared military hero, after all. Would reminding everyone that his
great conquest had been over a ragtag band of bandits rather than
over a well-trained, well-supplied army bring any of the councilors
to their senses?

"And *I* move that we remove that whore from the throne before she damages the credibility of our kingdom any more than she already has!" Tamzin shouted.

It was Ellin's turn to leap to her feet, her heart pounding in her throat. Out of the corner of her eye, she saw both Zarsha and Kailindar also stand, their hands straying toward weapons that should have been merely ornamental. Soon everyone in the room was on their feet, looking back and forth between Tamzin and Ellin. With a sickening lurch, Ellin saw that in just a few heartbeats, this meeting had devolved to a point where it could only end in bloodshed. It only remained to be determined whose blood.

"I am the rightful Queen of Rhozinolm," she said, hoping her voice was firm and steady though her knees were weak. "I am doing what is right for my kingdom, and you are nothing more than a power-hungry bastard who would plunge us all into a war we cannot win simply because you lust for the throne."

Tamzin spat on the table. "What do you know of war? Tell me of all your great victories on the battlefield, and then perhaps I will listen when you speak of wars we cannot win!"

The sickening lurch in her stomach became stronger when she saw both the lord commander and the lord high treasurer nodding in agreement. Worse, except for Semsulin, none of the other council members seemed inclined to stand with her.

"You defeated a pathetic collection of bandits," she said, trying to mimic Tamzin's disgusted sneer. "That doesn't make you the one military expert in all of history brilliant enough to win a war with Nandel."

Ellin's mind spun frantically as she looked around the room and assessed the expressions on her council's faces. She saw the fervor—and ambition—that entered the lord commander's eyes, saw the vision of overflowing coffers that made the lord treasurer's heart beat faster, and she knew that she was about to lose.

Any moment now, Tamzin would call for a vote—and he would have enough votes to win. He would have Ellin and Semsulin and Kailindar, and probably even Zarsha arrested and thrown in a dungeon, and he would plunge the kingdom into war.

Ellin reached into her reticule, finding the simple gold ring that was among the spells she had received from Alysoon's flier. She had planned to present these spells—and Alysoon's proposal of exclusive access to them—after she had won her battle with Tamzin. And she had hoped to keep this ring—and the spell it contained—a secret, for she had told neither Semsulin nor Zarsha about it.

Her heartbeat slowed, and a strange sense of calm descended on her as she donned the ring and opened her Mindseye. She heard the murmur of shock and disgust that went around the table as she plucked a mote of Rho from the air and fed it into the ring, activating its spell.

Closing her Mindseye, she pointed the finger with the ring toward Tamzin, though Alysoon's instructions had not specified a need for specific gestures to trigger the spell.

Ellin didn't put any great thought into her actions. Didn't weigh the consequences or consider alternatives. Later, she would be horrified by how easy and effortless the decision was.

"Tamzin Rai-Mailee," she said simply, naming the spell's target and then waiting.

Tamzin took a staggering step backward as if someone had shoved him in the chest. His look of righteous anger and disgust changed to one of puzzlement as he looked down at his chest, perhaps expecting to see someone had put a hand on him. But no one was touching him.

Ellin's heart rate sped up again as that blissful moment of numbness wore off, and she began to think about what she had just done. Everyone was looking confused, and she might have thought the spell hadn't worked except for that telltale backward step. Alysoon had warned that the first few moments would be uneventful as the spell burrowed into the victim's body.

The first sprouts are so small the victim does not immediately seem to feel them, Alysoon's letter had explained. *Of course we have not tested the spell on a human, so it is hard to know for sure what it first feels like. I can only imagine it starts with a mild upset, but that it quickly accelerates from there.*

"What the fuck did you just do?" Tamzin roared at her, the vulgarity so out of place in a council chamber that, even under the circumstances, a few of the council members gave him reproving looks.

"You'll find out sooner than you'd like," she said, and was amazed at how calm and cool her voice came out. Inside, her heart was tripping over itself, and her every muscle was tensed in dread. Alysoon had shared few details about the effects of this spell, but she'd made it very plain that they were terrible to behold.

"I've been in contact with Sovereign Princess Alysoon," she said. "She and her brother have been developing some new spells out in the town they call Women's Well. She has sent me a few in case we might like to enter into an exclusive trade agreement with Women's Well. This is one of them."

Tamzin winced, and his hand flew to his belly. "What—" The word choked off in a cry of pain, and he doubled over. The lord commander, who was closest to him, put a hand on his arm to keep him from falling.

Tamzin raised his head to glare at her once more, and Ellin tried to remember how to breathe. Everything within her wanted desperately to escape, wanted to flee the room so she wouldn't have to see what she had just done.

Another cry of pain rose from Tamzin's throat, and this time the lord commander's support wasn't enough, and he fell to his knees, both arms wrapped around his belly. His face was drenched with sweat, his skin leached of all color.

It was then that he began to scream in earnest, his body thrashing about on the floor. No one knew what to do, some backing away, some reaching for him then drawing their hands away. Ellin swallowed hard, as the lord commander looked at her with wide, frightened eyes.

"What did you do to him?"

"It's a growth spell," she said, and her mask of calm was still in place. Afterward, when she was alone, she would allow herself to acknowledge her feelings. For now, her blood had to run cold as ice so that no one in this room would ever accuse her of being weak again. "Something they developed in Women's Well with a new feminine element that was previously unknown. It can make seeds grow at enormous speed. Anywhere."

Tamzin's back bowed, and Ellin could see his doublet straining outward, the belt barely holding. Then, there was a sickening tearing sound, and the front of his doublet burst open in a rain of blood.

Even those who'd been reaching to help him backpedaled, knocking into one another in their haste to retreat as leafy tendrils shot up through the bloody flesh and torn cloth. Tamzin was still screaming, though his throat was so ravaged the screams were becoming horribly hoarse. And now wet-sounding, as blood filled his mouth and trickled down his cheeks.

The plants—unrecognizable through their covering of blood— continued to grow, and his body made sickening squelching sounds.

Zarsha shoved his way through the circle of men who stood watching as Tamzin continued to writhe and struggle. He'd drawn his sword from its drab black scabbard, and holding it with both hands, he swung it downward with all the strength in his body.

The sword sliced easily through Tamzin's neck, silencing his screams and clanging loudly against the stone floor beneath.

Ellin was still cold and numb when she finally escaped the council chamber and retreated to her private study. She desperately wanted to be left alone so she could finally release all the emotions that roiled within her. Emotions she'd kept under brutally strict control as every surviving member of her royal council had stared at her with wide-eyed shock—and undisguised fear. The sound of Semsulin retching would haunt her, as would the mingled scents of blood and the contents of Tamzin's stomach. And the screams. Those screams would feature prominently in her nightmares.

She shuddered as she stepped into the room, her tight control already slipping. Thanks to that demonstration of power and will, she still wore the crown of Rhozinolm, and her chief rival was dead.

She'd asked the council if they wished to vote to unseat her. Not surprisingly, they had to a man acknowledged her right to the throne and agreed that there was no lawful requirement that her husband be named king.

Ellin tried to close the door behind her as her whole body began to shake. She'd been so desperate to escape she hadn't even noticed Zarsha trailing behind her. The door hit his outstretched hand. She wanted to tell him to get out, to leave her alone, but she knew that any sound escaping her throat would turn to a wail, so she said nothing as he stepped into the study and closed the door.

Another shudder shook her as she saw the blood that spotted his cuffs. There were brilliant red stains on his white collar as well, though his doublet hid the worst of it, and he had at least wiped the blood from his face. Ellin's stomach churned as she remembered the sound of his blade striking the floor, and the room swayed. She closed her eyes and pressed her hands against her belly. She had never in her life fainted, and she was not about to start now. At least so she told herself.

She didn't open her eyes when she felt Zarsha's hand on her arm. She allowed him to guide her into a chair as she concentrated on breathing. One breath in, one breath out. Over and over, until the worst of the nausea receded and the floor no longer seemed to buck beneath her.

She opened her eyes to find Zarsha propped on the arm of the chair beside her. The pose might have looked casual and relaxed, if it weren't for the careful blankness of his handsome face and the haunted horror in his eyes. He, who had urged her to arrange Tamzin's quiet murder, was struggling to cope with what he'd seen her do.

"Are you afraid of me now, Zarsha?" she asked quietly.

He blinked, and she suspected he was trying to school his expression, though he met with little success. "Of course not. You did what you had to do. Many more would have died if Tamzin had succeeded in bullying his way to the throne. You and I doubtless among them."

She nodded, for that was all true. Any application of cold logic would find no fault with her actions and lay no blame on her shoulders. But cold logic was cold comfort.

"I killed him," she whispered. "Horribly."

"Well, technically, *I* killed him," Zarsha said. He made a try at a rakish grin, but the expression was more of a grimace.

"Thank you for that, at least." Zarsha had been far from the only man in that room wearing a ceremonial sword, and yet he'd been the only one with enough wits—and mercy—to use it.

"That spell," he started, but his voice choked off.

"Alysoon told me it was terrible," she said. "She told me they'd tested it on a horse that had to be put down and that it had given her nightmares."

"I'm sure today's demonstration has spawned nightmares for all involved. I'm also sure we cannot afford for the King of Aaltah to have access to such a weapon."

"It is not a battlefield weapon," she said. "There need to be undigested seeds in the victim's stomach for the spell to work." Zarsha gave her another sharp look, one that told her he had noticed the platter of seed cakes on the table. She braced herself for his condemnation, but he offered no comment on her obvious premeditation.

"I still would not want to meet it on the battlefield. And in the hands of an assassin . . ."

Ellin swallowed hard. The spell had been frighteningly easy to invoke and to target. King Delnamal was under the impression that the magic of Women's Well was small and unimportant. Barely worth noticing, until the people of Women's Well gave shelter to traitors. But if its spell crafters could create a weapon like this with so few people and resources and so little time, it was perhaps the most strategically vital Well of them all.

"At tomorrow's council meeting," she said, "I will bring Alysoon's proposal to the table. I think after what they saw today, they will be amenable to recognizing the sovereignty of Women's Well in return for exclusive access."

Zarsha glanced at the plain gold ring on her finger. "As long as you wear *that,* they will agree to anything you propose."

Ellin slipped the ring off her finger and tucked it back into her reticule. "I don't want them agreeing with me out of fear. I need advisers who will tell me what they really think, not tell me what they think I want to hear."

"You will have them," Zarsha assured her. "No one who knows you would think you'd cast that spell on them in a fit of pique."

Ellin wished she had that same confidence. "*You* know me. Did you think I would kill my cousin in cold blood and in front of everyone?"

He rubbed his hands together, not looking at her. "I had never seen you backed into a corner like that before, so no, I did not expect it." He looked up and met her eyes. "That doesn't mean I'm now afraid of you, nor does it mean I think you'll become a tyrant. I swear that I will still give you honest advice when you ask for it." He managed a half-hearted grin. "And likely even when you don't."

That brought a faint smile to her lips. It was true that she couldn't imagine Zarsha—or Semsulin, for that matter—mincing words with her. "And you're still willing to marry me?"

Zarsha rose from the arm of the chair and came to kneel in front of her, taking one of her hands in both of his and looking up into her eyes. She tried to focus on his face, to ignore the spots of blood that served as continual reminders of her capacity for brutality.

"I'm far more than *willing* to marry you," he said, squeezing her hand. "I've wanted to marry you from the first day I laid eyes on you. That is as true today as it was yesterday and the day before that." He raised her hand to his lips and planted a chaste kiss on her knuckles.

The touch of his lips to her skin made her heart race for entirely different reasons than it had earlier. There was still a part of her that doubted his sincerity, that wondered if it was truly *her* he wanted, or if it was merely the power and prestige that marrying her would bring him. But maybe it was enough either way. Royal marriages were rarely affairs of the heart, and at least in Zarsha, she would have a husband she liked and respected.

Yes, it would be enough.

CHAPTER FORTY-FOUR

There were no buildings of more than two stories in Women's Well—yet—but Alys did not need any great elevation to see the army that was encamped not far from their outskirts. The flatness of the desert landscape afforded her an excellent view of all those banners and pavilions and columns of men, horses, and chevals. She held the talker in the palm of her hand, facing outward as she looked out the window on the second floor of the town hall. Ellin's image became indistinct with the talker facing away from Alys, but she heard the other woman's soft imprecation at the sight.

Turning the talker back toward herself and moving away from the window, she shook her head at Ellin.

"I had hoped your declaration of allegiance would convince Delnamal to turn back, but it seems that is not the case." Alys tried to project an image of stoic calm, though in reality she felt only one step removed from panic. She had put all her hopes into an alliance with Rhozinolm, but if her half-brother's hatred of her was stronger than his love of his kingdom, then by this time the next day, every man, woman, and child in Women's Well might meet their deaths.

"I cannot believe he means to ignore the threat," Ellin said, though she looked worried. "I am certain he has spies and informants in Zinolm Well, and those spies will surely have reported the massing of warships in our harbor and the mustering of troops. He has left Aalwell all but undefended, and my navy can reach the city far faster than his army can. All of which I have pointed out in my correspondence with him."

"And yet here he is," Alys said with a sweeping gesture toward the window. "No matter how powerful our magic, we cannot defend ourselves against that many."

"I realize it is of little comfort at best, but know that if he moves on Women's Well, he will lose his kingdom. But for all that he is a spiteful brute, he has not struck me in our correspondence as stupid. I cannot but think that his presence on your doorstep is an attempt to intimidate you into surrender, rather than a prelude to an attack."

"He *has* requested a parley," Alys admitted, though the thought of coming face-to-face with her half-brother after everything he had done made her want to hit something. Best she go to the parley unarmed, or else she might be tempted to murder him before a word left his hateful mouth.

Ellin smiled in satisfaction. "If he intended to press an attack, then he would have no need for a parley. He hopes you will see his army and despair."

In that, he had succeeded, although Alys was doing everything in her power to avoid succumbing to that despair. "You are probably right." She smiled wanly. "But just in case you aren't, I want to thank you for supporting me. I know that can't have been an easy decision."

For just a moment, Ellin's eyes revealed a flash of something frightened and vulnerable, a glimpse of the twenty-one-year-old young woman who hid behind the trappings of a queen. Queen Ellinsoltah had demonstrated remarkable calm and maturity for one so young—and one not raised in the expectation of power—but just like Alys, she was still feeling her way along.

"I do hope that someday we can meet in person," Alys said.

Ellin smiled. "And without the fear of imminent disaster hovering over our heads."

"Yes. That, too."

"When do you parley?"

Alys glanced again out the window at the army, trying not to imagine what it would feel like to ride out into the open desert to meet them with only a small honor guard at her side. "In a few hours. By the time the sun sets this evening, it will all be over, one way or another."

"Stay strong," Ellin urged. "And know that in victory or in defeat, I am with you."

Alys nodded. "Thank you. I hope I will talk to you again soon."

"I hope that, too."

Alys plucked the mote of Rho out of the talker and took one last long look out the window. Then she left the room to begin preparing for the parley.

Alys stood in front of the full-length mirror and contemplated the impression she would make when she rode out to the would-be battlefield under a flag of truce. Her dress was wildly improper, and would have been considered so even if she weren't still in mourning. Respectable women did not wear red except as the occasional small accent. Red was the color of whores, was the color of the women of the Abbey. Honor had clucked disapprovingly as she'd helped lace Alys into the red gown, and the seamstress who had designed and sewn it for her had been both nervous and excited.

The bodice was of a deep red velvet, with a boned black stomacher as the only nod to her continued mourning. The skirts and sleeves were of a brighter, more arresting red. A panel of gold lace studded with pearls adorned the front of the skirt, and that same pearl-dotted lace frothed from the bottom of the fitted sleeves. Her hair was gathered into a gold snood at the base of her neck, and the top of her head was uncovered save for the hammered gold crown adorned with rubies she'd had pried from the small supply of jewels she'd thought to bring with her months ago when she'd come to Women's Well, never having dreamed she would never return to her home.

"You look more like a queen than I ever did," Shelvon said, and Alys turned to give the girl a smile. She couldn't imagine what a woman raised in the strict and austere land of Nandel must really think of the outrageous ensemble.

"You sell yourself short," she scolded. She owed Shelvon so much for having spirited Corlin away from Delnamal's grasp, and she was bound and determined that eventually the girl would recognize her own worth. "Eventually" being the key word, for it was unquestionably a long-term project.

Shelvon shrugged and blushed. "You are in equal parts stunning and shocking. I almost wish I could see Delnamal's face when he first catches sight of you."

"Hmm," Alys said noncommittally as she brushed at the skirts to smooth them, though they didn't need it

Tynthanal knocked and then entered the room, bowing to her. It would take a while before she felt fully comfortable having her own brother bow to her, but if she was the Sovereign Princess of Women's Well, then it was only appropriate.

"The delegation is ready for you, Your Royal Highness," he said.

She was about to make a quip about his formality—even if it *was* appropriate—but he dispensed with it before she had a chance.

"Are you certain you want to do this?" he asked. There was no missing the anxiety in his eyes. "I do not trust Delnamal to honor the flag of truce."

She held up her hands, displaying the rings she wore on all of her fingers, each one imbued with a spell. "I don't, either," she said.

Tynthanal's frown deepened. "It is unwise to go into battle

trusting in spells to protect you. There are too many counterspells out there . . ."

Alys knew that well enough. The vast majority of the spells that had been developed so far in Women's Well had limited military applications. While those that did—like the Trapper spell—would be mostly unfamiliar to the army, Women's Well would be facing skilled magic users whose primary purpose would be to undo their magic.

"I'm not going into battle," she said. "I'm merely going to talk."

"If he has not retreated after receiving a warning from Rhozi-nolm, then I don't know what there is to talk about."

"I expect he hopes to bluster and intimidate me into surrendering," she said. Thankfully, with Corlin here at Women's Well and Jinnell now in Nandel, he did not have the leverage necessary to accomplish such a thing. The thought of Jinnell in Nandel still made Alys sick to her stomach, but she could only hope that Chan-lix's generous gift would protect her daughter. Chanlix had donated her Kai to send a flier to Prince Waldmir. Having no informants currently in Nandel, she didn't know whether the flier had successfully completed its mission, but if it had, then Waldmir's interest in a pretty young girl to warm his bed should wane.

"Besides," she finished, nudging at her crown to make sure it was securely seated, "he gains nothing by killing me. I have an heir, and a trusted adviser who can act as regent if something happens to me." She gave Tynthanal a meaningful look, and though she could see his jaw working as he ground his teeth, he kept any further objections to himself.

Alysoon rode a horse to the parley, rather than a ladylike cheval. Falcor and the soldiers-turned-honor-guardsmen who rode with her kept casting nervous glances in her direction as if afraid she'd fall off. She had very little experience riding on the back of a real horse, so she had to admit to being slightly worried herself, but the horse chosen for her was a docile white mare that seemed disinclined to buck her off.

Behind her, she heard the white banner of truce and the red banner that held the newly designed emblem of Women's Well—a stylized woman's hand cupped under an array of motes—flapping crisply in the wind. Armor and weapons jangled, and the horses' hooves thumped against the hard-packed road. No one spoke as their party approached the midpoint between Delnamal's encampment and the invisible border of Women's Well. Delnamal already stood waiting for her, flanked by a dozen men on horseback and two more on foot. Alys's entourage was half the size, but then if this came down to a fight, the size of her entourage was the least of her problems.

Alys kept her eyes on her half-brother as she approached, telling herself not to see—and be intimidated by—the huge encampment that was clearly visible in the distance behind him. The clusters of tents and pavilions covered more ground than the entire town of Women's Well. And yet if Delnamal had wanted to—had thought he *needed* to—he could have mustered twice again as many men. He could kill every man, woman, and child in Women's Well, but not without suffering a great number of losses himself. Losses he could not afford with Rhozinolm's forces massing against him. Alys tried to calm herself with that knowledge as she and her entourage came to a stop. Falcor and two of his men dismounted, one holding her horse's bridle while Falcor offered her a hand.

Slipping off the sidesaddle was easy, but she appreciated the offered hand anyway. For all the comforting words she had offered Tynthanal, she could not deny that her palms were sweating and her pulse racing.

At first, Alys thought Delnamal had lost a little weight since she'd last seen him. The mail coat he wore—as if he were personally riding into battle—hung comfortably on his stout frame with no sign of straining. His cheeks, however, were as puffy as ever, and his second chin even more pronounced. When she realized he was standing unnaturally straight, she surmised that he was wearing stays under his mail, and it was all she could do not to laugh.

Based on the disdainful way he looked her up and down, he was similarly unimpressed with her own clothing choices.

"How appropriate that you dress like a whore," he sneered. "Like mother, like daughter."

She did not need to glance at the men behind her to know they were glaring daggers at Delnamal, outraged on her behalf. Several of Delnamal's men subtly moved their hands closer to weapons, and there was undisguised battle lust in their eyes.

"I'm not the one wearing women's stays under a chain-mail coat," she shot back, then cursed herself for the incendiary remark as his men began to mutter.

Delnamal held up his hand to silence them, though the color that rose up his thick neck told her her shot had hit home. "I brought you here to discuss the terms of your surrender."

"Then I might as well return to Women's Well, for we have no intention of surrendering. Need I remind you that Queen Ellinsoltah has pledged her full support for Women's Well? Our father married your mother specifically to end the last war between Aaltah and Rhozinolm. Would you really insult his memory so soon after his death by starting a new one?"

"You put too much faith in such an alliance. I see no army from Rhozinolm standing behind you on the field, and once you are defeated, the queen will no doubt see the advantage of reaching an accord."

Alys snorted. "Which shows just how little you understand about women in general and Queen Ellinsoltah in particular. If you insist on trying to take Women's Well, how many men do you suppose you will lose? And how fast do you think your army could make it back to Aalwell? I'd say Ellinsoltah's ships can make it there a great deal faster, and with so many of your men here at your back, Aalwell can't put up much of a fight. It's hard to win a war when your capital city falls to the first strike."

"What happens to Aaltah is not your concern," Delnamal said. "You and every traitor who stands with you will be dead. Unless you agree to surrender. If you, your brother, and my wife will surrender and face justice, then I will allow the townsfolk to live. Jinnell and Corlin and the officers who have led this rebellion against the Crown will of course be attainted and exiled, but they will not be executed. It's a far more generous offer than I have any need to make."

It was also an offer she had no reason to trust, even if she were willing to sacrifice her own life as well as Tynthanal's and Shelvon's. Her stomach fluttered nervously, and she wondered if she was being overconfident in assuming her half-brother's love for his kingdom was greater than his hatred for her and Tynthanal. For all the confidence she had in Ellinsoltah's commitment and willingness to provide military support, it would all be for nothing if Delnamal ordered his army forward anyway.

"I tell you again that I have no intention of surrendering."

"Will it change your mind if I inform you that I had Jinnell recalled from Nandel several weeks ago? She is currently in my dungeon awaiting trial for her treason charge after having confessed to aiding in the flight of my wife and Corlin."

It was all Alys could do to stay upright, and as much as she wished to put on a brave face and hide the accuracy of Delnamal's strike, she couldn't do it. She heard the scuff of Falcor's boot against the ground as he stepped closer to her, perhaps poised to catch her if she collapsed.

"You're bluffing," she choked out. "If you had recalled her, I would have heard."

Delnamal smiled cruelly. "Only if my men hadn't ferreted out your brother's informant in the palace. Do you wonder why you never heard a report about the precious little flier you sent me?"

Alys swallowed hard. She had not been overly surprised not to hear anything about the Kai flier's attack on Delnamal. It was always possible it had happened when he was alone, and he would not be eager to share the news once he realized what the spell had done to him. But the ominous silence of Tynthanal's informant had indeed struck fear into both their hearts.

"Your flier was destroyed before it had a chance to strike me.

And Jinnell's recall and imprisonment have been carried out quietly so as to cause the least embarrassment to all involved. If you surrender, you can take her place in the dungeon. If you do not, she will be tried, and convicted, and executed for treason."

Alys shook her head, her heart pounding as her stomach turned. She had told herself that Jinnell was safe, that she was out of Aaltah and that the Kai-spelled flier would debilitate her would-be bridegroom. Surely Delnamal was lying about having her in his dungeon, just as he was lying when he promised to let the people of Women's Well live if she surrendered.

"She's your *niece*," she said, unable to stop herself from giving Delnamal a pleading look. "She's an *innocent*."

Delnamal snarled. "She conspired against me with my wife. I, who am not only her uncle but her king. She is no innocent. Now choose! Whose life will you save? Hers? Or your own?"

Alys's eyes filled with tears, and there was nothing she could do to hold them back. It was a mother's sacred duty to protect her children, and everything she had done in the months since that earthquake had been to keep Jinnell safe. Even coming to Women's Well had been motivated by the hope that the magic here could keep her daughter out of Waldmir's clutches.

And now, if Delnamal was to be believed, her daughter was locked in a dungeon awaiting a trial that could have only one outcome.

He *had* to be lying. Had to be preying on her motherly instincts, counting on her to be unwilling to risk her daughter's life no matter *how* sure she was that it was a lie. He was staring at her with a predatory eagerness, drinking in the pain and distress he was causing, loving that he had this power over her.

But what if he wasn't lying? How could she ever live with herself if she called Delnamal's bluff only to have her daughter face the headman's ax?

"Decide!" Delnamal snarled. "Will you surrender or won't you?"

Alys sucked in one shaky breath and then another. Delnamal *was* lying—if not about having Jinnell, then certainly when he promised to spare so many lives. If she surrendered, he might let some of the townsfolk of Women's Well live, but there was no question in her mind that her children would not be so lucky.

Memories came to her unbidden of all the times her father had tried to explain why he'd had to divorce her mother, why he'd had to deny his first children his name and their lawful titles. *You cannot be a good king while putting the needs of those you love over the needs of your kingdom,* he'd said. She'd never forgiven him, never seen his explanation as anything but a pitiful attempt to justify himself.

She swallowed the hard lump that had formed in her throat. There was a kind of poetic justice in her being forced to face this very same kind of decision. Perhaps it was her punishment for having let her father go to his deathbed without ever receiving her forgiveness.

Delnamal was probably lying about having Jinnell in his dungeon.

Even if she *was* in his dungeon, the trial and execution would take time. Time in which Alys, with the help of Tynthanal and perhaps even Ellinsoltah, could find some way to save her.

And even if none of that was true, Delnamal was certainly lying when he promised mercy.

There was no other choice she could make.

Her fists clenched at her sides, her vision still blurred with the tears she could not stop, she stood as straight and tall as she could and met Delnamal's gaze with all the defiance she could muster. "We will not surrender." *Forgive me, daughter.*

She felt as if her body might shatter into a million shards at the smallest touch. And that she might prefer that shattering to having to live with the decision she'd just made. *He's lying, he's lying, he's lying,* a voice in her head kept repeating, as if thinking it enough times, thinking it hard enough, might make it true.

The fury that lit Delnamal's eyes was so fierce Alys almost backed away from it, even as a part of her rejoiced. If he'd been telling the truth, he'd have no reason to be so angry! The tears quit building in her eyes, fierce hope now burning in her chest.

Delnamal's face and neck were red with his rage, his hands nearly shaking with it. He turned and snarled something over his shoulder at one of his men. The man hurried to one of the riderless horses, detaching a heavy burlap sack from the saddle and handing it to Delnamal. Delnamal ripped viciously at the ties that held the sack closed.

Alys tasted bile in the back of her throat, and her breath froze in her lungs.

Delnamal bared his teeth at her. "Be proud of yourself, you whoring bitch," he snarled. "You've won the day. Congratulations. Here's your prize."

He pulled something from the sack and dropped it to the ground at her feet. Her thinking mind couldn't quite make sense of what she was seeing, but a scream of agony rose from her throat anyway. She threw herself at Delnamal, fingers clawing the air as she went for his eyes, screaming and shrieking.

Hands grabbed her, restrained her, pulling her back away from him, murmuring sounds that she couldn't hear as Delnamal laughed at her. *Laughed.*

She freed one arm so she could point at him, shouting his name. The impact of the spell knocked him backward but did not erase the glow of sadistic pleasure in his eyes.

"I've heard about your nasty spell," he said. "I thought you might be tempted to use it when you saw my gift, so I've been fasting. Just in case."

She shrieked again in helpless agony as Falcor gathered her into his arms and pressed her head against the mail on his shoulder, trying to shield her vision from the abomination that lay in the dirt where Delnamal had dropped it.

"Till we meet again, Your Royal Highness," Delnamal said with a mocking bow, then turned to mount his horse. His bulk made him awkward, and he needed a hand up, but he was too pleased with himself to be embarrassed.

"May you have a long and miserable reign," he said, pivoting his horse and riding away without a backward glance.

Alys's screams turned into moans, and she collapsed in Falcor's arms. She caught one more glimpse of Jinnell's head before one of his men covered it with his cloak.

EPILOGUE

Alone for the first time in she couldn't guess how many hours, Alys stepped into her bedroom, still fully clothed. Honor had tried to coax her into undressing for bed, but Alys knew her head would touch no pillow tonight.

Her whole body ached, and though she'd long ago wrenched every drop of moisture from her eyes, they burned fiercely as if another round of tears would soon arrive. She paced the room, ignoring the array of teas and calming potions that had been pressed on her by what felt like every inhabitant of Women's Well. It was good that Corlin had been persuaded to drink, but she had no desire to escape the pain it was her duty as a mother to endure. She would pace the contours of this room until she collapsed.

Passing by her bedside table, she caught sight of her mother's spell book. She rarely referenced it anymore, although when she did she often found new lessons waiting for her. She could not deny that the lessons were useful, that Brynna's extraordinary power made her instructions more complex and nuanced than anything Alys could learn from the other abigails. However, the book was heavily weighted toward the elements produced by Aaltah's Well, and it made only passing references to masculine elements. She had found it much less useful since she'd arrived in Women's Well, where so much of the magic was new and unknown.

Something about the appearance of the book made her stop walking, made her eyes focus when they'd been mercifully glazed. She picked it up and stared at the cover. The cover that had always before displayed the lurid title of a book of love poems.

Today, it had a new title.

Forgive Me.

Alys stared at the words with uncomprehending eyes. Then she thought of all her mother had told her when they had last spoken on the day of the earthquake. Remembered the sorrow and the apologies and the warnings. Remembered that her mother had been as gifted a seer as she had been a crafter. Remembered that the book had been specifically designed for her own use and not Jinnell's.

"You knew," she whispered at the book.

Her mother had claimed not to be able to see the future of those she loved. But that had been just one more of the many lies that had shaped the last months.

Brynna had known this victory was coming—and that it would cost Jinnell's life.

Enjoying a blissful moment of feeling nothing at all, Alys crossed to the small fire that warmed the chill of the desert night. She threw the book in the flames and watched the pages curl.

ACKNOWLEDGMENTS

First and foremost, I have to thank Melissa Marr and Kelley Armstrong and the rest of the gang at the bayou retreat. (You know who you are!) It was at that magical retreat that *The Women's War* finally blossomed from an ambitious idea into a true novel-in-progress. Major thanks also to my agent, Miriam Kriss, who has supported me wholeheartedly throughout all the ups and downs of this crazy career path of mine. Her enthusiasm and encouragement have always made it easy for me to be adventurous in my writing and to try new things.

I must always thank my husband, Dan, who is my first reader for all my books. He goes above and beyond the call of duty every time, and my books are always better for his input.

Lastly, a huge thank you to my editor, Anne Groell, who did the unthinkable and asked me to make this already long (for me) book longer—and gave me a blueprint for how to do it! I learned so much in the process of exploring some of the subplots in greater depth, both about the process of writing an epic and about my characters. It was a blast, and I look forward to working together on the next book!

ABOUT THE AUTHOR

JENNA GLASS wrote her first book—an "autobiography"—when she was in the fifth grade. She began writing in earnest while she was in college, and she proceeded to collect a dizzying array of rejections for the first seventeen novels she completed. Nevertheless, she persisted, and her eighteenth novel became her first commercial sale. Within a few years, she became a full-time writer and has never looked back. She has published more than twenty novels under various names, but *The Women's War* marks her first foray into epic fantasy.

jennaglass.com

ABOUT THE TYPE

This book was set in Galliard, a typeface designed in 1978 by Matthew Carter (b. 1937) for the Mergenthaler Linotype Company. Galliard is based on the sixteenth-century typefaces of Robert Granjon (1513–89).